A Brazen Bargain

Laura Trentham

A Brazen Bargain

Copyright © 2017 Laura Trentham

ISBN: 1-946306-05-3

ISBN-13: 978-1-946306-05-0

Editing by Heidi Shoham

Cover Art by Angela Waters

REVIEWS

AN INDECENT INVITATION...

"Trentham is careful not to settle for easy answers or simple explanations, making for a tale full of unexpected twists and turns and emotional complications." -- RT Book Reviews

"Danger, intrigue, and passionate love--what more could a Regency romance lover want? The first in Trentham's (*Slow and Steady Rush*) "Spies and Lovers" series is a well-written, engaging, and very steamy delight."--J. Harris, Library Journal

"Witty, compelling, and sensuous, Laura Trentham's is a fabulous new voice in historical romance." -- Valerie Bowman, bestselling Regency author

A BRAZEN BARGAIN...

"I loved Rafe from the first book and was eager to read his story. It was wonderful! Both of the Spies and Lovers books are fabulous. I love how Laura Trentham draws me into the story in every way. The characters come alive beautifully."—Lily, Goodreads

"I found this to be an exciting and interesting book. Hot and steamy and pulls just enough heartstrings to make it more than just a quick read."—Kilts and Sword blog

Also by Laura Trentham
Historical Romance
Spies and Lovers
An Indecent Invitation, Spies and Lovers Book 1
A Brazen Bargain, Spies and Lovers Book 2
A Reckless Redemption, Spies and Lovers Book 3 (Nov 2017)
A Daring Deception, Spies and Lovers Book 4 (May 2018**)**

Contemporary Romance
Cottonbloom Novels
Kiss Me That Way, Cottonbloom Book 1
Then He Kissed Me, Cottonbloom Book 2
Till I Kissed You, Cottonbloom Book 3

Candy Cane Christmas, Cottonbloom Novella 3.5
Light Up the Night, Cottonbloom Novella 3.75

Leave the Night On, Cottonbloom Book 4
When the Stars Come Out, Cottonbloom Book 5 (Jan 2018)
Set the Night on Fire, Cottonbloom Book 6 (Aug 2018)

Falcon Football
Slow and Steady Rush, Falcon Football Book 1
Caught Up in the Touch, Falcon Football Book 2
Melting Into You, Falcon Football Book 3

CHAPTER ONE

Summer 1812, London

Lord Rafe Drummond ducked his head to clear the low-hanging timbered doorframe of the gritty gaming hell. He scanned the room, tucking away as many details as possible. Left over habits from his days as a Crown assassin and spy, but they served him well in civilian life.

The low hum of men talking and the clink of glasses filled the space. The wood-paneled walls and liberally smoked cheroots contributed to an earthy, comforting smell and constant haze. High-stakes gaming took place in the back rooms, but he rarely ventured there. He had outgrown the hunt for artificial excitement.

White's, this was not. A group of familiar seamen gathered at a long, squat oak bar that dominated one side of the room, talking and drinking tankards of ale. Rafe shook hands and accepted his own tankard, taking small sips, mostly for show. He'd made his sister, Lily, a promise not to overindulge and wouldn't break it— not tonight at any rate.

The lively conversation eased the restlessness that had assailed him during his dinner alone at a table capable of seating eighteen. A deep breath loosened the tight lashes around his chest, and he propped a booted foot on a low rail.

"What brings you out tonight, Drummond? Liquor, games,

women? Or perhaps all three?" asked one of the men with a wink.

Rafe chuffed. "Boredom. Can't stand my own company. How're things coming on the docks? I'm leaving for Wintermarsh before the week is out, but I want to see the new ship. Will my investment pay off soon?"

"Never fear, she'll make us all rich," the man said, inciting a clinking of tankards. The seaman likened the new ship to a beautiful courtesan, and the innuendo-filled description pulled Rafe's lips into a rare smile.

As he tipped his tankard up for another sip, two young men stumbled into the common room. He only half-heard the ribald banter around him, his attention stolen. Simon, the Duke of Bellingham, had one arm flung over the shoulders of Viscount Hampton, possibly in camaraderie, but based on the duke's shuffling feet, even more for support.

Bellingham's voice, thick with liquor, carried across the room. "We're here to play. Where're all the tables? We have the coin, never fear." He bowed to a serving girl and even shook the manager's hand. "In fact, drinks for the house." The duke threw his arms out and twirled around to the cheers of the patrons.

The manager pointed the duo to the back rooms. Hampton shoved the duke through the door and tossed a careless, sweeping glance over his shoulder. Perhaps if Rafe hadn't watched the entire scene unfold, the incongruity wouldn't have made an impression.

Hampton's eyes were surprisingly clear, and without the duke's arm around him, he straightened and moved with little visible impairment. But it was the smirk, full of devious intent, that had Rafe staring into his nearly full tankard with a niggling sense of duty.

Dammit. Hampton's machinations were nothing to him. The man had cut a wide swath through London's gaming hells over the past year. According to gossip, White's had cut him off. What was Bellingham doing with such a wastrel?

The duke looked an easy mark tonight. He was only twenty—an immature twenty at that. Although only seven years his senior, too many of Rafe's years had been spent teetering on a knife's edge between life and death. His path had aged him well beyond his years.

Rafe had vague recollections of his chattering sister filling his broody silences with gossip about the duke's increasingly destructive vagaries. There was no harm in seeing how far down the road to ruin the duke found himself. What else would fill the lonely hours?

Rafe excused himself and followed the raucous laughter to a back room. Three well-heeled merchants had joined the two peers for a high-stakes game of loo. Leaning against the doorjamb, Rafe crossed his arms over his chest and watched the hand unfold.

None-too-subtle whispered encouragements from Hampton drove Bellingham to up the bet. After refilling the duke's glass to the brim, Hampton added a dash of brandy to his own. The young duke would end up fleeced one way or another. Rafe ran a hand down his beard and looked heavenward.

As soon as the round finished, he hooked a boot on the leg of an empty chair and seated himself. "Drummond, at your service. Care if I join you?" Gazes skimmed over his face and dropped to the stained green-felt tabletop. Rafe clutched his thighs to keep from tracing the long scar that marred the left side of his face.

His torso tottering in a semi-circle, Bellingham smiled a simple smile and held Rafe's gaze. "O'course, Drummond. Welcome, welcome. Have we been formally introduced?"

"No, Your Grace. I haven't circulated in Society for several years now, but our sisters are well-acquainted."

"Call me Bellingham," the duke said with a careless wave of his hand. "Your sister is Lady Lily Drummond? Minerva loves her to bits."

Rafe couldn't imagine the austere Lady Minerva loving

anything to bits. "My sister is Mrs. Gray Masterson now. She married in the spring."

"That's right. My sincere feli-felicit-ta... Jolly good for her." The duke thumped his fist on the table for good measure.

A guileless expression on his boyish face, Bellingham chuckled when Hampton totaled the amount he'd lost the previous game. A thousand pounds gone in a thrice. His amusement highlighted an unforgivable ignorance about the power of money.

"Are you sure you wouldn't rather bow out, Bellingham? Cut your losses?" Rafe asked.

Hampton's head jutted forward on a thin neck, and his face crumpled in on itself in an attempt to appear intimidating. "You'd better keep at it. Luck will turn your way. It's bound to. Your sister will be none too pleased if you come home in the dun."

The viscount directed his comments toward Bellingham but his beady eyes bored into Rafe. With his auburn hair and squinched features, Hampton looked like an angry red squirrel protecting a stash of acorns. Rafe held back a smile.

Bellingham shuddered with an exaggerated grimace. "You gents don't know my battle-ax of a sister. She'll have me strung up by my bollocks if I lose my stipend already. I'd be forced to eat at home the rest of the month listening to her unending lectures."

"I'm sure she would appreciate you discussing her in such glowing terms in a gaming hell," Rafe admonished, his gaze following the shuffle. It was Hampton's deal, and he didn't trust the man one bit.

Bellingham shifted on his seat but said no more. A combination of luck and skill held for Rafe over the next hands, and he took a majority of the tricks, causing the merchants to bow out. Two men with opportunity glinting in their eyes attempted to insert themselves into the game, but Rafe glared and waved them off.

"Perhaps now is a good time for all of us to move on to less taxing endeavors." If Rafe retreated now, the circling vultures would take his place and fleece both men.

Hampton slumped in his chair, ashen-faced and with a betraying tightness around his mouth. "We play on, right, Bellingham?"

"Why not? At this point, I'm so far in the hole, there's not much to do but try to climb out." Bellingham's eyes were bleary, his good humor having gone the way of his money.

Rafe tended to disagree, but who was he to tell a duke what to do? It was Rafe's deal, and although he hadn't learned how to expertly deal off the bottom like some of his home office counterparts, he counted and tracked the cards.

He revealed the trump card. Bellingham perked up. Hampton, sinking even farther down in his seat, took all new cards, but it was hopeless for both men.

"I want to raise the bet. I don't have it on me, but I'm good for it. I'm a man of honor." Bellingham's eyes reflected a sudden vitality.

"I don't think that's wise," Rafe said in a low voice.

"Why not let the man finish it, Drummond? Are you afraid you'll lose? Are you a coward?" Hampton leaned forward, his tone overly belligerent.

Rafe slammed a fist onto the table, rattling the glasses. "I'll give you one chance to retract that question and apologize, else we can take this game outside, and it's likely to end quite painfully for you, Hampton. Take your pick."

Hampton tried to hold Rafe's gaze, but like most men, he couldn't. He dropped his chin to his chest and his gaze to his cards. "My sincere apologies," he mumbled in a distinctly unapologetic tone.

"Gentlemen, please." Bellingham scribbled something on a scrap of paper and threw it into the middle of the table. "Here's my voucher."

Rafe shook his head at the young man's foolishness, but better he won the pot than Hampton. The hand played out as Rafe had foreseen, and he tucked his winnings, plus Bellingham's voucher into his coat. The duke stared at his hands as if they'd somehow betrayed him, looking considerably younger than his twenty years.

Rafe rubbed the knuckle of his forefinger along his lower lip. "I'll expect you tomorrow morning at eleven o'clock to discuss your losses, Bellingham."

The duke moaned. "Minerva's going to flay me alive." He dropped his head into his hands. Rafe could almost see the exuberance the liquor had imparted earlier eroding into the start of a blinding hangover. He was all too familiar with the painful process.

Hampton emerged from his stupor and shoved back from the table. His chair toppled. "For Christ's sake, Bellingham, ask your sister for your bollocks back." He stomped out, and the door swung wildly in his wake.

"Come on, lad. Time to go home and sleep it off." Rafe hauled the young duke to his feet and out into the warm August night. Hampton had decamped, and no carriage awaited the duke. Rafe whistled for a hackney.

Bellingham's knees buckled and his eyes fluttered closed. Rafe shoved him onto a squab, jostling him awake. After giving the driver instructions, Rafe claimed the seat across from the duke.

"What're you doing?" Bellingham's words slurred together.

"Seeing you home. You'll end up beaten and robbed otherwise."

"Not like I have anything left to take. Why're you being so nice? Minerva says you're an arse," Bellingham said with a cynical laugh and unguarded tongue.

"Does she now?" Rafe was well aware of what the duke's imperious sister thought of him. Not that he'd gone out of his way to garner her good will, in fact, just the opposite. The woman inspired a surprising and uncomfortable level of ire.

She was an undisputed diamond of the first water with her high cheekbones, sensuous mouth, and blonde hair he imagined felt like silk. Unlike other ladies of the ton, she never disguised the keen intelligence in her blue eyes behind tittering laughter and inane flirting.

Publically, he blamed his aggravation on her peripheral involvement in his sister's reckless enterprises over the spring. Her spirit in the face of his righteous anger had filled him with disquiet. But deeper, more primal reasons flowed under the surface.

She represented something forever lost in the war.

While he'd killed and schemed and lied to protect England, he'd ruined any chance of ever obtaining the kind of happiness a woman like her could bring. Her unmarred purity only underscored his tarnished soul a hundred fold.

"She used to be nice to me. Coddled me, made sure Cook made my favorites. Now, all she does is nag. Tells me I'm an embarrassment." Bellingham untied his limp cravat. "Perhaps she's right. Dammit, she has a *look* that can wither a man. Completely emasculate him. Have you seen it?"

"I've been on the receiving end once or twice. Didn't take."

Bellingham's laugh was small and humorless. "No, I don't suppose it did. Works on me though. Makes me feel about ten years old."

"If you'd quit running around with men like Hampton and take on some responsibility, perhaps you wouldn't get her look as often."

"Bloody hell, you sound exactly like her. I say, Drummond, is there some way we could settle our debt without my sister finding out? Perhaps there's something I could help you with?" Bellingham asked with a hopeful lilt.

"I doubt you possess any skills that could be of use to me,

Bellingham," Rafe said, but he pulled at his beard, surprisingly diverted by the idea of the duke under his tutelage.

"Tomorrow, I face the dragon. It almost brings me to tears. I 'ppreciate you seeing me home." Bellingham's blond head lolled back on the squabs as his words trailed off into the darkness.

Rafe was amused to realize Bellingham was more intimidated by his sister than the man to whom he'd lost a fortune. The duke listed against the side of the hack, the rhythmic swaying of the carriage lulling him to sleep. For the rest of the ride, Rafe trailed a finger down the long path of his scar and considered the young man.

Although irresponsible, stubborn, and dissolute, the duke was also amusing, considerate and reasonably intelligent. Rafe had observed the easy, convivial way he had treated the merchants and the serving wenches at Parsons.

Bellingham was trying hard to force himself down a rake's path, but his innate nature was friendly and kind, which was why men like Hampton would eat him alive. He reminded Rafe of a green recruit headed to war, ill equipped and innocent.

Still unsure what, if anything, he could do to help the duke, or if he even wanted to try, they arrived at Bellingham's palatial townhouse. He tossed the young man over one shoulder and hauled him up the steps to pound on the door, forgoing the delicate brass knocker. A footman took charge of the duke. By the long-suffering sigh of the servant, he'd seen to the duke's care in the middle of the night before.

The soft night gathered around Rafe, offering a blanket of comfort he'd rarely experienced since coming back from the war. The clack of carriages on distant streets and the call of summer birds filled the night. The loneliness that incessantly dogged him slept, and pulling in deep lungfuls of warm air, he decided to walk home.

With his townhouse in sight and thinking he might finally get a few hours of dreamless sleep, the hairs along the back of his neck rose.

Danger.

He kept his gait loose, not betraying his sudden alertness, and swept his gaze in every direction. Shadowy movement down a set of servant stairs across from his townhouse sent fight impulses skittering through his body.

Rafe slowed his pace and prepared for his assailants to make the first move. When he was within five feet of the stairs, a single man launched out of the darkness. The blade of a knife gleamed in the moonlight.

Dormant instincts roared to life. Rafe caught the smaller man's wrist in his left hand and squeezed. The knife fell to the cobblestones with a clang. A pained cry came from his attacker. Rafe jabbed the man in the throat with his right elbow. The man crumpled like a sack of turnips, rolling on the ground and huffing for air.

Less than a minute had passed. The attack had been weak and amateurish, and he toed over his would-be assassin with more curiosity than ire.

Viscount Hampton.

"You should learn to quit while you're ahead." Rafe adjusted his cravat and smoothed his waistcoat as if he'd dismounted a horse and not flogged a man.

Fear shined from Hampton's eyes, and his body trembled. Rafe hoped he wouldn't wet himself.

"Are you going to kill me?" Hampton croaked out, holding his throat.

Rafe pursed his lips and considered the man, letting him sweat a little. "No, I don't believe I will. It's late, and I'm in no mood for a visit from the local authorities. However, if you cross me again, you'll discover exactly how dangerous I can be. Is that understood?"

"Yes, yes, Lord Drummond." Hampton scrambled to his knees and reached for the knife. Rafe covered the blade with the heel of his boot as Hampton's fingertips grazed the handle.

"I think not. In case this little lesson didn't sink in." Rafe retrieved the knife.

Hampton didn't argue, but hate twisted his lips. Rafe palmed the hilt and jabbed the blade toward Hampton in intimidation rather than real threat. The man jumped to his feet and clattered down the street.

Desperation drove men to folly, and Hampton was desperate enough to mount an ill-advised attack to gain back his losses. Rafe guessed Hampton wasn't finished with the Duke of Bellingham either.

* * * * *

Lady Minerva Bellingham sought her desk with grasping hands, knees weakened by her brother's words. She wished she were the swooning sort. Oblivion sounded wonderful, even if it were only a brief respite.

"You did what?" she whispered.

Simon slumped in a chair in her study, his Adam's apple bobbing in either nervousness or from the effort involved in not casting up his accounts.

By all rights, the study should have been his, but her ridiculous, foolish younger brother had no interest in acting the duke...outside of the social obligations. So Minerva had invaded and conquered the masculine room. She'd banished the hunting pictures and paraphernalia to the attics, added a whimsical watercolor, crystal cut lamps, and a rotating assortment of fresh flowers. Soft-yellow wall coverings and comfortable armchairs completed the transformation.

Usually, the room was her sanctuary, but not today. Today, it was her hell. Gaining her chair, she sank down. Her agitated gaze cast around the neatly organized papers and ledgers.

"This is an unmitigated disaster. How could you be so imbecilic?" Although her voice started in a whisper, it rose until the last insulting word rang in the quiet. Her anger offered a solid mast to cling to in the maelstrom.

Not that she expected a satisfying answer, but her brother's casual shrug only fed her fury. With trembling fingers, she picked up the scrap of paper again. "This is my entire dowry, Simon."

"Isn't so bad, is it? Can't you use your connections with Drummond's sister or your feminine wiles to force him to forgive the debt like a gentleman?" Simon attempted a smile of boyish charm, but instead belched loudly and covered his mouth with fingers that emphasized his pasty face.

She closed her eyes and reached for a shred of sanity, feeling nearly as sick as Simon looked. Pinching the bridge of her nose, she said with exaggerated calmness, "Lord Drummond deemed me a poor influence on his sister and forbad me to associate with her ever again. Not that we abide by his absurd dictate, which is another black mark against me, no doubt. Does that sound like a man who might be swayed by my pretty compliments?"

With a grimace, Simon flipped the piece of parchment and tapped the faint writing on the other side. "I'm due to meet with him at eleven to discuss the transfer of funds."

She pushed herself out of the chair, her mouth agape, double-checking the clock. "But it's already half past nine."

"I couldn't drag myself out of bed any earlier." He shifted in his chair and ran a hand through thick blond hair so similar to hers. "You must see I can't go talk to him. I don't know what I could sign over or where your dowry money is kept."

She moved in front of Simon and propped her hip on the monstrous, dark oak desk used by generations of dukes. When and how had things gone so terribly wrong? Had their parents' early death set him on this path? Was it the influence of his roguish

Eton friends? Was it their isolated childhood?

Outwardly dutiful, Minerva had chafed under the strict rule of their tutor. At sixteen, she had insisted their solicitor-guardian dismiss the man. Simon had finished his education at Eton, and Minerva had blossomed with the freedom. She'd met with their ancient solicitor almost daily, acting as his secretary. He'd treated her like the child he'd never had and, proper or not, had indulged her strange notions.

Her mind had absorbed the intricacies of management and investment like rain on parched earth. Calculating risk and rates of return had been infinitely more satisfying than spending hours on useless embroidery. With his eyesight failing, he'd sought a younger man to take charge of the Bellingham estates, and Minerva had maneuvered for her choice, Maxwell Drake. A self-made man whose progressive opinions made him open to a partnership with her.

Sprawled in a corner chair, his legs outstretched and crossed at the ankle, Drake observed their familial drama play out in his usual taciturn manner. He tapped a silent rhythm on the velvet chair arm, and his hooded gaze shifted between them, missing nothing. She trusted Drake and relied on his objectivity. All she could focus on was her brother's irresponsibility. The reality of the financial debacle was overwhelming.

She held her hands up. "What in the world are we to do? The estates are entailed, and the majority of our funds are tied up in the tea plantation. If we pull out now, we'll take an enormous loss. My dowry is the only accessible means of payment."

Drake levered himself up and loomed over Simon. "Tell me again how much you lost, *Your Grace*."

Minerva rolled her eyes. There was no love lost between her flippant brother and the dour Scot. If only Drake would mask his disdain.

Pride straightened Simon's spine and forced his chin out.

"Twenty thousand, three hundred and ten pounds."

Upon hearing the sum in conjunction with his attitude, she opened her mouth to unleash another diatribe but just as quickly clamped it shut with such force pain radiated through her jaw. What was the use? Simon crossed his arms over his chest and tilted his head back as if the ceiling held the answers to their problems.

Drake pulled out one of their ledgers and opened it on the desk. He ran a finger down a column of numbers. "The wisest course of action would be to arrange a payment plan with Drummond. Offer him half your dowry, my lady, and then negotiate to pay the rest over…three years, should do it."

Half her dowry? Once word spread Simon had gambled away half her dowry, how many invitations would get lost in transit? How many indirect cuts should she expect while out walking or riding in Hyde Park? Drake didn't understand the fickle, intemperate nature of the ton. It would delight in her humiliation and downfall more than most.

As a duke's sister with a large marriage settlement, she enjoyed a certain power in Society. Even so, the whispers had reached her—cold fish, ice princess, heartless, disagreeable. Never to her face. To her face, they were full of pandering compliments. It had taken a long, painful season for her skin to thicken, but the hypocritical nature of Society had eventually stopped troubling her. And there were some—Lily Masterson, Rafe Drummond's sister, in particular—whom she counted as true friends.

"Is there no other choice?" She tried to massage the lump out of her throat.

"You could offer him your entire dowry…and your hand in marriage," Drake said with his usual black humor.

Her small puff of laughter sprung her mind free of its debilitating distress. "Do you think half is reasonable? I'm not sure how this sort of arrangement is typically handled." Ignoring Simon, who still stared defiantly at the ceiling, she chewed on a fingernail.

"Lord Drummond is not in need of funds. His estates are well run, and he's not usually a gambler. In fact, he's rarely in town, preferring to reside at his country estate…perhaps for obvious reasons," Drake said with a hint of empathy as he limped to lean against the mantle. He too had been injured in service to the Crown.

"That was it." Simon thumped his knee with his fist. "That hideous scar distracted my play. I'm sure I would have won if I could have stopped staring at his gruesome face."

The look she shot her brother caused him to sink even farther into the cushioned chair as if her gaze physically wounded him. "I'm sure Lord Drummond's scar caused you to lose. It certainly wasn't the fact you are a horrific loo player, and it had positively nothing to do with the bottle of brandy you guzzled before the game."

Minerva slammed the ledger shut. Simon jumped and gave her his full attention. "For pity's sake, take responsibility for your actions and don't blame a man who served his country while you were here whoring, drinking and gambling."

Simon inhaled sharply and rose. "Ladies do not speak in such a fashion. I'm a duke, don't forget."

Rage vibrated her entire body. "You are my little brother, and if I could, I'd take you across my knee and spank your bottom until it was red." She took several deep breaths, but her nerves remained frazzled. "Leave me now, but I expect you to stay in this house until I return with news. You had better hope it's good, or there's an estate in Northumberland that could use some hands-on attention."

"You wouldn't. You couldn't." His eyes widened, and his mouth hung open.

"Couldn't what? Mete out a spanking or a banishment? Don't test me. Now get out of my sight." She pointed to the study door.

His jaw clenched but no protest was forthcoming. She really

had no authority to banish him, but by God, she would try her damnedest to remove him from London's licentious influence. Simon stalked out, eyeing Drake with unvarnished contempt.

"I believe my days in the Bellingham employ are numbered." Drake pulled at his lower lip, his gaze on the empty doorway.

"Don't even think about leaving. I'm not sure what I would do without you." She laid an imploring hand on his arm. "I'm sure Simon will come around and see the merits of keeping you in place as an advisor. He knows nothing of the estates and investments. I can't handle him alone."

Her desperation softened his usually stern features. "I won't desert you, but I've already stayed in London longer than I intended. Anyway, you'll eventually marry—"

Minerva snorted. "Not without a dowry, I won't."

His lips twitched, as close to a smile as he came. "You will. I see the flowers and cards that arrive daily. You could have your pick of gentlemen. And, when you do, you'll no longer need me to act as your proxy, which is how it should be."

After three years in society without finding a gentleman who interested her past a dance or two, she wasn't as confident. In truth, the stinging loss of her dowry wasn't about societal acceptance or finding a suitable man to marry, but about having the choice *not* to marry. That money would have reverted to her control when she turned thirty years of age, allowing her relative freedom.

"What about the here and now? Do you think I should insist Simon go face his reckoning?" She smoothed her hair back, doubting herself once again where her brother was concerned. Why couldn't he act logically and predictably like a row of sums?

"It depends on your aim. If you want to humiliate him, by all means, send him to Lord Drummond. If you want to preserve as much of your dowry as possible and keep the investments intact, it will be far better for you to negotiate the provisions."

Her spine stiffened with a huge breath, the decision thrust upon her. "I must change. Would you call for the carriage?"

He murmured an assent, and she started up the staircase on feeble legs, attempting to rub the start of a throbbing headache away. The blue silk with the matching pelisse? It was the most flattering and revealed a hint of bosom. On the other hand, her dove-gray extended to her neck and exuded nothing but business. No, definitely the blue. She needed as many weapons as possible in her arsenal. She would do whatever was necessary to fix the mess, including employing her feminine wiles.

CHAPTER TWO

Minerva dragged herself up the Drummond front steps as if on the way to the gallows to deliver her final words. In a dream-like state, she watched her disembodied hand pull the bell cord. In a blink, the butler announced her into Lord Drummond's study. The rustle of her blue silk skirts as she stepped inside offered the only sound of greeting.

The warm, civilized, book-filled room surprised her. The master of the study, on the other hand, shot ice into her veins from his large armchair. Polished boots with dirt and grass embedded in the tread were propped on the desk. Even in a slouch, tension radiated from his body.

She forced herself to stay rooted while he examined her from head to toe. Her trembles would betray her sickening nerves, and she refused to give him the satisfaction. She needed every ounce of courage she could muster—even if it was all for show—but with each passing moment, his insolent study raised her anxiety another notch.

Rafe Drummond was a fearsome sight. While some might think the lined scar that ran from his brow into his beard imparted that impression, for her, it was his eyes. The swirled blue and gray coronas reminded her of a dangerous ocean, ready to pulverize dissenters.

Sleek, expressive brows overset his stormy eyes. A black ribbon tied back wavy, dark brown hair, much too long for current fashion. Although, she suspected he didn't cow to society's expectations in any way. An escaped piece brushed a sharp cheekbone. A crook marred a blade of a nose, and his mouth, the corners pulled down in displeasure, looked hard, unyielding. Undisguisable by the beard, his chin jutted prominently, lending him a stubborn, overly aggressive look.

Muscular and huge in every direction, he exuded a masculine virility that ton dandies played at. She'd always felt…well, *feminine* around him. For a woman used to bossing men hither and yon, his strength was strangely appealing.

His comportment, however, was abominable. A welcome indignation rose at his blatant, seated perusal, steadying her quivering knees and fluttery hands. Finally, so slowly it had to be deliberate, his boots thudded to the floor. He rose and gestured her to the armchair across from the desk.

She fussily arranged her skirts, not sure how to begin the interview. Once reseated, he swung his boots back on the desk and trailed his forefinger down his scar. The man was a foreign language. Was he angry? Surprised? Pleased to see her? Probably not the latter. She stifled an inappropriate, nervous giggle.

"I expected your brother, my lady. Is he behind your skirts, perhaps?" His voice was rife with sarcasm.

Fisting her hands so tightly fingernails bit through her thin, lace gloves to score her palm, she forced an even voice. "I am acting on the duke's behalf. I understand he was involved in a high-stakes game last night whilst in his cups, and you fleeced him of a large sum of money."

"Fleeced him, did I? Believe me, I tried to convince him to stop playing, but the young whelp refused. And, let me tell you, he would have lost even sober. He's a horrendous player." He weaved a surprising amount of lazy amusement in his insult.

Off balance, she smoothed her hair. "What's done is done, I suppose. I'm here to discuss repayment."

"Interesting. What are you proposing?" He arched his legs gracefully to the floor and leaned over the desk. Lacing his fingers, he pinned her with steely eyes.

The sudden intensity startled her. Weren't his lashes unusually long for a man? "Well...I..." Heat suffused her body, making her wish for a fan.

"Did you bring a bank note?" Both his eyebrows rose while his gaze coasted over her face.

"I...that is...no." Jabbing a finger to emphasize her negative response, she grabbed at the frayed threads of her rehearsed offer with profound relief. "I hoped you would accept half the money now, and we would repay the rest over the course of three years."

"Are you telling me you don't have the available funds? Is the duke in the dun with others?" His eyebrows arched higher.

For pity's sake, what if Simon had vowels all over town? The grim possibility had her patting the prickly, hot skin of her forehead. "I don't think so."

"If he isn't yet, he soon will be." The prediction was delivered somberly.

All she could do was stay the course. "The money is tied up in investments. If I withdraw now, I'll take an enormous loss. Given time, I'll be able to pay you with the dividends."

"*I'll* take a loss. *I'll* pay. You're doing the duke a disservice if *you* constantly clean up *his* messes. If I agree, will your brother turn a new leaf? If I were a betting man—" his lips quirked, "—my guess is he could be in the same predicament tonight, but to someone not willing to be as generous. Tell me, why didn't he come this morning?" He pressed steepled fingers to his mouth.

Her gaze drifted to his large hands—rough, callused, capable hands. They reflected a man well acquainted with hard work. A few thin white scars ran over the tanned backs dotted with dark hair. Her stomach spun as if she tumbled off a cliff, and her mind blanked once again.

He cleared his throat. The rumble tossed her back in the moment. "I-I manage the estates and investments. Simon's still young and doesn't know where our money has been allocated."

"He's twenty, isn't he? You can't be much older than that. Two and twenty, perhaps?" His brow furrowed.

She nodded once.

"How long have you been handling the estate business?"

"I started learning the ins and outs when I was sixteen and took it over entirely at nineteen with the help of my man of affairs." Minerva worried her bottom lip with her teeth, knowing the path his thoughts tread was a dangerous one for her. His cold eyes sparked with a heat that sucked the moisture from her mouth and forced her tongue out to daub her lips.

"My point is your brother is quite old enough to take on a responsibility you have handled since you were nineteen. In fact, you should have handed over the reins already." His voice had dropped and roughened. "It's quite unseemly for a lady to be involved in business."

His words pierced her cloud of befuddlement and released a torrent of resentment. "Not seemly? Are women too emotional or are our brains too small? Please tell me you don't believe the drivel some of these scientists purport?" Her voice was unsteady and reflected more vulnerability than she was comfortable showing. "If I had handed things to Simon, we'd be on the streets and penniless."

"You've coddled and controlled him to the point of uselessness. Do you enjoy having your brother under your thumb?" The corner of his mouth drew back as if he took delight in the provocation.

Anger twisted her gut. She rose, placed her fists on his desk, and leaned forward. He mimicked her stance until they were face-to-face across the desk.

"I hate constantly worrying about my brother. I've done my best to guide him, and for you to suggest this debacle is my fault is unmerited. You would rather see me ruined than help. Don't deny it. You're heartless and…and…an arse." The word hung between them. Had she really cursed at him? She was so close she could see his pupils dilate, darkening his eyes.

"And you are a haughty, conceited shrew." Irony, not horror, laced his voice.

She gasped, even though her insult had been more shocking.

"I have an alternate proposal. Either you pay me all the money today, or you and your brother come to Wintermarsh and pay off his debt by working for me." His mouth clamped shut in a frown.

Is this what he'd been planning since luring Simon into the high-stakes game? To what end? It was utterly beyond the pale. Her throat closed to the size of a reed.

"I assure you, Lord Drummond, I am a lady and not some…some…Covent Garden strumpet. I have an unbesmirched reputation." Still face-to-face with her over the desk, he dominated her, and her thoughts scattered like dropped marbles.

"Never fear, I don't require your services in that manner." His eyes warmed from ice to molten steel in an instant. He leaned even closer to whisper a few inches from her ear, "I only invite willing women to my bed and have no need to pay them." His breath skittered across her neck like the brush of gentle fingertips.

Gentlemen didn't speak of such things to ladies. It was disrespectful, despicable. She tried to summon the proper horror. Instead, she angled toward him and took a deep breath. Heady warmth and an intoxicating smell assailed her.

Soap, leather, and a scent that belonged entirely to him wafted over her, smothering her outrage. An irrational urge to bury her nose in the nape of his neck right where an escaped lock of hair curled over his open shirt had her creeping forward. No collar or cravat impeded her body's single-minded goal. She jerked herself upright in the same instant he sprawled back into his chair.

"What sort of work are you proposing then, my lord?" Smoothing the wrinkles out of her dress, she focused on an ornate dagger acting as a paperweight.

"Housework for you and outdoor work for your brother. I'll teach Simon about the day-to-day requirements of running an estate. He'll be kept busy with no time for trouble."

Minerva wandered to a set of shelves that ran along the wall of his study, putting much-needed space between them and buying herself time. Obviously, his aim was her humiliation, and she didn't savor submitting herself to his control.

But there was the no small matter of her dowry. If she paid him today, it would all be gone. Every quid. She would be left to find an inferior husband or left to rely on her intemperate brother for the rest of her life. In truth, left with nothing.

If she paid Lord Drummond and released her brother from responsibility, Simon might be back out tonight drinking, gambling, ruining them. This impetuous, ill-advised bargain would force him out of London and fill his days with hard work. Her choices ranged from bad to devastating.

"Why would you want me there as well if not to humiliate me?"

"Would you allow your brother to come and put himself under my care with no oversight from you?" he asked in an amused voice. Her dismay must have been apparent, because he didn't wait for a reply. "Learning some humility wouldn't be amiss, Lady Minerva. If you want to watch over Simon, you must work as well. That's my bargain."

She propped her hands on her hips, her usually impeccable manners deserting her once again. "Humility? Me? That's a kettle-

and-pot situation if ever I heard one. You're the most arrogant—"

"Yes, yes, heartless and a complete arse. You've made your opinion clear. But if I were indebted to you, you'd seize your pound of flesh and negotiate for more."

She rubbed her temple and cast about for any other option. None presented itself. "How long would the arrangement last? There are certain functions I'm obliged to attend, and Drake needs to be made aware of everything that must be handled in my absence."

"The beau monde will head out of town in a few weeks. Let's say the two of you plan to arrive at Wintermarsh the second week of September and work for me at least…three months. Your debt would be paid by Christmastime." He twirled the dagger in his hands, his gaze on the ceiling.

Three months. A pittance compared to a lifetime indentured in a loveless marriage. "If I agree to this, I would need everything in writing. In three months, you'll tear up the voucher and sign a paper absolving the debt. There can be no physical mistreatment of either of us. You wouldn't be able to extend our time without due cause, and you can't discuss our arrangement. Is that understood?"

"Do you want me to involve my solicitor or is a *gentleman's* agreement written and signed by the two of us sufficient?" He sounded amused by her demands.

"No third parties. I can't allow a word to get around London. I would be ruined. What about your servants? Will they gossip?"

"If they did, who would believe them? It's rather far-fetched to think a duke and his sister would be working at a country estate. You're Lily's friend. It's not implausible I would invite you to stay at Wintermarsh." With a flick of his wrist, he flung the knife end over end. The tip embedded in the wooden top of the desk.

Minerva's couldn't look away from the vibrating handle. His ease and familiarity with the weapon planted another seed of worry and doubt. What kind of man was Lord Drummond?

"I'll send a contract for your perusal. You can revise and amend to your heart's content. We both need to think the situation over at some length, don't you agree?" he asked.

"I do finally agree with you on something, my lord." Relief and fear warred internally while she walked to the door.

Finally playing the gentleman, he rose to see her out.

"I shall wait for your proposal, Lord Drummond. I…I mean your *terms*." Yet another blush bloomed across her face. Proposal indeed.

Quirking an eyebrow, he hummed, his lips curling. The smile, if it even qualified as such, held her immobile. The flash of humor in his blue-grey eyes was a wash of refreshing water, cooling the tension and anxiety of the interview.

The study door closed gently in her face. The dignified white-haired butler saw her out, and she glanced back at the imposing, black front door. Had she made a bargain with the devil?

CHAPTER THREE

A week later, Lily appeared at an unfashionably early hour in the Bellingham morning room, seething like a volcano ready to erupt. "First, I am in utter disbelief my brother came up with such a foul, underhanded plan. Secondly, I can hardly countenance the fact that you agreed. Why, Minerva, why?"

"This bargain is preferable to signing away my dowry to pay for Simon's foolishness. To be frank, with Simon at Wintermarsh for the autumn, he can't find more trouble in London or at a house party. The fact that your brother wants me to work as well—" Minerva held up her hands and shrugged. "It's no secret how he feels about me. I'll bear up fine. It's only for three months, after all."

Lily threw herself down on the settee and drummed her fingers on crossed arms. "I think it's ghastly and told Rafe such. He's usually not such an ogre. If only you could have known him before the war. He's always been a bit quiet, but he's a good brother. This intense dislike he harbors for you is unnatural."

"I did nearly bankrupt him on your wardrobe and then procured an indecent dress and sent you off to a Cyprian's ball," Minerva said with a small smile.

Lily ignored her attempt at levity. "My brother had the funds to foot a wardrobe, don't let him fool you. Plus, you didn't know it was a Cyprian's ball. I tried to defend you."

"I'm sure that went over like weevils in the flour. I get the impression he believes I should be above such foolishness. And perhaps I should be."

"I attempted to talk him out of this insanity. He stonewalled me. Gray even tried when they were in the study taking a brandy together. He said Rafe categorically refused to discuss it." Lily patted Minerva's hand. "I did extract a promise he wouldn't hurt you in any way. Told him I'd cut off his... Needless to say, he took heed. Acted as if I had impugned his honor by even asking for reassurances. Can you imagine the blasted gall? You only need to send a note, and I'll be there in a thrice to beat my brother senseless."

"I'll miss you." Minerva couldn't help but laugh at the picture Lily drew. As she departed, Lily hugged her with solemn, worried eyes she tried to hide behind a smile.

Minerva decided to get their indenture underway, praying the anticipation would prove more painful than fulfillment of the actual terms. She'd slept poorly since sending back the finalized agreement.

In most of her dreams, a red-eyed scarred devil with a whip made her clean floors, grates or rugs on her hands and knees until her fingers bled. Even more disturbing, some of her dreams had her bartering her body to the heavenly smelling brute, and she woke ill at ease and flustered.

With the sun barely chasing the stars from the sky, she and Simon set off in their carriage, a week before they were expected. Her brother left his horse in the city. Neither of them would be enjoying pleasurable jaunts across the countryside. With his legs braced apart, he sat across from her and stared out the open window.

"The countryside is lovely, isn't it?" she asked.

"I s'pose." He crossed his arms and kept his face averted.

"Three months is a pittance. We can endure anything for a measly three months."

"I s'pose."

"The country air will be good for us. Lily says Lord Drummond keeps an extensive stable. You'd enjoy working with the horses, wouldn't you?" Her voice sounded overly bright and brittle, even to her own ears.

"I s'pose."

"For pity's sake, Simon. We're doing this and might as well make the best of it." Her fake exuberance dissolved.

"Easy for you to say."

"Easy…you clodpoll. I wouldn't be in this mess if it weren't for you." She held a fist to her mouth to stop another tirade. They'd been around and above and below this issue for the past three weeks. Silence reigned for the next hour.

The coachman stopped at an inn for fresh horses, and she and Simon shared a bench, a pot of weak tea, and hard, tasteless biscuits. Perhaps feeling contrite, he commented on the weather, the road conditions and even the latest vote in Parliament.

"I didn't know you held an interest in government policy." She feared her mouth had fallen wide open.

He turned the teacup in his hands, his gaze fixed on the swirling liquid. "Contrary to your earlier stated opinion that I'm a clodpoll, I plan on taking my seat as soon as I come into my majority. I feel strongly about certain issues."

"That's admirable. What issues, pray tell?"

His animated gaze met hers, and he skipped over his words. "Issues of poverty. You can't imagine the way some Londoners live right under our noses. Young boys forced into servitude as sweeps, girls forced into prostitution in order to eat. In Seven Dials, women are—"

"Seven Dials? That place is dangerous. What in the world were you doing in such an area? Don't tell me you were gambling."

"Never mind." He retreated into his shell and stared back at his cup, his mouth pulled in a tight line. He picked up a biscuit, apparently thought better of it, and tossed it back down.

Their brief genial mood dissipated like morning fog, and a black cloud settled over the rest of the long, torturous trip. The carriage rocked back and forth in troughs gouged by recent rains. Dizzy and queasy, Minerva clutched the window frame with one hand while the other covered her eyes. Her concentration centered on keeping her stomach contents where they belonged.

A shout from the coachman and lurch of the carriage as they turned down the drive signaled their approach to Wintermarsh. Huge oak trees filtered the remaining meager sunlight. Eerily lit looming branches reached for the carriage, and the wind whistled through long shadows. The hollow pit in her stomach had nothing to do with the arduous carriage ride.

No light broke the dark stone façade of Wintermarsh, only adding to the ominous undercurrents urging her to flee. As soon as they pulled to a stop, Simon pushed the carriage door ajar and jumped to solid ground. She inhaled damp, cooled air to call Simon over to assist her down.

The front door hurled open with a boom. She startled and her lungs stilled, words lost. Lord Drummond stood framed in the doorway like the portrait of an ancient warrior. Dim candlelight glowed behind him and kept his expression a mystery. Clad only in boots, breeches and a white shirt rolled up his forearms, he stalked down the steps. The grim set of his mouth promised a confrontation. A warm welcome it was not.

Unable to tear her gaze away, she stepped out of the carriage, but her foot found no perch. Simon hadn't bothered to lower the steps. She closed her eyes and braced for a painful impact.

Arms snatched her against a hard chest. The rush of blood

and her quickened breathing blocked out any noise, but the blast of fear heightened her other senses. Rafe Drummond's heart thumped against her breast and coaxed hers into the same rhythm. Heat permeated the thinness of his shirt and seeped into her body. She clutched at his brawny biceps like lifelines.

Cracking her eyes open, they met his corded neck and jumping pulse. She tipped her head back and confronted his scar, red and angry. Her fingertips itched to discover how far into his beard it descended, simply curious.

Their gazes met. He appeared unsure, but perhaps his expression was a trick of the shadows. He plopped her away from him, and she skimmed her hands down to the hairy, sinewy muscles of his bare forearms. Her legs still quivered. Instead of shaking her off as she expected, he tested the span of her waist with his huge hands and slid them down a few inches to the curve of her hips.

Her stomach turned, perhaps still upset from their journey or fear, but it seemed a different sort of nervousness this time. She tensed and pushed him away with an odd reluctance. Pressing her hands over her stomach, she attempted to stem her trembles and nerves.

"What the devil are the two of you doing here?" With his arms akimbo, he loomed over her, a sneer in his voice.

She stepped from a sinking bog back onto solid, familiar ground. "I sent a message informing you of our early arrival, my lord. I thought it best to get our agreement started as soon as possible."

"I received no such message. The servants have the evening off."

Surely he wouldn't make them travel back to the last inn they'd passed. Weakness or not, she might collapse in a fit of tears if she had to climb back into the rocking torture box. "Lord Drummond, we've been travelling all day. Frankly, I'm exhausted.

Couldn't you show us to our rooms? We won't be any trouble." Aiming for genial, she sounded closer to desperate.

He sighed and swept his gaze over her, ignoring Simon altogether. "I suppose it's not worth making you turn around. I'll show you to your accommodations." He turned on his heel and trudged back inside, obviously expecting them to follow. She was certain her eyes mirrored Simon's wide and anxious ones.

Lord Drummond stopped in the entry hall and pointed to a room on their left. "Wait in my study while I take your brother to the stables."

"You're going to examine the horses? At this time of night?" she asked.

At odds with a brow still furrowed with displeasure, his smile chilled her. "The duke will be residing in a small room there. He'll be quite comfortable, I assure you." After a small, ironic bow, he beckoned Simon to follow.

Her brother's eyes implored for intervention, but frozen, her mouth agape, she was only able to watch Simon follow him out the door. Lud, in all her imaginings, she'd never considered them not sleeping in a set of guest rooms. Where would he tuck her away? On a pallet in the kitchens?

Her hysterical giggle reverberated in the cold entry, and she clamped a hand over her mouth. She approached his study on tiptoes, not sure what to expect. A medieval dungeon? Evidence of his hunting prowess littering every surface?

She toed the door open. The room enveloped her in warm, masculine-scented air. An open book and a glass with two fingers of brandy sat next to a large, comfortable-looking armchair. In any other circumstances, she might admire the dark ornately carved mantle framing a crackling fire. She might even peruse the books bursting from the shelves giving the room a comfortable, lived-in feel. Instead, circumstances demanded that she pace and bite her fingernails to the point of pain.

An eternity passed before the entry door opened. She scurried out of the study to find Lord Drummond alone.

"How is Simon?" Her shrill voice echoed unnaturally in the empty house.

"Really, Lady Minerva, he's fine. Do you think I've strung him up? Locked him in a cell with a multitude of rats? Applied a little thumbscrew torture? Spending the next months with the horses won't kill him." He chuckled and headed back into the study, where he stopped to empty the contents of his glass in one swallow. She followed close on his heels. "Most likely, only a handful of rats will be sharing his room," he added with a careless shrug.

"Where do you plan on housing me? In the butler's pantry?"

"The pantry. Now that's an intriguing option I never considered." He ran a hand down his chin, seemingly deep in thought. His twitching lips turned a portion of her debilitating anxiety into fury.

Cutting her hand through the air, she wished she were brave enough to kick him in the shin. "Stop it, you lout. Take me to my room."

Annoyance replaced his amusement. Cold, inhospitable eyes bore into hers. "You seem to forget who is the servant and who is the master."

She held his gaze and forced her leaden legs forward. His spark of surprise bolstered her courage. "I may be forced to be your servant, but you will never be my master, Lord Drummond."

"No doubt, any man would find it a challenge to master you. Have they all been driven away by the icy, frigid conditions?"

His jab bobbed past her defenses. Her chest tightened. She walked stiffly out the study door and forced a practiced haughtiness into her words. "It would take more of a man than you to master me, that's for certain. Now, I'm weary. Could you show me to my room, please?" All she wanted was to crawl into a bed and possibly have a good cry.

"You saucy piece of baggage." He ignored her swift intake of breath. "Right this way, my lady." He gestured grandly up the stairs, his tone falsely officious.

He started up the stairs, but she cleared her throat and stood at the foot of the stairs. Waiting until he turned around, she made sure to mimic his tone. "My trunk, Lord Drummond. Since there's no footman, would you be so kind?"

He stomped back down the stairs and heaved the trunk over his shoulder. She wouldn't be surprised to find her dress singed from the hot, furious look he shot her as he passed by. The heavy trunk didn't slow him in the least, and she scampered up the stairs to keep pace, breathless by the time they reached the third floor.

She followed him halfway down a narrow hallway, where he pushed a door open and dropped her trunk in the middle of a room. She caught a glimpse of a disused nursery across the hall.

With the two of them and the trunk, little floor space remained. A few beams of moonlight illuminated the room from a window high above the bed. It smelled pleasant enough however, and besides the bed, she could make out a chest of drawers and a side table.

"I hope you'll find the room up to your standards." Sarcasm dripped from his words, and she could feel, if not see, a malevolent smile.

"It will be adequate. After you fetch me a candle, you may take your leave."

"You want me to fetch? Like your lapdog?" He stalked her.

Tired and thoroughly intimidated in the dark by his size and crackling animosity, she retreated until her back hit the wall. He braced his hands on either side of her head, effectively imprisoning her. Did the humiliation start now? What was his plan? She shrank against the wall. Her palms grew damp, and a lump lodged in her throat.

"You work for me now. If I require something, you shall fetch it. If I request tea, you shall serve it. If I want my boots shined, you shall polish them. Unless you wish to leave that bank note with me and depart?" If it hadn't been for the content of his message, his roughened near-whisper sounded almost comforting.

Not a single witty reply to his threat popped into her head. She could smell brandy on his breath, but under the sweet tones weaved the intoxicating blend of scents that had captivated her in London and haunted her dreams.

Holding her breath, she closed her eyes and turned her face away, the wall cool on her cheek. They stood close but not touching for long moments. The sudden loss of warmth and the receding clomp of boots signaled his departure.

She pried one eye open and blew out a long, ragged exhale. Tension ebbed slowly out of her body with each breath and left her exhausted. She darted out to grab a candle. After locking the door behind her, she sank onto the bed and gathered her scattered thoughts.

She had been wrong. This was worse, so much worse, than the dreaded anticipation. What would the morrow bring? Tears stung, but she refused to give in to them. Her red, puffy eyes would bring him too much satisfaction.

After removing her clothes as best she could, she pulled on a night rail and slipped under the sheets. Even in the best of circumstances, she rarely slept easily. In a strange place, not sure what her future held, she took a particularly long time to drift into a fitful, nightmare-filled sleep.

CHAPTER FOUR

Rafe deserved to be shot. No, too easy. Strung up by his ankles and lashed like the time he'd been captured in Spain. Ignoring the rhythmic, banging protest in his head, he'd risen with the sun and ridden Aries in a pounding, painful gallop.

He finished his ablutions in cold water left untouched the previous evening. His gaze clashed with his reflection in the looking glass. Accusation and shame stared back. Minerva Bellingham had looked at him as if he were a devil last night. Perhaps he was. He'd certainly felt possessed by evil spirits.

The quiet house had been lonely, and his thoughts had travelled dark, treacherous paths, treading too close to the abyss. Certainly, he hadn't expected to have to play congenial host. The shock of seeing her ready to step out of her carriage had fired conflicting emotions. Antagonism he recognized, but the slash of satisfaction of having her at Wintermarsh confused him.

He'd acted a complete boor and used his superior size to intimidate the hell out of her. Although, she hadn't acted particularly intimidated, stinging him with her barbed tongue.

The few times they had been in the same room, he'd felt like a huge, hulking beast next to her delicate perfection—and last night had been no different. The memory of her soft body pressed against his had haunted his dreams. He couldn't recall the color of her travelling dress but remembered the vee of creamy white skin and the fluttering pulse exposed at her neck.

He'd lived like a monk since returning from France, not yet desperate enough to pay a woman to ignore his mean looks for a quick tup. It had been too long since he'd had a woman, that's all. Yet he couldn't quite banish the warmth he'd experienced when he'd looked down, expecting revulsion, but instead seeing only simple curiosity flicker as she studied his face.

As he'd stood over her in the nursemaid's room, the soap she'd used on her hair had cast a spell around him, the sweet feminine scent at odds with her rigid, cold persona. He'd had an urge to pluck the pins from her perfectly coiffed hair and tangle his fingers in the soft curtain. Her trembles had vibrated the thin air between them. No sharp quip launched back. She'd been terrified.

In a now habitual motion, he traced down the red, angry scar, a jagged, puckered line that ran from his forehead across his left cheekbone down to the edge of his jaw. He counted himself lucky he hadn't lost his eye. The stares and whispers bothered him—how could they not?—but at least the beard offered partial concealment.

He pulled on a clean shirt and shrugged into a sturdy navy waistcoat, rolling loose sleeves to his elbow. It promised to be a warm day, and he wasn't one to sacrifice comfort for societal expectations. Anyway, the task he had in mind for Simon might prove a tad messy. Rafe found a small smile.

He popped his head out of his chamber door and grimaced when he saw who lay in wait for him in the corridor. Her eyes shot fire, and her arms were crossed over her chest. Too late for a retreat.

"Good morning, Mrs. Devlin," he said in an overly jolly manner, hoping not to poke his former nursemaid and current housekeeper further into a snit.

"Is it, Master Rafe? For whom? The duke you stashed in the stables or his sister ensconced in the nursery?"

"In my defense—"

"Defense?" She snorted and took two steps closer. The keys at her waist jangled discordantly. "The entire situation is entirely improper. Lady Minerva is the sister of a duke and Miss Lily's friend, for goodness sake. You've lodged her in an inappropriate, inferior room, and now you demand she clean like a common maid? It's intolerable. What the devil are you thinking?"

His diminutive housekeeper kept pace with his long-legged stride to the stairs and looked as if she planned to shove him over the balustrade. His quick, painful descent to the marbled entry hall might be justified, but surely she wouldn't attempt murder with witnesses.

Cuthbertson waited at the foot of the stairs, holding Rafe's practical, wide-brimmed hat. With one eyebrow raised, the butler shook his head as his disappointed tutting echoed throughout the three-story foyer. If they weren't practically his family, he'd sack them both and hire servants who would at least pretend respect.

"Now see here, you two, her brother owes me a great deal of money. It's time for them to pay me back. A forced helping of humble pie will do them both some good, you'll see. Wouldn't you agree a little housework in return for her brother's vowels is preferable to demanding a bank note that would be sure to ruin them both? I'm doing them a favor. Consider me a damn saint."

"Fine then. Make her brother work off his debt. But Lady Minerva wasn't at that gaming hell, unless things have changed dramatically in society," Mrs. Devlin said.

"She deserves… Her attitude about the entire debacle… Goddammit, I can't explain it properly." He ran a hand through his hair and jammed his hat down.

"I don't think you understand why you're doing it," Mrs. Devlin retorted with startling insight.

Rafe had been as surprised as Minerva Bellingham when the outrageous bargain had presented itself. His original plan had been to intimidate the breeches off the duke before tearing up the voucher. When Minerva had glided into his study in a swirl of blue satin, a picture of elegant refinement, his plans had changed.

Bellingham was ultimately to blame. The duke had drunkenly planted a seed that had flourished overnight. Although, Rafe's cloudy motivation for insisting Lady Minerva take part troubled him.

"Give her something to do. Nothing too taxing. I wouldn't want her swooning away in the heat of the kitchens. I'll leave it to your discretion, but I expect her to work, Mrs. Devlin."

"Are you not staying to explain yourself to her? I'm to do your dirty work? Is that it?"

Rafe grabbed buckskin gloves off the table by the door and slapped them in his palm. "I've her brother to see to this morning. Let me warn you, the woman has a sharp tongue."

Hardly intimidated by his gruffness, Mrs. Devlin looked ready to spank him senseless. He did the same thing he'd done at ten when confronted by his furious nursemaid—he fled.

* * * * *

Minerva smoothed her skirt. While she appreciated the warm water and food that arrived not long after she rose, she only managed a few bites of dry toast with some tea. A riot took place in her stomach. What sort of work was Simon being forced to do? What work would be forced on her? Dread had her delaying the inevitable.

Lord Drummond meant to humble her by her less than elegant room. However, in the morning light, she found the room clean and aired, and the bed, while small, was comfortable with soft sheets and a thick, cozy coverlet. Sunlight poured through the large window. She hadn't missed her luxurious rugs or blankets.

The grey woolen day dress she'd chosen was plain and comfortable, but its quality would still surpass any servant's uniform. Most of the dresses she'd packed were bold, elegant and impossible to put on without a maid's help. None of them were appropriate for what Lord Drummond had in mind. What was the appropriate attire for humiliation and embarrassment?

A shrill laugh escaped. No, she would accept whatever the man handed out with the greatest of aplomb and not let him see her ruffled. She was a master of maintaining a cool, calm façade. The ton hadn't bequeathed her the moniker of *ice princess* for nothing. She raised her chin, a practiced mask of nonchalance blanked her face, and she threw the door open with a flourish.

The hallway was empty. Her shoulders slumped, and her breath gusted out. She had expected Lord Drummond to be lurking outside, ready to mete out her duties. Perhaps scrubbing floors on hands and knees or cleaning ash out of every fireplace or cooking and serving his meals or preparing his bath. The list made her stomach try to crawl up her throat.

Instead of Lord Drummond, the housekeeper met her at the bottom of the stairs. Disapproval radiated off her in waves. "My lady, I am so sorry about all of this. I'm not sure what Master Rafe is thinking, but he insisted I give you duties." The woman positively cringed.

"Mrs. Devlin, please don't fret. I don't want to bring Lord Drummond's wrath upon your head as well as mine. I'll satisfy his demands to free my brother from his debt." Minerva laid a hand on Mrs. Devlin arm to stop the woman from wringing her hands raw.

"But it isn't gentlemanly. *That man.* I would take him across my knee if I still could." Mrs. Devlin looked ready to do just that, and the mental picture made Minerva's lips twitch in spite of her nerves. Petite with grey-streaked brown hair, Mrs. Devlin possessed a delicately lined face dominated by chocolaty, kind eyes.

"Am I to assume you've been the housekeeper here since Lord Drummond was small?"

"I hired on as a nursemaid when I was naught but eight and ten. After Betsy Masterson passed on, I took over as housekeeper when Lily outgrew the nursery. My husband was stable master until he passed on two years ago." A sweet wistfulness colored Mrs. Devlin's voice. "Master Rafe is a good man, Lady Minerva, although he can be a bit strong tempered."

The understatement of the century.

"Since we don't have any guests—" Mrs. Devlin rumbled a frog from her throat, "—and with Earl Windor travelling and Lily in London, the bedrooms need airing and dusted up. Do you think you might be up for such a task?"

Minerva was thankful Earl Windor wasn't at home. Although, according to Lily, her and Rafe's father didn't care for Wintermarsh and was content to let her brother handle the estates and investments.

"I'm not some simpering London miss. Please follow Lord Drummond's instructions. Honestly, I don't want to give him any reason to break his word about absolving my brother's debts." Obviously, she'd never performed housework before, but really, how hard could it be? She was adept at figures and managing huge estates. A little dusting would be simple.

Four long hours later, she and Jenny, a young housemaid, cleaned yet another unused guest bedroom. Ironically, she had stayed in the lovely blue room as a guest for Lily's wedding. A tired, borderline maniacal laugh erupted at the ridiculousness of her present position.

"Why do we take clean sheets off the bed to put clean sheets back on and then send the first set of clean sheets off to the washerwoman? Does that make sense, Jenny?" A dozen or more bedrooms lined two long corridors.

Jenny gave a good-natured laugh. "No, ma'am. Not a lick. But my auntie in the village is thankful for the washing. Since my uncle died in the war, the only coin she earns is from Wintermarsh. She has two little ones at home still." The maid stripped the bed with a practiced hand and let a crisp, sweet-smelling sheet drift over the bed with a flick of her wrists.

After repeating the same routine several times now, Minerva had finally mastered a perfect crease and tuck of the sheet into the bottom of the bed. Not used to the unexpected physicality of the work, she rubbed at her lower back. A hot bath sounded heavenly, but a tepid basin of water would be all that awaited her at the end of the day. In reality, Lord Drummond could ring for a bath, and she would be the one carrying buckets of scalding water to his tub. The thought sobered her.

"Tell me about your family? Have they always lived in the village?" Minerva asked to distract her mind's morose wanderings but also with a fair amount of curiosity.

Jenny was high-spirited and sweet, no more than nine and ten, a fresh-faced beauty with gleaming chestnut hair and green eyes. Even in her dowdy black uniform, Minerva imagined the girl had to beat off the village lads.

"Yes, ma'am. My kin live in Lipton. It's a lovely little village. Papa's the blacksmith. Black John, he's called. It makes him sound terribly mean, but he's always laughing or telling a joke. My mama takes care of us children. There are ten of us in all." Jenny prattled while they changed the pillow coverings.

"Ten. My goodness. Older or younger than you?" Minerva tried to imagine the chaos but also the fun of having so much family around. Her only constant in life had been Simon.

"I'm right in the middle with my brother, Henry. He's a year younger and started work in the stables this spring. I'm happy to have some family here with me. I do miss them so."

Minerva bit her lip at the unexpected and embarrassing stab of jealousy. "How often do you get to see them?"

"When there's no visitors like now, we get every Sunday off. That's more than anyone else at big houses like this gets off. Henry and I go home and spend time with Papa, Mama, and the rest of the kids that are still at home. Mrs. Devlin says we're lucky to have Lord Drummond as a master."

That explained why no one had been about when she and Simon had arrived. Jenny spoke the truth. Minerva's servants in London only got a half Sunday off every other week. Minerva had never considered them having lives outside of the Bellingham townhouse. Cringing internally, she resolved to write Drake at the earliest opportunity.

Yet Minerva heard something unsettling in Jenny's voice. Fear. "What's Lord Drummond like?"

"I don't think…" Jenny looked around as if the housekeeper or butler might pop out of the floor.

"Does he take his temper out on the servants? He only seems to yell at me." Minerva smiled conspiratorially and shrugged, hoping to loosen Jenny's tongue.

"No, he doesn't yell. And he doesn't take advantage of the pretty maids either. I've heard terrible stories from girls that have worked in other houses. Honestly, he doesn't pay much attention to us at all.

"One time I walked into his study to clean the grate. I thought he was out riding, but there he sat like a wolf. I nearly jumped out of my skin, I did. That scar and that beard and those cold eyes. For a moment, I feared he was going to gobble me up." Jenny smoothed the counterpane up the bed and fluffed the pillow.

"Did he get angry?" Minerva mirrored Jenny's motions, and they stood across the bed from each other, finished with the task.

"Not a bit. Actually, he thanked me. Took me twice as long as normal, my hands shook that bad." Jenny fiddled with the bed curtains. "We all know…well, we heard you're a proper lady, and he's forcing you to pay a debt. Is it true?"

"Yes. It's complicated though. We could have paid him, but it would have been a terrible loss for me. My brother…" Minerva shook her head not sure what to say.

"Does he have a penchant for trouble? I have one of those too. Always getting into scrapes, needing money. Drives the family to the brink, he does. But we love him anyway."

"This time Simon pushed me over the brink." Minerva and Jenny stared into each other's eyes. No matter the difference in social standing, a common understanding bonded them. Minerva's sense of isolation eased. "I would appreciate if you didn't gossip about my situation."

"I would never. Anyway, Mrs. Devlin put the fear of God into everyone. No one would risk their position." They gathered the dirty sheets and walked side by side into the hallway, their heads close. "Aren't you frightened of Lord Drummond?"

Minerva considered her answer. "Sometimes. But sometimes he makes me so mad I want to kick him." She asked something she'd wondered about more than once. "Do you think he's lonely?"

"We don't get many visitors, especially now Miss Lily is married. The earl has never spent much time here. When Lord Drummond is in the house, he keeps mostly to his study, but he spends most of the day with the horses or working on the land."

Considering his muscular arms and hard chest, she imagined he did more than sit on his horse and supervise. Mrs. Devlin met them on the stairs to fetch Jenny. The silver required polishing.

"We still need to clean the master's room, Mrs. Devlin. Won't take a tick to finish it off," Jenny said.

Minerva grabbed the opportunity. "I can do it. Jenny has been an excellent instructor. When I'm finished, I'll help her with the silver."

"Are you sure?" Mrs. Devlin was back to wringing her hands. "You're welcome to take a rest in your room."

"Pish. That wouldn't do, Mrs. Devlin. Lord Drummond wants me to work, so work I shall. Honestly, I've enjoyed my morning."

Surprisingly enough, it wasn't a lie. Minerva smiled at Jenny, who winked at her behind Mrs. Devlin's back.

"If you're sure, my lady. Mrs. Potts has a light lunch for the...servants laid out in the kitchen when you're ready." The words emerged as if Mrs. Devlin were in pain.

Jenny pointed down the long hall to the right. "The master's is the last room. I'll be in the morning room when you're finished."

Minerva propped the supply basket on her hip. She cautiously opened the door to reveal a cavernous, empty room. Leaving the door ajar, she shuffled farther inside. Her room upstairs was hardly bigger than the enormous bed that dominated the space. Of course, Rafe Drummond was a large man. He was several inches over six feet and built like an oak tree. The bed in the nursery would probably collapse under him.

Sturdy and made of a dark wood, the bed oozed masculinity, as did the rest of the furnishings. A side table bore several books, one lying open. A large armoire and dresser sat against the far wall, both matching the dark, heavy style of the bed. Two sturdy, padded chairs were arranged in front of the grate. Rich reds and browns swathed the room and, despite the size, lent it a cozy, intimate feel.

Books littered almost every surface. The bed sheets were rumpled and untucked. Trimming and shaving instruments were scattered on the bureau, and a mound of clothing was piled next to the armoire. Did the man not employ a valet?

The complete lack of organization twitched her eye. She attacked the discarded clothes first, opening his armoire. The stirred air enveloped her with his distinctive scent. She closed her eyes and took a deep breath, clutching one of his frockcoats to her chest in a mock embrace. The man might be an arse, but cripes, he smelled splendid.

Shaking herself out of a daze, she hung the salvageable clothes and then made quick work of his dresser, dusting and neatly stacking the multitude of books. They covered a dizzying range of subjects from astronomy to current novels and everything in between. One of Austen's works lay opened at his bedside with a well-worn book of poems under it.

As one hand swept the duster over the side table, the other fell to the handle of the top drawer. Her heart picked up speed. Dare she? Violating his privacy was overstepping by leaps and bounds. The angel and devil warred, but the devil won. Its tart voice reminded her she was only in this position because Lord Drummond was the most unreasonable man in England.

She rummaged through the drawer. The top piece of parchment was covered in a jumbled chaos of figures. None of it made sense. Under that was a sheet with a listing of investments, some underlined, some with question marks. They ranged from England locales to India and the Caribbean. The variety surprised her, and she wished she could sit and discuss each one with him. Keeping her ears attuned to noise, she riffled through the remaining papers, nothing catching her eye.

The second drawer was empty save for a small book with no identifying title. She thumbed it open. Bold handwriting. A journal. She really shouldn't. Ready to close it, the spring date caught her eye.

March 12th

The nightmares come less frequently, but I'll never be free of them. Perhaps when you've killed as many as I have, my penance will be to see them in my sleep—forever. I deserve worse. Gray doesn't seem to suffer with his memories as I do, but at least he understands some of what I have been through. Lily tries, but she is too innocent, and I am glad for it. I would never burden her with the truth of what I became—

Footsteps invaded her consciousness. She shoved the journal back into the drawer and pulled at the sheets. The hope it was Mrs. Devlin died a quick death. A tingle zinged down her spine in warning.

* * * * *

Rafe opened his door to the unnerving sight of Minerva Bellingham changing his sheets. Her usually scrupulously composed appearance was rumpled. Cobwebs adorned her simply braided hair. Moreover, the braid itself had come loose in places and tendrils of hair lay against her nape. Dirty smudges covered her unflattering grey gown.

Surveying the room, he noted everything was organized and his clothes picked up. The intimacy of her handling his personal effects made his stomach squirm. If he didn't think Mrs. Devlin would give him another earful, he'd ask her to keep Lady Minerva out of his room. At the moment though, he was doing his best to avoid stoking his housekeeper's wrath.

"Enjoying yourself, my lady?" he asked too jovially to cover the awkwardness.

The look she shot him over her shoulder left no doubts that if she'd had knife, it would be buried in his black heart. "Immensely, my lord. Cleaning manor houses may become my new hobby."

She fully faced him and looked him up and down, arms crossed under her bosom. "You're filthy, and you smell like horses. That shirt will be good for nothing but rags."

She was right. He hadn't realized how damp and stained his shirt had become during his work. His waistcoat had been discarded over a stable door. Her gaze trailed from his chest all the way down his legs, and her mouth parted, most likely in disgust. He shifted on stocking-covered feet. Obviously, he hadn't expected to find her in his room. His dung-covered boots sat outside the kitchens.

"Where are your boots, sir?" She sounded as if something painful was stuck in her throat.

Her maidenly outrage stirred a hint of resentment. They were in his bloody room, after all. He sat in an armchair and peeled off his stockings. "They were filthy, so I left them outside. I would hate for *someone* to have to clean up my path of destruction through the halls. Aren't I thoughtful?"

"Wh-what are you doing?"

"Undressing."

"You can't do that here." She turned to the side, grabbed a pillow, and yanked off the covering. Her mouth tight, she huffed and blew tendrils of hair off her forehead. She looked lovely and infinitely more approachable in her disheveled state.

"That's odd, because I've been undressing here for nigh on fifteen years."

Instead of running away or looking to the ceiling to avoid his grotesque physique, she stared at his now bare legs and feet and punched the pillow with enough force that a feather popped out and drifted to the floor. Her voice creaked. "That's hardly what I meant, and you know it. You can't disrobe in front of me."

Rousing any sort of response from her, even if it was discomfiture, brought him a grim satisfaction. "Can't I?" He moved his hands to the buttons on his shirt.

Her throat worked and she held the pillow over her chest like a shield. He should desist. If she swooned and hit her head, Mrs. Devlin might chase him down with a dueling pistol. "I'm sorry, my lady. Pray, please continue, I'll wait." He gestured toward the bed and stretched his legs out, crossing them at the ankles and lacing his hands behind his head.

"You're by far the messiest man I've ever encountered."

"Have you been in many men's chambers to compare?" He was unable to stop his lips from twitching.

She opened and closed her mouth before responding in a stronger tone. "Of course not, and it isn't gentlemanly of you to imply that I have."

"I wasn't the one implying it, you were." It was becoming increasingly difficult to tamp down his amusement.

"You're also the most infuriating." She dropped the pillow to the rug, turned her back on him, and proceeded to make up his bed. Her body bent fluidly as she tucked and smoothed the sheet.

"If your idiot brother ends up gambling away your estates, you can come back here and apply for a position. You've turned positively domestic. Obviously a quick study."

She tugged the counterpane into place, her dress rising to expose a pair of nicely turned ankles. Her bottom wiggled. A single toss would have her on her back in the middle of his bed. Heat pooled in his groin, and he shifted his hands to his lap to hide his growing appreciation.

"In fact, I'd guess you're a quick study at all sorts of things." His voice rumbled the unintentionally suggestive words.

She whipped around and he snapped his head up, but by the deep pink wave flowing from her neck to her high cheekbones, the original direction of his gaze had been obvious. She took a step forward, hands on hips, her eyes sparking with a challenge.

A slow, admiring smile turned his lips. Most men's gazes skittered away from his during a confrontation. Not Minerva Bellingham's. In fact, her pert, stubborn little chin jutted out another inch.

* * * * *

The smile transformed his face. Laugh lines crinkled his eyes, and the white of his teeth against his dark beard was blinding. Her insides rearranged themselves most uncomfortably.

Lud, did he have to be so disgustingly masculine? He was probably trying to annoy her on purpose with his bulging muscles and hair-covered chest peeking out from the clinging, filthy shirt. He was uncouth, arrogant, and ungentlemanly.

Surely to God, she didn't find the man attractive? It wouldn't do. She would put a stop to this ill-advised, distressing feeling immediately—as soon as she figured out how.

Anger. Anger would banish this curling, fluttering warmth in her belly. "What is my *idiot* brother doing at the moment? May I see him at teatime?"

"His Grace will eat outside with the rest of my men. Leave him to me. The last thing he needs is a simpering, overly sympathetic demonstration of sisterly devotion. That's what got him into this mess to begin with. You coddle the man like he is a ten-year-old."

She welcomed the hot lick of fury. "I love my brother, sir. He came into the title and the responsibility too young. He needed a little coddling."

"No longer. It's time he learns to be a man. I'm sure you're more than adept at many things, but that isn't one of them, my dear."

"I am *not* your dear, you insufferable brute. What do you have Simon doing?"

"He's mucking out the stables."

"But-but…that's disgusting." She scooped up the dropped pillow and twisted it in her hands.

"Disgusting, but necessary. He'll learn about hard work, which isn't always pleasant or enjoyable, is it? I've mucked stables from the time I could hold a shovel on until today. I don't ask anything of my men that I wouldn't do myself." He paused, and then continued on conversationally, "Are you planning on murdering my pillow then?"

Minerva looked down at the twisted misshapen mass of down in her hands. "I'm pretending it's your neck, my lord." She launched the pillow at his head, but he snatched it out of the air before it made contact.

"Damn you to perdition." Clamping her mouth shut, she whirled and stuffed her basket with the dirty sheets. Had she cursed at him? Perhaps she had only said it in her head—very loudly.

"Lady Minerva, my innocent ears are burning," he said in

mock outrage.

Keeping her eyes to the floor, she tried for a dignified stalk out the door. It felt closer to an undignified scamper. Her slam of the door as she exited lent her a small measure of satisfaction.

The ebbing of tension left her feeling...*starved.* She stopped off to deposit the dirty sheets and cleaning supplies and continued on to the kitchen where Mrs. Potts, the cook, directed several girls who were preparing platters of meat, cheese and bread.

"Do you need any help?" If she took the food, maybe she could have a word with Simon.

"Not a bit. Are you hungry, dearie?" Not waiting for an answer, the rotund cook sat a large portion of bread, cheese, and cured meat on the table. Minerva's stomach growled with unladylike fervor. She gave in and finished every bite. Fresh milk quenched her thirst, and she sat back utterly satisfied by the simple meal.

The girls carried the platters outside and a lull descended. Mrs. Potts poured herself a cup of tea and sat across the table with a biscuit and a sigh.

"How long have you worked here, Mrs. Potts?"

"Goodness me, thirty years at the end of the year. I got taken on right before Christmas. The earl had announced his betrothal to Lady Windor, God rest her soul. They had planned a huge celebration. It was a happy, gay time. I started as a kitchen drudge, but after ten years of climbing the ranks, I got made head cook. It's been a fine life. Mr. Potts and I weren't blessed with children, but I consider Master Rafe and Miss Lily my little lambs. We all helped raise them after...after everything that happened." Mrs. Potts's dreamy, unfocused eyes looked toward the plastered wall.

"I know Lily felt lucky to have all of you. Both my parents died when I was quite young." Minerva wasn't given to confidences, surprised the words had come out of her mouth.

Mrs. Potts nodded, her gaze dropping to her teacup. "It's

good to have Master Rafe home for good. He nearly died last fall. He came back in terrible shape. Skin and bones. A bullet to his shoulder and the wound on his face. I barely recognized him. We all worked day and night to nurse him back to health. Then came the nightmares. Lord above, he could shake the rafters. And the drinking."

"Drinking?"

As if recognizing Minerva as near stranger, Mrs. Potts brushed nonexistent crumbs from her apron and heaved herself up. "Never you mind, dearie. He's better now." She turned her back to wash a bin of vegetables. Minerva took that as her dismissal.

She spent the rest of the afternoon polishing silver and sweeping floors with Jenny. She was tired, sore, and had acquired a few painful blisters. Yet she had laughed more than she thought possible given her situation.

Just when she thought the day was done, Jenny stretched her arms above her head. "Time to light the fire."

"But it's dinnertime, are we not done yet?" Minerva's shock was tinged with desperation.

Jenny shook her head with a little laugh. "Dinner time for the gentry, not for us. There's only the study for tonight. It's worse in the winter with the constant ash." Jenny's gaze darted to the mantle clock for the umpteenth time.

"Is there something else you need to do?"

A rosy blush tinged the girl's cheeks, but her smile was bold. "Mr. Donahue makes his rounds in the stables about now. If I'm free, sometimes I join him. To check on Henry."

"I can light the fire, so you can check on your brother." Minerva winked, and Jenny's smile morphed into a worried earnestness.

"Are you sure you can manage it?"

She'd seen it done countless times. It took less than a minute at home. "Certainly, I can. You run along."

"The supplies are by the grate." Jenny took off her apron and checked her wavy reflection in the window. She stopped with a hand on the doorjamb. "Are you sure, ma'am?"

"Positive. Now go before you miss your chance."

Jenny was out of sight before Minerva made it across the parquet floor to the study. With Jenny's infectious energy gone, exhaustion threatened to swamp her. The study extended the same welcome she'd felt last night, and the armchair looked indescribably comfortable.

What if she sat for a few moments to gather her strength? No, the sooner she got the fire started, the sooner she could eat and sleep. Tomorrow was likely to be an exhausting repeat of the day.

As promised, flint, peat, several logs, and tinder lay next to the grate. Now what? Kneeling, she placed two logs side by side and stuck some of the smaller pieces of tinder out at various angles. For good measure, she placed a chunk of peat on top. If she could get one of the pieces of tinder to light, surely the logs would catch.

With her fingers stiff and sore from polishing silver all afternoon, her attempts to produce viable sparks were anemic. She struck the flint harder and pinched a finger. Blood welled, and she sucked on her finger, tears springing to her eyes for the first time all day. She was at the end of her endurance. Snuffling a little in self-pity, she decided Lord Drummond could freeze. But what if Jenny got in trouble? Leaning over, her hands shaking, she struck the flint again and again.

"Having problems, are we?" A jolly, self-satisfied voice startled her. For a big man, he could move without a sound. Numb fingers tightened around the flint.

Keeping her face to the floor, she surreptitiously wiped at her dewy eyes. She took a deep, steadying breath, but her voice cracked anyway. "I've never started a fire."

Expecting more mockery, she was surprised when he squatted next to her. She looked away, refusing to let him see her gathering tears.

"Let me show you." He brushed a finger over her frozen hands, his touch gentle, his voice a whisper. On its own accord, her hand relaxed. He took the flint from her palm and rearranged the wood. "The tinder and peat go under the logs, which you need to prop up to allow the air to feed the flames. Then get your flint close to the pile of tinder and…"

He deftly struck the flint a half dozen times and sparks rained down. The tinder caught, and he crouched even lower to blow deep gusts of air under the mound of wood. The fire grew until the merry crackling filled the growing silence between them.

"Where did you learn to do that?" The leaping orange flames mesmerized her.

"In the war. When it was safe enough, a fire offered a bit of company and comfort. It takes a bit of practice, but you can learn." His deep, resonant voice washed over her with the comfort of a bedtime story. The warmth from the fire soothed her aches. She would be perfectly content to curl up and fall asleep where she sat like a cinder girl.

"I suppose I should thank you. I'll take my leave. Have a pleasant evening, my lord." Her carefully delivered speech was ruined when she staggered getting up. Rising with her, he caught her elbow in his big hand. She finally looked him square in the face. His stormy eyes didn't reflect the smug arrogance she'd expected. Something more dangerous lurked.

She pulled out of his grasp and backed away, holding his gaze until she bumped into the doorjamb. She slipped away without another word, too tired to spar with him, and trudged to the kitchen. Mrs. Devlin glanced at her wan face, ordered a tray fixed, and promised clean water for her ablutions, patting her arm all the while. Mrs. Potts's sympathetic tutting drew more tears to her eyes. She'd never had anyone worry over her like Mrs. Devlin and Mrs. Potts.

After dragging herself up the three flights of stairs, Minerva ate reclined on her bed, not even caring if she had to sleep in crumbs. Ready to nod off, she forced herself up to remove her dress. The gown already showed wear. Minerva examined the other dresses hanging in the wardrobe with chagrin. They were all too fine to be worn doing the type of work she'd performed today even if she could find someone to help her fasten them. Heaving a sigh, she sponged the grey wool as best she could.

She wondered how Simon had fared, but slipping between the sheets, she was asleep before worry could take hold.

CHAPTER FIVE

Minerva spent the next two weeks in a whirlwind of activity. She discovered a newfound respect for how much work went into maintaining a house and how physically grueling the work could be. She spent her days helping Jenny, and they became good friends. It was impossible not to like the feisty, funny maid. She assured herself Simon wasn't being physically mistreated but never had time for an in-depth questioning. As for Lord Drummond, she'd only seen him at a distance.

Their brief encounter in the study had left her off balance. She didn't want him to be kind, didn't want to wonder if something gentle hid under his brutish, rude exterior. She'd tried to avoid it but eventually found herself outside his bedroom door again to dust and straighten. Jenny's budding romance with Tom Donahue had her traipsing to the stables every free moment, and Minerva happily abetted the situation, covering for her when she could.

While Jenny stole some time with Tom, Minerva promised to tidy Lord Drummond's room. He would be either in his study or outside with Simon for hours yet. While stacking the numerous books littering his nightstand and dresser, one in particular caught her eye. It was a poem called *The Lady of the Lake*. The title intrigued her, and she flipped through the small book.

She had never read for pleasure as a young girl. Her tutor had been adamant she and Simon fill their time with academic texts. She could recite the characteristics of the various flora and fauna inhabiting Ireland but knew little about Shakespeare or, heaven forbid, any popular authors of the past fifteen years.

She chewed at her bottom lip. The sun was high in the sky. She tiptoed to one of the chairs and sat on the edge, ready to jump up at any noise. Returning her attention to the book, she lost herself in Ellen and Malcolm's love and the story of Scottish deception and war.

* * * * *

Rafe ascended the stairs to his chambers, stroking his beard and worrying over his two indentured servants. The duke was proving to be a hard nut to crack. He had withstood the punishing physical labor better than expected. Although he grumbled and complained, he hadn't broken.

Lady Minerva was another enigma altogether. His two encounters with her had surprised him. In his room, she had been sassy and spirited. Then, in his study, her eyes had been wet with tears, her face pale. She'd been at the end of her strength, and he'd felt...*guilty*, dammit.

He had caught sight of her several times in the company of one of Black John's daughters. Uncommonly aware of her, he seemed attuned to her bubbling laughter, the sound providing both pleasure and discomfort. Was she actually enjoying herself or was she putting on an act? He found himself lingering outside of any room she occupied, but he never entered, knowing he'd steal her happiness.

He stepped into his room but stopped short, sensing someone's presence, instantly on guard. A pair of legs covered by a serviceable wool dress dangled from the side of one of the armchairs.

Any question of who the invader might be was put to rest with a breathy exclamation. "Lud, no."

He crept up behind the chair and peered over the back to find Lady Minerva engrossed in a Sir Walter Scott poem. Not that Rafe blamed her. The man wrote an exciting tale. She'd finished more than half the pamphlet, and he smiled. He was wont to get lost in a story as well.

He rested his arms across the back of the chair and said teasingly, "Shirking your duties, Lady Minerva?"

She startled and looked like a child caught filching sweets, her eyes huge. Scrambling up, she straightened her skirts and pushed escaped pieces of hair behind her ears, clutching the book to her chest. "I'm so terribly sorry. I'll not let such a thing happen again, my lord." Her gaze darted to the window, and Rafe could practically see the curses she stemmed with her tight mouth. "I had no idea it had gotten so late. I'll finish cleaning your room tomorrow, or after you dress for dinner."

She returned the book to the bureau, grabbed her duster, and scurried around him. Before she could escape, he wrapped his hand around her upper arm gently, but with no intention of letting her slip by.

"You're welcome to read during your free time."

"I don't have free time until bedtime, my lord, and it would be a waste of your candles. Pardon me, please." She twisted her arm. He loosened his grasp but didn't release her.

She was so delicate and fragile. Christ, the top of her head barely reached his shoulder. He slid his hand partway down her arm before letting her go and then turned around, effectively dismissing her.

Her flurry of footsteps stopped. "May I inquire how my brother is faring?"

He spun back around to find she'd stopped well shy of the door, holding a handful of his clothes to be washed and her duster. "Better than I expected from a spoiled, self-centered young man thrust into such a situation."

"I tried not to spoil him, my lord. I did my best." Anger and hurt warred in her voice. Rafe had meant it as a compliment, but she assumed the worst of him time and again. Really, was that so surprising considering she was being forced to clean his room? Guilt reared its ugly but justified head once again.

To cover his discomfiture, he pulled at the hair on his chin. "I apologize, my lady, I'm sure you did. My guess is it would be hard to be a duke from age five and not grow up feeling entitled. He fares well."

"Is he eating enough?"

At this, Rafe rolled his eyes and chuffed. "I don't make him clean his plate like a child. If he's hungry, he'll eat. You must stop managing his entire life."

"What happens when I stop? Look where that has gotten us." She waved her duster around and kicked up a cloud, making her sneeze three times in quick succession. "Good gracious, pardon me."

The dust settled on her dress and hair. Christ, why was she so damn appealing all rumpled in her dowdy grey dress? He approached and reached for her thick braid. Rolling the silken rope between his fingers, he pictured her hair flowing around her shoulders. "You're a mess, my lady."

She sucked in a breath and yanked the braid out of his hand, raising another smaller plume of dust. "We're not discussing me. We're discussing my brother."

"Leave your brother to me. He doesn't need a bloody nursemaid." Her obvious distaste for his touch stabbed at his gut and harshened his voice.

"You are such an unfeeling, dastardly, rotten…stinker!"

The weak epitaph settled into the silence and neither of them moved. She seemed to glow with her rage, her blue eyes like the hottest part of a flame. A crackling energy emanated from her and filled the room. She looked as if she wanted to launch a dozen less-than-lady-like insults or maybe even beat him around the head with the duster. Was this the same woman the ton had named the ice princess? They were either blind or fools.

He shocked himself when laughter bubbled out of his throat. God, he couldn't help but admire her spirit. She did not look amused. Turning on her heel, she stormed out and slammed the door behind her—again.

* * * * *

Stomping feet and laughter woke Minerva the next morning. Her sleep had been restless, filled with the memory of Rafe Drummond's laughter. Worryingly, the need to kick him in the shin had been trumped by the urge bask in the beauty of his smile and wallow in the sound of his resonant laughter.

She wanted to pull the covers over her head for another hour, but she didn't have such luxury anymore. Once downstairs, she watched two footmen haul a rolled rug on their shoulders out into the bright, warm sunshine. She followed, joining Jenny and three other housemaids. The men struggled to heave the rug over a long rope tied between two oaks. The maids urged the footmen on with insults to their manliness. Minerva did a poor job stifling her giggles.

"What in the world is going on?"

"It's beating day." Jenny seemed positively delighted. "Do you want to join us?"

"I'm not sure I have a choice in the matter." Mrs. Devlin was nowhere to be seen, and if this was what the maids were doing, Minerva supposed she should help.

The footmen finally wrestled the rug over the rope, and the maids took up wooden sticks with a large circle on the end. Jenny handed her one, and she tested the weight in her hand, moving to a smaller rug hung to the side.

"It's dusty work. You might want a kerchief for your hair,"

Jenny called out.

Gingerly, Minerva hit the rug a few times. Puffing clouds of dust rose into the sun-dappled leaves, the occasional beam illuminating the motes eerily. Becoming comfortable with the wooden club, she heaved it harder. As all the girls got to work, dust lay in the air like a fog.

Lord Drummond came into her mind's eye. The pace and vigor of her swings increased. She needed to dispel the incredibly disconcerting feeling of his large hand encircling her arm like a vise, and his fingers tugging playfully on her braid. Tingles had shot all the way to her toes as if her hair contained a thousand nerve endings.

In short, she wanted to beat the ungodly physical attraction that thrummed through her in his presence out of her system. The attraction was simply a primal reaction of the natural world, after all. She was strong-willed and logical and planned to smother it out of existence.

She muttered at her rug before laying into it with fervent relish. The other maids had taken notice and stopped work to listen to her ramblings. All the insults and set-downs she'd been too flustered to let fly the previous day poured out of her. The fact Rafe Drummond wasn't around to hear only diminished her satisfaction slightly.

"And another thing, you callous brute, your smile will not make me forget myself." At that, a flurry of hits poofed a great cloud of dust into the air.

Through the dust, a man approached. His sheer bulk identified him as the object of her imaginary beating. She straightened, swinging the beater at her leg until he came into focus as if emerging out of a dreamy fog.

His hair was neatly combed and pulled back. Although he was still in his customary buckskins, he'd tied on a cravat, albeit loosely. He looked ready for a ride in Hyde Park, and handsome enough to set a debutante's heart aflutter. The dust settled, and she took a deep breath in preparation for another uncomfortable confrontation. Her nose itched. A series of loud, unladylike sneezes had her doubling over.

A wellspring of amusement hid poorly behind his bland expression. "Good morning, Lady Minerva. You're really laying into that poor Abbusson. Did it insult you at tea?"

Anger should be her first emotion, but looking down at herself covered in dust, she wanted to laugh along with him. She refused to give in to the urge. It smacked of friendship and forgiveness. "*It* didn't insult me."

"Imagining beating your brother for his irresponsibility?" Rafe nodded as if commiserating with her, crinkles showing at his eyes.

"Not this time. But that's a good idea for the next rug, my lord. No, I had someone else in mind. Someone who deserves a good beating."

"And who would this miscreant be?" His slowly curling lips flipped her stomach.

Before she found herself smiling back, she turned back to the rug and gave it a good whack. "Lord." She hit it harder. "Rafe." Another blow. "Drummond." The beater cracked and hung in her hand. "Blast! I wasn't nearly done bashing you, my lord."

He threw his head back and laughed. He laughed so hard, he had to wipe away tears. Everyone in the side yard stopped to listen and stare, her included.

"Do you ride, Lady Minerva?" he asked after his laughter dissipated.

She went on-guard. "Yes, of course. I love to ride. Why?"

"Take your aggression out on a hard ride. Go check on your brother."

"What about my chores?" She gestured with her limply hanging beater, and he sputtered out more laughter.

"Leave the rugs to the maids and footmen. I'm not sure our limited supply of beaters would survive the afternoon. I'd say you've done enough damage." Rafe leaned close enough she could smell the scent of his shaving tonic and added, sotto voce, "And to be perfectly frank, you're scaring the rest of the staff. They think you're a bit—" He winked and tapped his temple.

Heat coursed up her face. A look around showed several maids sending them side-eyed glances. Cuthbertson waved from the door. As Rafe backed away, he said, "Unfortunately, I have a meeting, or I'd join you. Why don't you change into a habit and look over my stables. Pick a horse. I'm curious which you'll choose. Take a groom and tell him the men are working in the north pasture. Is that acceptable?"

"Yes, quite." She was pleased and confused and suspicious. He turned and bounded up the steps, disappearing inside.

After a quick wash and changing into a habit, Minerva toured the stables with Tom Donahue, suitably impressed by the cleanliness and diversity of stock. Tom was somewhere in his late twenties and a handsome rough-hewn man. He was quiet and serious, quite a foil to Jenny's exuberance. He obviously loved the horses and detailed the breeding and temperament of each one. They looked in on Aries, Lord Drummond's horse.

"Aries was half wild when Lord Drummond brought him here. Nearly destroyed his stall. He took a long while to break and train, but Master Rafe was patient and didn't allow whips. He's turned into a gentle giant, he has. He's been bred twice now and his progeny are equally as impressive."

Minerva admired the huge black stallion, wondering at Lord Drummond's depths. Still reeling from his sudden kindness, she had to assume there was some hidden motivation behind it.

Minerva picked a frisky grey mare named Sparrow. Her spirits rebounded once she was in the saddle. A golden field crisscrossed with lines of gray stone walls led into a copse awash with songbirds. Red squirrels jumped from branch to branch chattering happily. Clean, sweet air filled her lungs, and her troubles went away for a moment or two. She and the groom broke from the trees into another field.

"There they be, ma'am." The groom pointed to a group of five men moving stones from the field toward a partially finished wall.

Poor Simon had dressed for a jaunt in Hyde Park. The mud and dust covering him was in complete juxtaposition to his Weston jacket and fine Hessians. She trotted up, and the men stopped their work.

She spoke to the group as a whole, not sure who was in charge. "Good day. Lord Drummond said I might speak to my brother. Would you mind if I borrowed him for a few minutes?"

"'Course not, my lady. We've tired of his complainin' anyway." A powerfully built man chuckled and waved Simon away before shifting an impossibly large rock into place.

Simon was sullen and uncommunicative as they walked side by side toward the far end of the clearing. Minerva studied him out of the corner of her eyes. "Simon, I think you can safely lose the cravat and waistcoat, for goodness sake. There's no one out here to impress, and you'll be much more comfortable."

"I have *never* been put through such humiliation. Drummond made me shovel horse shit, Minerva, horse shit." Simon's voice escalated. Men glanced in their direction.

"Simon, do be quiet. Someone has to clean up after the horses, and wasn't Lord Drummond doing the same for a time?"

"So he could witness my total degradation. It's not worth it. Let's sign over your dowry."

Minerva grabbed his arm, her glove slipping through something gooey and brown. "Ugh…" She shook her hand in the air trying to fling off the muck, momentarily distracted. "Are you insane? You would rather sentence me to spinsterhood or, even worse, marrying a man for his money rather than put in an honest day's work? Granted it's not the easiest and cleanest of work, but I think if you would quit complaining, Drummond won't push so hard."

"Why did I let him in the game? Hampton told me it was a bad idea," Simon said on a whine.

"Hampton was there? You didn't tell me that."

"'Course he was. He's my friend, isn't he? Drummond took all his money as well. I don't see Hampton out here working off his debt. Drummond obviously hates me."

Minerva pulled off her mucky glove, her mind whirling. "Or perhaps he's doing you a favor he didn't think Hampton deserved."

"A favor? This is a favor? I've a good mind to walk away right now." Simon's defiant, churlish tone worried her.

"I will literally strangle you if you do any such thing. Through your folly, we have no recourse. My entire future is at stake. And how will society treat you knowing you gambled my dowry away, little brother? Did you consider that? My work hasn't been easy either. I've spent my time cleaning rooms, polishing silver, and beating rugs. Do you think I enjoyed it?" Minerva refused to admit she had enjoyed it—just a little.

He stayed mulishly silent, so she pressed on. "Please do as Lord Drummond commands you and, for goodness sake, be respectful. He holds our fortune in his hands." Her tone was cajoling, her eyes imploring, begging his cooperation, but she recognized the surly set to his mouth.

Lord Drummond was right. She hadn't done Simon any favors. At the very least, he was spoiled and teetered on dissolute. Was it even possible to get her earnest, caring brother back?

After leaving Simon at the rock wall, she galloped ahead of the groom. The wind dried the tears in her eyes and plucked her hair out of its braid. Back at the stable, Tom took her horse and thankfully didn't comment on her appearance. Tears always splotched her fair skin.

A quiet pall replaced the bustle of the morning. She crossed the marbled entryway on her way to the staircase, knowing she should seek out Mrs. Devlin for her next task but craving the solitude of her little room.

"Lady Minerva? What an unexpected but most happy surprise." A familiar male voice echoed off the marble.

She turned slowly, feeling as if she'd been plopped into a nightmare. "Lord Stonewell. What are you doing here?"

He strode toward her with a wide smile and took her bare hand, her dirty glove clutched in the other. Bowing, he pressed a lingering kiss against her skin. When he straightened, he didn't drop her hand but held it between both of his. She resisted the urge to tug it back.

"I met with Drummond about a possible investment. He's gained a reputation for knowing which endeavors to back. If I can get his weight behind my new project, I'll have men lined around the block to join."

"Did you succeed?" Her mind considered and discarded reasons for her presence at Wintermarsh, one more unbelievable than the last, but none as outlandish as the truth.

"Not yet, but I'm hopeful. What brings you to Lord Drummond's estate?"

"I'm, well that is to say, we're here because… Simon is here as well, and we're planning to—"

"The duke and his sister are waiting for the Mastersons. My sister, Lily, and Lady Minerva are great friends, you know." Lord Drummond's voice was full of dry amusement. He strolled across the parquet floor, his hands clasped behind his back. The humor crinkling his eyes disappeared the closer he drew.

Now she did snatch her hand from Stonewell and hid it in her skirts. Lord Drummond stopped next to Stonewell, and Minerva couldn't help but compare the two men.

Rafe Drummond dwarfed the other man in both size and

personality. He was a jungle cat to Stonewell's house cat. Stonewell was handsome enough, but next to Drummond's flagrant masculinity, he seemed almost effeminate.

"Yes, your sister caused quite the stir last Season," Stonewell said.

"What the devil are you implying, Stonewell?"

"Only that she was quite an original and much admired for her wit." Stonewell cleared his throat and smiled stiffly, fingering the cuffs of his jacket. He turned to Minerva once again. "Drummond has invited me to stay for dinner. Perhaps we can discuss what you thought of the latest Royal Academy exhibition. I saw you from a distance, but it was such a crush, I never had the chance to pay my respects."

Her throat had closed to a pinhole. Her gaze bounced back and forth between the two men. "I, well, I'm not sure, I'm rather tired—"

"Ready yourself. We'll gather in the drawing room in an hour." Lord Drummond's voice brooked no argument, and one look at his face told her she should consider this part of her duties.

She retreated to her room. Perhaps the evening would be a pleasant reminder of London and a break from her work. The dread crawling through her body and sending her stomach scurrying for cover portended a different outcome.

CHAPTER SIX

Rafe paced the drawing room, waiting for Minerva and that dolt Lord Stonewell. He'd dressed in black breeches and frockcoat with a gray and silver waistcoat. He'd ripped off his neck cloth and thrown it on the rug of his room, mainly out of sheer orneriness. He hadn't wanted Stonewell to stay for dinner in the first place. However, the man hadn't taken the hint, and Rafe had been unable to avoid issuing an invitation without sounding churlish.

After Stonewell had spotted Minerva, dinner was a foregone conclusion. Stupidly, he'd forgotten what a small world the ton really was. Of course Minerva and Stonewell were acquainted. Perhaps even more than acquainted by the overly effusive greeting Stonewell had bestowed on her bare hand. The need to plant a fist squarely in Stonewell's pleasantly handsome, unblemished face had nearly overwhelmed him.

Lord Stonewell entered the drawing room with a murmured greeting.

"Help yourself, Stonewell." Rafe gestured toward the sideboard.

After pouring himself a glass of brandy, he joined Rafe to peer out into the darkened gardens. Every few seconds, Stonewell glanced at the drawing room doors and rocked on his feet. He broke the increasingly oppressive silence. "So, Drummond, how long will Lady Minerva stay cloistered at Wintermarsh?"

"For as long as she wants. Why do you ask?" Rafe knew perfectly well why the blighter asked. Stonewell was casting his net for Minerva. And why wouldn't he? She was beautiful and smart and, if she managed to keep it away from Simon, favored with a sizable dowry to boot.

"To be frank, I find Lady Minerva exceedingly charming and lovely, not to mention quite rich. I'm fast approaching thirty. Time to think of producing an heir, I would say."

"You're interested in breeding her?"

"I certainly wouldn't put it that way or imply—"

"It's her money you're more interested in then?"

Stonewell smoothed his intricately tied cravat. "She's an intelligent, beautiful woman. Any man would be lucky to gain her for a wife."

Dammit, the man sounded like a true gentleman. He tried to dislike Stonewell but had a difficult time hating a man so bland and uninspiring and *nice*. He would just have to try harder.

Minerva rapped, gaining their attention. She had enlisted help. There was no way she had laced herself into the low-cut blue silk gown. His gaze lingered on the lovely swell of bosom it exposed. Her hair, which he was used to seeing in a braided rope with soft, escaped tendrils, was twisted and pinned in a tight knot on the back of her head. He didn't like it. She looked icy and cold, and Rafe was fast learning she was anything but.

"You look lovely, Lady Minerva." Stonewell scurried over like a dog seeking a pat, bending low and kissing her hand, holding it longer than Rafe deemed appropriate.

Rafe noticed she didn't pull away though. Not as she had done to him countless times. A simmering anger built. He stalked to the sideboard and poured himself an unhealthy amount of brandy, sloshing it over the rim of the glass.

Stonewell led her to the nearest settee and joined her, his knee bumping hers. She didn't shift away from him. Indeed, she angled toward him to answer questions about the art exhibition. Rafe took a large swallow and the burn of the liquor settled deep in his stomach, feeding the demons.

They were a perfect example of the finest match of the ton. Stonewell was dark, where Minerva was blond. He had regular, even features and was tall and trim, an outdoorsman. Intelligent, charming, a full head of hair—he seemed a decent fellow all around. In short, Rafe couldn't stand the bastard and wondered how he would keep from garroting the man at dinner.

* * * * *

Minerva cut her gaze to Lord Drummond, who stood with a hip propped against the sideboard taking huge swallows from his glass. Had Stonewell intercepted the murderous looks Drummond shot in their direction? They had seemed on decent terms in the entry hall. Had something happened in the interim?

With her usually well-ordered mind ransacked, she found it difficult to concentrate on Stonewell's attempts at conversation. If she wanted to stay out of the gossip mill, she needed to first find and then keep her wits about her.

"Will your brother be joining us, Lady Minerva?" Stonewell asked.

She grimaced at the question and looked to Drummond.

"He's not feeling well and told me to pass on his sincere apologies." Lord Drummond didn't sound the least bit sympathetic.

Minerva sighed. "Yes, he's been under the weather for a few days now. Probably why you didn't run into him earlier."

"Goodness, does he need a physician? I have a friend not far from here that we could summon," Stonewell said with true worry in his voice.

"Not necessary, my lord. He'll be up and about in no time, I'm sure. It's his…" She blanked for a moment.

"Stomach."

"Head."

She and Drummond spoke on top of each other. Stonewell's brow crinkled, and he cocked his head.

"His upset stomach is making his head hurt. Are you and the duke well acquainted then, Stonewell?" Drummond took another large swallow, his penetrating, predatory gaze never leaving the other man.

Stonewell shifted on the settee, and his thigh tensed. "Only marginally. We've sat at the same gaming table a few times."

"Have you? And did you find the young duke to be a capable player?" Drummond's eyes sparked with malicious intent.

Minerva sent Lord Drummond her *look*. This was hardly the time to be talking about gaming and debts, for goodness sake. Stonewell wasn't an idiot and might even come to the correct conclusion.

Rafe's lips twitched around his brandy glass, intercepting what should have withered him on the spot. He quaffed the remainder of his drink and poured another.

Stonewell shot her a small smile. "The duke's young yet. He'll turn into a fine player, I'm sure."

"Ha," Drummond barked before she had a chance to answer. "He's abysmal, especially when he's drunk."

"That's something you seem to know quite a lot about, isn't it, Lord Drummond?" Unable to tolerate another second, she popped off the settee and stared him down. Proprieties be damned.

Stonewell's mouth opened and closed a few times, his gaze ricocheting between them. Blessedly, Cuthbertson opened the door and announced dinner.

The tension travelled with them from drawing room to dining

room, making the meal the most uncomfortable Minerva had ever sat though. Unfortunately, just when she thought the torture was ending, the footman placed a blackberry tart on her plate. She grimly attacked it, unable to enjoy the delicious treat due to the thinly veiled animosity aimed from the head of the table.

Rafe Drummond's hooded eyes regarded her steadily, a finger circling the rim of what had to be his fourth or fifth brandy. Across the table, Stonewell manfully kept the conversation light and moving forward. She tried to help him, but the cutting interjections from Drummond made it impossible.

"There appears to be a storm brewing, and it's getting rather late, isn't it Drummond?" Stonewell looked at Minerva. "It might behoove me to throw myself on your hospitality. Perhaps we can conclude our business tomorrow."

Minerva was unaware of the atmospheric conditions outside, but there was surely a wicked wind blowing inside. Amazed at Stonewell's bravery, or perhaps stupidity, she shrank in her seat and dropped her fork to her plate. The clatter echoed.

"Consider our business concluded. The answer is an unmitigated no." Drummond stood and placed his fisted hands on the table. "Therefore, there's no reason for you to stay. There's a comfortable inn back up the London road or an even more comfortable one in Lipton. Take your pick."

Stonewell tried to modulate his voice but sounded affronted nonetheless. "May I ask why your answer is no? It's a sound venture."

"It doesn't fit with my other investments."

"But surely you're looking to expand—"

Drummond pounded a fist on the table. Dinnerware rattled. "Stonewell, I don't like you. I don't want to invest with you. I don't want you in my home. It's time for you to depart. Bertie!"

At Rafe's bellow, the butler glided into the room. "Yes, Lord Drummond?"

"Have Tom bring Lord Stonewell's horse around, please." Drummond never took his gaze off the other man. Minerva was torn between anger and trepidation.

Stonewell rose to leave, tossing his napkin on his half-finished tart. Minerva mimicked his actions. At the very least, she intended to see him out the door. Someone had to act civilized, and it certainly wasn't going to be the lord of the manor.

"Where are you going?" Drummond asked with a dangerous edge, moving to lean against the doorjamb. An ogre they'd have to pass to exit to safety.

"I'm going to see my friend safely away, Lord Drummond, if you'll excuse me."

He looked as if he might stop her, and she was angry enough to raise her brows, daring him to try. A muscle in his jaw twitched, but he made no move. Sweeping around him in a flurry of silk, she stalked to the front door, Stonewell on her heels. Bertie opened the door, his head down as if embarrassed by his master's behavior.

A gusty wind whipped her skirts about her legs and tugged pieces of her hair free of the tight chignon Jenny had managed earlier. Dark clouds obscured the moon, and Minerva could smell the storm coming from the south. Poor Stonewell was sure to get drenched before making it to either inn.

"Minerva... May I call you Minerva?" Stonewell took her hand and held it in a warm clasp.

"Of course, you may," she said in appeasement for the dreadful dinner he'd endured.

"Minerva, I'm not sure what has prompted your visit with Drummond, but I assure you I would be happy to escort you and your brother back to London at your earliest convenience. You can always travel back here with Mrs. Masterson."

He really was a nice gentleman. Handsome, charming, urbane. Completely compatible with her lifestyle. He would never raise his voice, their children would be comely and well behaved and she would never want for anything.

Except…

The wind carried his scent, and she leaned closer, nearly burying her nose in his nape. He startled but then smiled and squeezed her hand.

Nothing. She couldn't muster the smallest iota of desire for the man.

He smelled pleasant enough. He'd bathed recently and had applied an agreeable cologne. However, no frisson of awareness zipped down her spine. Her stomach stayed firmly in place. No mind-numbing wave of need overtook her. She studied their hands. His was large but soft and well-manicured. Used to holding cards, a quill, the reins of a horse on occasion. Disentangling them, she stepped back with a hint of regret.

"I appreciate the kind offer, but Lord Drummond has been a perfectly affable host, and Mrs. Masterson will be arriving any day now. Simon and I are enjoying the country air."

"Yes, *affable* is the first word that comes to mind when thinking of Drummond," Stonewell said dryly with a glance to the door.

She smothered a laugh. "He can be a bit gruff, I'll give you that, but we're being well taken care of, I assure you." Tom approached with Stonewell's handsome bay gelding.

"If you find yourself in need, don't hesitate to send word. I'll be here within a day, Minerva."

She tucked an escaped piece of hair behind her ear, flummoxed at the kind offer and what it implied. "Thank you, sir. I'll bear that in mind. Have a safe journey back to London."

Stonewell regarded her a moment, looking as if he wanted to say more. She didn't want to hear more, was loath to hurt him, so she stepped even farther back, her fingers curled around her arms. He released a gusty sigh, tipped his hat and rode away in a flurry of horse hooves. The beginnings of a headache brewed, and she wanted only to collapse in bed.

Retreat to her room was not an option. Rafe Drummond waited, a shoulder propped against a thick stone column, the wind whipping his hair around his face. With his mouth twisted and his eyes mere slits, he sought a confrontation. If that's what he wanted, that's what he'd get, blast the man.

* * * * *

Stonewell had offered to save Minerva from his dastardly clutches. That little toad. If he'd still been here, Rafe would have given him the beating of his life. Minerva Bellingham was *his*...at least for the next two months.

She was in quite a snit if her flashing eyes and jutting chin were any indication. Rightly so. He'd acted a complete arse all evening, insulting them both repeatedly. The brandy had done its dark work.

Stomping up the steps, she clapped her hands in a slow, ironic accolade. The wind pushed her dress against her body, outlining her long, lithe legs. The tantalizing sight of her flushed bosom distracted him, turning his anger into something infinitely more dangerous.

"Bravo, Lord Drummond. You put on quite the performance, I must say. You play the rude, boorish villain quite convincingly. Perhaps next time you could try something a bit more congenial and friendly." Her voice was sharp enough to draw blood. She attempted to sweep by, but he stepped in her path, and she bumped against his chest.

Her breath caught, and she scurried backward. Dammit. Why should he care if she preferred the dandyish Stonewell's touch to his? But he did care. It twisted his gut into knots of pain.

"I heard his kind offer. I'm surprised you didn't take him up on it. Confess all and throw yourself on his mercy."

"And leave Simon here with you?" She fought the wind,

trying to tuck her hair back into place.

"Perhaps Stonewell would buy you out of our agreement. As long as you give him something he wants, and I believe I know exactly what his price would be." Rafe backed her into one of the stone pillars that flanked the entry door. He crowded into her space and forced her to accept his physical dominance.

"And what would he have asked from me, Lord Drummond?" Her face tipped up, exposing the long, graceful line of her neck.

Rafe trailed the callused pad of his finger down and over the delicate arch of her collarbone. The rate of her breathing increased noticeably, drawing his finger farther down. He stroked across the white swells of her breasts, tracing the line of her bodice, wanting desperately to dip his hand inside.

"His price would be your body. The use of your lovely, delectable body," Rafe whispered.

The wind crested around them like a wave, floating her skirts around his legs. Her back arched and pushed her breasts more firmly into his fingers for a moment. Until she shrank away from him.

"You…you said you wouldn't hurt me. In any way." She stumbled over her words, sounding innocent and unsure and completely unlike the Minerva he was used to.

His anger and lust dissipated, replaced by a throbbing headache and a healthy dose of shame. He punished her for something out of her control. Dropping his hand, he stepped back with a small courtly bow. "I won't. I'm a cad when I'm in my cups. Lily learned to avoid me, but I forced myself on you. I'm sorry. Please, forgive me."

He left her leaning against the pillar, her blue eyes wide and, for once, with nothing to say.

* * * * *

Buffeted by the increasingly wild wind, Minerva pressed against the cold pillar, her fingernails scratching at the rough stone. She'd waltzed with more gentlemen than she could count and let them trail their hands down her arms to hold her hand. That same hand had been bussed hundreds of times. She'd even had a few kisses stolen in darkened gardens. Just that evening she'd dispassionately catalogued all of Lord Stonewell's favorable qualities. None of them had ever aroused anything resembling desire or passion.

With the touch of a single fingertip, Rafe Drummond had made her body thrum to life. Her nipples were peaked and achy and that secretive place between her legs had grown damp and throbbed. She been grateful for the pillar, both for the support and the lack of a retreat. Far from wanting to escape him, she'd wanted to guide his hand fully over her breast, sure he knew how to ease her discomfort.

In a moment of sheer madness, she'd wanted to kiss him— badly. Even after everything that had transpired that evening, she wanted to explore his hard, wicked lips. Cold needles of patchy rain brought a semblance of order to her chaotic body. Raising her face, she welcomed the onslaught, only leaving when the wind died and a steady, pouring rain forced her inside.

CHAPTER SEVEN

The next afternoon, Minerva accompanied Jenny in an old wooden cart into Lipton to pick up fresh vegetables and staples for the kitchen. The draft horse plodded toward town, a familiar trek for the beast, and she handled the reins while Jenny chattered on. She was glad to be outside on an adventure and away from the possibility of meeting Lord Drummond in the halls of Wintermarsh.

After dropping off the cart to be loaded, they stopped at Jenny's cottage. It was filled with joyful chaos, little bodies running hither and yon. When word spread Jenny was in the kitchen, several of the children hurled themselves at her for hugs and kisses. She spent time with each one while her mother made a pot of weak tea for the three of them to share around the rough-hewn kitchen table.

Jenny's mother was charming and energetic, much like her daughter. Minerva watched Jenny and her mother with a twinge of sadness. Her own mother had died so young that Minerva barely recalled her face. After their tea and another round of hugs from the children, she and Jenny picked up their cart and pulled up at the smithy.

Jenny jumped down from the wagon bed straight into her father's arms for an enveloping hug. Minerva hopped down and stood to the side.

"Papa, here's Minerva. She's new to work at the big house. Came with excellent references." Jenny winked in her direction. "We've had ever so much fun. This is my papa, or Black John as most people call him."

Black John was a bear of a man and might have been intimidating if it weren't for the twinkling in his eyes and the laughter lurking at the corners of his mouth. He reminded Minerva of a bigger, hairier version of Jenny.

Minerva dropped a quick curtsy. "Nice to make your acquaintance, sir. Jenny has told me so much about the family."

"Any friend of Jenny's is welcome at our house anytime, young miss. Now, what brings you to town during the week?" Black John turned back to his work on a horseshoe.

"We're picking up supplies. In fact, I only stopped by so you could meet one another. We already had tea with Mama. We'd better head back before Mrs. Devlin thinks we're wasting time." Jenny regained her seat on the wagon. Pulling her skirts up, Minerva joined her.

"Isn't that exactly what you're doing, missy?" Black John asked.

"Right you are. We'd best make haste." Jenny tossed a laugh over her shoulder as their horse plodded away.

"How's Henry faring?" Her father called out.

"He's grand, Papa. Loves the stables. See you Sunday."

Minerva waited until they were out of town before teasing her friend. "Henry's not the only one who *loves* the stables."

Jenny's face pinkened. Her gaze was downcast, and she kept uncharacteristically silent.

"What's the matter?"

"Tom is too honorable." Jenny sighed and propped her chin on a fist.

"He's managed to resist you?"

"Don't tease. I'm quite serious. He says I'm too young and don't know what I want yet. But I do know. I need to convince him of it, is all."

"The man must be missing a cog or two."

"He's stubborn, that's for certain." Jenny picked at the end of her braid, her voice small. "He's hasn't even tried to kiss me."

A bit out of her depth, Minerva cut her gaze to Jenny. "Perhaps, the timing—"

"He's had ample opportunity. I've stepped in front of him and puckered up half a dozen times. He acts as if I'm going to bash him over the head and rob him. I wonder if I don't need to try something more drastic."

"Like what?" Minerva shifted to the edge of the bench.

"One of the other maids told me to wait in his room—" Jenny looked to make sure no trees could overhear, "—in a state of undress."

"Please, don't do it, Jenny. There must be another way." If Tom wasn't as honorable as Jenny supposed, she could be ruined and fired without a reference for such recklessness.

"Don't worry, I'm not brave enough…or my morals aren't loose enough, I suppose."

"What if *you* kissed *him*? That wouldn't be so scandalous, would it?" Minerva steered the cart onto the drive approaching the house.

"I could corner him in a stall, but what if he's disgusted?" True worry drew Jenny's face tight, and she searched for reassurance from Minerva. That, at least, she could offer.

"Jenny Mitchell. You should have no fears on that account. And if he should push you away, you'd have your pick of any of the other lads."

"But I don't want any other lad." Jenny tried to smile, but her shoulders slumped. No one but Tom would make her friend happy.

A flash of Rafe Drummond standing over her with his finger caressing her collarbone quickened Minerva's breathing as if it had just happened. My God, was she in a similar predicament? Would no one but the despicable Rafe Drummond ever rouse her passions?

Later in the evening, after finishing her dinner tray, she sponged her grey wool dress to little effect. She'd come to hate the dress with fervor. This was the loneliest part of her day, the hours between working and sleep. The other servants gathered below stairs for gossip, cards, and sometimes even music. Simon was tucked away in the stables. Socializing with Lord Drummond was out of the question.

The scratch echoed in the oppressive silence. She slipped on a wrapper and cracked the door. A young kitchen maid balanced a tray on her hip. Several beeswax candles rolled into the poem by Scott. Minerva took the tray with shaking hands and a word of thanks, wondering if it might be booby trapped. It was the only explanation. A folded scrap of parchment lay on top. She plucked it up with two fingers and shook it open.

I apologize heartily for my behavior during and after dinner. Please take this as a peace offering. I'm certain you're anxious to find out what befalls Malcolm and Ellen.

Rafe Drummond

His script was aggressive and bold, like the man himself. Was this truly a peace offering or was it an attempt to manipulate her? To do what, she couldn't fathom. She refused to become mawkish over his thoughtfulness. Her uncertainty over his motivations didn't stop the tingle of excitement when she settled into bed and picked up the book.

* * * * *

The next afternoon, humming a jaunty tune she'd learned from

Jenny, Minerva hitched the wash basket farther up her hip and headed to the hanging line. Over the course of her day in London, so many people depended on her, but here in the last of summer's warmth, only some sheets needed to be hung in the fresh sunshine. The temporary respite from responsibility was surprisingly freeing.

Movement on the edge of her vision stilled her feet. Two men stood close together at the corner of the stable. Shining blond hair gave Simon away. The other idly twirled a cane with a beaver hat perched on his head. Not Lord Drummond. The man was too thin and dandified.

Recognition dawned in a wave of fury. Viscount Hampton. What the devil was he doing here?

Minerva dropped the basket at her feet and stalked toward the stables. Before she got close enough unleash her wrath, Hampton tipped his hat, whispered something to Simon, and was gone.

She took a deep breath. Dire prophecies rolled through her head, tightening her stomach. "How did he know you were here, Simon? What did he want?"

"I left him a note before we left London telling him where to find me if he was in the area. His grandfather has a house not far from Lipton." Simon refused to meet her eyes, kicking at rocks.

"Was he trying to get you to meet him somewhere?"

"He was making sure Drummond hadn't killed me is all."

Minerva considered him for a moment. Dark circles ringed his eyes. He was lean but not skinny. In fact, he was noticeably broader across the shoulders and thicker in the neck. Lord Drummond was trying to break her brother through labor. Of course, she was concerned, but her methods of bringing her brother in line hadn't worked.

"Do you think about what would've happened if Drummond hadn't offered this unconventional proposal? He holds thousands of pounds of your vowels. He's doing us a favor," she said more sympathetically than he deserved.

"A gentleman would forgive those debts. I was foxed."

"You are an outright fool to believe that. Any other man would have been on our doorstep the next morning to collect the money. Your supposed friend Hampton included. We would have had to sign over everything not entailed. This is your last chance. You need to make this work for both of our sakes. At the very least, do you not care what happens to me?" Minerva laid a pleading hand on his arm.

He shook her off. "Speaking of work, I need to finish mucking out the stalls. Who would have thought the Duke of Bellingham would be shoveling shit?" Not giving her a second glance, he strode around the corner and out of sight.

If Simon didn't come to his senses, Lord Drummond could make things very unpleasant for them both. Minerva pressed the heels of her hands to her brow to stem the gathering tears. She didn't have the time for a cry and was afraid if she started, she wouldn't be able to stop.

Worry and a pressing sense of isolation replaced her earlier contentment.

* * * * *

Taking a deep breath of fall air, Rafe decided a hard gallop on Aries might divert his thoughts from his two indentured servants. Drawing even with the drying line, he spied a basket of laundry but no maid. Old instincts for trouble tingled, and he scanned the yard.

Minerva and Simon talked at the corner of the stables. Rafe backed into the shelter of a tree, hidden in shadows but able to observe the siblings. Their discussion was heated and ended with Simon stalking off. Minerva stared after her brother, her shoulders slumped as if her worries were lead weights.

A familiar stab of guilt had him ruffling his hair. Not only was he forcing her to work off a debt she hadn't accrued, but his behavior at dinner with Stonewell had been deplorable...and afterwards. He couldn't bear to think of her disgust at his touch.

The way she acted hardly assuaged his shame. Nursing a pint of ale in the inn and waiting for Black John to repair Aries's shoe, he'd watched Minerva and Jenny arrive in Lipton for supplies. Minerva dropped a respectful curtsy and laughed gaily up at the blacksmith. She'd even handled the reins of the heavy cart. Was this the same lady that could bring the most hardened gentleman to his knees with a flinty, cutting *look*?

Pushing his guilt into shame was seeing her worry and love for her brother. She was obviously at her wit's end with him, and he could understand why. Simon resisted him with a strength that surprised and even impressed Rafe. He did the work but not without resentment. The duke was stubborn, but not as stubborn as Rafe. It was a battle of wills and endurance Rafe was determined to win. If he didn't, Simon would likely destroy his and Minerva's future. What Rafe couldn't fathom was why it felt so vital that he succeed.

Minerva trudged back up the hill. Exhaustion seemed to hold her in its grip, but he knew no amount of sleep would help. She tucked escaped pieces of hair behind her ears before taking a deep breath and pulling up the first sheet. She struggled to get the cloth over the line. Keeping the sheet between them like a shield, Rafe approached on wary cat-like feet.

"Allow me, my lady." His height a distinct advantage, he pulled the sheet up to rest in halves over the string and peeked over at her.

A quick intake of breath was her only visible reaction. She picked up the basket and moved down the line, gathering the next sheet. "I don't require your help, Lord Drummond. I'm perfectly capable of hanging sheets. I wouldn't want you to accuse me of shirking my duties and extend our time in servitude."

"I promise I won't count my help against you."

She carefully kept the ends of the next sheet from brushing

the dusty ground. "Do you enjoy watching me work like a housemaid?" Her gaze stayed on her work, but red burnished her high cheekbones. She was either embarrassed or furious. Knowing her as he did, he guessed the latter.

Now. He should tell her now. Apologize and free her from the obligation of her brother's debt. He opened his mouth and took a bracing breath.

"I suppose you enjoy having women under your thumb to torment and humiliate. Makes you feel more of a man, does it?"

Her words were like a punch to the chest, stealing his breath. His apology would have to wait. "Is there something amiss with Simon? Can I help?"

"You've done enough, don't you think?" Sarcasm masked the dark worry reflected in her eyes.

Dammit. If only she would accept that he had Simon's best interests at heart. His interest in her, on the other hand, was questionable. His motives unclear, even to himself. She'd been a constant fixture in his dreams since their meeting in London, her beauty and fire rousing him.

Her hands curled over the top of the cord, dainty and elegant. Peering closer, he picked one up and examined it front and back. Angry blisters ran along her fingers and onto her palm, the skin chaffed red.

"What in bloody hell happened to your hand?" he bellowed, harsher than he'd intended.

Flinching away from him, she tugged at her hand, but he squeezed it and grabbed her other one. He performed the same inspection and found it in much the same shape.

"I'm not used to washing and cleaning with the soaps and liniments. They'll adjust." Now he held both hands, and she tried to twist them free. He held on tighter.

"I won't have you ruining your hands for your brother. No more soaps and chemicals, do you hear me? I'll talk with Mrs.

Devlin." He rubbed his thumbs over the delicate skin of the backs. Her attempts at escape ceased, and her hands lay pliant in his. So small, yet strong. Like the woman herself. Lord knows, regret and guilt dogged him over things he couldn't change. However, this he could, and would.

"I don't require special treatment, Lord Drummond. I must see to my duties." He loosened his grip, and she yanked her hands away, stalking off with her empty laundry basket. Even though her grey woolen dress was almost in tatters, she carried herself as if she was about to meet the Prince Regent himself. Nothing could disguise her pride.

* * * * *

Spending a good half-hour pacing in her room, Minerva's mind alternately worried over what Hampton's arrival portended and the ungodly warmth that coursed through her at the feel of Rafe Drummond's hands. Both situations caused nervous fluttering in her stomach. One she could only ignore and wish away, but she resolved to find Simon, hopefully in a more congenial mood, to continue their discussion.

His room, adjacent to where the tack was stored in the stables, was small but clean and cozy. It was also empty. Walking down the row of horses, she called his name.

Tom Donahue popped around the corner, a bucket swinging in his hand. "Master Simon's not here, ma'am."

The pit of dread that had been planted at the sight of Hampton flourished, making her queasy. "Do you know where he might be?"

"He got dressed in fine clothes and took a horse into town. Said he had Drummond's leave to meet a friend." Tom's hooded gaze glanced over her as he refilled his bucket with oats.

"Fool," she whispered, half at Simon and half at herself. She should never have let him walk away before pressing him for more details. "Tom, I need Sparrow saddled. Simon shouldn't be out tonight. He has a long day in front of him tomorrow."

A weak attempt at a smile accompanied her request. What would Tom do if he realized Simon had left without permission? She breathed in and out of her mouth and concentrated on not casting up her stomach in his clean stable.

With his usual efficiency, Tom bridled Sparrow while Minerva hauled over a saddle. Running her damp palms down her skirt, she forced positive thoughts. She could easily make Lipton before darkness fell, and Simon would escort her back. Everything would be fine. Drummond wouldn't even notice their brief absence.

"Let me ready a horse and escort you," he said.

"No," she exclaimed and then added in a softer tone, "No, thank you, Tom. You have work to finish, I'm sure."

"A groom then? Let me scare up young Henry."

"Thank you, but it isn't necessary. It's still light out and my brother will escort me home." Minerva used the mounting block, afraid Tom would stop her, but he allowed her to depart.

The sky was awash with purple clouds swirled in orange and red, the beauty and tranquility at odds with her dire situation. What if she kept riding? Rode until either she or her horse gave up? Maybe they'd even make Scotland. The outskirts of Lipton brought reality crashing down.

She stopped at the inn to leave Sparrow in the care of the hostler. "Did a tall blond gentleman leave a horse as well?"

The hostler's gaze wandered over her worn, dirty gown. "Aye. Some time back. You looking for the nob?"

"Yes, could you point me in his direction?"

The hostler leered, his gaze lingering on her bosom. Clearing her throat, Minerva drew herself up and favored him with her most cutting glance. Adam's apple bobbling, the man dropped his gaze to where he fingered her reins. "He and another gent headed toward the Happy Harpy. Down the alley there."

She stepped off the main thoroughfare and was swallowed in the darkened maw of the alley. Skimming close along the bricks of one building, she hunched her shoulders in a protective stance, and the leaden weight of her feet carried her forward with tremendous effort. A base instinct of preservation called her to turn around. Duty to her brother forced her to ignore the voice and carry on.

Catcalls accompanied her approach to the tavern. Gathered around the entrance like a gauntlet, men held tankards of ale and socialized. She stared straight ahead, vowing to yank Simon out by his bollocks for putting her in this untenable situation. Her anger lent her courage, and she lifted her chin, pushing past the men and blocking out the disgraceful insinuations.

Inside the tavern, things improved marginally. A handful of men occupied tables, and although she garnered attention, they kept their distance. The interior was dim and fogged with smoke, which only partially masked the putrid smell of rotting food and unwashed bodies. A middle-aged man with a baldpate stood behind the bar. He cleaned glasses with a grey rag trailing blackened water. Minerva swallowed hard and examined the row of dusty bottles lining the back wall.

She touched the edge of the bar but snatched her hand away. Years, perhaps decades, of sticky grime coated the wood. She wiped her hand down her already filthy dress. "Good sir, I'm looking for my brother. He's tall with blond hair, dressed well. Is he here?"

The man gave no indication he'd understood a word of her request, working his tongue around his mouth and out his lips. Blank, slow-blinking, rheumy eyes stared into hers. Did he not speak English? Was he a mute?

"Ye got coin?" The man finally spoke in a thick country accent, revealing a shocking lack of teeth. It took a moment for his words to register, but when they did, she silently castigated herself. Lipton had seemed like such a wholesome country village. She hadn't known such places even existed here and hadn't considered the need to grease palms for information.

"As it happens, I don't, but my brother does." *If he hasn't lost it all.* The thought tumbled her already upset stomach. "I'm sure he'll reward you if you'd take me to him."

Smacking his lips together, the barkeep motioned for her to follow him. He led her through a dingy hallway and opened a door set at the end. She hesitated on the threshold. Three tables of men played cards. Laughter, groans or whoops of victory overlaid each other, depending on the state of play. A thick fog of smoke hung low. She coughed and waved her hand in front of her face. With her every muscle tensed, she looked around the room like a wild animal assessing its chances of survival.

The men scattered at the tables were rough and common, on par with the men outside the tavern. Simon and Hampton played at the farthest table away. Their two opponents looked almost identical with blunt features and greasy, lank hair. The kind of men who kept a rusty knife or two tucked away in case of emergency. Hampton slouched in his chair and aimed a sly smile at Simon, who pounded the table and laughed.

A shiver of fear flowed from her spine outward, making her knees and hands tremble. She forced a step into the room anyway. An almost empty bottle of liquor sat between Hampton and Simon. While she wanted to turn and run, she gathered the pieces of her armor and became the ice princess, ready for battle. If real courage were beyond her, she would pretend.

She grabbed Simon's arm. "We're leaving."

His bleary eyes registered shock, and his mouth hung agape like a simpleton. Recovering his composure, he guffawed, snorting and hiccupping. Ignoring her, he turned back to the table. "Gents, my sis has ordered me to my room. I hope she doesn't take away my toys."

"Look at me." She screeched the words like a crow, muffling nearby conversation. He turned to her, wearing a smirk. With a mind of its own, her hand flew at his cheek. The resounding smack silenced the room, and every head swiveled in their direction. It was the first time she had ever hit him.

Breathing hard, she twisted his ridiculous cravat in her hand and whispered in his ear, "You will come this instant. You will not ruin both our lives." She straightened but held his gaze. "Settle up. Now."

His eyes clear once again, he rubbed at the red imprint of her hand on his cheek. "My luck is ready to turn, if you'd—"

"Now, Simon, or I swear to God, I will curse you until the day I die."

"Good Lord, Min, no need for theatrics. I'll come. You joining us, Hampton?" Simon rose from the chair and swayed. Minerva tucked her shoulder underneath his arm.

"You're going to allow your sister to dictate to you, old boy?" Hampton stared into her eyes even as he baited Simon.

"This is none of your business, Hampton. *Old boy.*" Minerva poured as much disdain as she could muster into her voice.

His jaw worked, and he looked ready to strangle her, but he tossed his cards face down on the table. "I suppose I'll accompany you. It's the gentlemanly thing to do."

Minerva huffed, not caring one way or another.

"You gents ain't leavin' yet. We want to play on, don't we, Dugan?" The man closest to her spoke in a soft voice and picked at dirty fingernails.

"I'm terribly sorry, good sirs, but my brother is in no state to continue playing. I'm sure you understand. I'm taking him home now." She tightened her arm around Simon's waist and tugged him toward the door—and freedom.

"I'm terribly sorry, good sirs," Dugan mocked her in a singsong voice, but then added harshly, "He's sittin' and playin'."

"Or what?" Minerva eyed the door and kept Simon moving.

"He'll pay one way or another, you saucy piece o' baggage." Dugan's threat was unvarnished and very real.

"Come on, Simon." If she could get Simon out of this room, they would be safe. They passed through the doorframe. She fished a coin out of Simon's jacket pocket and pressed it into the barkeep's hand. Hampton pointed her to a back door, and she and Simon stumbled out into a narrow alley. Even with the slight stench of urine, the night air smelled fresh and clean compared to the tavern.

Her back and shoulders already ached from taking Simon's weight. Hampton stuffed his hands in his jacket pockets, offering no help. The man was a pig, and if looks could kill, Hampton would be aflame.

Even if she managed to make it back to the stables, could Simon sit his mount in his inebriated condition? Her only consolation in the entire debacle was that Simon wasn't a mean drunk. Even after she'd slapped him, he'd made no move to retaliate as some men might. In fact, he laughed at their bumbling progress through the alley. Hampton walked several paces in front of them.

With the opening of the alley in sight, two men sauntered toward them through the shadows. The undercurrent of danger spiked fear through her, nearly taking her out at the knees. The two men from the card game were ready for their payment—one way or another.

Simon greeted the men, too deep in his cups to sense ill will from his newfound friends. He left Minerva to totter a few steps closer. "Hello, gents."

"We didn't finish winning the rest of your money, did we, sir?" The man's gravel-roughened voice sent a tingle down Minerva's spine.

Swaying and with a good-natured grin, Simon was blindsided by Dugan, who emerged from the shadows to punch him squarely in the face. The sudden brutality shocked her into immobility, and time slowed while Simon collapsed like a house of cards.

Her own scream cleared her daze. Protective instincts prevailed over her terror, and she lunged forward, putting herself between the men and Simon.

"Lord Hampton, help!" She reached out a shaking hand, but ghostly pale, Hampton made a run for the alley opening. He caught the two men by surprise and squeezed out, the clatter of his boots fading to nothing.

One of the men pushed her out of the way and into the brick wall. The other man kicked Simon in the stomach before riffling through his pockets, pulling out a few pound notes and a purse of coins. Blood coursed down Simon's face.

"Get away from him!" Even though her shoulder hurt from being slammed into the wall, Minerva threw herself at the nearest man and raked her fingernails down his face.

"Bitch," the man roared, backhanding her.

She stumbled backward, pain sweeping over her face. A pulsing whoosh in her ears blocked any noise, the throb in her lip matching the rhythm. She plopped to the ground, scraping her hands and bruising her bottom. Swiping her tongue over her lower lip, she was overwhelmed by the metallic taste of blood.

The man strode toward her. She scrambled backward on her hands, pebbles imbedding in her palms, her legs tangling in her skirts.

He grabbed the neck of her dress to haul her up and it ripped, exposing the top swells of her bosom. He heaved her to her feet, and she dangled in his grasp, her toes barely touching the ground. Balling her hand, Minerva hauled back and popped him in the nose. Her hand went numb from the impact, but blood trickled out of his nostrils.

Bellowing, he dropped her, and she landed on hands and knees. A nauseating terror clawed its way up her throat. Simon was useless, rolling and moaning on the dirty stones. The men in the tavern would ignore her screams. Or her screams might even draw more men out to join the two blackguards. She turned to sit on the rough stones and held the bodice of her dress together, her hands trembling. The two men stood over her like wild animals moving in for the kill.

A clatter echoed down the alleyway. A huge black horse reared, drawing the two men's attention away from her. The stallion pawed the stones as if it wanted nothing more than to charge and trample them all, but the dark cloaked figure on top held him in tight control.

The rider dismounted, a black greatcoat swirling around his boots. He stalked the two men. His wide-brimmed hat kept his face in shadow, making him appear all the more menacing, but Minerva recognized Aries.

Rafe Drummond was no Lord Hampton. He wouldn't abandon her to the two blackguards. Hardly sparing her a glance, he focused on the two men who had shifted, perhaps sensing a more dominant predator.

"Awfully brave fighting a woman and a drunk. Well, now you lads have a man to fight, think you can handle me?" Drummond's voice was as hard as the cobblestones. Feet planted wide and arms hanging loosely at his sides, he clenched and unclenched his hands.

No one moved. Then, one of the men made a bid for freedom, much as Hampton had done. Drummond caught him by his jacket, lifted him to his toes and drove a fist into his belly. The man deflated, and Drummond tossed him against the brick wall. He slid down to his knees and sputtered for breath.

The other man was more cautious and crouched low to pull a knife from a worn, muddy boot.

A warning creaked out of her tight throat. "Be careful."

He inclined his head, and the white slash of a smile broke the black of his beard. Was he actually enjoying himself?

"I certainly will be. I would hate to rip my new coat."

The second man's eyes widened at the blithe statement and good-humored smile. The man lunged forward, but fast as an adder, Drummond grabbed his wrist and turned it at an impossible angle. The man cried out and his hand opened reflexively, the knife clattering to the stones. In two blinks, Drummond jabbed his fist into the man's solar plexus and again into his face. He landed next to his friend against the alley wall, his legs splayed wide.

The first man, having regained his breath, scrambled for the knife. Rafe kicked it out of reach and turned to drive a boot heel into the man's knee. Ignoring the high-pitched keening, Drummond bypassed Simon altogether to squat down in front of her. The brutality of the men's attack on Simon was child's play compared to the ferocity of Drummond's retribution.

Fear still tightened her limbs and thickened her tongue. Even though she was safe, danger crackled around Rafe Drummond. However, worry for her—for them—shone in his eyes, tightening his mouth. Sliding his hands to cup her elbows, he helped her to her feet. Although he had demolished two huge brutes only seconds before, his touch was gentle. He skimmed his gaze down her body and tilted her face toward the dim light, his thumb dabbing her lip.

"He hit you." Rage laced the simple statement. "I went easy on them. Perhaps I should leave them with a more permanent reminder of this evening after all."

"*That* was going easy on them?" A slightly hysterical giggle escaped. She clamped her mouth shut when the laughter almost turned into sobs. "I want to go home. Please."

He brushed his knuckles gently over her sore cheek. Her eyes filled with tears. Whether it was at his touch or in reaction to her long, traumatizing evening, she couldn't say.

He pulled her to his chest, the warmth of his hands settling along her back. She swallowed back tears while she allowed the embrace. The steady pounding of his heart against her cheek banished the last vestiges of her terror, and some of his strength seeped into her. She itched to slide her hands under his coat to encircle his waist. Before the transgression occurred, she pulled back, still clutching the bodice of her dress together. The long ride home no longer seemed impossible.

He cleared his throat. "Did they touch you otherwise?" He gestured toward her bodice. "I'll kill them if they did."

She stared into his face, shadowed by his hat and the night. My God, was he serious? "No, I'm fine. But I'm not sure what would have happened if you hadn't come, Lord Drummond. I...thank you." The man had most likely saved their lives, and that's all she could manage?

"Let's get you and your idiot brother home," he said gruffly and turned to Simon, who had passed out. He examined her brother before hauling him up over his a shoulder.

"Is he going to be all right?"

"He'll survive. Although, he might wish the blackguards had finished the job when he wakes in the morning." He didn't sound remotely sympathetic. "I'll have to punish him harshly."

Minerva didn't reply, dizzy with dread. She hadn't thought past their rescue, but it seemed that while they'd escaped with their lives, she might lose her dowry after all.

Aries waited at the entrance to the alley and snorted when Drummond laid Simon across the saddle, feet and head dangling over either side. With a hand on the back of Simon's legs, she followed Rafe to retrieve the horses from the inn's hostler. He moved Simon from Aries to a bay gelding. Several people looked at them curiously and a few voiced greetings. He returned them politely but curtly, not inviting further conversation.

Pulling off his greatcoat, he settled it around her shoulders. It was much too long, but that wouldn't matter while she was riding. He buttoned the front as if she were a child that needed tending.

Before she realized his intent, he lifted her into the saddle. He kept a hand on her calf until she steadied herself and found the stirrups.

The sun had long disappeared over the horizon, leaving the night air chilly and damp, portending the coming of winter. Lord Drummond, in breeches and shirtsleeves, mounted Aries. He led their procession back to Wintermarsh, checking behind him frequently.

A light touch to Sparrow's flanks moved her pertly up beside Aries. Minerva spared a glance at Simon, but he was out cold and probably would be until morning. Drummond maintained a stony silence.

The moon provided enough light for a fast pace back to Wintermarsh. What was their harsh punishment to be? Was he was going to call in the vowels and turn them out? Minerva wanted to ask but was too afraid of the answers.

Tom Donahue, who had been leaning against a stone pillar at the front of the house, straightened on their approach, hands shoved in the pockets of his jacket. He avoided her eye. "The boy going to be all right, sir?"

"He'll live. I'm going to put him inside tonight. I'll need to tend to his nose." Drummond dismounted and clapped Tom on the shoulder.

With a grim expression but sympathy in his eyes, Tom offered her a hand down, and she accepted. "I'm sorry, miss."

"Whatever for?"

"You didn't want Master Rafe knowing your brother took off. But I couldn't in good conscience allow you to go to town by yourself."

"Oh, Tom. Honestly, I wish you'd been about five minutes faster in telling on me." She pulled her smile up short, pain shooting through her lip and jaw.

Drummond snorted and gestured toward Simon. Without words, Tom helped him carry her brother inside, Drummond scooping under his shoulders and Tom hooking his knees. Simon's head lolled against Drummond's chest. Purplish bruising was forming under the rusty dried blood.

Mrs. Devlin met them at the front door. "My goodness. My goodness. You poor dears." She scurried straight to Minerva and wrapped an arm around her shoulders. Her kind, motherly manner was almost Minerva's undoing.

"Lady Minerva, wait in the study while I see to your brother." His voice held no hint of anger, but it was clear he would brook no argument. It reminded her a bit too much of their arrival at Wintermarsh.

Like a recalcitrant child or perhaps a criminal on the way to the gallows, she walked into the study. Beaten or hung? What a choice. She collapsed in the oversized chair at the end of her strength, his coat still around her shoulders. What excuse could she offer for Simon's behavior?

There was none. None at all. Lord Drummond would be well within his rights to demand payment immediately. If Simon awoke, he might even banish them into the night as he had Stonewell. If necessary, she would humble herself and beg him to wait until morning.

Mrs. Devlin bustled to the sideboard and came back with a glass half-full of an amber liquid, clucking sympathetically all the while. She pressed it into Minerva's hand. "Drink it all, dearie. It will settle your nerves."

Trusting Mrs. Devlin, she tipped the glass back. The fiery path of the liquor made her sputter and cough. However, when the brandy hit her empty stomach, warmth bloomed all the way to her fingers. In spite of her worries, tension left her shoulders and her fingers unclenched. She sank deeper into the chair and emptied the glass.

Waiting for judgment, she buried her nose in the folds of Lord Drummond's coat. It smelled divine and comforting—his soap, horses, fresh hay, leather. She wanted to wrap herself in it for the night. Not as good as his arms had felt around her, but close.

Where had *that* errant, dangerous thought come from?

Finally, he entered the study holding a pot of salve and strips of linen. After setting the supplies on the table next to the armchair, he moved a sturdy stool from the corner to sit in front of her, his long legs bracketing her knees. His face was serious and unreadable. She swallowed hard, waiting for the ax to fall.

* * * * *

An increasingly oppressive silence descended. Rafe studied her. Her lip was swollen and bleeding from a cut, and a red welt stained her jaw. She would look infinitely worse on the morrow. Her blue eyes were huge and fearful, but unfocused. He removed the empty glass from her pliant fingers. How much liquor had his housekeeper allowed her to drink?

Mrs. Devlin brought a bowl of warm water and a clean cloth. He caught her eye and swung the empty glass in his fingers, gesturing toward Minerva. Mrs. Devlin only shrugged and backed her way out of the room.

Minerva followed his every move like a frightened animal. Slowly, so she wouldn't spook, he dipped the cloth into the water and gently cleaned the cut on her lip.

"Your face is going to hurt like the devil tomorrow." He held out some headache powder and a glass of water, but she made no move to take it. Unfurling her fingers, he put the packet in her palm and lifted it to her mouth. Taking over, her movements wooden, she tossed the powder to the back of her throat and washed it down with the water. A grimace flashed. Through all his ministrations, she was silent.

"Why didn't you come to me when you discovered your brother was gone?"

"I was afraid you'd make us pay his debt and leave

immediately. I hoped I could get him back without you noticing." Her gaze dropped to her lap, and her voice was wobbly and uncertain. "Shall I go pack my trunk?"

"Good Lord, I'm not an unfeeling monster."

"Aren't you?"

He slipped a finger under her chin and tilted her head up, forcing her to meet his eyes. "Let me help you, Minerva. I want to help you."

"Why?" she whispered.

What could he say? Because he empathized with her daily struggle to keep their lives from falling apart? Because he admired the determination she had exhibited since starting this farce? Because he felt a primal urge to protect her? Because he wanted her in his bed in the worst possible way? All true.

"At the very least, Lily would castrate me if I didn't help her best friend. And I see myself in Simon. Truth be told, I was wild in my youth. Lionel Masterson was my steadying hand. I can be that for Simon."

While he talked, he dipped his finger in the salve and brought it to her lip. She pulled back and caught his wrist. Although her touch was light and he could have easily pulled from her grasp, he understood her vulnerability.

"Let me take care of you," he whispered roughly. "You need someone to take care of you for once, dammit."

Her chin wobbled and a single teardrop escaped to trickle down her cheek.

"You don't have to do this alone, sweetheart. Let me help you." He feathered the tear away with his thumb, not wanting to hurt her tender face. More tears trailed after the first.

A hollow ache settled in his chest at her pain. He didn't stop to think and pulled her into an embrace. She didn't fight him and burrowed even closer, slipping her hands around his waist to press them against his back. Tears wet his shirt and wrenching sobs vibrated his chest.

He pressed a kiss to the top of her head and rubbed small circles on her back until her sobs quieted. Still she didn't push him away. Instead, her hands, light as butterfly wings, explored his flanks. His muscles contracted in the wake of her touch.

Christ, she felt good. Her breasts pressed against his stomach, causing it to lurch and his groin to tighten. He allowed his hands to wander her back from her neck to the top of her buttocks, offering comfort, yes, but also feeding his desire.

Time became irrelevant. He rested his chin on top of her silken hair and closed his eyes, her light floral scent enveloping him. She turned boneless in his embrace, and he pulled her fully onto his lap, groaning when her hip settled against his cock, hardening him further. Tensing, he expected a protest, but she snuggled closer, burying her face in the crook of his neck. Her eyes had closed, a little brandy and a long day exhausting her.

Rafe shifted her in his arms and rose, scooping her up against his chest. She was so delicate and soft. With complete trust, she looped her arms around his shoulders and nuzzled him under his ear, a hand toying with his hair. Pleasurable shivers coursed through him. He stood still, afraid to break the spell. My God, how foxed was she?

"Can I keep your coat tonight?" Her sleepy, kittenish voice broke his consternation.

After the odd request, she dropped fully into slumber, her body lax and her breathing deep and even. A small smile tugged at her mouth, incongruous with her damaged lip and tear-splotched face. Hugging her close, he nosed the hair along her temple. Eventually, regretfully, he called softly to Bertie, who opened the door and clucked like a mother hen when he saw Minerva curled up and sleeping in his arms.

"Ask Mrs. Devlin come and tend to her, would you, Bertie?" Rafe whispered.

"Certainly, sir." Bertie glided off.

Rafe climbed the stairs to the nursery and stopped in the doorway to her room. Perhaps larger than a typical servant's room, it was nothing befitting a lady of her stature. Everything was neatly stored, her bed was made, and a vase of fresh picked flowers sat on the bedside table. She'd made the best of her situation.

His bargain with Minerva ended now. Retracing his steps, he took her to the blue bedroom and lay her on the counterpane. She was swallowed from neck to toe in his greatcoat. He didn't trust himself to remove it. He smoothed the hair back from her forehead, sleep softening her face. His lips ached to mimic his hands ministrations. Before he could give in to the temptation, Mrs. Devlin bustled in, shooed him out, and closed the door in his face.

CHAPTER EIGHT

Minerva stretched languorously, sunlight streaming in through the windows on either side of her bed. She bolted upright and looked around in confusion. Finally, she placed herself in the blue bedroom she had cleaned several times.

The last thing she remembered...falling asleep in Rafe Drummond's arms, warm and safe. Prickling heat crept up her neck. He must have carried her to bed. His greatcoat still enveloped her, and she lifted the folds to her nose to take one last deep breath, savoring his scent. Perhaps that's what had attributed to the best night's sleep she had experienced in months...maybe even years.

She yawned and pain shot through her cheek and jaw. The skin of her bottom lip was stretched taut. No doubt, she looked a fright. There was no need to confirm such in the looking glass.

She swung her feet to the floor, removed the greatcoat, and fingered the jagged edges of the tear in her grey dress. It was ready for the rag bin. She padded on the thick rug to the wardrobe and cracked it open. Her dresses hung in a neat row.

Was this to be her new accommodations? But Lord Drummond had said they would be punished. She wouldn't discover his intentions hiding here, and she needed to check on Simon, the blighter. Perhaps she could slip downstairs and retrieve a rug beater. A few whacks on Simon's behind would make her feel better.

She flipped through the dresses in the wardrobe, finally pulling out a scoop-necked blue sprigged muslin. Although it was lovely, it was not appropriate for morning much less housework. However, it was the only one she could button herself, and she refused to ask one of the maids to help her. They were busy enough, as well she knew.

After seeing to her ablutions, dressing and braiding her hair, she folded Rafe's greatcoat over her arm. Poking her head out the door, she looked up and down the hall. No one was about. Tom and Lord Drummond had carried Simon inside, so he must be in one of the other bedrooms. He had been in terrible shape and was surely still abed. Although he wouldn't be for long after her tongue lashing.

Checking the rooms down the long hallway, she found a rumpled bed and discarded clothes in the cheery yellow bedroom, but no Simon. Had Drummond already tossed him out? Was he waiting on the doorstep for her to awaken so they could depart? Then why were her dresses in the wardrobe?

The distinctive jangling of keys drew closer. She scurried into the hallway. "Mrs. Devlin, where is my brother?"

"I was coming to check on you, Lady Minerva. Master Rafe gave me strict instructions to reapply the salve this morning as soon as you awoke." Crackling with energy, the housekeeper pushed Minerva back into the yellow bedroom to sit on the bed. With a furrowed brow and pursed lips, she examined Minerva's cut lip and dabbed on salve. "It hurts, I suppose, but no permanent damage, thank the Lord."

"Mrs. Devlin, where is my brother?" She emphasized each word.

"I'm surprised the commotion didn't wake you. Goodness, it reminded me of when Masters Rafe and Gray were young."

"What happened?" Her arms tightened around the greatcoat.

"Master Rafe pulled your brother out of bed at dawn and took him to the south field to remove some fallen trees. I must say your brother looked rather green, and his face was a bit worse for wear." Mrs. Devlin didn't sound the least bit worried, her tone jolly even.

"So…Lord Drummond isn't throwing us out?"

"Of course not." Mrs. Devlin eyed her curiously. "What gave you that impression? Was Master Rafe not kind to you last night? Do I need to have a chat with him?" The housekeeper's voice grew more strident, and she set her hands on her hips.

"No, please. He was—" her stomach fluttered recalling his strong arms and tender care, "—very kind, but Simon…"

"May I give you a piece of advice?"

At Minerva's nod, Mrs. Devlin continued, "You mustn't coddle him. He needs to learn there are repercussions for his actions. One time, home from Eton, Master Rafe spent the night carousing and dragged himself home in the wee hours of the morning. At dawn, Lionel Masterson hauled him out of bed to supervise the spreading of manure over a field of crops." Mrs. Devlin laughed. "Master Rafe came back that afternoon looking as grey as a dead man. I never saw him drink like that again, until…" A heavy frown replaced the laughter.

"Until what?"

Mrs. Devlin adjusted her mobcap and tugged the greatcoat out of Minerva's arms. "Oh, never you mind."

"Until what, Mrs. Devlin?" Minerva grabbed her arm before she could turn away.

"His injuries from the war were severe. The pain, the nightmares. He drank too much, still does on occasion." Her gaze cut to the rug. "Listen to me. I'd have Jenny's ear if she were gossiping like this."

It was hardly gossip. She had firsthand experience with a foxed Rafe Drummond—more than once. However, the knowledge his suffering drove him to the bottle made her feel sympathetic. She'd noticed the shadows that dogged him. He was a haunted man.

Mrs. Devlin walked away, and Minerva lifted her skirts to keep up.

"And how do you like your new room?" Mrs. Devlin asked.

"It's lovely, of course. Why was I moved?" They started down the staircase side-by-side.

"Master Rafe finally came to his senses, I'd say. It was disgraceful he insisted you have servant's quarters to begin with. We argued fiercely about it."

They were still in his debt, yet he'd rescued them at great risk to himself. His hand on her cheek had been so gentle, and his eyes hadn't been cruel at all, but understanding and comforting. He'd cradled her against his strong, warm chest until a sense of security had seeped into her marrow. It had felt quite foreign and utterly wonderful.

Resentment and dislike were easy and straightforward. If she couldn't hate Rafe Drummond, she was left with a complicated tangle of emotions that terrified her. Not the least of which was her inappropriate attraction to the man.

"What does Lord Drummond have in store for me today?" Better if he wanted her to clean floors on her hands and knees, something that would fire her anger.

Mrs. Devlin pinned her with a look she'd probably used frequently as a nanny. "Absolutely nothing. Master Rafe said your hands were in deplorable condition and you need to rest after last night. I couldn't agree with him more."

Minerva harrumphed. Blast the man, that was *nice* of him. "I feel perfectly rested. My face is sore, but sitting around isn't going to make it heal any faster. Surely there's something I can help with?"

"Nothing," Mrs. Devlin said with finality. "Go find a good

book and retire to the drawing room." She twirled, her dress fanning out, and disappeared down the servant's corridor.

Minerva didn't have a natural inclination toward idleness. She drummed fingers on crossed arms and paced. The barren entryway gave her an idea. After gathering fall flowers and greenery, she located several vases and filled the space with color and a sweet smell.

She dragged over a statue of a rearing horse that moldered in the corner of the morning room and positioned it on one side of the entry. She removed a landscape painting from the drawing room and propped it on the table and surrounded it with figurines of hunting dogs. A stack of books, perhaps?

In the study, she reached to one of the highest shelves and pulled down two heavy, ornate tomes no one ever actually read. The dust that accompanied them had her coughing. All the books seemed overly dusty and disorganized. After finishing the entry hall table, she bustled off to see Mrs. Devlin.

"Can't you relax in the drawing room? Daydream on the settee?" Mrs. Devlin asked with a slight eye-roll.

"I can't. I don't paint or embroider or play the pianoforte. I'll go round the bend for sure if you don't allow me to do *something*. It's just a bit of tidying. I promise."

Mrs. Devlin's face softened. "Fine. But don't tax yourself."

Minerva clapped her hands and gathered a basket of supplies.

First, because she couldn't help herself, she straightened his desk. At least the wood grain was once again visible through the stacks of papers. Then she cleaned a vase with several years of dust layered inside. After filling it with flowers, she rearranged the mantle, making the vase the focal point. She stepped back, tilting her head side to side, and regarded her handiwork. Lovely.

Originally, she planned to dust around the books, but they were stacked without rhyme or reason. *The History of Ancient Greece* was between a colorful book of children's tales and a scientific treatise. Really, it was only logical to reorganize the entire room.

In the beginning, things went quickly, but as she delved farther into the collection, she became increasingly distracted. The range of subjects was staggering—from collections of Roman philosophers in Latin to the modern literature of Radcliffe and Scott.

Luncheon came and went. Minerva ate cheese and bread while she flipped through a book about the isle of Capri off the coast of Italy. The illustrations and descriptions of the sea and the quaint whitewashed villages set into cliffs captured her imagination. She had never even contemplated travelling. What with the war and her responsibilities, it had always seemed an impossibility. However, the war would be over one day, and if Simon finally took up the reins of his birth, perhaps someday she could visit this beautiful island.

A small leather-bound book had fallen behind a row of tall books on the top shelf. Distractedly, she flipped open the cover to catalogue it. The inscription in the front cover had her glancing at the door.

To Raphael Drummond

From Uncle Leo and Aunt Betsy

For your lovely poems

Raphael. An Archangel? Not sure what to expect, she turned the page. What she found was a sweet poem about autumn at Wintermarsh. It was in a young boy's handwriting, the bold confidence of his current script not yet realized.

Touching, charming, funny poems depicting a young boy's childhood in the country filled the first half. Blank pages disappointed her, but a new grouping of poems began, these written in his more familiar, heavy-handed script. They were broodingly dark and full of allegories of war and suffering. Slices of black humor leapt from the page. The beauty of his words stole her breath and brought tears to her eyes.

Blast. She could not allow herself to feel sorry for the man. He was a brute and uncouth and…she traced the ridges of leather on the cover. There were hidden depths to Rafe Drummond. Reverentially, she laid the book on top of Shakespeare's *Julius Caesar*. It felt right. Even after forcing herself back to the task, she found herself flipping through the small book more than once.

The afternoon passed in a haze of discovery. Books were stacked hip high around the room, and she was only a quarter finished. She'd cleaned the shelves and dusted the books, but before she moved them back, a book of German folktales translated into English transported her. The magical dark tales were unlike anything she had been allowed to read as a child. She found a warm patch of late-afternoon sun and lay on the rug to continue reading. On her stomach with her legs swinging idly, she was enraptured.

* * * * *

Sweaty and covered in grime, Rafe ran a hand through his damp hair and clapped his hat against his leg, eyes to the ground, his thoughts on Minerva Bellingham. She had snuck into them the entire day.

Mrs. Devlin fell into step next to him, carrying a basket of apples. "Did Master Simon survive?"

"He did. Between his broken nose and roiling stomach, it was a testament to his strength of will. Took it like a man. There's hope for him yet." He glanced at his former nursemaid. "How did Minerva fare? Did she rest?"

"She's not one to loll around feeling sorry for herself." Admiration laced her voice. "She asked to tidy your study. I didn't think you'd mind. It's been neglected of late." She swallowed audibly.

She didn't need to elaborate. He terrified the maids at Wintermarsh. Even young Jenny couldn't hide her fear. Except for lighting a fire and a hasty cleaning, they avoided him and his lair. Afraid he might jump out and eat them, he supposed, even though he went out of his way to be kind.

He stepped through the front door and froze. The formerly austere, boring space was pretty and welcoming. Flowers scented the air, their colors lending warmth to the cold, white marble.

"It's charming, isn't it?" Mrs. Devlin asked.

"I…yes, quite." His greatcoat hung from the coat stand. Did it carry an echo of her scent? If Mrs. Devlin wouldn't look at him like he'd gone queer in the attic, he might check. Mentally kicking himself for his mawkish thoughts, he made for his study on cat feet.

He cracked the door open warily as if Minerva Bellingham might jump out and eat *him*. Dismay had him pushing the door open and standing in the threshold of his sanctuary. Teetering towers of books covered every table, chair, and a good portion of the floor. Squarely in the middle of the chaos, Minerva lay on the floor reading a book, completely unaware of his presence.

As he'd predicted, her face looked worse, her cheek purpling and her lip swollen. Even so, a smile bloomed as she read. His eyes widened and his mouth went dry when his gaze wandered lower. The bodice of her dress gaped, revealing a sizable portion of her round, full breasts.

Perhaps he should thank the blackguard for ripping that grey monstrosity. Her bare feet swayed in the air and her dress had bunched at her knees to expose shapely calves and well-turned ankles. Her slippers crowned the tallest stack of books braced against the doorjamb to his right.

Rafe cleared his throat. Minerva popped up to her knees, covering her legs, looking like a fox ready to run from the dogs.

"Lord Drummond." Minerva's head swiveled left and right as if just recognizing the state of upheaval. "My Lord."

Rafe was fairly confident her exclamation was an entreaty to the Almighty and not in deference to his title. He held a hand against his mouth to stem a smile.

"I realize this looks chaotic, but I'll set it to rights in no time at all. Really, I will." She gained her feet and clutched the book to her chest. Turning in a circle, she looked to the floor.

"Looking for these, mayhap?" Rafe dangled her slippers from two fingers.

"Yes, thank you." She weaved her way through the stacks to retrieve them. Their fingers brushed on the exchange, and she snatched the slippers away. His hand drew into a tight fist. Apparently, she could only tolerate him when she was in shock or inebriated.

Covering his discomfiture, he plucked the book out of her hands, being careful not to accidently touch her. "Grimm's stories, yes, a recent addition. They're ostensibly for children, but I found them to be entertaining, bloodthirsty tales." He wandered over to a still intact shelf and pulled out a careworn book. "This one is full of similar tales from England and Ireland. Did you read them as a child?"

"Our tutor didn't allow such books." He raised his brows, and she shrugged. "We read the classics. *The Odyssey* was more along the lines of our bedtime stories. During the day, we read history or philosophies."

"There's certainly nothing wrong with a little Homer, but children need their imagination fed. Speaking of which…" He plucked another well-read volume off the closest shelf. Pages had detached from the binding, but he reread it from time to time. "Now this fed many a childhood adventure."

She moved a few steps closer, her braid brushing his arm. "Arabian Nights. What's it about?"

"Take it and read it." He handed it to her. "Tales from India and Persia. There are plenty about princesses, but I prefer the ones about pirates and swashbuckling heroes." She ran a finger over the gold-embossed title along the spine, her face downturned.

"Do you mind?" She gestured vaguely. "I intended to dust, but once I got started I couldn't seem to stop myself. You have a wonderfully diverse library, Lord Drummond."

Rafe took in the disarray but also noted the papers neatly stacked on his desk and the rearranged mantle. More fresh flowers contrasted pleasantly against the heavy, masculine wood. "I don't mind. And, for God's sake, will you call me Rafe?"

"That wouldn't be at all proper." She angled her face farther away from him.

"What about our situation strikes you as proper, Minerva? Using my given name is a drop in the bucket of our impropriety, I'm afraid." He paused and wished she'd meet his eyes, but only her shiny blonde hair was visible. "Use it in thanks for last night."

"Yes, I'm not sure I thanked you properly. So...thank you again." Holding the book against her chest, she tapped her fingers on the leather. "Did Simon come back with you?" Her words fell out in a torrent of worry.

She still didn't trust him? A stab of anger harshened his reply. "Of course he did. Did you presume I'd leave him to toil in the field all night?"

"I—no, of course not, but you told me we would be punished harshly, and I've been wondering what you meant." Her voice was strained.

"Look at me, for Christ sake." She obeyed his coarsely given command immediately. Fear tightened her mouth and eyes, and he hated to think he was the cause. "First of all, I said that Simon would be punished. Forced out of bed for hard physical labor after last night was severe punishment indeed. Secondly, I never said anything about punishing you. You did nothing wrong except protect your brother. I wish you had trusted me, but I well understand why you took matters into your own hands."

"I assumed you would want me to suffer as well." Her matter-of-fact statement shifted him backward a step, and he dropped his gaze for a moment. He hated guilt.

He forced himself to meet her eyes. "You've handled things a sight better than I had anticipated with regards to our agreement. I told Mrs. Devlin to make sure you understood you aren't required to continue working as a housemaid. Consider yourself my guest. The blue bedroom is yours."

"What about Simon? Has he repaid his debt, as well?" A sudden ebullience threaded her voice. In anticipation of their imminent departure? Not bloody likely.

"Not by half. He still has work to do, and he'll stay to see it through. You're welcome to depart for London as you wish."

"I can't leave him here."

Rafe's laugh held no humor. "Of course you can't. Who knows what evil plans I have in store? As I said, you're welcome to go or stay as you desire."

He whirled away, but a soft touch on his arm stopped him. "Rafe, I didn't mean to imply you would treat Simon unfairly. In fact, you've been more understanding than I had anticipated."

His given name on her lips settled warmly in his chest and his ire faded. "Would you care to join me for dinner this evening? We can discuss my plans for your brother, among other things."

"What other things?"

"You can tell me all about the books that caught your eye."

"If that's what you wish." The old uncertainty was in her eyes. She couldn't quite let herself trust him, and he had no right to ask it of her—yet.

"I wish," he whispered.

* * * * *

Minerva stood in her new room and smoothed her skirts, stalling. The sage-green silk dress had required help from a giggling Jenny to hook. It was too grand for dinner in the country, but she desperately needed a boost of confidence to face Rafe Drummond across a dinner table. Alone.

At first, she thought to strong-arm Simon into joining them, but he was sprawled facedown and fully dressed on his bed, snoring to wake the dead. She'd covered him with part of the counterpane and left him to sleep.

Jenny had been excited to help her dress, feeling none of the awkwardness coursing through Minerva. The maid's good-natured manner had eventually put her at ease, and she'd even allowed Jenny to dress her hair again. This time, Jenny had managed a loose chignon only poking her half a dozen times with the pins, which had them both laughing. Not the most elegant effort, but a nice change from her braid.

Waiting until the last possible moment, she shuffled downstairs. Dread and anticipation in equal parts turned her stomach. Rafe was seated at the head of the long oak table reading a London paper. His brow furrowed as if something he read was troublesome, and he traced a finger down his scar.

Minerva cleared her throat, and his head shot up. He wore a dark jacket and blue striped waistcoat, both fine, well-made articles, but still no neck cloth, leaving his tanned throat exposed. There was only one other place setting to his immediate left.

His gaze roamed over her, making her legs feel like planks of wood. Finally, as if he had to remind himself to perform the courtesy, he rose, folded the paper, and set it aside. They seated themselves, and Minerva fiddled with the napkin in her lap. "Is the news grim?"

"Much the same. Pardon me for reading. I've been taking dinner alone for so long I've thrown propriety out the window I'm afraid. Although, to be frank, following the proprieties has never been my strong suit."

"Shockingly, I have noticed," she said dryly. "Don't you think small polite gestures civilize us as a people?"

"Not particularly. Society's little strictures can hide the most depraved, barbaric soul. In fact, it gives men—and women—a way to disguise their true intentions. I'd prefer to look someone in the eye and be able to see what's behind the polite façade."

Considering she never attended a social event without her façade, his words thrummed a chord. "If everyone were so open with their opinions, the average London ballroom would be a mass of wailing women and outraged men."

"More interesting than the typical ball, I would guess." A ghost of a smile crossed his face.

The footman approached to fill their wine glasses and ladle soup in their bowls. She thanked him by name and the young man blushed and retreated to the kitchen.

"The ice princess is going to conquer Wintermarsh too, it seems," Rafe said with an amused shake of his head.

"Don't call me that. It's ridiculous." Hearing the hated moniker clipped her words.

After taking a measured sip of wine, he half-smiled. "I assumed you were proud of your status in the beau monde as the untouchable paragon. Tell me, why have you never married?"

Was he trying to goad her into an argument? She took an unladylike gulp of wine. "Why have I never seen you at a London event, my lord?"

"Have you not? I've seen you." He picked up his spoon and attacked his soup. As the silence lengthened, he cut his gaze to her, masked through his long lashes.

"When? This season? I'm sure I would have noticed." She cast around for any memory of him. There was no way the man could enter a room and not garner everyone's attention—scar or no scar.

"No, it must have been your first season. You were wearing a white dress and were surrounded by half a dozen gentlemen. But you didn't pay the slightest bit of attention to them. In fact, you looked a bit lonely. I was feeling the same. I suppose that's why I noticed you. You stood there apart from all the frivolity."

The first season had been her worst. She'd received several marriage offers, but the forced socialization had made her curl up in bed and cry nearly every night. She hadn't yet learned how to flirt superficially, only allowing her suitors to see the very surface of her thoughts. "I was the fox and all those gentlemen were the dogs nipping at my heels. I hated it. Why didn't you ask for an introduction?"

"You were innocent and pure and…clean. I had completed half a dozen missions by then. My life was so far removed from London's game, it seemed another world to me by then. One I wasn't fit to enter."

A deep emotion—Despair? Regret?—flashed over his face, pulling his brow and the corners of his mouth down. Then it passed, and he dropped his attention to his bowl, making a whirlpool with his spoon.

At a loss for words, she took two bites, not tasting anything. Finally, she broke the lengthening silence. "You're the heir to an earldom. You can enter that world at will."

He smiled, but his eyes were still troubled. "I'm glad you don't understand, Minerva. That white frock you wore so beautifully represented everything I had lost, everything I could never get back, yet exactly what I was fighting to protect."

Damnable tears pricked. Faking a cough, she surreptitiously pressed them back with her napkin. The footman replaced their soup with roast quail, providing her time to gather herself.

"You never answered my question. Why have you never married?" The tease in his voice sounded forced. "Surely you've had offers. Stonewell would come up to scratch at the snap of your fingers."

Shrugging, she fumbled with her knife and hacked at the bird on her plate. "Most gentlemen want a wife who will sit back and provide accolades for their accomplishments while they receive nothing in return but a dress allowance. I enjoy my freedom, and I've not met a man who even tempts me to give it up." No need to mention the fact no one had ever roused her sensibilities. Until him.

His hum seemed to impart understanding while his large hands gracefully dissected every piece of meat from the many small bones. "You spent the day hip deep in my books—literally. What caught your eye?"

"Books?"

He huffed a laugh. "Yes, those large masses of paper with little things called words inside?"

A giggle sputtered out before she could suppress it. "I found a travelogue from Capri. It looked beautiful. The drawings were breathtaking, but I can't imagine the colors are real."

"They're quite real. If anything, they're even more vivid."

"You've been there? I've never travelled outside of England."

"That's a shame. You'd enjoy it. Language and even food can vary from country to country, sometimes region to region."

"I'm abysmal with languages. I tried to learn French, I truly did, but my tutor eventually threw his hands up in despair at my ineptitude. It was my only failure." She abandoned the bird for the potatoes.

"Beauty, a sharp mind, charm…you can't be perfect. Allow the rest of us to acknowledge you exhibit some human frailty."

Her head shot up. He stared at her, a slight smile curling his lips even as he took a sip of wine. Her blush spread like wildfire. "Th-thank you."

"I've embarrassed you? I wasn't sure you were capable." His mocking tone was not lost on her.

"I'm a woman, like any other, Rafe Drummond," she said tartly.

The smile over his wine glass grew, and his eyes twinkled with puckish charm. "I beg to differ, but we won't argue the point. Did you come across any of my novels?"

"One of Austen's books was in your room. When I cleaned it," she returned in the same mocking tone.

Her barb hit the mark. Rafe shifted, and Minerva smiled.

"She's vastly amusing. You would enjoy her sarcastic take on society. I'll send my copy to you. What else did you find?"

"I skimmed through a book about Egypt and the tombs of the pharaohs. Do you think it's all true? Even the part about the ghosts?"

"Ghosts? I should think not. If ghosts were real, I'd have a battalion following me." Real pain hid behind his lighthearted jest. The urge to reach out and touch him was strong. Instead, she fisted the napkin in her lap at a loss for words.

Dessert arrived, and they ate the small tart in silence. The clanking of silverware against the plates filled the ponderous silence. Stuffing the last too-large bite in her mouth just to have it finished, she rose.

He followed suit, leaving his tart almost intact. "Would you care to take a turn around the gardens?" The words tripped out of him as if he were nervous. If her damnable mouth hadn't been full, she would have declined with a hasty excuse, but all she could do was chew furiously and nod.

They strolled outside, the setting sun streaking the sky with color. A chill edged into the space the sun had abandoned, making her wish for a shawl. Rafe didn't offer an arm and kept a satisfactory distance between them. Unlike the silences at dinner, this one felt more companionable.

"Your brother held up well today. I was proud of him. Soon, I'll teach him about estate management from a more cerebral approach."

"There's hope for him then? I wasn't sure last night."

"There's always hope for redemption." He walked with his hands clasped behind his back, and his face tipped to the darkening sky. Did he seek redemption? Before she could pursue the line of questioning, he said, "The fresh flowers in the house are lovely."

"You don't mind?"

"But earthlier happy is the rose distill'd, Than that which withering on the virgin thorn, Grows, lives, and dies in single blessedness." His lilting voice was melodious.

"That's lovely. Did you write it?"

"Me?" He blocked the middle of the path, crossed his arms over his chest and pursed his lips in mock disappointment. "Tell me you jest. The finest English wordsmith in history wrote that. William Shakespeare."

His feigned outrage at her ignorance made her laugh. "Shakespeare was not on our docket, but I'm well-versed in the mating habits of the African rhino, if you have any questions." His smile, genuine and wide, reached his eyes. Her breathing quickened. "Anyway, not so farfetched. Your poems are beautiful."

His smile crumpled, and his brows drew low, shadowing his eyes. "What?" he croaked as if his throat had collapsed as well.

Her tart wanted to make a hasty reappearance. "I found your poems this afternoon."

"You read them? All of them?"

She tried to make herself say no but couldn't lie. "Yes. They were lovely. You have no reason to be embarrassed."

"Those were personal, Lady Minerva." He didn't yell, but his words, cold and impersonal, sliced her nonetheless. She had been a fool to read his work and an imbecile to admit it. It seemed their new, unacrimonious relationship would be brief.

His jaw worked as if it was a dam against a flow of words. Gone in a blink, he left her, full of shame, in the beautiful garden.

CHAPTER NINE

Two weeks had passed since Simon's debacle in town and Minerva's debacle in the garden. After the hellish day Simon had spent in atonement with Rafe clearing the trees, he had stopped complaining and looked to Rafe with a newfound respect and admiration. They worked side by side during the day and even took dinner together in the study, playing chess or delving into estate business well into the evening.

Her exclusion chaffed. How much of it was Rafe's attempt to untether Simon from her apron strings, and how much was a punishment for reading his personal writings? During the day, she continued her work in the study, cleaning and cataloguing the books. She lingered well into the afternoon, hoping to intercept them, but something always called her away.

Feeling slightly pathetic and sick of waiting, she offered her services to Mrs. Potts, who sent her to pick apples for turnovers. The apple grove sat well beyond the stables, and she walked along, swinging an empty basket. The light breeze carried a hint of burning wood and turning leaves made a fiery blaze on the horizon. She rounded the corner of the stable, and her feet seemed to plant themselves deep in mire.

Simon and Rafe grappled and punched, obviously trying to kill each other. They broke apart to circle warily, both crouched low, looking ready to pounce at the slightest provocation.

"Come on, whelp. My sister hits harder than that. Are you sure you have a pair of bollocks down there?" Rafe taunted.

Simon looked grim and determined, but a red welt stained his jaw. He leapt at Rafe, who dropped low and let Simon's momentum carry him forward, using the motion to flip Simon onto his back. Her brother gasped and flopped on the dirt floor like a fish out of water.

"Ha. Nice try, but too hasty." Rafe nudged Simon with a boot. Once recovered, Simon scrambled to his feet and pulled a knife from his boot, ready to attack again.

Rafe made a rude hand gesture. Simon swung the knife on a short arc, trying to slice open Rafe's belly. Her leaden feet wouldn't obey the screaming commands in her head. She was beyond terrified.

In a blur of motion, Rafe grabbed Simon's wrist and twisted. Maneuvering Simon around, he snaked one arm around her brother's neck. His other hand clamped around Simon's wrist and, in slow motion, forced the knife tip toward Simon's belly. Simon shook, straining to push Rafe's arm away, but the blade continued its slow trek.

Simon slipped a foot around Rafe's leg, pulling him off-balance. Her brother wiggled free and elbowed Rafe in the sternum. Rafe grunted and released his wrist. Simon laughed and circled Rafe again. Rafe would kill Simon for that. She'd seen what the man was capable of in the alleyway.

She flew at Rafe, grabbing at his biceps and pulling. "Stop! For, God's sake, stop it!"

Rafe didn't budge, only straightened out of his crouch. He didn't look the least bit angry. In fact, he was smiling. But she remembered the delight he'd seemed to take in annihilating the men in the alley.

She quit pulling at him but kept her hands around his arm,

trying a different tact. "Please, Rafe, you're too strong. You'll kill him." She stared into his blue-grey eyes, not sure what she saw. His smile fell not into a frown, but into something more complicated.

Simon's laughter penetrated her singular focus on Rafe. "Min, you dolt. Drummond's teaching me how to fight. This knife could barely slice through butter. Although, come to think of it, I'm rather hurt by your poor assessment of my abilities." Her brother sniffed in mock self-pity.

"You're not trying to kill each other?"

"Honestly, Minerva, did you think Drummond would try to actually hurt me?"

One of Rafe's eyebrows quirked up as he waited for her answer. Because of course, she'd thought that very thing—more than once.

"I am a dolt." She took a step back, lifted her skirts, and ran like a coward. First, she'd read his personal writings, and now she'd accused him of attempting to murder her brother.

Lost in her sea of humiliation, she startled when a warm hand circled her arm. Rafe held out her basket, a sheepish expression on his face.

"Minerva—"

"I'm sorry—"

"Ladies, first," he said.

"The two of you were fighting, and it looked so real. I was afraid…" Minerva looked to the cloudless sky. "And can I apologize again for reading your personal writing? I knew I shouldn't, but they were so lovely, I couldn't stop."

"Those writings…I don't reveal that sort of thing to…well, to anyone. They're hardly lovely. They're bleak and dark and wretched."

"There's beauty in the darkness. You just have to look a bit harder."

A beat of silence passed. "Minerva, your brother is doing well. Things are better. I promise."

"I know they are. He's different. You're different." Perhaps he'd changed from the gruff, intimidating man that had met them at the front door that fateful night, or perhaps it was her assumptions about him that had undergone a transformation. Either way, things were different between them.

A flash of something passed between them, but like the searing, brief energy of lightning, the feeling was gone before she could classify it. Swallowing, she took the basket and headed to the orchard again. He fell into step beside her.

"He talks about you as if you're a hero, you know. I can't tell you how much of a burden you've lifted off my shoulders," she said.

"A hero? I'm anything but." Surprise colored his tone. He nodded toward their destination and the empty basket dangling from her hand. "Apple picking, I presume."

"Mrs. Potts promised turnovers for tonight's dessert if I gather some. I've never picked apples before. I'm quite looking forward to it."

"Never picked apples? Next you'll be telling me you've never climbed a tree."

"I haven't."

Rafe halted, and she turned to look at him. "You've never climbed a tree? Never read Shakespeare? What kind of bleak childhood did you have?"

"I'm coming to understand it was... Well, not bleak perhaps, but not much fun either."

Compassion softened his eyes. "Today is as good a day as any to remedy such a deficiency in experience, wouldn't you say? Blue skies, warm sun, trees all around." He gestured about them expansively.

"Did you climb trees when you were young?"

"Thousands. I would pretend I was on a great sailing ship, climbing the rigging to look for land or sea monsters or, my personal favorite, sirens in the deep blue sea."

"You had a happy childhood then, even with your mother gone?"

"I did for the most part. It was difficult after Mother left us, but mostly because of Father."

This very spring, Rafe and Lily had learned an obsessed, spurned suitor, Lord Penhaven, had killed Victoria Drummond. They had spent their lives thinking she had abandoned them and run off with a lover.

"Lily was too young to remember much, thank God. The earl was unhappy. It was a relief when he was called away on Crown business. When he was gone, Lionel and Betsy Masterson acted as our guardians, and better ones you couldn't find." He paused, scanning the treetops. "Even though on the surface I was heir to a title and house and fortune, I spent many hours secretly jealous of Gray. He had something even more precious to me. A real family."

The pain in his voice spoke directly to her heart, and, without thinking, she brushed a finger over the back of his hand. She snatched her hand to the handle of the basket, and he thankfully didn't acknowledge the errant touch. They continued their stroll toward the apple orchard.

"How old were you when your parents were killed?" he asked.

"Simon was five and I was seven. Highwaymen waylaid them on the road. Mother refused to give up her jewels and a struggle ensued. They were killed and then robbed. The irony was her jewels were paste."

"Who took care of you after that?"

"The estate was put into trust. We had a tutor." Even she could hear the dread in the simple statement.

"Yes, Simon mentioned your tutor. He sounded charming." The sarcasm in his voice settled her sudden uneasiness.

"Our solicitor was an old family friend and managed things until I took over. Well, technically, I convinced him to hire Drake, who is a progressive sort of fellow. Simon will take over at twenty-one. It's honestly terrifying."

"Why not keep your Mr. Drake on as an advisor to Simon?"

Minerva sighed. "They dislike each other intensely. Drake makes no effort to hide his disrespect. Simon's first order of business will be to fire him."

"Would Simon allow you to guide him?"

"I don't know. He has a need to prove himself, I think. What will I do when he takes over? What's left for me?" She kept her gaze on the ankle high grass.

"You could marry and have children. Catch yourself a title and live your life in contentment. Stonewell would be amenable to such an arrangement, I'm sure." A hint of derision soured his voice.

Minerva barked with laughter. "And do what? Embroider? Play the pianoforte? Paint watercolors? I'm atrocious at all three endeavors."

"Perfect. You obviously need the practice. The world is crying for more witty samplers." His wry voice made her huff a laugh.

On reaching the orchard, Minerva drew in a deep, satisfying breath of rich, pungent air. Fallen apples covered the ground. Right now, she didn't want to think about what would happen past this afternoon.

He shook the lower branches of the closest tree. "You'll have to climb for the apples anyway. I would offer, but I learned the hard way that those branches aren't sturdy enough for a man like me."

"No, I can see that wouldn't work a'tall." Her flirty side-eyed glance and tone came naturally, unlike her practiced, faked repartee in London's ballrooms. Red burnished his cheeks, and she smiled. "Why, Rafe Drummond, I've embarrassed you? I had no idea you were capable."

"I'm a man, just like any other, aren't I?" He threw her words back at her.

Her mouth parched, any retort crumbling into sand. She was suddenly and acutely aware of his potent masculinity—from the strong column of his throat to his hair-covered forearms flexing with his movements, to his thick, muscular thighs.

"Are you ready? You'll be everyone's heroine tonight as we enjoy Mrs. Potts's apple turnovers. You'll need to tuck your skirts up so you can climb."

She twisted her skirts up, revealing a good bit of her lower leg. No doubt, he'd seen his fair number of bare female limbs. She tamped down her sudden modesty and turned to the nearest tree. The lowest branch was still too high for her to get a foothold on.

"How in the world do I begin?"

"Allow me." Rafe cupped his hand much like a groom helping her mount a horse. "I'll toss you up."

"Toss me?" Her nerves jangled, but she had trouble pinpointing the exact cause.

"Trust me?" His half-smile was taunting and set her heart racing. Nodding, she placed a booted foot in his hand. She grabbed his shoulders for balance and admired the hard, bunched muscles with her fingers.

Shooting upward, she reached for the lowest branch. With his help, she turned and sat using neighboring branches for support and balance. Gingerly pulling herself to standing, she felt like a little red squirrel hiding in the leaves. Rafe grinned up at her from the ground, his hands on his hips.

"How do you feel?"

She took a deep, sweet breath. "Free," she said on the exhale.

"Well, go on, find us some apples. Drop them down, and I'll gather."

Minerva climbed up a few more branches. She rained apples

down on Rafe. Giggling, she aimed for his head while he snatched them out of the air, making a game of it.

"The basket's full. Are you ready to climb down?"

"I'm going to go up a bit farther." Pulling herself up another two branches, her head poked through the canopy. The sky seemed bigger and the stables smaller. The ground looked a long way down, but her stomach turned with excitement, not fear.

"I could stay all afternoon," she called out breathlessly.

"I wouldn't advise it. I tried to sleep up a tree one night, and it was dammed uncomfortable after a couple of hours, let me tell you."

Minerva laughed. "I suppose I'll defer to your obvious expertise."

"Be careful, coming down is trickier than going up." The worry in his voice gave her pause. Her skirts had come untucked and tangled around her legs, making the descent that much more difficult.

She was only two branches from the ground when she made the mistake of glancing down. He stood directly underneath her, a concerned expression aimed in her direction. Looking at him instead of the next branch, she put her weight on a thin offshoot instead of the main branch. It gave way. She hit her bottom hard on a branch and flailed for a handhold, finding none.

Closing her eyes, she expected to hit the ground. Except she didn't, she fell onto Rafe and drove them both down. Sprawled over him, she caught her breath and rubbed at a stinging scratch on her neck. He wasn't moving.

"No, no, no. Wake up." She straddled his stomach and shook his shoulders, making his head bob. She ran her fingers through his hair, probing for bumps, or, heaven forbid, blood. There was nothing. His long lashes cast shadowy crescents on his cheekbones.

"Rafe. Rafe. Please, wake up." She glided her hands up to his face to cup his cheeks, his beard tickling her palms.

"I have a new appreciation of Newton's theories," he rasped, the corners of his lips quirking up.

Relief hummed through her, and she dropped her forehead to his chest. "I thought I'd killed you." With her nose buried between his waistcoat and shirt, she breathed in his distinctive scent. Mixed with the apples, it was heady.

"It would take more than a slip of a woman falling out of a tree to kill me if the French didn't manage it." Although his words were teasing, his tone was low and rough.

Was he in pain? Minerva raised her head to examine his face. No, not pain…but something strained his features and tensed his muscles. Emotions seethed like a brewing storm in his blue-gray eyes. How could she ever have thought them cold and flinty? He was a complex, fascinating man, and she didn't understand him.

But she wanted to. There, she'd admitted it.

She wanted to kiss him too. His lips were parted, inviting and soft, framed by dark hair. What would his beard feel like against her lips, her cheek? An aching awareness emanated where she was pressed against his stomach.

Desire. This was desire. Potent and commanding.

What if she were to lean closer…just a brush…a taste. Her lips touched his, and she closed her eyes on contact. She skimmed her hands over his bristly cheeks and delved into his hair, the thong holding it back lost among the fallen apples. She nibbled at his lips, brushed the corners, and laid a simple kiss on his upper lip. Finally, because she had to know what he tasted like, she flicked her tongue along his full lower one.

He didn't respond. In fact, he hadn't so much as twitched a muscle. She pulled back. He was stunned, his eyes wide and brows high. A heated flush of embarrassment flooded her body, and her breathing hitched in panic.

She swung her leg over his torso. "Rafe—Lord Drummond, I'm terribly sorry. Please forgive my improper, forward, outrageous—"

The hard, unyielding statue came to life, rolling her to her back and reversing their positions. He lay half atop her, his heavy thigh between her legs, and his chest pressing her down. Up on one elbow, he touched her flaming cheek as if she were a delicate piece of china.

"You kissed me." His whispered declaration was accusatory.

"I-I don't know what to say. I'm an idiot. It must run in the family." Her joke fell flat, and she prayed a sinkhole would swallow her.

"Did you hit your head on the way down?"

"Let me up." She pushed ineffectually at the hand stroking her cheek, humiliation bringing a sting of tears to her eyes and a lump to her throat. He caught her wrist and trapped her arm in the soft grass.

"You have no idea, do you, sweetheart?"

His endearment eased her mortification, and her struggles ceased. "No idea of what?"

"Of what you do to me." He gave a rusty laugh before capturing her lips.

Urgent sensations rippling through her body trumped her embarrassment. At first, he mimicked her innocent explorations, gently kissing and nipping at her lips. He ran his tongue along the seam of her mouth but was more insistent than she had been. Although Minerva had never allowed it, she knew his tongue wanted entrance, and while the thought had disturbed her in the past, she craved his invasion.

She parted her lips, and he accepted the invitation to rub his tongue alongside hers. A low moan escaped her throat as a growl vibrated his chest. Her free hand, which had been lying clenched on the ground, opened and pressed against his lower back. Then, because she couldn't seem to control the urge, she ran her hand up his broad back, relishing the play of muscles.

He released her wrist and tilted her head, forcing her mouth open even wider. His kiss grew more aggressive, and she became bolder in return, stroking her tongue against his. An unfamiliar womanly satisfaction bloomed when he moved his hips farther over hers. She exalted in his weight. The hard, aroused length of him pressed into her leg, and she ground her hips on his thigh. Her body had lain dormant for so long, she didn't know how to control the rising torrent of need. She wanted everything and all at once.

He trailed a hand over her cheek and down her neck to cup a breast, his thumb flicking at her peaked nipple. She arched into the weight of his hand and turned her face away, overwhelmed by sensation. He slid his lips down her throat, stopping to lick and nip at her ear. Shivers coursed all the way to her toes, curling them in her half-boots.

She pulled at his shirt with frantic hands and slipped them underneath to explore the heated skin along his sides. The hiss of an indrawn breath drew her gaze to his face to find a sensuous, beguiling smile.

He continued to squeeze and tease first one breast and then the other. Scooting lower, he grazed her nipples with his teeth. Even through the cloth, bolts of pleasure made her squirm.

She looked down at his dark head and imagined someone walking by, a servant or, even worse, Simon. Humiliation would be a certainty, maybe even ruination. It was a dunk in a vat of cold water. She pushed at his shoulders, ineffectually at first. Panic welled, and her movements became agitated.

"Stop, you must stop!" She hit his shoulders with balled-up fists until he took notice, pulling his mouth away but making no move to release her.

"What's wrong?" He stayed focused on her breasts.

"We can't do this. I don't want to do this," she whispered, even knowing it was a lie.

"You could have fooled me, sweetheart." His gaze swept to

hers with lazy intent, but he was still as if waiting for her move.

Her mind tried to assimilate what he'd unleashed in her body. Another kiss might see her hauling her skirts up and begging him to ruin her. "Get off of me. Let me up." Confusion sharpened her words.

His sensual, hooded eyes hardened to flint in an instant. For the first time, she couldn't hold his gaze and stared on a rotting apple lying at her side. Breathing heavily, he rolled off her and stared up into the trees.

Minerva propped herself on elbows and looked down her body. Her behavior had been outrageous, wanton, brazen. After all, she had kissed him.

"Offering me your body won't release Simon from our agreement any earlier." His voice was scathing and harsh.

"I intended nothing of the sort. How could you think—?"

"What would you have me think? That you couldn't control your maidenly passions? Please, don't patronize me. We both know I'm the last man in England you would choose to dally with. I'm impressed you tolerated my touch for as long as you managed. You even acted convincingly aroused."

He hauled himself to his feet, facing away from her. His shoulders were tense and hunched. Turning his head so his face was in profile, his scar prominent and angry-looking, he said between clenched teeth, "Understand, if you play this game again, don't expect me to be the gentleman and stop before I'm riding between your legs, *my lady*."

He stalked toward the barn, and she scrambled up on weak legs, holding out a hand. "Rafe, I didn't mean…" He didn't give her a backward glance, and she couldn't be sure if her hoarse whispered plea even reached his ears.

Well, she'd thoroughly botched that. While she tried to summon laughter, her eyes filled with tears instead. She hauled the basket up to the kitchen, waving Mrs. Potts off with a thin excuse of being overtired when the kindly cook questioned her red eyes and wan face. Finally reaching the safety of her room, she threw herself on top of the counterpane and allowed herself a good cry, muffling her sobs in the feather pillow.

* * * * *

Goddammit, the woman had him tied in knots. He kicked a stone as far as he could down the path to the stables. What in bloody hell had just happened? She had initiated the encounter, but to what end? Was it a manipulation to release Simon? It wasn't what he'd expected from her, knowing her character as he did now.

Was he to believe she was genuinely attracted to him? He barked a laugh. He had too many examples of her distaste for his touch. Yet her response had seemed truly ardent. She'd trailed her soft hands up his bare flanks and rotated her hips against his cock. Her kiss had been skillful and erotic, her tongue aggressive. Perhaps she wasn't the innocent she portrayed. Had she already lain with Stonewell?

The thought made him want to rip the nearest tree from the ground. He couldn't quite convince himself she wasn't what she seemed. Or, more accurately, didn't want to believe it. He ran a hand over his face, tracing his scar. A quick swim in the chilly pond would cool his heated blood and clear his cluttered mind. He stripped and dove in, catching his breath at the contact.

It didn't take long for the cold water to work its magic, and soon enough, he headed to the house to change out of his damp clothes. Relieved Minerva was nowhere in sight, he stopped short at the top of the stairs, listening intently. On silent feet, he crept to stand in front of her door.

Muffled cries penetrated the heavy wood. He braced his hands on either side of her door. Pain shot through his body, impelling him to enter and offer comfort, but earlier doubts stayed his feet. Even so, he stood outside her door like a sentinel until her sobs quieted and finally ceased.

CHAPTER TEN

After her satisfying cry, Minerva napped fitfully, waking close to dinner. She crept to the kitchen to gather a tray of food and retreated again. The thought of seeing Rafe while her nerve endings were still so raw from their kiss and his accusations was terrifying.

The clock chimed midnight. She was paying for her nap and a frustration she couldn't shake. Finally relenting, she kicked off the covers with a sigh. A distraction is what she needed. She slipped on a wrapper and crept down to Rafe's study to bring back Mary Radcliffe's latest novel.

Clutching the book to her chest and holding a candle high, she glided back up the stairs. The complete silence of the usually bustling house triggered an unexplained anxiety in the pit of her stomach. An eerie, pained moan echoed through the landing. She dropped the book with a thud, and the shadows against the walls moved erratically with her shaking hand.

"No!"

She recognized Rafe's voice this time, followed by some intelligible mutterings. A nightmare.

"God, no, please no." Hearing him beg some unseen tormentor squeezed her heart. How could she leave him in such pain?

Her decision made, she hastened inside his room and set the candle on the night table. He writhed in bed. The glow of the candle revealed he had little to no clothes on. His chest was bare, heavily muscled and dusted with dark hair trailing to where the sheet was riding low on his hip. His unmentionables were covered at the very least. One leg stuck out from the sheet, which was otherwise wrapped and tangled about him.

She gingerly laid a hand on the warm skin of his shoulder and shook. "Rafe. You're having a nightmare. Wake up."

One of his hands flew out and hit her hard above the elbow. The lower half of her arm went numb. He could truly hurt her without even realizing it.

Moaning, he rolled toward her, grabbed her wrist, and pulled her toward him. She half fell across the bed, catching herself on his chest. He rolled them and came up over her.

"You will not...not again...not her..."

She hardly recognized his guttural voice, and a frisson of fear coursed through her. "Wake up. You're hurting me. Rafe, please." She pounded on his chest with her free hand and twisted her wrist trapped in his grip.

The hand loosened, but he didn't free her entirely. His eyes opened.

"Rafe, thank God. Are you awake? You're having a nightmare." Relief sailed her voice high.

"Minerva? You're alive? She didn't kill you?" His voice was like gravel, but his relief was palpable.

"I'm fine. It was all a bad dream."

He encircled her nape and stroked his thumb repeatedly down the column of her throat, over her windpipe. "You're fine. You're alive. Just a dream." It was almost a chant, and he dropped back to his pillow, bringing her with him, his hand still around her neck, his thumb on her windpipe.

"Who did you think was going to kill me?"

"What are you doing here? Did I hurt you? Tell me I didn't hurt you." He released her wrist and neck, his arms falling to the bed.

"You didn't hurt me." She pushed a lock of his hair behind his ear.

His anguish was genuine. She scooted off the bed and went to his washbasin to rinse out a cloth. Smoothing his hair from his brow, she ran the cloth over his clammy face and neck.

Next, she set to unwind the woefully tangled sheet, trying in vain not to stare at his hair-covered muscular legs. She catalogued the multitude of scars crisscrossing his broad chest. One large red scar took up a good portion of his left shoulder. How had he borne the pain and survived?

Her hands shook as she pulled the sheet up his chest and under his arms, tucking him in like a child. She touched his scarred shoulder, the skin reddened and puckered. Then, without thinking, she ran a fingertip down the scar that marred his otherwise unblemished face.

He flinched at her touch, but she rubbed her thumb along his beard-covered jaw, offering reassurance. Aware for the first time she was in a state of dishabille in a gentleman's bedroom, she clutched her wrapper together and sidestepped toward the door.

"Minerva, please. Come back a moment." His voice was rough, needy and she obeyed, driven partly by compassion and partly by something a bit less noble.

She approached the bed. He took her hand and tugged her down next to him. His grip didn't hurt, but it was unrelenting, and she had little choice but to swing her legs on the bed.

"This is most improper."

"Only for a moment. I don't want to be alone." The strain and sorrow in his voice were more than she could deny.

What would it hurt if she lay with him like this for a few minutes? It was well after midnight, and no one was about. She lay next to him, and he released her. He didn't touch her but turned on his side to face her. His chest rose and fell in a heavy sigh, and his eyes closed. As soon as he went lax, she would slip to her room. With that last thought and an unusual contentment seeping into her bones, sleep washed over her.

In the next instant, something tickled her cheek, and she breathed in the captivating scent of man. She didn't want to leave her dreams.

"Wake up, Minerva. The servants will be seeing to their duties soon." The words penetrated her consciousness as warm hands rubbed her back. Her eyes shot open inches away from Rafe's beautiful blue-gray ones. Dawn leaked light into the room.

Good Lord Almighty, she'd spent the night in his bed. Her leg was notched between his, his heavy calf trapping her, and her neck was pillowed on his arm, the other draped over her waist. They were twined together like lovers. A slow heat simmered in her body.

* * * * *

Had he ever been this aroused? She moved against him, obviously not realizing the pain and pleasure she incited. His hiss drew her attention.

"Are you well?" Her voice was rusty with sleep, her blue eyes still dreamy.

"I am. It seems you banished my demons last night. Thank you." He wanted to kiss her. Christ, who was he fooling? He wanted to rub his aching cock against her silky, bare skin. He wanted to slip inside of her and drive them both to oblivion.

"Do you have them often?"

Rafe didn't want to lie, but he didn't want her pity either, so he shrugged. "Less often than I used to. I've grown used to them."

The nightmares had started as soon as he'd arrived home. Men he had killed in the name of England began making mocking appearances, tormenting his sleep. The nameless, but not faceless, men who believed in their cause as vehemently as Rafe had believed in his. They were different sides to the same coin, and Rafe had grown sickened by the games in the end. The men he'd killed had sisters and mothers or even worse, wives and children, waiting for them, but because of Rafe they would never return. He deserved their torment, but it was the dreams about his final mission that proved to be his undoing.

"Is that why you drink? So you can sleep without the nightmares?"

Her insight startled him. For some time, he'd found the only way to attain a dreamless sleep was to drink himself there. As soon as he was out of his sickbed, he had descended into a drunken stupor most evenings.

"Yes," he whispered, "coming home was difficult." He only allowed weakness or melancholia to force him into old habits, and like the morning after she'd arrived and after Stonewell's visit, he invariably regretted it.

Now he worked himself into exhaustion every day, going to bed late and waking at dawn or before. It seemed to keep the nightmares at bay for the most part. But last night, his nemesis had come calling. This time, it had been Minerva that he couldn't save in his dreams, Minerva that he couldn't reach in time, and it had been terrifying. He'd needed her in his arms, needed to know she was safe, and as a result, he'd slept better than he'd had in two years. At least until he had started to wake with her soft body curled into his.

"I'm sorry, Rafe. I have trouble sleeping sometimes too, but for different reasons." She feathered her fingertips down his face and neck to rest on his bare shoulder. His cock twitched.

"You have to go. I promised not to besmirch your reputation, remember?"

"Yes, I'll go. Will you be all right?" Minerva disentangled

herself and sat, pulling her wrapper around her body.

A week ago, he was sure he had disgusted Minerva. His scar, his body, his hands, his boorish nature—none of it appealed to gently bred women. If she was the beau monde's ideal, then he was its antithesis. Now, he was confused.

He wanted her to want him. More than sex, he wanted her to laugh up at him, brush his hair back, touch his arm while they walked or talked. Christ, he was a weak-kneed fool.

"Are you sure you're well?" She rubbed sleep from her eyes like the innocent she was.

"There's nothing wrong that you can help with. You'd best hurry to your room."

With one last look, she slipped through the door, her white night clothes a flash in the fading darkness. As soon as the door closed, Rafe rolled onto his stomach, buried his head in his pillows and fisted the sheets.

He burned for her. It had been so long since he had lain with a woman. After the stress of his missions and the trauma of his injuries, maybe he needed a woman—any woman. It just so happened Minerva Bellingham was attractive and convenient.

Perhaps this was simple lust. There was an establishment not far where he could find a woman to slake his desire. Pride be damned, he would pay to lessen the consuming need he felt around her.

Unfortunately, he needed to alleviate his immediate problem by taking matters into his own hand. Images of Minerva danced behind his closed eyes. He imagined her trailing her hand between his legs and spent in record time. Certainly nothing to brag about. He laughed into his pillow. He would visit a whore and soon. Until then, he would avoid Minerva like the plague.

CHAPTER ELEVEN

It became painfully obvious Rafe was avoiding her. She had already suspected it, but when he actually turned around and ducked into his study on her approach, it was a foregone conclusion. On the one hand, he kept Simon busy from sunup until sundown. Her brother was working hard and staying out of trouble. Wasn't that exactly what she had wanted from this affair?

Affair? Her stomach swooped. On the other hand, she was unaccountably hurt. She'd hoped they'd reached a turning point. Clearly, she was wrong.

Still, she needed to keep track of what her brother was learning, didn't she? That's the only reason she found herself passing by the study a dozen times over the past few days. All she wanted was to be included in their discussions. That's all it was. It had nothing to do with an irrational desire to stand close and breathe him in like a smitten dunderhead.

Finally, by the fourth afternoon, she went looking for Simon. Simon, not Rafe Drummond. If she'd spent a few extra minutes on her toilette and had Jenny help her into a pretty yellow gown, it had nothing to do with possibly seeing Rafe. The thought was utterly ridiculous.

She marched straight to the study. Checking the combs in her hair and taking a deep breath, she knocked and opened the door with a flourish. The room was empty. She barely controlled the urge to stomp her feet in a fit of pique. Cuthbertson came into the entryway humming and carrying a vase of flowers. In spite of her frustration, she smiled at the white-haired butler. He had embraced her changes.

"Cuthbertson, do you happen to know where my brother might be?"

"Well, as to that, my lady, the gentlemen are occupied." Bertie didn't meet her eyes and spent an inordinate amount of time arranging the flowers.

"Occupied? What does that mean?"

"It's nothing a lady should be concerned with, I'm sure." Bertie made the mistake of peeping at her, and she pinned him with the stare that had withered her most ardent suitors.

"I believe you should tell me," she said in a steely voice.

"They're fencing behind the stables." The words tumbled out of his mouth, and guilt niggled at Minerva for cowing the man.

"Thank you, Cuthbertson." Gracing him with her sweetest smile, she laid a hand on his arm in atonement before walking to the door.

"It really is no place for a lady," he called.

Waving a hand above her head, she skipped down the steps. Shouts and curses carried on the breeze, and she followed the noise. A group of men had gathered on the far side of the stables in a grassy common area. A wall of male backs obstructed her view.

The clang of steel and grunts of effort rose in the air. Jabbing her elbow into a set of ribs, she inserted herself between two brawny laborers. Both Simon and Rafe had stripped to shirts and breeches, and sweat showed through the white linen, even though the weather had turned chillier. Rafe was surprisingly graceful and agile for such a large man. Muscles rippled under his shirt, recalling a knee-weakening image of his bare chest.

"Ah-ha," Simon exclaimed as his blade almost broke through

Rafe's defenses.

They sparred a few minutes longer, the tide shifting back and forth between them. Her feet shuffled with theirs, and she held a hand over her mouth, willing herself not to call encouragement to Simon...and then to Rafe.

Circling one another and catching their breaths, they taunted each other until her ears burned. She looked her brother over. He stood straight and tall with one hand on his hip, swinging the blade by his leg. A man with muscle and brawn had replaced the skinny boy who'd arrived at Wintermarsh. The metamorphosis was astonishing. Moreover, he was skilled enough with a blade to offset Rafe's obvious advantage in size and strength.

She nudged the man to her right and whispered, "How long have they been at it, sir?"

He startled to see a woman in their midst. "A half hour at least. No one's drawn blood yet, but the blond one's gettin' tired," he whispered in return.

Blood? Minerva looked closer at their untipped blades. Were they complete idiots? A wrong slip and one of them could be accidently run through.

Simon launched an attack, driving Rafe backward with its ferocity and speed. What was Rafe doing allowing her brother to advance so aggressively? Although outwardly calm, he had taken a dozen steps back in a defensive posture. She darted around the men to follow the action. Coming to the end of the row, she wrapped a hand around her throat and squeezed.

Rafe's head swiveled as if pulled by a puppet master, and his gaze locked on her as if they were the only two people in the courtyard. Had she actually called out? In that second of distraction, Simon's blade whizzed past his defenses and grazed his upper arm.

* * * * *

Rafe's plan had been to let Simon expend the last of his energy, certain he could outlast the onslaught, and then go on the offensive himself. Until a blaze of yellow flashed in his peripheral vision. The hairs on his neck rose, attuned to her presence. He had to look, even knowing it was foolhardy. Sure enough, she stood amidst the men like a daffodil in spring, her blue eyes wide and her hand clutched around her neck in—Worry? Dismay? Disgust?

Sweat trickled into his cut and stung almost as badly as the loss. He and Simon dropped their arms, blades to the ground, both breathing hard. Minerva ducked behind the group of men, but her dress betrayed her. She'd better hide, the minx.

"Well done, Simon." Rafe barred his teeth in something resembling a smile and gave him a congratulatory slap on the back. "Not many have gotten the better of me."

"I never thought I'd best you," Simon said, wide-eyed and with the beginnings of a bemused smile.

"No need to dwell on my defeat." No yellow showed behind the men anymore. Where the devil had she gotten off to? "Let's get cleaned up and meet back in the study to continue where we left off, shall we?"

"Yes, certainly, but you're bleeding. Should I fetch Mrs. Devlin?"

"'Tis only a scratch. I'll take care of it." Yellow flashed in the corner of his eye close to the stable door. He followed it like a beacon. The gauntlet of good-natured ribbing from the men added to his annoyance.

Minerva stood outside of Sparrow's stall, stroking her hand down the horse's nose. The grey mare nudged against her shoulder looking for treats. She flipped her blonde hair over a shoulder, making it dance down her back. Her yellow dress scooped low in the front, drawing his eyes to the swell of breast exposed.

The dress was hardly scandalous, it was even modest compared to what the ladies of the ton donned in London, but to

Rafe it was like water to a parched man. He wanted to rip it off her and run his tongue over the swells and dips, discover the color of her nipples. He wanted to wrap his hands in her hair and force her to accept his kiss. God, the very reason he had avoided her all week. Her very presence tormented him.

"It's not proper for a lady to observe such proceedings." His bleeding arm and throbbing cock fanned his anger. He blamed her for both painful situations.

"Not proper—" She went taut and turned to confront him.

She flipped her hair once more and the strands fell in a waterfall of silken threads. One more time and he'd press her against the stall door and lift her skirts. He'd make her beg for his touch. Promises, be damned.

"I have the right to take a walk, do I not? How was I to know the two of you were involved in some flagrant display of masculine aggression? Like two rhinos establishing territory. You don't see ladies fighting each other, do you?"

"No? I would say women are infinitely worse, because they don't fight openly. At least you know where a man stands when he exhibits his masculine aggression. Women strut like peacocks flashing their pretty feathers as a distraction before they peck your eyes out with their sharp little beaks. I'd much rather face a man with a blade than a predatory female in a ballroom any day."

"Well I can't deny that the fairer sex can be quite ruthless." She stepped closer and skimmed her fingertips above the thin red gash on his biceps. "Why in heaven's name weren't you using tips? One of you could have been seriously injured. This looks painful enough."

"I've never trained with anything but a real blade. Believe me, you learn a sight faster when your reality is an actual wound," he said dryly.

"Why did you allow Simon to put you on the defensive? You could have easily beaten him back."

Rafe's eyes flared at both her chiding tone and backhanded compliment. He cocked his head. Jenny Mitchell's exuberant chattering carried through the doorway. Minerva launched into an unexplained flurry of action. Opening Sparrow's stall, she pushed at his arm. "Go, get in. Hurry, before they see us."

He allowed her to maneuver him in, and she followed, crouching low and peering over the door. Sparrow nudged her, and she absently stroked the mare's mane. Rafe had no idea why they spied on young Jenny but moved behind her.

"I'm too damn old for you, Miss Jenny. I've told you before." Tom Donahue's voice held a note of desperation.

"Yes, sir, I see you're practically on your deathbed. My plan all along has been to marry an old man who'll die off and leave me a merry widow." Jenny's voice teased. "Goodness, you're no more than thirty if you're a day, Tom. You're being ridiculous."

"Miss Jenny, war has made me old. What I lack in years, I more than make up for in experience, believe me." His voice held a note of regret and sadness only too familiar to Rafe. "We're nothing alike. All the lads here would love to court you, surely you know that."

"I don't want any of those lads. I don't dream about kissing them. Surely *you* know *that*," Jenny replied with a hint of exasperation as if this was an argument they'd had before.

"Sweet Jesus, Jenny, I—"

Rafe could guess what cut Tom's words off. He kept his voice to a whisper. "We shouldn't be eavesdropping. It's private."

"Yes, yes. Private." She parroted him in a vague tone.

Standing behind her and being so much taller had its advantages. He could see straight into her bodice. He could press her up against the wooden wall, dip his hands inside and cup the two swells. Then, he could turn her and explore them with his mouth for hours. A groan almost escaped. His head swam dizzily from the willpower it took to still his hands.

Murmurs moved away and out the stable. "Blast. Why is Tom being so obstinate?" Minerva asked.

He was in no state to theorize on his stable master's courting habits. Opening the door, she brushed against him and walked out. A guttural protest was the only answer he could offer. She whirled, her skirts swishing prettily, revealing a flash of ankle.

"What in the world is wrong with you?" She played with a tendril of hair that had fallen over her breast while her little tongue glanced over her bottom lip. Her intent was not seduction, at least he assumed not. Nevertheless, her artful play snatched the remainder of his control.

His voice rasped. "I need to take care of…my arm." He pushed past her and left at a near run.

* * * * *

Later that afternoon, after yet another chilly swim in the pond and bandaging his arm, Rafe sat behind his desk explaining rates of return to Simon. He was determined to put beautiful, maddening Minerva out of his mind. He was failing miserably.

"Tea, gentlemen," the object of his obsession announced with a merry lilt. She balanced a laden tray, glided to his desk and set the tray down on a pile of papers.

What was she playing at? The woman had never inserted herself in Simon's lessons before. Why today, when his self-control was in tatters?

In high spirits from his victory, Simon launched into a description of their match. She acted surprised, which had Rafe slumping in his chair and rolling his eyes. After pouring their tea, she settled in a chair across the desk as if she were roosting for the foreseeable future. Downing his tea in one swallow, he eyed the brandy decanter on the sideboard.

Simon explained what he had learned under Rafe's tutelage. He talked excitedly about Rafe's plans for the southeast quadrant of Wintermarsh, where a new crop rotation schedule and irrigation system would be implemented by spring planting.

After he was finished, Minerva patted his knee and ducked her head to try to hide eyes shiny with tears. "Simon, I am so proud of you. You are going to be the best Duke of Bellingham in centuries." He puffed up at her words of praise, red tingeing his cheekbones. It had probably been years since Simon had heard something other than scolding and pestering from her.

It was going to cost Minerva dearly to give up her role in his life. She had spent years acting as his caretaker and the proxy duke. Seeing her brother take up the mantle was sure to be bittersweet.

She rubbed her forehead and raised her chin, eyes dry, her composure restored. "Lord Drummond, could you show me specifications on the shipping venture you're invested in?"

Rafe inclined his head and pulled a file from underneath a huge pile on the corner of his desk.

Minerva tutted and shook her head. "How in the world do you manage your estate and investments living in a total state of disorganization?"

"Nothing gets lost."

She didn't heed the warning in his brusque voice but sashayed around the desk to stand at his elbow. "Your desk is worse than your bedroom, and that's certainly bad enough."

"Bedroom? How would you know what Lord Drummond's bedroom looks like?" Simon shifted on his seat and crossed his arms.

"Good Lord, Simon, close your mouth. It was nothing scandalous." She gave a harrumphing laugh. "Well, not in the way you're thinking. I tidied Lord Drummond's room my first morning here. Now, the portfolio, please, Lord Drummond." She snapped her fingers a few inches from his nose.

Snap her fingers? At him? Rafe was in awe of the woman, if he were honest. Had she been born a man, she would have made an outstanding prime minister. Before he could offer a response of any sort, she plucked the file out of his hands and opened it on the desk. Leaning over, she scanned the first page and emitted small humming sounds.

Her soft breast brushed his biceps. Her hair swept forward and several tendrils bounced along his forearm and hand. Knowing it was a mistake, like in the fencing match, he turned to look anyway. Her glorious breasts were at eyelevel and only a few inches away from his mouth. Her slightly gaping bodice offered a tantalizing, distressing view.

He took a deep, calming breath, which only made matters worse because the floral soap she had used on her hair seduced him. He turned his hand over and fingered a swath of hair that had been teasing him. If she had an inkling of the things he wanted to do to her, she would run screaming in horror from the room.

"Is that right?" She poked his arm.

"Is what right?"

"Have you been listening to a thing we've been saying?" She straightened and propped a hand on her hip.

"No."

"Well, good grief. Simon asked how often the ships made the trip to the Far East, and I said once every four months or so. Is that right?"

"Something like that." He could barely remember his name much less how often the ships sailed. He had to escape, and not just the study. "I'm heading to London in the morning to settle some business. Bellingham, you're in charge of the estate. I expect you to handle any issues that arise."

Simon squared his shoulders and tugged on his jacket lapels. "I'll not disappoint you."

"How long will you be gone?" Minerva asked.

"A few days...a week perhaps." As long as it took to slake his lust with some doxy. "I'm leaving at first light." Rafe rose and backed toward the door, not attempting any social niceties.

At the very least, the trip would get him away from her. Once he put some distance between them, it should be easy enough to forget about her. He only regretted it was too late to start for London that evening.

* * * * *

Minerva moped around the drawing room. She picked up the book she had found riveting the night before but threw it down after reading the same page twice. Simon had retired, telling her he needed to be on top of his game the next day. Minerva had barely suppressed her eye roll. As if he would have to deal with anything more than an irate tenant or two.

She was not in a charitable mood, and she blamed Rafe Drummond and his spontaneous trip. No one from Mrs. Devlin to Cuthbertson had even had an inkling he planned to leave, and he had been acting odd all day. Was this a drastic measure to ignore her? Had the fact she'd witnessed one of his nightmares drawn a permanent wedge between them?

Grabbing a pillow and plopping on the settee, she fingered the fringed edging, her mind racing. She would write Drake and request he send some of their ledgers. Simon would need to familiarize himself with the investments she and Drake had chosen.

Rafe could pick them up and bring them back on his return trip. She composed her note at the small writing table. If he planned to start at dawn, she needed to get him the note tonight.

The study was deserted. Perhaps he was abed. If his chamber door was shut, she would forget the whole endeavor. However, if a candle burned or the door was open, he surely wouldn't mind her interruption.

His door was shut and nothing moved. There, it was decided. She stared at the dark, wooden door and backed away, bumping into a pedestal holding the statue of a horse and rider. Grabbing at it, she saved the teetering display with a gusty sigh of relief.

The door flew open and rattled on its hinges. She bobbled the statue again. The shot of surprise made her clumsy and the statue crashed on the floor, the rider beheaded. Her gaze pinged from the statue to the man framed in the doorway.

"Good God, not you." Rafe ran a hand over his beard and turned on his heel to retrieve the brandy glass sitting on his nightstand. His shirt was half-untucked, and his hair was mussed and untied. Somehow, his rumpled state only heightened his appeal.

She looked down the hall toward safety, which seemed to stretch to infinity. Dark currents crackled around them. She sidled a few feet into the room, her hand outstretched, the note shaking. "I hoped you might undertake an errand for me in the city."

Ignoring her, he sprawled on the bed, still in his boots, ankles crossed. He took another gulp of the amber liquid, peering over the top of the glass.

"Am I to be your errand boy, Your Grace?" he asked mockingly. "You really should have been born a man, Minerva. You certainly have the bearing and authority of a duke. Or perhaps a field commander. You and Wellington would have gotten on sle-splendidly. No wonder you turned your brother into milquetoast. You're more a man than he is. 'Cept for your gorgeous breasts. You had to stick them right under my damn nose today, didn' you? Twice, in fact." Rafe held up two fingers as if she needed help counting.

The man was obviously deep in his cups. She dropped her outstretched hand and infused all the disdain she felt into her words. "It's too bad you weren't born more of a man, my lord."

"More of a— Bloody hell, are you casting aspersions on my manhood? Are you quite serious, woman? I'm more than enough man to handle you, although why I would want to, I have no idea. You're tyrant enough to shrivel any man's cock."

Her sharp intake of breath seemed loud in the aftermath of

his outrageous statement. If he meant to shock her with his crude language, he'd succeeded, but it was the substance that sent her reeling backwards. She was frigid, the ice princess. No man would want her because she was smart and independent and didn't flirt and coo inanely, constantly stroking the delicate male ego.

She fisted the letter and held his glittering, wintry gaze. He swung his legs to the floor and stalked her. There was no other word for it. The door was close enough for swift retreat, but she refused to show that level of cowardice. Nevertheless, she hit the tall wardrobe without even realizing she'd shuffled backward.

Finally, toe to toe, the sweet scent of liquor rolled off him. "You're foxed, Rafe Drummond."

"Very astute. But I'm a grown man and can drink when and how much I please. I'm not your poor sot of a brother who you boss around like a ten-year-old." He propped his hands on either side of her. Certainly, intimidation was part of his goal, but she wondered if he didn't need the support, he was that far gone.

"Don't do anything foolish."

"You're the foolish one. Why are you here?" His whisper sent a skitter down her spine. Of fear? Partly, but something else too.

"I told you. An errand, a favor. I hoped you could take this letter to Drake?" She held up the crumpled missive. He plucked it from her numb fingers and tossed it over his shoulder.

"I thought perhaps you were here for this..." Rafe wrapped both hands in her hair and pulled, tipping her face up. Her scalp tingled in pleasure and pain.

His lips crashed down on hers in a bruising kiss. One of his hands stayed wrapped tightly in her hair while the other dropped to cup her buttock and fit her against him. She should hate this—hate him—but her body ignited.

"Did you come here for this?" He sneered, pressing her into the wardrobe and grinding his erection against her hip.

Yes. The word reverberated through her body. She barely

stopped herself from speaking the humiliating truth aloud.

"Blast it, why aren't you running away screaming?" The cruel light seeped from his eyes, and his hand eased in her hair.

"I don't know." And she didn't. Why did this man draw her so forcibly?

Rafe shook his head and sighed. Eyes never leaving hers, he kissed her again. This time, he gently slid his lips along hers and pressed softly into her mouth with his tongue, perhaps apologizing the only way he knew how. He massaged her scalp, and a moan escaped her throat between his devastating kisses. She leaned into his chest, rose to her toes, and wound her arms around his neck. He ran his hands up and down her back as their tongues danced and explored with a devastating carnal lushness.

This was why she was here. For the gentle, sensitive soul no amount of gruffness or alcohol could hide.

"For the love of… I'm so terribly sorry." Mrs. Devlin didn't sound the least bit sorry. She sounded angry.

Rafe stepped back, and Minerva leaned against the wardrobe, her breaths coming too fast. Now though, it wasn't passion reddening her face to match the draperies and dizzying her.

With trembling knees, she pushed off the wardrobe, retrieved the crumpled missive and handed it to Rafe with as much dignity as she could muster. "If you could take this to my townhouse for Drake, Lord Drummond? Please excuse me, my lord. Mrs. Devlin."

She forced her chin up and her shoulders back and glided out of the room as if exiting the Prince Regent's drawing room. Would she be able to look Mrs. Devlin in the eye again? As soon as she was out of sight, she covered her hot cheeks with both hands and ran to her room to curl in a ball on her bed. Yes, she was embarrassed. Not because she had kissed Rafe Drummond, but because she had been caught doing it.

* * * * *

Master Rafe, really. Do I need to remind you that *Lady* Minerva is not a woman to be trifling with? She's an innocent and a duke's sister and I hope you aren't taking advantage of the situation because he's in debt to you."

"Mrs. Devlin, are you suggesting that I am forcing Minerva to pay off her brother's debt in my bed?" He swayed on his feet, wondering which of the Mrs. Devlins he should direct his outrage toward.

"I'm honestly not sure of your motivations. It smells like a tavern in here, so you're obviously in your cups. Who knows what you're thinking? Or more likely what you're thinking with. *I'm* thinking it was a good thing I came along when I did." At that, Mrs. Devlin marched out and slammed the door, the bang like a physical slap to his head.

Lady Minerva Bellingham had come to *his* bloody room. Had he taken advantage, forced himself on her? Most assuredly. He ran a hand down his face, scrubbing at his beard, unbelievably tired and undeniably foxed.

He stuck the missive in his travelling bag and decided retreat was the only option. He collapsed on the bed, not bothering to remove his boots or clothes, and slipped into the welcome dark oblivion brandy offered.

CHAPTER TWELVE

A week later and with the lights of Wintermarsh visible through the oak trees, Rafe sighed, feeling a portion of his discontent seep into the leaf-strewn path. He always missed home when he was gone, but an unnamed melancholy had dogged him for days. Really, ever since he'd lost sight of Wintermarsh's chimneys on the road to London. He should have waited until the next morning to depart London, but after meeting to finalize a new ship design, he'd shoved papers and Minerva's ledgers into bags and ordered a horse.

Practically running from the stables to the house, he didn't examine his urgent need to check on his charges—well, one charge in particular. Bertie directed him to the drawing room, and he threw the door open. Minerva popped up, playing cards fluttering to the floor at her feet. Simon, more circumspect, remained seated, tapping his cards on the felt game table.

Was it the hearth fire or the heat in Minerva's eyes sending tingling warmth through his body? Had it only been a week? He drank her in. Her hair was piled atop her head, tendrils escaping to brush her cheeks and neck, and her rose-colored gown exposed a sliver of creamy skin at her throat.

Simon broke the silence. "Welcome home, Drummond. I assume you'll want an accounting?"

Rafe nodded absently, his gaze stuck to Minerva.

"Yes, well, why don't I wait in the study for you?"

Rafe grunted, and thankfully, Simon left.

She cleared her throat. "You've returned."

"Yes."

"Did your business go well?" Minerva bent to retrieve her scattered cards.

Without her searing blue eyes on him, he found his tongue, even though it felt clumsy. "Quite well. I saw your man Mr. Drake and brought back the ledgers."

Minerva aligned the cards in her hand. Unable to stop himself from touching her, he took the cards, brushing his fingers over hers, and laid them on the table. He didn't move away, instead turning them over and fanning them out. Her gaze remained fixed on the cards.

"How did you find Drake? Was he managing satisfactorily?" she asked.

Rafe moved away and sat in one of the armchairs, not immediately answering her. An echo of the jealousy he'd experienced on meeting Drake crimped his stomach. He had expected a bald, doddering, bespectacled solicitor—not a handsome, virile man in his prime. The same primal territorial aggression from that morning filled his chest and tensed his shoulders. He forced himself to relax.

The not-so-subtle questions he'd launched at the stoic Drake had been answered with a hint of amusement but total truthfulness as far as he could discern. In return, her man of affairs had asked several pointed questions that had had him shifting in his chair, feeling less than certain with his denials and reassurances. He'd departed with the ledgers after giving Drake a firm handshake—perhaps a bit too firm. Rafe had inwardly cursed when the sly Scot hadn't been able to hide a dry smile.

"Mr. Drake is well. Worried about you. He wanted

reassurances I wasn't mistreating you." Rafe stared at Minerva, trying to interpret her hand wringing. Did she harbor tender feelings for the dour Scot?

"What did you tell him?" Shielded by her lashes, her eyes cut to him.

"I told him that I was treating you well enough, but when I said it, I felt like a toad, because I haven't treated you well at all, have I?" He'd gone over their last encounter a thousand times. What he remembered of it, anyhow. He'd been too rough, that he knew.

"I don't have any complaints." This time she didn't try to hide her eyes. The tranquility on her face washed away some of the blackness around his heart and made him want to kiss her again.

He turned away, not trusting himself. "I saw Lily and Gray while I was in town. She sends her best."

"I don't suppose you could take her a message from me if you go back to London before our time ends."

"They've planned a sojourn to the coast and will stop here on the way, so you can tell her yourself." Rafe picked up a pillow and flicked the useless decorative tassels on the corner.

"Has there been any gossip about our situation?"

"Not that I heard, but then they'd hardly whisper on-dits that concerned me in my ear. I was hardly out socializing anyway. Lily didn't mention anything, though, and she's in the know."

She let out a gusty sigh. "That's a relief. I was a bit worried Hampton might try to spread poison about Simon. And Stonewell seemed to have some suspicions as well."

"Your hair looks different." He rose and tossed the pillow aside.

Minerva's hand flew to her hair, patting and tucking at the loose locks. "It's ridiculous, isn't it? Jenny has it in her head to learn to be a lady's maid, and she's practicing on me."

Rafe stayed her hand. "No, I like it. You look quite lovely, in fact."

"Thank you."

While he fingered a loose tendril, Minerva brushed her fingertips over his knuckles. The simple, careless touch set him on fire. It seemed his time away had only strengthened his need, dammit. He strode away, toward a semblance of sanity only rows of numbers could provide.

"Lord Drummond."

He glanced over his shoulder, his hand on the door latch.

"Rafe. Will I see you in the morning?" The desperation threading her tone and written plainly on her face took him aback. "About my ledgers."

"Yes, the ledgers. I'll be busy tomorrow catching up on estate business. You and Simon can discuss them at your leisure."

"All right. Have a good evening. I'm glad you're home."

Rafe heaved a sigh, gave a perfunctory nod and escaped. What the devil was he going to do? Avoiding her hadn't worked. Running away hadn't worked. He should ignore the odd feeling of betrayal and tup another woman. He'd bloody well planned on it in London, even taken a step over the threshold of a quality brothel. One sweeping glance around the room, and he'd turned on his heel, cursing himself roundly.

Surely, he could act the rake for one night. Christ, he would close his eyes and imagine her face if he had to. Then perhaps he would gain some peace.

CHAPTER THIRTEEN

How do I look, sister?" Simon put his arms out and spun. Of course, he looked quite dashing. More like a man and less like her little brother. His shoulders pulled the seams of his jacket taut, and the sun had burnished his hair. A strange melancholy threatened, but she shook it off. This was exactly what she had hoped for when she'd agreed to Rafe's mad scheme.

Minerva pretended to straighten his already impeccable waistcoat and cravat. "You look marvelous, Simon, but I thought Lord Drummond made no bones about the fact there was to be no socializing while you worked off your debt."

"He's been pleased with my efforts, especially how well I handled things when he was in London. We're headed to the nearest house of ill-repute." Simon waggled his eyebrows, sounding pleased.

Minerva felt as if someone punched her in the stomach while pulling the rug out from under her feet at the same time. "You and Lord Drummond are going whoring?"

"That's a rather common, unladylike way to describe it." His words were scolding, but his tone was amused. "But in a word—*yes*. Christ, it's been weeks since I was around beautiful, available women." Simon smoothed the lapels of his frockcoat and set an emerald stickpin in his cravat.

"Good grief, Simon, that's a terribly ungentlemanly thing to say."

"Good grief, Minerva, I'm not referring to *ladies*." He mocked her priggish tone and sauntered out of the room whistling softly.

Minerva plopped on the edge of Simon's bed. Rafe was perfectly within his rights to go whoring every night of the week if that's what he desired. The mere thought of it settled an aching pit in her stomach, so much so, she had to lean over and rest her head on her knees. She had no claim on the boorish, asinine blighter.

Forcing herself up, she took several deep breaths, gathering her cool façade back around her piece by piece. After leaving Simon's room, she stutter stepped when Rafe started down the hall toward her. She wanted to escape, duck into an unused room, fly down the steps, jump out of a convenient window. Anything to avoid him. But she couldn't move, not an inch. The sight of his loose-limbed, confident gait congealed her muscles.

The civilized trappings of his dress tamped down his customary fierceness. She'd never seen him in evening clothes. A simply but elegantly tied cravat circled his neck. His shoulders looked impressively wide in the black jacket. His breeches barely held his muscular thighs in check. They flexed indecently as he closed the last few feet to stand in front of her. Everything molded to his muscular frame.

No doubt, she gawked, but she couldn't halt her silent perusal for all the tea in London. His dark hair was tamed into a queue, and he'd trimmed his beard. His scar wasn't the first thing one noticed when the rest of him was this incredibly striking. He looked strong and virile yet elegant. No woman would resist his overtures. In a word, he was utterly *devastating*.

Here she stood in a once-green muslin gown Jenny had let her borrow so she could sort through a trunk of books that had been stored in the Wintermarsh attic. Decades of filth smudged the skirts. It was even a little short, exposing her ankles. Her hair was untidy and probably adorned with cobwebs. She ran a hand down her braid and, sure enough, it came away sticky.

"You…" Minerva cleared her throat, as her heart seemed to be stuck in its narrowest point. She tried again. "You look awfully—" *magnificent, breathtaking, stunning,* "—nice."

"Thank you. I haven't pulled these on in a season or more. I was afraid they wouldn't fit any longer. I lost a considerable amount of weight convalescing last fall."

"No, you're filling them out rather—" her gaze skittered down and held on his flexing thighs, "—nicely." Good Lord, was she a total muttonhead? She started down the stairs. Rafe fell into step beside her.

"I hear you and Simon are headed out for a night of debauchery." Her emotions crashed into one another roughening her voice.

"That's a bit of an overstatement. But Simon's been working hard. We could both use a night away. A distraction," Rafe said casually.

No doubt, his evening would involve a woman. Minerva wanted to stick out a foot and trip him. Not so he'd seriously injure himself, but enough to lay him up for a day or two. She didn't, of course.

Simon waited in the entry hall, impatiently rocking from foot to foot, looking like a little boy going on his first picnic. Minerva had no desire to wish them well in their depraved endeavors. Perhaps a carriage wheel would break or a horse would go lame.

"What are your plans?" Rafe asked, taking an elegant beaver hat from Bertie.

"I was invited to an exclusive ball, but I sent my regrets. I'd rather clean and sort the rest of the books." She forced a light tone. He twirled his hat in his hands, half smiling at her weak jest and side-eyeing her.

"Help yourself to anything in the study." Now his gaze focused on the floor, and he bit at his lower lip as if there was something more he wished to say. "Good evening, then." He ducked out the door, and all she could do was watch him go to another woman's bed.

Minerva was mad and hurt and maybe even a little jealous. She trailed into the study on heavy feet, threw herself in the chair behind his desk, and propped her chin on her fist. Heaving a sigh, she flipped through some of the papers that littered the desk. The business language and columns of numbers usually excited her. Not tonight. Tonight, she found it dry and dreary.

Her gaze fell on his sideboard, and the full decanter of brandy. He did say that she could help herself to anything in the study. The night of the attack, one little glass had afforded her a welcome numbing comfort.

She had never allowed herself more than one glass of champagne in London. There were too many dangers lurking for an available woman with a large dowry. Too many reasons to keep her guard up. Not tonight, though. Rafe was gone, and she would be alone. All night long.

Another painful stab to her gut. Why should she even care? So she dreamed of his two kisses every night. He was a man of the world who'd lain with countless other women. She was inexperienced, not naïve. He probably planned to kiss a dozen before settling on one to take to bed. She blinked furiously, absolutely refusing to cry over the man.

Instead, she marched over to the sideboard and poured herself a small amount of brandy. Tilting her head and pursing her lips, she decisively splashed another finger on top of the first. After sending a toast to the heavens, she took a large swallow.

She slammed the glass down on the sideboard and clutched at her throat, doubling over with coughing spasms. After what seemed an eternity, she straightened and wiped her watering eyes. A smaller, more-measured sip followed the first. This one slid down easily enough, the trail having already been blazed by her absurdly large gulp. A soothing warmth spread in her belly.

Minerva snuggled in Rafe's huge armchair, nosing the leather to catch his scent. Blast him, why did he have to smell so divine? Her next swallow of brandy went down like water and sent the blessed warmth to her toes. Kicking off her slippers, she rolled off her stockings and rubbed her feet on the rug, scrunching her toes in the soft pile.

What kind of woman would catch his eye? A dark haired beauty with big breasts? A plump, curvy blonde with bouncing curls? Her hand tightened on the glass, and she raised it for another swig.

The brandy made her light-headed. Not in a bad way, but in a way that made her feel audacious. Her glass emptied quickly, and she returned to the sideboard to pour another. She didn't need a man. She had survived—no, she had bloody well thrived the past few years on her own. She did a duke's job and did it well. Men wanted her and women emulated her. While mayhap not beloved by the ton, she commanded respect.

She sat with her legs splayed wide, her feet bare, in a dress that was too short. Dirty, dusty and disheveled, she doubled over with laughter. What would the high-fliers of London Society say if they could see her now? She didn't care. Is this how men felt when they drank? Was this freedom? Because she rather liked it.

She cracked open a window and unbuttoned the collar of her dress, the cool night air tickling her skin. Resting her head against the sill, she closed her eyes, her ears filled with a nightingale's song in rustling leaves. Unbelievably, if the clock could be trusted, several hours had passed.

What was Rafe doing now? She took another swallow.

No, it didn't matter. She was fine. No, more than fine, she was damn near splendid.

Had he picked a woman out? Would he carry her to a bed or

rut in the hallway?

One more tot would surely dam off her tears. She tilted the heavy decanter, getting most of the brandy into the glass, and sopped up her spill with the folds of her dress. She weaved her way back to his armchair and stared at the licking flames in the grate. Her existence had taken on a dimorphous quality, and she floated between the worlds. The quiet night settled over her. Perhaps she drifted off, perhaps not.

The study door swung on its hinges. The shock brought her to her senses in an instant of clarity. She popped out of his chair. Rafe Drummond stopped short, halfway to his desk.

His shirt was open and his cravat was hanging around his neck, untied. His jacket had been discarded at some point and his waistcoat was unbuttoned. His hair brushed his neck, the thong holding it back gone, lost in some whore's bed, no doubt.

The brandy had obliterated her careful barriers and filters. A fury welled up from her belly, extending to her toes and fingertips until she felt on fire.

* * * * *

"Did you have a pleasant evening, Raphael?" Infused with scorn, her tone made him feel like a schoolboy caught putting frogs in her bed.

"No one calls me that," he said automatically, taken aback to find Minerva still in his study. A quick check put the time after two in the morning.

"Oh, really, *Raphael?* Don't you like your name?" She practically sneered.

Not sure of her game, he kept his tone even. "Not particularly. Do you want to know what happened to the last person to call me by my given name?"

"What? Did you kill them?"

Rafe jerked his head back, shocked at the vehemence in her

voice. "Hardly. It was Gray, and we were eight. I bloodied his lip."

"What are you going to do to me, Raphael? Are you going to hurt me?" Minerva weaved over to him, pulled his cravat from around his neck, and threw it at his feet.

"You should be abed." He ignored her barb.

"Did you find a woman to meet your needs tonight, my lord?"

"There were many beautiful women there tonight."

"So it was difficult to pick only one whore for your entertainment?"

What in the bloody hell was going on? Why was Minerva spitting daggers and talking about whores? He'd stepped into a farce without being given a script.

"Quite difficult, my lady. Who knew they would all be fighting over me?" His tone was light and joking, but Minerva didn't take it as such.

She turned up her nose and examined him from head to toe. "You bloody, no-good bastard. Why do you have to be so disgustingly..." Minerva paused as if searching for the right epitaph. She rubbed a hand over her forehead.

Rafe froze and waited for the stab of her words. So disgustingly...ugly? Grotesque? Hideous?

Minerva snapped her fingers. "*Masculine*. I mean look at you with your bulging muscles and chest and your hands... Dear God, your hands."

"My hands? What about them?" Rafe's voice was scratchy.

She strode forward two paces, pulled back her fist, and let it fly toward his face, catching him on his heels. When her hand was a hair's breadth away from causing considerable pain, he caught her wrist. He twisted her arm around her back and hauled her against his chest.

Catching a whiff, he startled and looked over at his formerly full brandy decanter. She smelled as if she'd taken a bath in the stuff. "Minerva Bellingham, you're utterly and completely foxed."

Laughter threatened to overtake him, but her eyes were bright with unshed tears. She would never forgive him if he laughed. Christ, she looked bedraggled. Her hair was coming free of its braid and tendrils framed her flushed, smudged face. The only redeeming feature about her horrid dress was the fact she'd partially unbuttoned it so he could see the top swells of her breasts.

And, dammit if she wasn't more beautiful and alluring than all the women combined that evening.

Why was she so angry? Did she actually believe women threw themselves in his path? Most avoided catching his eye. Could she possibly be jealous? The thought gave Rafe pause. Afraid of the answer, he swallowed through his constricted throat and asked haltingly, "Do you not want me with other women?"

"Of course I don't want you with other women, you blithering idiot. I want you to make love to *me*." Minerva stamped directly on his instep.

Ignoring the pain in his foot and the fact she had called him an idiot, he focused only on the important. "You want me to make love to you?"

"I want you to touch *me* and kiss *me*, not some two-bit cheap whore. I've been right here in front of you. Why don't you want me?" A tear escaped its confinement to trail down her cheek.

"Minerva, you're a lady. An innocent. I can't—we can't—" He caught the tear on her cheekbone with his thumb. His heart thumped so loudly, surely she could hear it.

"What was she like? Did she satisfy you? I would gladly scratch her eyes out. Pull every hair from her head." Her wet eyes flashed with heat, and she hit his chest with a balled-up fist, weakly this time.

"Would it make you less murderous to learn there were no other women tonight?"

"No other women?" She choked back a sob.

"I sat in a corner observing Simon try his luck with both women and cards. He was more successful with the women than the cards, not surprisingly. I played a few hands, but the company was bland. When I couldn't handle babysitting your whelp of a brother any longer, I hauled him into the carriage to come home."

His original intentions had been a bit murkier. He had gone in search of a woman, any woman to relieve his physical torment. He could have paid one enough to ignore his scars, but it turned out it wasn't any woman he wanted. He wanted *her*. Not a single woman in the establishment had held any attraction. He hadn't had a chance to examine what it meant. He only knew it to be true.

* * * * *

No other women. The words sang through Minerva. Her drink-addled mind decided it was past time to stake her claim. She ran her hands up his chest into the open collar of his shirt. Holding his gaze, she stood on tiptoe to touch his lips with her tongue.

Her inhibitions were nonexistent, her movements frantic. She tugged roughly at his hair, deepening their kiss, and pulled at his shirt, fighting it out of his breeches. She wanted him on his back…or maybe pressed over her like in the orchard…but prone, definitely somewhere prone. And with less clothes.

Finally, with a sob of relief, she pulled his shirt free. She explored the bare expanse of his back and reveled in his heat and hardness, scratching him with her nails. He hissed his pleasure.

Rafe broke the kiss, and her world tipped dizzily. Steel bands cradled her until she came down to rest on his lap in his oversized armchair. She would have preferred a bed or the floor, but so long as he didn't push her away, she wouldn't complain.

Pressing herself close, not wanting an inch to separate them, Minerva nuzzled his neck with her lips. She glided a hand around his shoulders while she slipped the other under his shirt to trace the contours of his chest. His bare chest had been the starring player in most of her nightly dreams. Running her hand over the hard ridges, she wasn't disappointed. She brushed through a sprinkling of hair to find one of his nipples.

She cupped his cheek and initiated another kiss. This time, he took the lead, plundering her mouth without mercy. She met him at least halfway, sucking his tongue into her mouth and nipping his lower lip. His erection pressed against her hip, and her body responded by rocking against him.

"No other woman can hold a candle to you." His voice was low and gruff.

"I want you to take me." She was throbbing and empty, but he was experienced. He knew how to ease her. She trailed a hand between her legs where the uncomfortable feeling was most acute. His eyes were wide, his gaze glued to the press of her fingers.

"Sweetheart, are...are you a maiden? A virgin?"

"Yes. Does it matter? Tell me it doesn't matter."

He tipped her face up with one of his callused, arousing hands. She rubbed against it like a cat, seeking more. He seemed to be searching for answers to questions he hadn't asked. "Of course it matters. You know what happens between a man and woman?"

"I understood the biological act long ago, and your sister described what passion, what need felt like."

Rafe choked on his words, "Lily...bloody hell. How much did she—"

"As much as I wanted to know, and I was curious. But hearing about something and experiencing it is very different. A man's tongue in my mouth sounded disgusting, but yours isn't. Your kisses make me want to crawl inside of you. When you touched my breasts, I wanted even more. I got scared in the orchard, but it's all I've thought about. Will you take me? Love me?"

The intensity on his face stripped her naked inside and out. He shook his head, tight lines radiating from his eyes and mouth. "I can help ease your ache. Do you want me to help?"

"Yes, please, yes," she replied in a small, thready voice.

Rafe unbuttoned the rest of her gown and pulled it down, along with her chemise, exposing her breasts. The night air stirred with his movements, the wispy touch bringing pleasure to her aroused, oversensitive skin. Her eyes grew heavy, but she forced them open. The sight of his tanned hand cupping her pale breast sent more moisture between her legs. The rough pads of his fingers added to her sensory overload. Both her nipples hardened into points.

"I love your hands." She skimmed her smaller, softer hand up his forearm, the hair tickling, the flex of muscles fascinating.

With his thumbs caressing the sensitive underside of each breast, he curled his fingers around her back, arching her over the arm of the chair. Her breasts thrust up like an offering, and he took full advantage. Flicking a tongue over one nipple and then the other, he expertly ratcheted up her pleasure.

He swirled his tongue over each nipple, wetting them, and then blew cool air. They were painfully tight now. Squirming on his lap, she clutched at his hair, words meaningless, only a primal need registering. Finally, he closed his mouth over a nipple, pulling it into his hot mouth. A shameless, guttural moan bounced around them. It was her.

Her head spun—from the liquor? from his attentions?—spiraling her higher, until nothing existed outside of his mouth, his hands, his body. He tormented her other breast and glided one of his hands up her calf, lifting her skirts along the way. She parted her legs, and he squeezed her thigh, brushing the hair at the apex of her legs. He was so close to where she burned. *Did he know?*

She tipped her pelvis up, begging him without words. He moved his fingers through her curls and slipped them into her folds, stroking her. His thumb landed exactly where she ached. *He knew.*

"So wet." He sounded pained.

"I couldn't help it. I'm sorry."

"Never be sorry, it's a good thing, a very good thing. You actually want me. It's more than I deserve. Christ, I want to taste you. I've dreamed of it countless times."

There were things she still didn't understand. Why didn't he deserve this? What did he want to taste?

The same time he pushed his tongue into her mouth, he slipped a finger inside of her. She gasped against his mouth at the foreign, exquisite feeling of being invaded and stretched. His pulsing erection pressed against her bottom. It belonged inside of her in place of his finger. She wanted him to claim her. Even once. Even if it meant her ruination. But it was too late.

Tension stiffened her muscles, the play of his fingers making her squirm. Something was ready to break. Like stormy summer air before the cut of the first bolt of lightning. Instead of fighting the coming storm, she surrendered and hurled through dark clouds. The pleasure of her climax demolished her pain and frustration.

Eventually, her spirit reconnected with her earthly body, relief, pleasure, contentment warring for supremacy. He continued to stroke her.

She snuggled closer and said dreamily, "Raphael...Raphael. What did you do to me? Are you an angel?"

Rafe hummed, his chest vibrating against her. "A fallen one perhaps."

"I love the way you smell." She nosed the hair at his neck. His mouth curled against the hand cupping his cheek, and she lifted her head to witness the rare event. "You're so handsome."

Her words stole his smile. "No, I'm not."

"You are, you silly man. When I saw you in your evening clothes, I was so jealous. I knew you'd be fighting women off in droves. I'm so very glad you didn't lie with one of those harlots." She settled her head against his shoulder. Sleep was creeping closer, blurring the edges of her consciousness. On a huge exhale, she said, "You're 'specially handsome when you smile and aren't grumbly."

* * * * *

S he thought him handsome? Even scarred as he was? The knowledge wormed its way to his heart, lighting dark corners that had festered over the past year. A soft, indelicate snuffling caught his attention. He shifted to see her face, but her head lolled to the side, either passed out or thoroughly satisfied. Most likely both.

She was always lovely, but she'd been bewitching in her climax, a beautiful flush tingeing her breasts and cheeks. She'd clamped his finger to the point of pain. The total abandon of her surrender in his arms humbled him.

He reluctantly removed his hand from between her legs and adjusted her skirts but kept her in his lap. Stroking her hair, the delicate shell of her ears, and her hands, he marveled at the perfection of her breasts, her nipples a dusky rose to match her lips.

She would feel like hell on the morrow. Would she even remember this encounter? He'd known many men who'd lost their memory when they overindulged. Would it be better if she didn't remember? Or, even worse, what if she remembered and regretted letting him touch her so intimately? His heart constricted, and he rubbed his chest.

He righted her bodice and slipped noiselessly to her room, holding her close in his arms, his training coming in handy once again. It was still the wee hours, and the house was quiet. No one had heard her keens of pleasure.

After laying her on the bed, he slipped off her dress and tossed it over his shoulder. One breast peeked over her hastily arranged white chemise. The combination of innocent and erotic made him throb. He would seek relief later—alone. The devil in him left her chemise in disarray. Covering her with the counterpane, he barely touched her lips with his and then retreated to end his own torment.

CHAPTER FOURTEEN

The rhythmic rocking woke her. How had she ended up on a boat? She pried one eye open to see the familiar blue canopy above her. Not a boat then, but everything spun oddly. She was in danger of tossing her accounts all over the beautiful bed.

Swallowing down the rising bile, Minerva closed her eyes. It wasn't getting any better. She sat up ever so slowly. The counterpane fell to her waist. Her chemise drooped down, her exposed nipple pebbling in the cool, morning air. Her dress lay puddled haphazardly on the rug.

The evening's events rushed back to her in an instant. She fell backwards and pulled the covers over her head. Oh…my…God. Had she actually begged Rafe to take her maidenhead? Unfortunately, she remembered every minute detail of the previous evening. She'd gained a roiling stomach and a pounding head but hadn't lost her faculties.

She recalled it all. Her shrewish accusations, her attempt, albeit feeble, to break his nose, and her admission she wanted him—very, very badly. Even hidden under the sheets with no one to see her, heat suffused her body, the embarrassed kind. Not the kind he had invoked with his hands. Those devilish hands. He may have been named for an angel, but he was wicked. So deliciously wicked.

The door creaked. Minerva tucked the sheet under her chin. Jenny popped her head around, her eyes bright and darting.

"Oh-ho. You're finally awake. I've been peeking in on you all morning. Are you unwell?" Jenny bustled into the room, expertly balancing a breakfast tray. There was dry toast, fruit, tea and a glass filled with a strange green liquid.

"Why would you think that?" She righted her chemise under the covers before sitting up against the pillows.

"Lord Drummond specifically had Mrs. Potts prepare this tray for you. Said you might not be feeling quite up to snuff."

Jenny sat the tray in Minerva's lap, flourishing a hand over the contents. She would be forever grateful there weren't kippers staring back at her. A run to the chamber pot would have been a surety. Her entire body felt parched, and she drank the entire cup in three gulps, craving a river of tea. She pointed to the glass filled with green sludge. "What in the world is that?"

"Not sure what's in it exactly. Mrs. Potts calls it a morning-after tonic." Jenny tidied the room. She swept the borrowed, discarded dress from the floor with a disapproving tsk.

Rafe knew how to survive mornings after drowning in the bottle, there was no question there. Minerva raised the glass with a shaking hand and sniffed. It smelled of fruits and greens, mild and sweet. The first sip stayed down, so another followed, until the glass was empty.

Her stomach's violent roiling reduced to a mild simmer, which only emphasized the pounding in her head. Never, ever again would she give in to temptation. Of the bottle, that is. Despite her embarrassment, Rafe Drummond was a temptation she wasn't sure she could give up. Especially not after the blinding pleasure he'd wrought. She remembered that too. Vividly.

She set the tray aside and gingerly swung her legs over the side of the bed. The floor stabilized under her feet, and she attended her morning ablutions, allowing Jenny to help her dress.

Thankfully, the maid didn't comment on her nightly attire or lack of conversation.

She owed Rafe an apology. Or did he owe her one? Either way, it was going to be awkward. A cool, detached façade is what the situation called for.

Jenny hooked her into one of her favorite day dresses, a sage-green muslin with sprigs of flowers. Comfortable and airy, it flattered her figure with a slightly scooped neck and tight three-quarter sleeves trimmed in lace. Although, the color seemed to enhance her green-tinted pasty face. Under-eye smudges stood out alarmingly, and her lips looked bloodless. She bit them and pinched her cheeks, drawing false color on her face.

Her usual, deliberate stride made her head pound in concert with each step, so she slowed to a shuffle. Her cottony mouth begged for more tea, even lukewarm tea left from breakfast. She entered the dining room on soft feet and stopped short. Rafe was in the middle of his noontime meal, a hearty repast of potatoes, ham, and scones. She pressed a hand over her mouth, her stomach heaving once, and then, thankfully, settling.

A London paper held his attention. He was dressed for riding in buckskins and boots, and his white shirt was rolled up, exposing the sinewy muscles that ran from his thick forearms down to his large hands. Those hands. A slight edge of desire sliced through her queasiness. Had one drunken escapade in his arms turned her into a complete wanton?

She cleared her throat. Rafe leaned back, his eyes shadowed by the distance between them. He seemed as much for a loss of words as she was. Tea was on the table. Rafe rose and pushed the chair next to him out with his foot.

"How are you feeling? I guessed you weren't up for a full breakfast." Rafe's voice was austere and more formal than she was used to.

"I'm better. The green concoction helped matters

considerably. I awoke wondering when I'd boarded a boat." Her half-hearted laugh echoed in her head, making her wince.

"The first time is the worst. Did you solemnly swear to never drink again?"

"I did, how did you know?"

"It's what everyone vows in the morning after drinking too much for the first time."

"When was your first time in the bottom of a bottle?"

"At Eton. Amongst that many curious boys, alcohol is a foregone conclusion. Gray and I drank ourselves into a stupor one night during our second year. The next morning we fought over the chamber pot. It was a miserable experience. It was three years or more before I could even look at the stuff again." His gaze remained on the paper, but his lips curled.

"So before your injury…?"

His smile faded and he ran a finger down his scar. "I rarely drank. War is a terrible thing. Did my actions save English lives? Yes, but I took other lives. Men with families and with the same loyalty to their country. Things have gotten better this autumn. Perhaps you and your brother have helped me as much as I've helped you." The paper wrinkled in his hands.

Her first instinct was to crawl over the table into his lap and hug him as tightly as her puny arms could manage. She settled for laying her hand on his forearm. He shuffled the paper to the side, pulling out of her light grasp. Fisting her hands in her lap, she bit her bottom lip.

"What are your plans for the day, Lady Minerva?" His tone was brisk and distant.

Lady Minerva? As if he hadn't had his hand between her legs? Would he pretend nothing had happened between them? Her façade crumbled in the face of his indifference. "Why didn't you make love to me last night?"

"You remember?" A sudden intensity underscored the

question.

"Of course, I do. I was drunk, not brain-addled." She pushed up from the table and leaned toward him. "I begged you to take me. *Begged you*, for goodness sake." Hurt and humiliation and even a hint of fury warred in her voice. "And you refused. What's wrong with me?"

* * * * *

The daft woman was angry because he hadn't taken advantage of her? In fact, deciding to act a gentleman, albeit a bit late, he hadn't planned on even mentioning their middle of the night activity. If she'd wanted to pretend nothing had happened, it wouldn't have surprised him, nor would he censor her for it. More than most people, he understood how alcohol destroyed common sense. Yet here she stood, raging at him for not rutting her like a beast.

"I didn't want to take you? That's what you believe?"

Minerva shrugged and retreated, putting distance between them. He followed, grabbing her arm and pulling her around to face him. The pain in her eyes made his heart stutter. He was a broken man with little to offer, but at the very least, he could reassure her of his physical desire.

He backed her against the wall and kicked the dining room door closed. Lifting her to her toes, he pressed his body into hers, melding them. And if trapping her with his body wasn't enough, he encircled her forearms and held them against the wall next to her head, completely immobilizing her.

She didn't tug at her arms or squirm away. He brushed his bristled cheek against her soft one, probably chaffing her red, but he didn't care. In fact, he wanted to mark her, if not with his seed then somehow. "Does it feel like I don't want you, Minerva? Because I can assure you, I want you badly."

His erection strained to escape his breeches. He had been in a near constant state of arousal since last night. Even relieving himself hadn't helped for long. He'd hardly slept and had ridden for two hours at dawn, seeking a physical outlet for his sexual frustration. Her hips bucked into him. Tightening his hands on her arms, he moaned. Given very little encouragement, he might spend in his breeches like a young, untried buck.

He leaned into the shell of her ear and rasped, "I was very tempted to bury myself inside of you, damn the consequences. You have no idea what it cost me to leave you in your bed. Alone. But I don't want your senses dulled by drink when I take you. I want to be looking in your clear blue eyes when I sink myself inch by glorious inch inside of your wet heat. I want you to remember every single moment. You'll cry out my name and beg me to take you faster, harder, until you shatter with my cock inside of you."

"Yes. Rafe, take me to your bed. Now. Right now." Her voice had thickened with lust and need.

Her leg circled his, and he released her arm to glide a hand up her thigh to her buttock. He squeezed and tilted her pelvis, settling his cock near her core. "Are you already wet and aching for me, sweetheart?"

She dropped her head to the side, exposing her neck, and he gently bit and sucked the supple flesh. Her freed hand threaded through his hair, and she tugged his face up for a kiss. It was a deep, carnal exploration, a conquering—but he wasn't sure who was the vanquished. He rocked against her, mirroring his tongue's rhythm.

In some tiny sane corner of his mind, the part that recognized it was noon and, although the door was closed, it was not locked, Rafe heard a commotion. The ruckus moved closer.

"Bloody hell." He wanted to cry tears of frustration. Pulling away, he kept her in the circle of his arms. She panted and gripped his shoulders. Her lips were rosy and swollen, her cheek was indeed chafed and her neck bore the imprint of his mouth.

Not knowing what else to do, he propped her against the wall and walked away. The door was flung open without even a knock and in swept his sister, Lily. Following close behind was his best friend and her husband of five months, Gray Masterson.

Rafe wanted to strangle them both.

"Surprise!" Lily swept over to give Rafe a kiss on the cheek and turned to Minerva to repeat the gesture. Although she no longer sagged against the wall, her face was flushed, her eyes glassy and unfocused.

"Darling, I've missed you in town. It's not the same riding in Hyde Park and having no one to gossip with. You're trembling. Is anything amiss?" Lily looked back and forth between her and Rafe. "Did we interrupt a fight?" Lily shook her head, crossed her arms, and sighed like their disappointed nursemaid. "I hoped the very least to come out of this debacle was that you would be able to speak to each other without rancor."

A high-pitched giggle popped out of Minerva, and she cut her wide eyes to Rafe, the message clear. *Save me.* Feeling surprisingly off balance himself, he cast about for some excuse before landing on the one Lily had already provided.

"Yes, Minerva and I were at each other's…throats when you arrived. Unexpectedly, I might add. Your arrival, not our argument." He winced at his less than stellar conversational skills, sidled to his armchair, and scooted under the table to hide his still aching erection.

"Thank heavens, lunch is still laid out. I'm starved." Lily made herself a plate at the buffet and took a seat next to Rafe, digging in with gusto. Gray followed Lily's lead while Minerva took the seat next to Rafe. Remnants of passion sparked between them.

With effort, Rafe regulated his breathing and the tone of his voice, focusing on his sister instead of the overwhelming desire to lay Minerva over the table and eat her for lunch. "I wasn't expecting you for another week. Not that I'm not delighted, of course. Did you already inform Mrs. Devlin to make up your room?"

Minerva was less successful masking her reaction, her voice still shaky. "How long are you staying, Lily?"

"Regrettably, not long. We're on our way to Devon to stay with the Earl of Linley and his new countess. Do you remember her, Minerva? She had the red hair and all the freckles? Quite charming, I thought. No one else gave her a chance to bag a peer, much less a handsome earl." Lily's prattling dissipated the thick undercurrents in the room.

"What's in Devon, Gray?" Rafe asked.

"A smuggling ring. More than brandy, I'm afraid. We have an information leak somewhere." Gray's half-smile was at odds with his words and a shot of unease had Rafe squirming.

Lily clapped like a child. "I'm to help. I was briefed by Sir Hawkins himself."

The unease about his own situation transformed to outright worry for Gray's. "Does Hawkins realize the force of nature he's unleashing?"

Gray shot a side-eyed glance toward Lily. "I tried to explain it to him, I truly did."

"Stop it, both of you. Hawkins says I'm an asset to the Crown."

Rafe looked heavenward and held up his hands. "God help England."

Lily gave him a playful punch on the arm.

He leaned toward Gray. "I wish you the best of luck, my friend." Dropping his voice, he added, "You'll need it."

"Ha, ha, very funny." Lily shot him a withering glance she must have learned from Minerva but ruined it by sticking out her tongue and grinning.

"Did you come from London? You must have started in the wee hours of the morning." Rafe looked back and forth at them.

Lily shifted and looked to Gray, who rolled his boiled egg from one side of the plate to the other, red creeping up his neck. "We actually got here yesterday and spent the night at your cabin. Hope you don't mind."

"Of course, I don't." Rafe looked to Minerva. "Gray and Lily spent their honeymoon at a small cabin I renovated in the middle of the forest."

"I knew you stayed here, but I didn't realize—that sounds lovely." Minerva's smile appeared back to normal.

"It was lovely." Lily and Gray exchanged secretive smiles.

A shot of something that might be jealousy or longing or loneliness—or perhaps a stew of all three—rocked Rafe.

"Minerva, let's go for a turn in the garden so we can chat. I'm anxious to know how my brother has been treating you." Lily's voice was full of dire retribution.

Minerva pushed up from the chair, looking like a firing squad awaited her in the rose bushes. Lily linked their arms and dragged her away.

As soon as the women were out of earshot, Gray burst out laughing and laid his head on folded arms until he gained control of his guffaws.

"What in bloody hell is wrong with you?" Rafe sensed the laughter was at his expense.

Gray raised his head, a smile cutting deep dimples into his cheeks. "I thought you and the ice princess detested each other?"

Rafe brushed non-existent crumbs off his waistcoat, unable to meet Gray's eyes. "We do. It's quite obvious I can't stand the woman."

"Really? What was obvious to me was the beard burn on her cheek, the love bite on her neck, and how could I fail but mention the huge mast standing at attention in your breeches." Gray ticked off the evidence on his fingers before dissolving into teasing laughter again. "Awfully quiet in here for a huge fight. As a matter of fact, I'm not sure I heard any conversation at all on our approach."

"Christ, was it that obvious?" Rafe leaned his head back on the chair.

"Only to a master spy…and to a man who went through the same agony mere months ago." Gray's laughter turned into a sympathetic smile.

Rafe ran both hands through his hair, knitting them around his nape. "I'm not even sure how it happened. She's always disturbed me, but I had come to the wrong conclusions about her. With her constantly under foot, I've realized she's loyal, a hard worker, smart, sweet—when she's not yelling at me that is—and bloody gorgeous on top of all that. And, dammit, Gray, she seems to want me too."

"Why wouldn't she want you?" Gray's voice held a hint of tease. "Not that I'm at all interested in you in that way, you understand, but you're well-built and have all your hair and teeth. Women have always found you devilishly attractive. Perhaps you never noticed, but I did because I always took your cast-offs."

Rafe didn't believe him. Perhaps not classically handsome, Gray was hardly a wallflower with his dark good looks and easy charm. "I think my title had something to do with my appeal back then. I don't get quite as much romantic attention these days."

"You may believe it has to do with your scar, but I think it has more to do with your general cheerless manner. You've become downright melancholy." Gray's teasing manner disappeared in an instant as he leaned over the table. "Does she make you happy?"

A simple question without a simple answer. What was happiness? Would he even recognize it? "She makes me laugh. She's fascinating. I've actually enjoyed our conversations. In turns, she's annoyingly autocratic and incredibly vulnerable. I'm never sure if I want to take her across my knee or protect her with my life. I constantly think about her in the most salacious ways that end up frustrating the hell out of me. Is that happiness? Or a living hell?"

"That's life with a woman you care about, my friend," Gray said if delivering dire news.

Rafe sat back and absorbed the blow. "Oh, bloody hell."

* * * * *

Bundled in cloaks, Lily and Minerva strolled between hedges, out of sight of the house. Minerva tried to quicken her steps. If she hurried, Lily wouldn't have a chance to interrogate her, but her friend kept their arms linked, forcing Minerva to match her ponderous pace.

"I hope Rafe hasn't been too demanding of you?"

"It's certainly…that is to say, no, he's not been." Minerva cursed her tongue.

"What tasks, pray tell, has he been asking you to perform?" Lily's voice was sharp, belying her casual manner.

"At first, I worked with Jenny, the upstairs maid. She comes from a wonderful family in Lipton. Do you know them? Ten brothers and sisters. La, can you imagine?"

"Yes, I know Jenny and her family well. What else has he had you do?"

"There was a spot of trouble with Simon, but Ra—your brother handled it admirably. You won't recognize Simon. I'm so proud of him, and Lord Drummond has been ever so patient. It's amazing. After the spot of trouble, I moved to the blue bedroom, and he said I wasn't to work anymore, but I can't stay idle, so I began organizing the books in the study. He has quite a collection, as I'm sure you're aware. I've found some excellent travelogues and novels. Have you read *The Lady of the Lake*?" Minerva had to stop for a breath, her words tumbling on top of each other.

Lily stopped and turned Minerva to face her, her hands tight on Minerva's upper arms. "Where in the devil were you sleeping before you got moved to the blue bedroom?"

"In your nursemaid's old room." Minerva tried a smile, but her puny effort didn't seem to dent the impossible-to-misinterpret outrage on Lily's face. She looked ready to unman her brother.

"That blighter."

"I was quite comfortable. Please don't make a fuss."

Lily harrumphed. "I'll let it go—for now. Are you fighting constantly?"

"We had a few clashes at the beginning, but I've come to understand him a bit better. He's different than I supposed."

"You aren't completely miserable then?"

"No, not at all." Minerva could almost feel Lily's gaze try to strip to the truth behind her words. She tucked her arm back into Lily's and got them moving again. "Honestly, Lily, I promise. Recently, I've even been happy."

Lily allowed her to steer them through a grassy space to a fountain littered with colorful leaves. "Has he been drinking?"

"He had a bit too much when Lord Stonewell was here."

"Only one overindulgence? That's an improvement, I suppose. He can be terribly insulting when he's drunk. I hope he didn't embarrass you too badly. Poor old Stonewell. I suppose Rafe wasn't very polite?"

"No, not very." Minerva cast her eyes to the gray skies at the understatement.

"Will your prodigal brother take dinner with us tonight? I would love to see the miraculous change myself."

"I'm sure he will. If only you could have seen him working here the first few days. He kept his fine London clothes on to muck out the stables. It's not often you see a man in a perfectly tied cravat shoveling horse dung around. Rafe has done wonders with him." She laughed, and Lily joined in, but the decidedly speculative gleam in her eyes set Minerva's nerves jangling

CHAPTER FIFTEEN

Dinner was a lively affair. On his best behavior, Simon was charming and gregarious. Sipping her wine, Minerva imagined the devastating impact her brother would have on the London misses in the spring. No doubt, he would be pursued with renewed vigor. A rich, handsome, bachelor duke was a rare commodity. Where would Simon be without Rafe? A debtor's prison? Where would *she* be without him?

She turned to find him staring with an intensity that set her blood racing. Smiling, she raised her glass in an unspoken toast. The corners of his mouth quirked, and he raised his glass in return. The conversation ebbed around them. They hadn't been alone since their passionate embrace, and his stare made her wonder when—not if—they would continue where they'd left off. Laughter cresting around them broke the connection.

After a dinner of roast pork and vegetables, along with a decadent dessert of braised apples, Simon pushed back from the table and patted his belly. "I have a long day ahead of me tomorrow. Lord Drummond has me doing all his dirty work these days." He winked at the table in general and bowed to Lily and Minerva. "I'll leave you to enjoy your spirits and gossip. I must stop to give Mrs. Potts my most sincere thanks on such a fine meal."

After a round of murmured good evenings, silence descended until Lily broke it. "What have you done with the real duke? That cannot be the same dissolute wastrel."

"Isn't it amazing? It took Rafe less than two months to transform him. The first three weeks were…" Minerva paused, searching for the right word.

"Hellish?" Rafe supplied.

"Rafe Drummond, there are ladies present, don't forget." Lily's admonishing tone was ruined when her laughter snuck through.

"I'm fairly certain you could teach me a few choice words, Mrs. Masterson." Rafe lifted his glass in a toast.

Lily told an abbreviated version of how she'd donated all of Rafe's brandy to the local tavern after reaching her wit's end with his bouts of overindulgence. "When Rafe discovered every decanter empty, let's just say every matron of Almack's would have swooned dead away had they been within earshot."

Even as he joined the laughter, tight lines pulled at his mouth, and he eschewed an after-dinner glass of port. Gray suggested cards, and they settled around the playing table in the drawing room.

Lily leaned toward Minerva. "Watch out, Gray is a disgraceful cheat."

"Mrs. Masterson, why I never. That you would expunge my honor thusly is outrageous. You'll pay for that in spades later." Waggling his eyebrows at his wife, Gray dealt the cards.

Minerva had never had such an atrocious hand. Rafe tossed his cards back on the table, face up, to show a similarly poor deal.

"My, my, that is an astonishingly bad hand, Rafe," Gray said with a convincing gasp. "Let's hope your partner fared better."

Minerva fanned her cards out. "How in the world did you do that?"

Gray demonstrated the trick and had Minerva attempt it. Rafe's gaze never left her, and she fumbled with the cards. Several scattered across the table.

Lily scooped them up and took the deck from Minerva, shuffling with the same precision as Gray. "It's all right, Minerva, learning to cheat takes loads of practice and an excellent teacher." She smiled at Gray while her hands moved in a graceful arc, dealing a round. Again, she and Gray had the winning hands.

"Where did you learn to do that, Gray? At Eton?" Minerva threw her cards in the middle of the table and shook her head.

"It was part of my training when I joined the home office. There were some basic skills I needed in to order to maintain a plausible cover. Cards, languages, accents, disguises. I learned how to navigate a boat using the constellations, how to repair a wagon wheel, shoe a horse and perform simple surgery. An education of a different sort than I received at Eton. This time I promise I won't cheat, and we'll play a real game, shall we?" Gray shuffled and dealt.

"Was your training similar, Rafe?" Minerva asked after they discarded, casting a look at him through her lashes. He'd been quiet throughout Lily and Gray's demonstrations, although a smile lingered around his eyes.

"In some respects, but my talents lay elsewhere."

"What was your talent?" She sensed rather than saw him tense and looked up from her cards, realizing too late that she'd taken a misstep. Rafe's discomfort was obvious. He shifted in his seat, the tease in his eyes gone.

"My size made me a good fit for more physical endeavors. I was sent in situations where they required a bit of muscle, but someone who could think on his feet as well."

"What sort of things did you learn?" Lily turned toward her brother before Minerva could change the subject. The two siblings wore a similar intensity even though they looked nothing alike.

"I don't want to talk about it." Rafe's jaw ticked.

"Come now. It's time you discussed it, brother. I want to know."

Minerva and Gray exchanged a glance.

"Rafe was a master at extracting prisoners. He could plan and execute a rescue better than anyone. That trap you orchestrated in Toulouse was genius. They still talk about it around the office." The good humor in Gray's voice sounded forced.

"But what else, I know there's more." Now that Lily had sniffed out a bone of information, she was a bloodhound.

Rafe threw his cards down and lay his palms flat on the tabletop. "I was trained to kill. With a rock, a blade, a bullet, a piece of string even and, of course, my bare hands. Is that what you want to hear, Lily? That I'm a killer? That England sent me to do the dirtiest work possible?" Rafe stood, his chair toppling with a bang. He left without a backward glance and slammed the door.

An awkward silence descended.

"Well done, Lily." Gray rested his forehead on a propped, fisted hand, his gaze on the green felt tabletop.

"It's been over a year. He should talk about it. Excise the poison." Indignation threaded her words.

Minerva focused her most intimidating, icy stare on her best friend. "Shame on you. Don't you understand him at all? You're his sister. He wants you to look at him like the big brother he was, not as he sees himself now. He feels damaged. No matter how hard you press him, you can't fix him, and he doesn't want you to try."

Lily's mouth opened and closed. "I-I didn't realize—"

"You didn't realize because you want to satisfy your own oversized curiosity." Minerva rose. "You owe your brother an apology."

His eyes wide and with a hint of a smile, Gray whispered, "Bravo, Lady Minerva," which earned him a slap on the arm from

Lily.

Minerva went straight to the study, sure he would be there pouring himself a drink. It was empty. Deflated, she toyed with the idea of searching the house, most notably his room, but discarded it. Lily and Gray were staying directly across the hall.

The study offered her comfort—the smell, the masculinity that oozed from the dark heavy furniture, his beloved books that lined the walls. She plopped in his armchair and pulled a rug over her legs. She would wait. All night, if necessary.

A killer, he'd said, but she suspected things weren't so simple. He had honor. He had a conscience. He struggled with guilt and remorse. He wouldn't kill without reason and a weighing of justice. The snippet from his journal, his darkly beautiful poems, the ramblings during his nightmare—they all spoke of a conflicted soul.

The extraordinary number of poetry and children's books still in his library was telling. He might possess the body of a warrior, but he longed for the innocence of childhood and simple beauty. How difficult it must have been for him. First, to grow up with such a harsh, unemotional father and then to be trained as an assassin, to take another's life on command.

Her heart ached for him. As if drawn by her emotional musing, Rafe pushed the door of the study open and stepped inside.

"What are you doing here?" His tone was clear. *Get out.* Like her, he had erected walls. Thicker, taller, and even more difficult to breech, but she would try to scale them.

Minerva walked straight into him, wrapped her arms around his waist, and pressed her cheek against his chest. He stayed stiff and unyielding in her embrace for a moment, but when the surrender came, it was swift. He locked his arms around her, and his lungs deflated under her cheek. Curling around her, he rested his chin on top of her head.

"What's this then?" His voice rumbled under her cheek.

"I thought you might need a friend."

"Why would I deserve such?"

She pulled back to take his face in her hands and forced him to look her in the eye. "Inside your warrior's body beats the heart of a poet. That's why the past haunts you. I can't tell you to forget the past, it will always be with you because of your nature, but it might help to talk about it. I'm not pushing like Lily. You could talk to your father or to Gray. Anyone. But I would listen." She dropped her hands to his shoulders, tensing for his reaction. He hadn't shoved her away—yet.

He surprised her by roughly pulling her closer and burying his face in her neck. Her lips sought his and found them on a similar hunt. They collided in a maelstrom of emotion. Passion, yes, but there was an added dimension to the kiss. A tenderness, perhaps. Soon, understanding its meaning wasn't as important as the press of her body into his. Their tongues coiled and explored, but she needed more. Needed his wicked hands.

His attention was entirely on the play of their lips. He caressed her face and weaved his fingers through her hair, but her desperate, impatient squirming against him didn't go unnoticed. Breaking the mind-numbing kiss, he chuckled. If her world hadn't blurred and tipped, she might have kicked him.

"Now is not the time to fulfill my promise. Unfortunately."

She managed a very eloquent grunt in response. Putting several inches between their bodies, his caressed her waist, testing the span and offering support.

"Anyway, I need to find Lily and apologize." His mouth tightened.

"You will do no such thing, Rafe Drummond."

"But I acted a boor."

"Not without due cause to my way of thinking. It's Lily that owes you an apology, and you'll let her make it. Promise me."

"All right." A fleeting smile twitched his beard before he stepped back and rubbed his nape. "Tomorrow is the harvest fair in Lipton. Would you like to go?"

The abrupt change in topic left her mute for a moment. Finally, unable to mask her incredulity, she asked, "With you?"

"That was the idea. If you're interested. If not, it's fine, of course." His head down, he fingered his scar while red spread over his cheeks. My God, the man looked...*nervous*.

Minerva caught his hand and pulled it away from its agitated rambling. "I would love to accompany you. I've never been to a country fair."

"It seems I'm to introduce you to all sort of firsts." He smiled, a real one this time, his white teeth on display and his relief palpable.

His insinuation left her lungs tight, gasping for air. Now she was the nervous one. A tentative knock sounded on the door. Lily peeked around the doorjamb.

"We'll leave early afternoon. Now, I think Lily and I should chat," he said.

Holding his gaze, she smiled, shakily perhaps, but with an equal amount of anticipation tempering her nerves. It seemed to bemuse him. Although he rarely played the gentleman with her, he took her hand and bussed the back, very properly. A bit bemused herself, she walked past Lily, who had taken in their exchange with huge eyes.

CHAPTER SIXTEEN

The next day dawned clear and cool. Autumn had officially pushed the late summer warmth away, but the skies were blue and the changing leaves blanketed the countryside in rich hues.

Rafe stood outside the stable door holding two sets of reins and chatting with Tom Donahue. His back stretched the fabric of his dun-colored jacket, and her step quickened with a shot of anticipation. He shifted to watch her approach, his smile reaching all the way into his eyes. If Tom hadn't been standing there, she might have walked into his chest and searched for his lips again.

Instead, he offered a formal greeting and small bow before offering a hand up. On the way to Lipton, Rafe pointed out various landmarks. Men and women called out greetings, and Rafe often inquired after their spouse or children by name. He was obviously well liked and admired amongst the crofters and merchants in town. His servants should have no complaints either. They all had the afternoon and evening off to enjoy themselves.

As they neared the edge of town, foot traffic picked up considerably. Colorful tents dotted the main street, and flags waved in the slight breeze on the corners. The lilt of music drifted in the air.

"This is so exciting." She rose in her stirrups to see as far as possible.

"Didn't you grow up on one of your country estates? I'm surprised you didn't sneak down to one of the village fairs."

"I'm a rule follower by nature, and our rules were numerous and strict. It was rare we had an afternoon out of doors, much less leave to attend a fair." She couldn't keep a certain wistfulness away.

"Good Lord, I can understand why Simon went wild once he was set free in London. Makes me feel even sorrier for the chap. And what about you, did you not feel the need to rebel as well?"

Sliding the reins through her fingers, Minerva reviewed the last years of her life. "I think I did, in my way. It's why I haven't married, why I took over the estate. I was sick of being told what I should do and say."

Facts and figures and logic ruled her day-to-day business. To realize something as emotional as her desire for control had driven the path of her life skewed her perception of herself and her motivations. Some of her consternation must have showed on her face.

"You should have no regrets. Although, no one understands more than I do how difficult that advice is to take. It's a beautiful day, and there's much to see." He waved his hand at the milling crowd ahead of them.

He was right on all counts, and Minerva let herself be swept into the excitement of the day. After leaving their horses at the inn, they joined the bustling melee. The first stall housed a woodworker. Tiny wooden soldiers lined up in a regiment, lifelike animals marched, and carved flowers graced a wooden vase. Intricate and delicate, the black and white painted pieces of a chess set called to her. She wanted it for Rafe.

Giving the set one last covetous glance, she allowed him to guide her to the next stall. Pretty adornments for ladies hung from pegs—ribbons, bows, bunches of dried flowers.

"Pick some ribbons for yourself. Which do you like? You look lovely in blue." Rafe pulled a satin cornflower-blue ribbon from the bunch.

"I couldn't. You mustn't think you have to buy me anything." The delicate ribbon incongruously weaved through his fingers.

"Have none of your suitors ever taken you out and bought you something pretty?"

"Suitor?" Her head popped up.

Rafe tensed, seemingly as stunned as Minerva that the word had come out of his mouth. "I didn't mean… What I meant to say…" He clamped his mouth shut and then muttered, "Oh, bloody hell," without unlocking his teeth.

Rafe leaned over and chose ribbons of various colors and designs. Handing them to the girl, she packaged them prettily and took his coins with a curtsy. He delivered the package to Minerva with a tip of his head. Pressing the package to her chest, she stammered out thanks. Bouquet after bouquet of flowers had arrived at her townhouse, but never had a man bought her anything so precious.

They stopped to peruse more wares and enjoyed a magician's show. Food merchants packed the end of the street, delicious scents wafting on the breeze. Her mouth watered, and her stomach growled. Chuckling, he grabbed her hand and pulled her straight toward the meat pies.

"William Watkins. It's good to see you back this year. How've you fared since last fall?" Rafe called out.

William's hands stayed busy in the pie dough. "Fair enough, my lord. My, but you're looking much improved since last year. Everything well at Wintermarsh?"

"Indeed. The earl is healed and off giving Scotland hell, last I heard. Lily and Gray got married this spring. They left this morning, but Lily tried most desperately to talk Gray into staying so she could have some of your pies and Miss Beverly's fruit tarts, of course." Rafe set a booted foot up on a rock and winked toward an older woman who had sidled over to eavesdrop on their conversation.

"Ack, go on with you," the old lady cackled. "Such a charmer when you want to be. Who is this, my lord? Is this your lady?" Miss Beverly ingratiated herself in the thick of it, examining Minerva from head to toe.

"Miss Beverly, this is Lady Minerva Bellingham. A friend of Lily's…and mine."

"A pleasure to make your acquaintance, Miss Beverly, Mr. Watkins," Minerva said.

"Well, ain't you a pretty thing. You'd best hang on to this one." Miss Beverly shook a finger at Rafe, hitched her skirts, and scampered back to her tent. "Let me fix you up with some tarts."

Meat pies and tarts in hand, they retreated to a quiet grove of trees to sit on a log and eat. The first bite of Mr. Watkins's pie exploded in her mouth, and she threw her head back, moaning. The pork filling along with the unusual spices overloaded her senses. "This is incredible."

"I know. I keep pestering him for the recipe, but he claims it's a gypsy secret and won't reveal it."

"Is he a gypsy? As a people, I imagined them darker and more mysterious."

"He was born not ten miles from here to a cobbler," Rafe replied dryly. "Wait until you try Miss Beverly's tarts."

Unable to resist, she bit into one and the berry filling oozed out. The sweet-tart combination hit exactly the right note, and she closed her eyes. The brush of Rafe's thumb on her bottom lip had her eyes popping open. A daub of berry colored his thumb.

Ever so slowly, he licked it clean. Her thighs clenched, and a flush raced across her chest. If she'd been bolder, more experienced, she might have helped him. Instead, she wet her dry lips and swallowed convulsively. He took a bite of his tart and the moment passed, yet it seemed to leave an indelible mark.

They discussed inconsequential things throughout their

impromptu picnic and soaked up the cool sunlight. Rafe settled against the log, crossed his booted feet, and laced his fingers behind his head in an attitude of total relaxation. Soon enough, winter's weary clouds would invade, and the trees would drop their colorful cloaks.

"You love the country, don't you?" she asked.

He swiveled his head toward her. "I do. London leaves me feeling…boxed in, I suppose. I tried to enjoy the social whirl when I was younger, but at the end of every evening, I longed to be here. You love London, don't you?"

"I enjoy the bustle and the energy. I hated the country and the empty house when I was a child. As soon as the strings were cut, I moved us to London. Wintermarsh is different though. I've enjoyed my time here—mostly." She tried a teasing smile. Although, he smiled in return, his eyes didn't crinkle.

He cleared his throat and brushed crumbs off his breeches. "Let's explore more, shall we?"

Instruments being tuned made her stand tall, head cocked toward the cacophony of sound. "What is that?"

"Dancing in the field." He tried to guide her in the opposite direction, back toward the merchants. Ignoring the hand on her waist, she spun away toward the gathering crowd. He followed, but slowly. She pushed her way to stand on the edge of a field that doubled as a dance floor.

The disharmony righted itself, and the band of musicians launched into a boisterous, fast-paced jig. A collective whoop cascaded through the crowd. Couples twirled into the clearing. So different from the staid, controlled ballroom waltzes of London, the pulsing energy set her toes tapping and her hands clapping. Rafe stood behind her with his arms crossed, his legs braced wide, and not a single betraying twitch in time to the music.

As soon as one frolicsome song finished, another began, neither the players nor the dancers tiring. A man whirled close and grabbed her hand. Her willing feet followed his lead, and a reckless laugh burst out of her belly. The man was a Mitchell. There was no doubt about it. From his hooded eyes and charming but sly grin, she'd guess it was Jenny's rakish, ne'er-do-well brother.

Jenny sent her a little wave when they spun past each other. She danced with a local lad, but Tom Donahue stood on the side, in an almost identical stance to Rafe, looking ready to strangle Jenny's partner.

As the music trailed off, Jenny's brother deposited her with Rafe. She curtsied and thanked him prettily. Another jig started, and she tried to pull Rafe into the clearing. She had about as much luck as attempting to shift an elephant.

"Dance with me. What's wrong? Are you scared?" Minerva grinned.

"Absolutely terrified," Rafe whispered so low she barely heard him.

This time when she tugged, he followed her, and she was in for another surprise. Although a large man, he was light on his feet and familiar with the steps. She reveled in the touch of his hands on her waist and back. She tried to mimic his quick footwork and laughed all the harder when she couldn't keep up with him. They danced straight through two more songs. Linking their hands, he led her through the thickening crowd. Several men slapped Rafe on the back as they passed.

"You, Rafe Drummond, are a disgustingly good dancer. Is there nothing you can't do well?" Minerva leaned into his arm. He tipped his head toward hers, his smile warm and genuine, and he fingered an escaped lock of her hair. A few inches and she would be kissing him surrounded by a throng of people.

Vicar Appleby's sonorous voice shattered her sense of isolation. "Lord Drummond, I'm so pleased to see you here. If I might have a word about the belfry? It requires repairs, and I hoped to replace the bell while we're already up there. Do you have a moment to spare? Would you care to join me for an ale?"

"Actually—"

"You go along with the vicar. I'm going to find Jenny. I'll meet you at the stables." Waggling her fingers, she shooed him away.

As soon as he was out of sight, she made tracks back to the woodworker's booth, letting out a gusty sigh when she spotted the chess set still on display. Turning away, she cleared her face of all emotion and took several deep breaths before she stepped up to the merchant.

A long, hearty negotiation followed. A small crowd gathered to witness the two combatants finally reach a satisfactory agreement. Minerva clutched the chess set to her chest and hoped Rafe was still busy discussing Lipton's belfry.

Jenny perched on the wooden fence outside the blacksmith's, talking with her father and swinging her legs.

"I saw my scoundrel of a brother pull you out for a dance," Jenny said.

"And you had nothing to do with it?" Minerva asked with raised eyebrows.

Jenny laughed and nearly toppled backwards. "You were practically on your knees begging for a dance, but I knew you'd never get Lord Drummond out there. Somehow, you managed it though. Lady Minerva got him to dance, Papa. Isn't that amazing?"

Black John hit a metal horseshoe with a hammer, the ring melodious. He paused to wipe his forehead. "Before your time, Jenny, Master Rafe would have been out there dancing all afternoon. He was quite a charming young man. Stole many a kiss from a country lass, I'd guess."

"He's still charming," Minerva said a bit defensively. The speculative looks both father and daughter sent her direction had her biting the inside of her mouth. Her next request would be sure to fan Jenny's curiosity to inferno-like levels. "Could you take this back to Wintermarsh for me, Jenny?"

"What is it?"

"A chess set."

"Why not get Lord Drummond to put it in his bag? No one will bother it, I'm sure."

Minerva scuffed her boots on a rock, unable to meet her eyes. "If you must know, it's a gift for him, and I want it to be a surprise. As a thank you for dealing with my brother."

"Of course," Jenny said with an eye roll.

"Who was the lad you were dancing with? And why was Tom Donahue standing on the edge looking like he wanted to commit murder?"

"Tom Donahue can go straight to—"

"Jenny Mitchell, you watch your mouth, girl. I can still take you across my knee," Black John said.

"Sorry, Papa, but that man riles me up." Jenny reached for the set, but Black John took it instead and offered to store it in the smithy for the afternoon. Jenny could pick it up on her way home.

"Here he comes. Thank you for the help." Minerva waved goodbye and hurried toward the stables.

"You found Jenny," he said.

"I did indeed. She was amazed you danced with me, but Black John says you were quite the charmer in your youth. I told him you're still quite charming."

"Am I?" he asked softly.

"Sometimes," she whispered back.

Rafe cleared his throat, taking the reins from the hostler and giving Minerva a boost up. He brushed his hand along her calf, squeezing slightly. Even through her thick habit, the heat of his palm left a brand on her sensitive skin.

"I thought we could ride back through the woods."

She could only manage a nod.

After he mounted Aries, they set off slowly until they cleared the village and left the road toward a grove of trees. Minerva pulled Sparrow to a halt, dazzled by the colors spread in front of them.

"It's times like these I wish I had taken up more maidenly pursuits like watercolors. To be able to capture such beauty on canvas would be incredible."

"I'd like to capture the beauty before me as well."

When she looked over, his gaze was firmly on her and not the countryside.

* * * * *

See? Quite charming indeed." Minerva tossed a sweet smile in his direction, making him fumble his reins. "Race you?"

Without waiting for his answer, she urged Sparrow into a gallop through the fallow field toward the woods. Faint laughter carried on the wind. He gave her a head start, as was only fair, before he gave Aries his head and raced after her. The huge stallion ate up the distance, catching her before she entered dense forest.

Her hair flowed around her shoulders, the pins stolen by the wind. They weaved their mounts through the trees, and this time, Minerva had the upper hand on the smaller, more nimble horse. Aries was a brute, much like his master, and plowed straight over the saplings.

"I call it a tie," he said.

"Accept your loss, my lord." Breathless with flushed cheeks and bright eyes, she brought Sparrow to a stop.

"Let's walk. The horses need to cool. We're entering the darkest, deepest part of the forest. There always seems to be a touch of magic here." After dismounting, he spanned her waist and lifted her down. Christ, she was a puny little thing. Compared to him at any rate. The need to protect her rose up inside of him, so strong he had to force himself to release her, even though the only danger to her in these woods was…him.

He took a deep breath and tried to leave proper space between them. The path through the trees was barely wide enough for two horses and left them jostling into each other, shoulder to shoulder. His conscience cackled like an old man had told a bawdy joke. Rafe knew what awaited in the woods and wondered if he should turn them around.

"Where are we headed?" she asked.

"This path leads to my cabin. Would you like to see it?" Keeping his gaze on the brown needles softening their steps, he couldn't tell if she was outraged or surprised or pleased. The silence stretched. It would be best if she said no, best if she slapped him and told him to go to perdition. "Of course, we can head back to Wintermarsh. Probably should. No reason to stop. It's only a small cottage. Nothing special."

"I would love to see your cottage," she whispered.

Fingertips brushed the back of his fisted hand. He relaxed at her wispy touch, and her fingers weaved through his. As selfish as it might be, relief and satisfaction and happiness poured through him.

"Rafe, has there… I mean, have you brought other ladies here before?" Her tripping question prodded his heart into an erratic, quick dance.

"Never. It's always been my retreat, my safe haven. Years ago, I used it as an escape while the earl was in residence."

"Lily told me you bore the brunt of his high expectations."

He barked something he hoped she'd take as a laugh. "High expectations? Yes, impossibly high. He expected things of me at ten that a grown man couldn't accomplish. I was strong physically but still a child in many ways. I didn't know how to handle his constant berating."

Minerva squeezed his hand. "I'm sorry."

"It was a long time ago." He shrugged.

"That doesn't make it hurt any less."

"What were your parents like?"

"I don't remember either of them very well. They spent a good amount of time in London without us. Occasionally, before dinner, I was required to perform like a monkey, rattling off whatever our tutor had taught me to recite. We were more an obligation than a joy to my mother. She probably wished Simon had been born first, so there would have been no need for a second child." Bitterness crept into her voice.

"Well, then, I'm awfully glad you were born first," he said roughly.

"What about your mother?"

"She was beautiful, I suppose, but wrapped up in my father's wants and needs."

"Did she resent you?"

"No, she loved me in a fashion, but not in a playmate sort of way. One sunny afternoon, I begged her to come fly kites, but she preferred to laze on her lounge chair discussing the earl with her lady's maid. I was close to tears when Gray's father came outside and played with me even without Gray."

"You had people around you that cared. Makes me feel a bit, I don't know, not jealous, but incomplete? All I had was Simon, and I suppose I focused everything on him. Much to his detriment." Years of loneliness underscored her words. Rafe pulled her around to face him.

"Many people care about you, Minerva. Lily nearly unmanned me the evening I confessed our bargain. Your Mr. Drake was oddly protective. Simon would do anything to please you. You've wrapped the servants around your little finger." He ran fingertips down her face. "And me."

"I've got you wrapped around my finger?" She huffed a laugh as if it was a joke, but an unexpected vulnerability snaked through her words.

"You've had me wrapped in knots for months."

Her smile fell, and she dropped her gaze to his mouth.

He tugged her forward. "We're close. Can you see?"

A glow shone through the trees and a trail of smoke wound its way to the sky. Aries nudged at his shoulder, the smoke a signal oats were near.

"It's like something out of one of your storybooks." The wonder in her voice pleased him. He had whitewashed the outer walls and painted the wooden beams a deep green. The roof was slanted and topped with red clay tiles. A heavy oak door graced the front, and the knocker was an iron forest sprite.

"It was a hovel when I found it. There are several abandoned crofter cottages in the area. Over the years, I reconstructed it. When I came home from France and was able to ride again, I would come here and…"

"Get utterly foxed by yourself?" Minerva tsked.

Because he viewed his drinking as a weakness, teasing usually roused a base need to defend himself, but this time only amusement surfaced. "Look who's calling the kettle black. I recall a certain beautiful blonde getting plastered all alone in my study."

"You shouldn't…my goodness." She ducked her face and tucked a swath of hair behind her ear.

"In addition to pickling myself, no one could hear me if I had a nightmare out here."

"Has your sleep been troubled recently?"

"My dreams lately have been haunted by a blue-eyed temptress, but they've tormented me in an entirely different way, believe me."

For the second time, Minerva stuttered some inane words. "Rafe," she finally whispered on an exhale.

He'd heard his name on her lips before, of course, but this time, the single syllable demolished his already crumbling good intentions. There was such longing imbued in her utterance. The evening would end one way. Finally, he would satisfy his overwhelming need, but he promised himself he would bring her a pleasure she'd never forget. One enchanted night was all he could allow himself, and he planned to take full advantage.

"You don't have to be shy with me, sweetheart." Rafe voice was gruff as he unlocked the door and ushered her inside.

CHAPTER SEVENTEEN

Minerva stood entranced. A sturdy table stood in front of a crackling fire with two large chairs. A picnic basket was on a counter that ran along part of one wall. A chair took up a corner with a small bookcase containing a handful of books. In the far corner, sat a bed.

She fought the urge to chew on her nails. Her gaze skittered away from the mass of pillows. A question hung in the expectant air. A decision was required. On the other hand, perhaps by coming here, her decision had already been made deep in the recesses of her mind.

"It's lovely. You planned for this?" She gestured vaguely toward the fire and food.

"I hoped you would want to come. I shouldn't have assumed, I suppose. Am I a total arse?" He let out a gusty sigh, smoothing a hand down his beard. "I'm a bit out of practice in the fine art of wooing a lady."

"Is that what this is then? A wooing?" Her voice quavered.

His teeth worried his bottom lip, and he ran his hands down her arms, roughing the velvet of her jacket. "Minerva, you need to understand something. There's only so much I can offer. Only so much you'd ever want from me. But I want you, and you want me. There's no shame in that. This—tonight—can only be a..." His gaze cut away.

"An interlude?" she whispered, her lips numb.

He sighed. "Yes, an interlude. Once we leave here, at the house, we can't continue to have…" Again, he searched the floor.

"A liaison?" she offered.

"Exactly. Can you accept one night of pleasure with me?"

He ran his hands up and down her arms, around her back, up into her hair. If he had told her she would be a human sacrifice at the mouth of a volcano, she would agree as long as his hands continued to roam her body.

She hummed her acceptance of his terms, leaning into him and draping her arms over his shoulders. At her acquiescence, Rafe applied himself to nibbling at her ear and neck. Shivers coursed down to her toes with a lingering stop between her legs.

The corner of her brain that enjoyed summing columns of numbers detailed the reasons this interlude was an exceptionally poor idea. Top on the list was her total and complete ruination. In society's eyes, at any rate. As Rafe said, there would be no shame in their joining. Marriage to a gentleman of the ton might be impossible. Although, she really had no desire to marry anyway.

What if he gets you with child? the voice screamed. The probability was low, and it was a gamble she would readily accept. The future was a distant worry.

The present stifled the annoying voice of logic and reason. The present included Rafe Drummond tracing his tongue around her ear and slipping the hooks of her habit free. She was tired of being responsible, of following the rules, of being in control. She wanted to follow this man off the brink and into the unknown.

She clutched at the muscles of his back and buried her nose where his hair curled over his collar, breathing his unique essence. "In your study in London, when we started all this, I wanted…I wanted…"

"What did you want, sweetheart?" He roved his big hands to

her hips and pulled her firmly into him. The hard ridge of his erection settling against her hip bone sent knee-melting heat through her body, leaving her unsteady. He circled an arm around her waist, holding her against him. His size and strength made her feel feminine and protected, and her desire ratcheted up another notch.

"I wanted to crawl across the desk and bury my face right in your collar, press my lips against your neck. You always smell so intoxicating." She kissed his neck and even took a quick, gentle bite.

"Good Lord," he rumbled. He cupped her buttocks and fit her even tighter against him. Her knees quit working entirely, but he didn't even flinch at taking her full weight.

"I tried so hard to squash this, but when you saved me...us. It became more than a physical need, impossible to deny. I'm sorry."

"Sorry? I would never have dreamed a woman like you could ever be attracted to me. It's downright humbling. In my study that morning when you mentioned working off your brother's debt in my bed? I've pictured that scenario every bloody day since."

Her bottom hit the dining table, and she was grateful for the support.

"Are you hungry?" he asked with a rasp.

"N-no. Not really." Her stomach was a churning mass of nerves and desire. She couldn't imagine trying to choke down even a husk of bread.

"I am."

"Are you? Would you like me to unpack the basket?" Her brain function had slowed to encompass only the receipt of the pleasurable sensations his hands and mouth were leaving in their wake. And, she wasn't even undressed.

"I'm not hungry for anything Mrs. Potts made." Having already unhooked it, he slid her bodice down her arms and tossed it over his shoulder. He looked starved. His gaze devoured her breasts, and Minerva didn't need to look down to know her nipples were poking at her chemise, begging for his mouth.

"You're not?" She arched her back, pushing her breasts closer to his mouth. The need for his touch overrode her pride. "What do you plan on eating then?"

His chuckle was a dark portent. "You, sweetheart."

Finally, he cupped her breasts with his hands and rubbed her sensitive nipples with his thumbs. An embarrassing moan escaped on her sharp exhale, and she squeezed her thighs together, trying in vain to control her body's response.

"Do you trust me?" he whispered into her ear before tugging the lobe between his teeth. The hair on his chin tickled her cheek.

She nodded, her eyes closing. A moment later, her skirt fell to the floor in a whoosh. Her drawers followed, and he lifted her to sit on the table, kicking her clothing out of his way. The cool table on her backside added to the tactile pleasure that threatened to swamp her.

He left her unanchored. Seeking balance, she opened her eyes and curled her hands over the side of the table. He pulled up one of the heavy armchairs, his gaze lingering on her breasts and the juncture of her legs.

Although a chemise covered her, she might as well have been naked. Growing more and more self-conscious, she dropped her face into a scrunched shoulder and curled an arm over her hardened nipples. Her hair fell around her like a curtain

"No. You're bloody gorgeous. I want to see you. All of you. Don't hide from me," he fairly growled.

She obeyed, dropping her arm, but she kept her face averted, slightly dismayed at how easy and arousing she found it to follow his commands. He pulled her foot on his lap and removed her half-boot and stocking. He squeezed and scraped her delicate skin with his fingernails.

He repeated the process with her other leg, keeping both her feet in his lap. His hands skimmed up and down her legs, inching her chemise higher with each pass, until his fingertips grazed the hair of her mound.

Placing a foot on each arm of the chair, he drew her legs apart. Instinct tightened her thighs. He rose and pressed his hips between her legs, forcing them open. Supporting her back, he pushed her flat over the table, gently nipping and tugging at her lips. His kisses were casual, unaggressive, relaxing.

"I promise you'll like this. I've been driving myself crazy dreaming about it for weeks. But you have to give me control. Now, close your eyes and enjoy."

Again, her body ruled her mind. Her eyes closed. His weight lifted, and she closed her knees, the exposure too unsettling. The warmth of his hands settled on her knees, at first gently caressing the sensitive undersides, but soon they pressed her legs apart. His touch floated down her inner thighs, and he slipped a finger through her wet folds.

Laying an arm over her eyes, she tried to block out the embarrassment. Was it too late to request a glass of liquor? Soon though, she forgot about the liquor, even forgot she was spread open mostly naked on a table. He circled her nub with his thumb while he pushed a thick finger inside of her. Her moan accompanied the invasion. The intensity of the pleasure was startling, but she was greedy and wanted more. Knew there was more.

The need to assuage the ache trumped her maidenly modesty, and she squirmed closer to the edge of the table. His wicked, talented hands disappeared.

"No, Rafe, please, don't leave me." Had that rough, guttural plea come from her?

His rumble sounded suspiciously like laughter, but she couldn't summon enough indignation to care.

He was back, the sensations different but no less intense.

Firm, wet strokes. She raised her head. His dark hair brushed the inside of her thighs, his beard adding another element to the pleasure spiraling from between her legs. Another mystery revealed.

He slid his hand under the curve of her bottom and tilted her pelvis up. Her legs fell farther apart. As his tongue dabbed, he slipped a finger inside of her. Her climax was sudden, like falling from an unseen precipice. Her hips bucked and she tried to clamp her thighs shut, but he was merciless, forcing them open to continue his glorious torture. She lay across the table utterly spent. Nothing existed beyond the echoes of pleasure rolling through her.

He rose and leaned over her with a smile of pure male pride. Realizing she wore a smile as well, she curled a hand around his nape and dragged him down for a kiss. Her tangy essence on his lips and tongue was indescribably arousing.

"That was amazing, Rafe."

"Believe me, I enjoyed it as much as you."

"Not quite as much, I don't think." A hint of nerves edged into her teasing lilt.

"We don't have to do more. We can get you dressed and ride back to Wintermarsh."

"What if I want more?"

The column of his throat worked against her hand. "You understand what you're asking?"

"I understand the mechanics. You'll bring me pleasure, won't you?"

"I'll try my damnedest," he said grimly and rose.

She sat on the edge of the table and attacked his waistcoat, her fingers trembling but successful. He shrugged it off and dropped it on top of her discarded clothing.

She rucked up his shirt so he could pull it over his head. Finally, his chest was bare and hers to behold. And behold she did, with eyes and hands. The planes and ridges of muscle jumped under her questing hands. Her gaze touched every scar, and soon her fingers and lips followed suit. She wondered at his strength, and not only the physical kind.

His hands rested on her thighs, occasionally jerking in reaction to her touch. Were his nipples as sensitive as hers? His eyes were half-lidded and stormy. She flicked her tongue across the flat disk of his nipple. He clutched her thighs, uncomfortably tight, and his head fell back. She suspected he enjoyed her attentions very much.

She dropped her hands to the fall of his breeches, and a shudder racked his body. His erection strained against the fabric. Fear and curiosity fought. She traced the contours of the hard ridge. She wanted this, wanted him, but she fumbled with the discs nonetheless.

"I'm surprised you haven't already popped a disc off," she said breathlessly to hide her trepidation.

Their fingers collided, two sets of hands frantic to slip the discs free. The fabric parted, and his erection jutted.

Not knowing exactly what to do, she skimmed her fingers up and down the length of him, barely making contact. Although he was iron hard, his skin was supple and soft. She explored the mushroom-shaped tip where fluid wept. Rubbing a finger over the end, she gathered the fluid and then, curious, licked her finger.

"Oh, Christ." He had been raptly watching her gentle explorations but stepped back to shuck boots and breeches in an instant. Settling himself between her legs, he ripped her chemise over her head. Finally, there were no barriers between them.

Except one—her maidenhead.

"Sweetheart, I don't want to hurt you. You're so small and tight, and I'm a damn brute." His voice was gruff and thick with an unidentifiable emotion.

"If you're trying to scare me, you've failed miserably. You make it sound so delicious. I find I'm rather partial to brutes."

"Are you sure? Please be sure. I'm not sure I can stop if we move to the bed. It's been a long time, and I want you badly." Desperation laced his plea.

She pulled his head down and offered her parted mouth. He stroked her back, pressing them close. The hair on his chest against her sensitive nipples coiled a now recognizable tension in her belly. He settled his erection against her opening, but he didn't try to enter her, only rubbed his length through her slick folds.

He slid his hands under her buttocks and lifted her off the table. "Wrap your legs around me."

She clamped him tightly, and they collapsed on the narrow mattress. He caught himself over her on his elbows but then fell to her side. His mouth closed over a nipple, and she bucked up. He pushed her flat before palming the other breast. The dual assault fuzzed her mind, but she worried all the pleasure would be hers, and he'd already done so much. She sought his erection, rubbing and squeezing, until he halted her with a laugh.

"Keep that up if you want this to end before it gets started."

"What do you mean?"

His laughter was muffled in her neck. "Let me touch you this first time, then, I promise, you can have a turn."

He pushed her legs wide, his thigh in between. Stroking and playing at her core, he settled his mouth back on her breast. There was no gentle climb to pleasure this time. He drove her hard, and she was thrown into a twisting maelstrom.

She writhed, dimly aware Rafe had shifted and now knelt between her legs. The head of his erection pressed inside of her still-pulsing channel. As he'd promised, he entered her an inch at a time. The invasion intensified her climax, extended it, and he cursed breathlessly, holding himself a few inches inside of her, until she came off the crest of pleasure.

Deeper he pushed, and her body stretched to accommodate him, the feeling uncomfortable but not painful. She knew what was to come, tried not to tense, but the anticipation was worse than the actual breaking of her maidenhead, and her gasp was more from surprise than pain.

"I'm sorry...so sorry..." His voice sounded foreign to her ears.

"It's fine. Are you almost there?" Her lungs couldn't pull in enough air.

"Almost," he bit out. He pushed forward another inch.

"Are you sure you'll fit?"

He gave a weak laugh, his breathing as labored as hers. "I will, I promise. You were made for me, but I'll stop right now if you want me to. Do you?" He held himself immobile, waiting.

He would. If she asked it of him, he would withdraw to save her from pain. Lightning streaked through her body, cracking into her heart and rushing through her ears. She loved him. No matter his faults, she loved him. More convenient if the blinding revelation had come when she was alone and could logically assimilate the ramifications. Now, all she could do was try to hide her sudden tears.

"No. I want all of you...even if it kills me." The words were forced from her tear-tightened throat.

"I don't think it will come to that." With one last push, he was seated to the hilt.

Sweat dotted his forehead, his face a study in pleasure and pain, his groan a combination as well. His muscles quivered under her hands. There was more, wasn't there?

"Are you still in pain?" he asked through clenched teeth. "Christ, I need to move."

"I'm ready." Her gaze darted from his face to the play of muscles along his arms and chest.

Rafe pulled almost all the way out of her and slowly pushed back in, a shudder slashing through his body.

"I wanted to make this good for you, but I'm not going to last. You feel bloody incredible." His voice was almost a growl. He dropped on top of her, his elbows bracketing her head.

His pace increased until he slammed into her. Cupping a buttock, he tipped her pelvis up. The change in angle and sensation wrung a moan from her on her next exhale. His every muscle stiffened into stone, and a warm torrent poured inside of her.

As if shot, he collapsed on top of her, lax and trembling. His shallow, rapid breaths blew hot across her neck. Closing her eyes, she wrapped her arms and legs around him, wanting to etch the moment into her memory. This interlude may be her one and only opportunity. She was happy under his weight and savored the feeling.

Too soon, he reversed their positions, slipping out of her and arranging her across his chest. Boneless, she sprawled, her head tucked under his chin, a single tear leaking out of the corner of her eye to wet the hair on his chest. He traced each vertebra along her spine and spread her hair across his shoulder.

They lay like that a long while, neither speaking. Eventually, he deposited her on the bed and rose. Pressing her face into the pillow, she listened to the ripple of water and the wringing of a cloth.

"It's cooled, I'm sorry for that. Let me clean you." No matter he'd kissed her there and ridden between her legs, the gentle cleansing felt just as intimate. A shy glance showed the cloth streaked with red, evidence of her societal ruination.

Naked, Rafe walked back to the basin and cleaned himself. Did her virgin blood mark him? Even while openly admiring his back and buttocks, she pulled the sheet up to her neck.

Tall and muscular, he appeared as hard as a marble statue, but not as unblemished. Countless thin scars crisscrossed his back. Not to mention the puckered flesh on his shoulder. His legs bore further evidence of his time during the war.

He returned to the bed, pulled her leg between his and wrapped her close. She tried to avoid his eyes, not sure she could hide her love. Titling her face, he forced her to meet his gaze, full of worry and regret. "I was too rough. I hurt you." It was a statement.

He attributed her avoidance to a pain he thought he'd caused, and she couldn't allow that. "No. Well, a bit at first, but that's to be expected isn't it? I have no complaints with your handling." Her smile seemed to satisfy him, and he let out a gusty sigh.

"You're sure?"

"Quite." The loss of her maidenhead troubled her less than her loss of control. Perhaps it was time to gain some back. "Is it my turn to explore you yet?"

"It's your turn," he said gruffly.

* * * * *

Minerva pushed him to his back and propped herself up on an elbow. The sheet was still tucked around her, but it gaped at the top, revealing the tops of her breasts and the barest hint of a nipple. He'd prefer to rip the sheet away entirely, but she was obviously still battling virginal shyness. Even so, he decided not to play the gentleman and enjoy the view.

What was she thinking? No distaste or repulsion crossed her face. Her eyes were wide, and she worried her bottom lip with teeth and tongue, making his cock twitch. Bloody hell, the thing had a mind of its own around her. In fact, he'd meant to pull out and spend on her stomach, but once inside of her, he'd been unable to control himself. The thought of the possible consequences didn't fire regret, only a grim satisfaction, even though a child would vastly complicate matters.

She ran her fingers through his hair and massaged his scalp. Smoothing his eyebrows with a thumb, she said, "I can tell when you're surprised, or happy, or amused, *or* feeling especially grumpy by your eyebrows, you know."

He didn't know. "Am I grumpy often?"

"Too often, but your smile…your smile makes my stomach flutter. You should do that more often." She traced his lips and leaned down to brush her mouth against his, but when he tried to deepen the kiss, she pulled back with a naughty smile. "No, no. It's my turn, remember?"

Her finger burned a path down the length of his scar all the way into his beard. He winced away as if it actually hurt, which it did, somewhere around his heart.

"Darling, no." She forced his face back around with a hand on his cheek. "You're ill at ease about your scar, but it's never bothered me. You're so handsome, and you're mine—at least for tonight."

More than one woman had gazed on him in pity. It turned out they didn't matter. Only she did, and her eyes blazed with acceptance and warmth and truth.

She advanced down the column of his throat, and he swallowed. Next, she skimmed a hand to his shoulder, circling the puckered skin of his bullet wound and onward to squeeze his biceps.

"Do you have any idea how appealing your strength is? As soon as I saw you in that alleyway, I knew that you wouldn't let them hurt me."

"I won't let anyone hurt you," he said fiercely, even knowing it was a promise he couldn't keep.

She hummed noncommittally while she tweaked his nipples. Shivers coursed straight to his cock, hardening him further. Deep breaths did nothing to get the monster under control. He absolutely could not take her again. He would end up breaking his promise in record time. The very thought of being the cause of her pain cemented his resolve to control the primal calling of his body.

After her hand grazed every scar that peppered his chest, she continued her journey south. There was no way she could overlook his engorged cock. Would she touch him? And would that lessen or intensify his agony?

He waited with a held breath for her decision. She rubbed a hand down his shaft from tip to base. A groan escaped, and his hips bucked into her touch. His cock twitched reflexively, and she pulled back as if bitten.

"Am I hurting you?"

He chuckled hoarsely, although there was nothing remotely funny. "'Tis pleasure it's reacting to. A firm touch is even better." Hell had already claimed his soul. He might as well teach her how to pleasure a man.

"Oh, like this?" A quick student, she clasped him tightly.

"You...you might need both hands."

"Something like this?" She sat up, the sheet falling to her waist, both hands wrapped around him. The view alone was worth going to hell for.

A coherent reply was beyond his ability. Her rosy-tipped bouncing breasts mesmerized him. While one hand stroked him, the other snaked to cup his bollocks. His seed erupted over her hand and onto his belly.

Flinging an arm over his eyes, he lay paralyzed. The mattress dipped, and she tried to tug the sheet from under him. With a huff of frustration, she scampered off the bed naked. He could have shifted off the sheet but selfishly wanted to ogle her pert breasts, rounded buttocks and long legs in motion.

She repeated the same task he undertook before, padding over to the washbasin to wring out the cloth. After cleaning her hands, she returned to wipe his belly. Her head stayed down, the curtain of her hair shielding her expression. She was a master at masking her emotions.

Before she could return the cloth, he grabbed her arms and forced her over him. "Was that too much? Did I scare you?"

Pushing her hair back, he cupped her cheeks and tilted her

face. Bubbling laughter poured out of her.

She propped her elbows on either side of his head. "Let me make something perfectly clear, Rafe Drummond. You weren't too rough, you didn't hurt me, and you didn't scare me. Far from it. I enjoyed everything we did. In fact, I only wish…" Her laughter faded, and her smile turned wistful.

"What you do you wish?" He would give anything to keep her happy and smiling.

A small shake of her head accompanied her words. "I wish for impossible things. Now, I'm hungry." She clambered off him, tossing her hair and smiling over her shoulder. "For food, I mean."

She snatched his shirt off the floor and slipped it over her head. It hung to her knees and she rolled the sleeves over her wrists. The front dipped between her breasts, and her hair was tangled around her face and down her back.

Was there a woman anywhere as beautiful? The painful twist in his stomach didn't feel much like hunger. It was more akin to regret. Or longing.

There was no use dwelling on something that could never be. She had accepted his physical scars, perhaps, but she had no idea how deep and black were the pits in his soul. And he never wanted her to find out.

By the time he rose, she had unpacked the hamper. She watched him from the fringe of her lashes, a blush staining her cheeks. After everything they'd done, how could she possibly be embarrassed? Not bothering to pull on any clothes, he tugged her into his arms and slipped his hands under his shirt to smooth over her bare bottom. Her blue eyes darkened.

Kissing her nose, he pulled out a chair for her and then pulled on his breeches. Along with the cold repast of cheeses, meats and bread, they sipped on a sweet wine. The conversation came easily, covering safe topics—the state of parliament, the state of the world, the state of their investments. Both of them steered clear of talk of the future.

As she packed the leftover food, she ran her hand across the wood grain of the table and another flush of color suffused her face. For once, he could read her thoughts like a favorite book.

"That was almost the best thing I've tasted on this table. Almost, but not quite," he said in a teasing tone. Her eyes flared, and he winked.

"Rafe, you are incorrigible."

Night had long since fallen and the fire burned low. "We should get back."

She nodded and gathered her clothes from the floor. Words threatened to spill out of him. How beautiful and wonderful she was. How special the day and evening had been. How he wished he could offer her everything she deserved. Nothing emerged from his constricted throat and dry mouth. Instead, he silently hooked her habit and pulled his shirt on, still warm from the heat of her body.

Clearing her throat, she broke the thick silence. "You'll not speak of this to anyone, I assume." Reflected in glowing orange embers, her face was a serene, opaque mask.

"My word as a gentleman." The ridiculousness of his answer hit him. He'd acted anything but. "You enter the house first. The servants will either be abed or still be in town. The revelry lasts well into the night."

It seemed neither of them knew what to say or do, and their manners were unusually formal and polite. They snuck back with no one the wiser. He took the horses and watched her scamper to the house, disappearing into the night. Their interlude was over.

CHAPTER EIGHTEEN

The morning sun woke her. Her gaze caught on the smallest details. Dust motes danced over the bed and leaves bounced outside the window, casting dappled, movable shadows. Individual blue threads of her canopy wove in and out of gold and cream to form delicate flowers. Her body too was sensitive. The sheet and her night rail abraded her breasts and lay heavy on her skin.

It had been no dream. Her imagination could never have done it justice. Forcing herself up, she was a bit sore, but no worse than after a long ride. She avoided the looking glass, didn't want to see the guilt and longing and sadness warring behind her eyes. Was she to act as if nothing had happened? And how was she to pretend she didn't love him?

She struggled to dress herself. Jenny's cheerful chattering would drive her around the bend. Her stomach sick with nerves, she left her room, looking back at her cold, empty bed. There was nothing for it but to confront reality. If he treated her as a stranger, she would retreat for a good cry and then force herself to do the same to him.

As if approaching a scene of carnage, she stood outside the study door. Propelling her shoulders back, she closed her eyes for an instant before knocking and entering. Instead of Rafe, Jenny sprang from the armchair. She mopped at her eyes with her white apron. A bucket of cleaning supplies sat at her feet.

Seeing it was Minerva, her tears flowed faster. Minerva rushed forward and took her hand. "Whatever is the matter?"

"It's Tom. He's told me to quit nagging him and find someone else to bother. He was quite mean about it." More tears welled.

Minerva pushed her back down to the chair, riffled through the cleaning basket and handed her a clean linen square. "Do you know what I think? I think he's terrified."

"Terrified of what?"

"You."

"Me? But why?"

As murky and confusing as her situation with Rafe, Minerva could see Jenny and Tom's dilemma with clarity. "He's afraid of the way you make him feel. He's afraid of being hurt by you. He thinks you're too beautiful and vivacious."

"But that's silly. I would never hurt him. I love him," she choked out, holding the handkerchief to her mouth again.

"Men are illogical creatures."

"What can I do? How can I make him understand?" Jenny gripped Minerva's hand, her eyes wide and trusting as if Minerva had the answers. It really was the blind leading the blind. Seduction was the only possibility that sprang to mind.

"Do you remember the advice from the other maid? About waiting for him in a state of dishabille?"

"I couldn't."

"No, I know. Instead, what if you borrow one of my dresses, and we fix a picnic basket. Offer him dinner and conversation, but privately. Make him understand you know what you want."

"It would have to be in the evening. What about Master Simon's old room in the stable?" Jenny's tears dried with the spark of hope and a plan.

"Yes, that would be perfect. Simon and I will help set the stage, but you must do the work of convincing him."

Minerva galvanized Jenny like a good field commander should and then made straight for the kitchens. At least her mind had something to worry over besides Rafe. She stumbled to a halt to find Simon and Mrs. Potts laughing over scones and a pot of tea.

"Hello there, Min. Come join us?" Simon asked casually.

"Yes, my lady, do come." Mrs. Potts reached for another cup and poured before Minerva had a chance to answer.

"Simon, I need a favor," Minerva said pointedly as she slid into a seat.

"Lord preserve us, Mrs. Potts, Minerva has a project. I recognize the gleam in her eye."

"Actually, perhaps both of you could be helpful." Minerva looked back and forth at them over the rim of her cup.

"Whatever can we help you with, dearie? Something to do with Master Rafe?" Mrs. Potts had a definite, disconcerting gleam in her eye as well, and Minerva choked on a swallow of tea. It only just occurred to her someone from Wintermarsh had assembled the food and lit the fires in Rafe's cabin last night.

Simon raised his eyebrows in an unspoken question, and Minerva was afraid her hot cheeks provided the unspoken answer.

"What? Not Lord Drummond. Whatever gave you that idea? Of course not. No, it's Tom and Jenny."

"What kind of help do they require?" Simon asked.

"Help of a romantic sort."

Guffaws spurted out. "You! *You* are playing matchmaker? *You*, who have spurned every gentleman who approaches with even a hint of romantic interest in his eye? This is going to be rich. I'll help if only to see what you're up to."

Minerva ignored his ribbing. "Tom has some misplaced sense of honor that Jenny could do better. That he's too old and staid for her. But she loves him to distraction, and I believe he loves her as well."

"You should have been named Cupid or Venus; not Minerva." Simon erupted in laughter again.

"Will you shut it, Simon." Minerva tried to sound annoyed, but it had been a long time since she and Simon had teased each other like siblings. A giggle escaped, which made Simon laugh even harder.

Grinning, Mrs. Potts tutted. "I think it's a grand idea to push the two lovebirds together. What did you have in mind, my lady?"

She laid out her idea. Mrs. Potts agreed to fix a basket with some of her best treats while Simon would discover Tom's schedule for the next several days. Minerva would make sure the room was cozy and comfortable.

She and Simon strolled back toward the drawing room together. "Where's Lord Drummond?" she asked.

A list of explanations scrolled in the instant before Simon answered. He was avoiding her. He'd gone to London. He was sick. He was—

"A roof collapsed on one of the barns on the north side of the estate, and he's gone to see about repairs."

"I see." A long exhale followed.

Simon's brow furrowed as he examined his boots. "Minerva, is there anything you need me to know? Do I need to talk to Lord Drummond about—" he waved his hands around, stirring the air, "—things?"

"No," she said shortly. "I appreciate you playing my brother, but please, leave things be."

"Playing your brother?" He sounded affronted. "I *am* your brother, and you are sister to a duke. If there's action that should be taken—"

"It's complicated, and I'm not sure how things will unfold.

But I would appreciate if you would let me handle things." Simon's troubled eyes, the same piercing blue as her own, searched for truth in her face. She looked away before he could find it.

"I admire Drummond and would count him a friend. But if he hurts you, make no mistake, he'll pay dearly."

Minerva hugged him around the waist, thankful for the sentiment but hoping it wouldn't come to anything so dire. Rafe would destroy Simon, no matter how much stronger Simon had become over the autumn.

Later that evening, Simon found her in the drawing room to inform her that Rafe and Tom were taking Aries to stud the next day at a neighboring farm. They would be gone all afternoon. A perfect opportunity to set the trap.

A commotion echoed off the marble at the front door. Tension had built all day. The anxiety of not knowing how he would look at her shredded her stomach. She stepped outside the study door, feet braced apart as if waiting for the blow. Their gazes locked while he handed Cuthbertson his hat and coat. He strode over, dusty from his day, stopping a few feet away.

"How are you?" he asked, his voice rusty.

"I'm well. And you? Is the roof repaired?"

"I'm well. No rain will wet the hay."

The emotion weaved in their tones contradicted the polite, trite exchange of words.

Rafe cleared his throat. "I thought after I bathed I might read aloud to you this evening."

Simon, who had been leaning against the doorjamb, piped up, "So long as it's not the Bible or some tome on philosophy."

"Shakespeare, perhaps? *The Tempest.*"

The Tempest. She had no idea what it was about, but the name seemed apropos.

Two hours later, Rafe snapped the book closed and stretched

like a cat. The cadence and beauty of his voice had enthralled her. Even Simon had been unusually attentive.

"That was lovely, Rafe. Will you read more tomorrow evening?"

Ducking his head, he touched his scar. "If you wish."

"I wish," she said, unsuccessfully trying to catch his eye.

"You should both retire. I have some paperwork to attend to this evening. I bid you good night." He was gone before she could formulate a reply.

He hadn't ignored her, but neither had he acknowledged there might be anything more between them than the barest of friendships. He had made things perfectly clear. One interlude.

The problem, of course, was she yearned for more than one brief interlude. Actually, the bigger problem was she loved him, but he didn't know and probably never would. There was a month left until their agreement was satisfied. Couldn't he allow them a month of happiness? She wouldn't mention the future or love. For once in her life, she would live in the moment.

What if she took the little maid's advice? What if she waited for Rafe in a state of undress? On the steps to her room, her courage faltered. What if he denied her? Sent her back to her cold bed? Perhaps tomorrow night, she'd locate her bravery.

After undressing, she held her night rail in both hands. The soft fabric irritated her overly sensitive skin, and she dropped it to the chair. The cool linen sheets soothed her. Really, sleeping naked wouldn't rival the most scandalous thing she had done in the last twenty-four hours.

* * * * *

Pacing in his study, Rafe scrubbed his face and nearly bellowed. He couldn't even make it a night without her. It was either drink his weight in brandy or indulge in a much more pleasurable but no less destructive vice.

The urgency to have her overruled any misgivings he harbored. It wasn't fair to her, this clandestine affair. He stood outside her bedroom door, looking up and down the hall. Perhaps she'd locked him out. That really would be for the best.

He prayed she hadn't. The latch opened under his trembling hand, and his tension dissipated into the welcoming darkness. Slipping inside, he allowed his eyes to adjust, her deep, even breathing marking time.

He should take her quickly in the dark. Slake his desire and retreat to his room, leaving her to sleep alone. He wouldn't though. He needed to see the desire in her eyes, wanted to explore her supple curves, craved the blush that suffused her skin as she climaxed.

After lighting a handful of candles along the mantle, a soft glow bathed the room. Her back was to him, but the sheet outlined the rounded curve of her hip and long length of her legs.

He disrobed, dropping his clothes in a path from mantle to bed, finally slipping under the sheets. Encountering smooth, bare skin, he clutched her hip. Bloody hell, she was stark naked. His control wavered.

Stirring at his touch, she arched her back and stretched into him, her bare bottom nestling around his hard cock. He thrust into the cleft.

"Is this a dream? Tell me it's not a dream." Longing colored her sleep-roughened voice.

"Have you been dreaming about my cock?" He cursed his tongue. He should shower her with pretty words and compliments. She didn't seem to mind, scooting into him and pushing his hand between her legs. He found her wet and ready and drove his finger deep. Her throaty moan was nearly his undoing.

He cupped her breast and lightly pinched her nipple. "I haven't been able to stop thinking about you. I want you writhing under me. Do you hate me for coming to you like this?"

She writhed against him already, her voice thin with desire. "I can't stop thinking about you either. If you hadn't come, I would have waited in your bed tomorrow night. What does that make me?"

"Utterly delightful. Almost makes me wish I had a bit more self-control. Almost."

He pushed her on her back and knelt between her thighs, poised at her entrance. He rubbed the head of his cock through her folds, circling her nub. A guttural groan ripped from her. Once he entered her, he wouldn't be able to concentrate on her pleasure.

"Look. Look at us," he commanded.

Minerva raised herself on her elbows, watching raptly. Holding the base of his cock, he pressed inside her a few inches before pulling out to rub the glistening head over her again. He pushed inside of her a little farther before pulling out and repeating the torture over and over again.

Her neck arched, her skin flushed, and she clamped him inside of her with a cry, falling back into the pillows. The sight of her open to him, the smell of her arousal, and the tight hold of her body overloaded his senses. He lost all semblance of gentleness, pounding hard until his seed released in a wash of pleasure.

He rolled to his back, cuddling her against his side, her head pillowed on his scarred shoulder. "Did I hurt you?"

Her reply was a sigh and a sleepy snuffling.

Several minutes passed before his heart rate and breathing slowed to normal levels. Again, his traitorous body had released inside of her. As long as they were under the same roof, he wouldn't be able to stay out of her bed. The image of her round with his babe annihilated a fleeting thought of sending her away.

Would it be so horrible if she were forced to stay at Wintermarsh? Perhaps not for him, but for her it might be. She belonged in London, not cloistered in the country with him. Would she hate him if the decision was thrust upon her through his recklessness?

Pushing away thoughts of the morrow, he would hold her until dawn forced him to sneak back to his bed like a thief. Gathering her close, he fell into a deep, dreamless sleep.

CHAPTER TWENTY

She searched with sleepy hands, finding only cool linen and a squashed pillow. She was alone. And heartbreakingly lonely. Still, he'd come to her, so hope was not yet gone.

Mustering her energy, she waited until Tom and Rafe departed with Aries and then cleaned the little stable room. Fresh flowers, fresh sheets—just in case—and sweet-smelling evergreen branches made the room inviting and romantic.

Minerva dragged Jenny to the blue bedroom late in the afternoon and ordered a bath. Playing her maid, Minerva combed and styled her hair and dressed her in a blue scoop-necked muslin dress. Jenny spun in the looking glass, her color high with excitement, but once in the stables, she paced, leaving an ever-lengthening track in the dirt floor.

"What do I do and say once he's here? I feel like my heart is going to explode out my chest." Jenny rubbed the skin above the neckline of her gown.

Minerva leaned on Sparrow's door, scratching the mare's forelock and watching Jenny's nervous meandering. "You'll know what to say when the time comes. Tell him what's in your heart."

"There's enough food to feed ten men in here." Simon hauled a basket into the stables and set it down with a thunk. He rubbed and stretched his arm but froze when he saw Jenny. His head jutted forward, and his eyes popped. "Bloody hell—pardon the language, ladies—but you look positively glorious, Jenny. Tom's a goner."

More than any of Minerva's advice and words of wisdom, Simon's compliment lent Jenny some ease. "Do you really think so, sir?"

Simon tutted and shook his head. "He's done for, the poor blighter. Might as well read the banns now." He checked his fob. "They'll be home soon. Why don't you lay out the food, and Minerva and I will wish you luck. As if you need it."

Jenny nodded, a relieved smile on her face. "Thank you both."

Minerva gave her a hug and followed Simon around the corner.

She glanced at her brother several times on their walk back to the house. His expression perfectly serene and with his eyes straight ahead, he asked, "Do I have a hairy mole growing out of my cheek or something?"

Minerva sputtered a little laughter. "No, I'm wondering how you did that."

"Did what?"

"Relieved Jenny's nerves and gave her the confidence to believe it would all work out with a few words. I've been droning on all afternoon trying to settle her down."

"No offense, but being on the receiving end of your droning lectures, I can attest to the fact they never work. Anyway, you forget, while Jenny relayed information to you, I witnessed firsthand the progression of their courtship when I stayed in the stables. Tom is smitten with the chit. If this ploy doesn't crumble his defenses, he doesn't deserve her."

She took his hand and swung his arm like a child. "Simon, you've been full of surprises this autumn. I don't think I have to worry about you anymore."

Simon smiled a knowing smile and squeezed her hand. "No, you don't. I'll be fine. You need to start thinking to your own happiness."

She tucked her hand in his elbow and leaned the side of her face against his shoulder to hide a sudden rush of tears. When had her dissolute, immature, wayward brother become so wise?

* * * * *

That went better than I expected, but I hate leaving Aries in a strange stable, even one as agreeable as Lord Wyndam's," Rafe said.

"Aye, my lord. Aries acquitted himself well. Do you trust Wyndam to mount him again tomorrow without you?" Tom asked.

"Wyndam's an outstanding horseman. I wouldn't allow Aries's progeny to be raised by anyone less." The need to be home had outweighed his duty to Aries. Anticipation thrummed in his blood.

They dismounted and led the horses inside the stable. Darkness had fallen, but a soft glow lit Simon's old room. He would flay someone's hide if a flame had been left unattended amongst the highly flammable hay. Apparently, Tom had the same thought and shoved the door open.

Tom's chin dropped. He put a hand on the doorjamb and leaned into it as if suddenly ill. Worried, Rafe looked over Tom's shoulder, his eyebrows bouncing high at the cozy room and spread of food.

"Lass, what are you doing here?" Tom's voice was barely more than a whisper.

"Waiting for you, Tom." Jenny's chin tipped up, her face set in determined lines.

Tom's convulsive swallow was audible. "Wh-why?"

"Because you're worth fighting for, Tom Donahue. And I warn you now, I mean to win." Jenny cocked out a hip and cast a surprisingly sensual smile toward Tom.

"I have a feeling it won't be a hardship to surrender to you, lass." Tom voice was rough. "You did all of this for me?"

Tom seemed to have lost the ability to move, so Rafe shoved him into the room and grabbed the door latch to pull it shut. It seemed Jenny and Tom might need a cottage soon. Rafe took up the horse's reins and led them farther into the stables. After rousing a couple of the lads, he gave them instructions and headed straight to the drawing room.

He stood in the doorway observing Minerva pace around the room. She stopped occasionally, fingers pulling at her lower lip.

"Am I to assume you have pushed my stable manager and your favorite maid into a tryst?" Rafe asked, startling her around, her hair flying over one shoulder.

"You're home." Relief and happiness lit her like a candle.

Her brief statement hit him in the chest like a punch, flipping his good mood on its head. Home. A beautiful woman waited for him at home. How long would it last? How long before she left him? A corrupt, unfair anger at the Fates welled, and unfortunately, Minerva was the only one to take it out on.

"I take it you saw Jenny. How did Tom react?" The picture of excitement, she scurried over to lay a hand on his arm, no matter the road-weary condition of his jacket.

"How is it to end, Minerva? Will Jenny be ruined or will Tom be trapped?"

She removed her hand and lifted guarded eyes toward his face. "Neither, I hope. Does it have to end badly? What about love and marriage? That sounds like a good ending to me."

"That only happens in fairytales. Don't be naive. Tom is a man, like any other, who will take what's offered and walk away."

Her breathing hitched, nostrils flaring. "*Tom* will do that, will he? I think not. He's not a coward. He'll hold on to Jenny because she loves him—no matter his faults." With her mouth clamped shut and shaking her head in frustration or maybe disgust, she stalked past him and slammed the door on her exit.

Staring at the empty space she'd left, Rafe fisted a hand in his hair. Could Minerva possibly care for him? And did it really change anything? Maybe she could and maybe it did change things. He sank in a chair, his knees embarrassingly weak.

* * * * *

Minerva woke the next morning. Alone. She'd been alone all night. Her pride and anger had not been good bedfellows, and she'd tossed and turned in restless frustration throughout the night. When she had managed to sleep, Rafe plagued her dreams.

Anxious to find Jenny and hear about the evening, she sped through her ablutions and scurried downstairs. She found Simon behind the study desk, scribbling notes in a ledger with intense concentration. The sight stole her words, and she watched the efficient dip of quill in amazement.

Glancing up, he smiled and rose after marking his progress. "Good morning."

"Have you seen Jenny or Tom this morning?"

"As a matter of fact, Cuthbertson told Mrs. Devlin who told Mrs. Potts, who summarily told me, that Tom asked for the morning off, and he and Jenny went to the village to see her father."

Minerva hopped and clapped her hands like a child. Faith in humankind, the male species in particular, was restored. "How wonderful."

"What's wonderful?" A low voice drawled from the study door, drawing their attention.

Dressed casually in buckskins and a waistcoat, Rafe leaned against the doorjamb, one booted foot crossed over the other. His barely contained energy simmered. He appeared well rested. Damn him.

"Tom has gone to Lipton to ask Black John for Jenny's hand. That's what's wonderful." She barely resisted the urge to stick her tongue out at him.

He pushed off the door with his shoulder and meandered farther into the room. "I have to go to Wyndam's to see if Aries has done his duty by their little mare and bring him home." He picked up a letter opener and traced a scar on the top of his desk with the pointed end, his eyes attending the task. "Would you care to accompany me, Minerva?"

Hours alone in his company? Pride could go to the devil. "I would love to."

"Lady Wyndam is close to your age. She was out last season. Do you know her?"

"I'm not sure we were ever introduced."

"You'll like her. You'll like them both, I believe. If we leave soon, we can be there before luncheon." Rafe tossed the opener on the desk with a clang.

"Let me go change into my habit, and I'll meet you in the stable." She nearly tripped over her feet on the way out the room, rolling her eyes at her own foolishness.

They rode off under grey skies, and Minerva tugged her gloves higher to stave off the brisk wind slipping up her sleeves. It was a two-hour ride north.

She intercepted half a dozen hesitant glances before he broke down. "I'm sorry I upset you last night, Minerva. Sometimes the devil gets ahold of my tongue." The sincerity in his voice and face were real.

"I missed you last night. I'd hoped…" Heat rushed over her face in spite of the cool air.

Rafe strangled out a laugh. "I'd hoped too. You can't imagine my crushing disappointment to find my bed empty. But it was no less than what I deserved."

"I'm sorry."

"You have nothing to be sorry for, sweetheart."

He sat his horse fluidly, his apology seeming to bring him

peace. Now she was the one casting nervous, furtive glances in his direction. "You can say you don't wish to discuss it, and I won't press you, but will you tell me how you were so gravely injured?"

He didn't even acknowledge that he'd heard her speak, staring into the distance, his eyes disengaged. "It's not a happy tale."

"Happy or not, it's shaped you, and I want to understand," Minerva whispered, the moment vitally important. Not necessarily the content of his story, but the fact he was willing to open the door to a dark part of his soul. Faltering at first, his voice grew stronger, his memories painting a vivid scene for her. Soon, she wasn't on a brown, dirt-packed lane in England, but in lush, green France.

* * * * *

The spring had been unusually rainy. The heavy fighting was centered south in Portugal and Spain, however, intrigue abounded in France where Bonaparte ruled. Rafe had been crisscrossing France for a month, staying a few steps ahead of his French counterparts. His first mission had been successfully completed with only minor bloodshed. Thankfully, none of it his.

He read over his next assignment again, hoping he'd decoded the missive incorrectly. No such luck. He crumpled it in his fist, dropped it in the fire and black smoke rose to the trees. An English baron's French-born widow was using her late husband's military affiliations to pass intelligence to the French. Beautiful and amoral, she used her body to obtain information from the sex-starved English officers. Rafe was to infiltrate her compound and eliminate her.

A multitude of horrific deeds riddled his conscience, but he had never killed a woman. It was a murky line he refused to venture over. He was to rendezvous with another agent for details. The man could go to hell. He wasn't taking the assignment.

The next evening, Rafe pushed open the rotting door of a seedy, back-alley tavern. Only a handful of men populated the tables, but they provided enough of a din to mask any conversation. He lurked at the door, letting his eyes adjust to the dim light and smoky conditions. Scanning the occupants, he muttered a curse.

His contact slumped in a chair and pretended to sip on the swill they served, surveying the room as if he hadn't a care in the world. Rafe knew differently—the man's green eyes missed nothing. Rafe didn't know whether to hug the bastard or gut him.

The only chair faced away from the door, and Rafe rolled his eyes, hooking a foot around it. "You managed to get the best seat in the house as usual."

"Of course, because I'm always early and invariably prepared." Gray Masterson smiled slyly. They both spoke in fluent French.

"How in hell did you get assigned this debacle and why the devil involve me? I won't do it."

Gray's easy grin faded. "I know. That's why it must be you. Some of our counterparts would be only too glad to slit her throat after they take advantage of her person in other ways, I'm sure."

Unfortunately, that was true. "What's the alternative then? If we don't eliminate the target, someone else will."

"The plan in motion will neutralize her influence." Gray leaned in. "A French agent has her young son and has been using him as leverage to force her cooperation. She's gotten desperate, made mistakes. Her heart's not with the cause but with her son. If we get the boy, she'll retreat to Switzerland, never to be heard from again."

"Who has him?"

"He's in Chevret with a man named Armand Desmarais."

Rafe rubbed his nape and sighed.

"You're familiar with him?"

"He's a cruel bastard. How did he get stuck playing nursemaid? Christ, I would rescue the child whether we needed the mother's cooperation or not. There's no end to the man's depravity." The increasing complexity of the situation brought on a headache.

"Can you get him out?" Gray asked.

"How old is he?"

"Around eight."

"That's easier than a squalling babe, I suppose. What about Demarais? Should I eliminate him?"

Gray looked to his ale, rubbing a finger across his lips. "It's not officially part of our orders, but you'll not hear any wailing or gnashing of teeth from the Home Office if it becomes necessary."

"Once I have the boy, where do we meet?"

"The farm. Two days hence. I'll bring the woman and escort them both to the border."

"Good enough." Rafe stood, pulling his hat low over his eyes. "Good luck, old friend."

"The same," Gray replied, his mouth tight and his eyes worried.

Chevret was an old French village with a large cathedral dominating the center. Demarais had acquired a spacious house within sight of the looming spires. Rafe surveyed his residence for the first day and a half. People who were comfortable tended to settle into a routine, and Demarais was very comfortable indeed. He strolled through the streets with no protection and received well-dressed visitors during the afternoons. Two whores visited the first evening but left looking disheveled and alarmed. Not surprising given the rumors of the man's proclivities.

Rafe never saw the boy, but he didn't question Gray's intelligence. He was there. Rafe could almost feel him. It would be tonight. He couldn't stomach leaving an innocent in there any longer.

Rafe moved silently through the deserted garden to a little-used door. After spreading grease on the hinges, he picked the lock and eased it open. A twinge of misgiving bothered him. Demarais was too valuable to leave himself so vulnerable.

He stood inside the door, got his bearings, and listened for movement. There was none. A frisson of warning zinged up his spine, but he continued on, determined to finish it. Flying up the main staircase three steps at a time, he hid in shadows at the top. Only the steady cadence of a clock cut the silence and ratcheted up his anxiety tick by tick.

Based on information he'd obtained from the whores, he knew where Demarais's rooms lay. He padded down the opposite hall, systematically checking the doors. All of them were unlocked, the rooms unoccupied. Until he came to the last one. In only a few seconds, he had the door unlocked, tucked the picks back into his pocket, and pushed the door open with the toe of his boot, half-expecting an ambush.

He eased inside, his gaze sweeping around the room, gauging the danger. A small creature huddled in the middle of the bed. Rafe's heart constricted. No blankets covered the painfully thin boy. Rage urged him to the other end of the house to slit Demarais's throat. Deep breaths calmed the vicious compulsion. That was not the mission.

He covered the child's mouth and gingerly shook him. If the boy panicked, he would have to subdue him, but his conscience rebelled at putting the child through further torment. The boy came awake with only a slight grunt and stared up with round, dark eyes.

Rafe whispered a half-truth, "Your mother has sent me to bring you to her, but you must stay very quiet." The boy blinked vacantly. "Nod if you understand me, lad."

Life flared in the boy's face, and he nodded.

"Get dressed in something dark."

The boy's lips were pasted tightly together, and he shook his head, holding up the thin, dirty shirt he wore.

"You have no other clothes, is that it?" The boy nodded again. "Well, come along, we'll make do."

The boy scrambled off the bed, and Rafe's gaze cut to the window in dismay. The welts running up and down his bony legs incited another blast of fury. Damn Demarais. Shrugging off his jacket, he put it around the boy, buttoned it, and rolled up the sleeves. The boy's hands poked out the ends and with his gaunt face and shadowed eyes, it called to mind caricatures from Rafe's childhood storybooks depicting wraiths in hell. Perhaps this place was a version of hell.

The bedroom looked over the garden, one floor from the ground. An easy jump for Rafe, but he worried the lad might break like a dry, brittle twig under a boot. He couldn't take the chance. A stroll back through the house it would have to be.

Rafe picked up the boy and swung him around to hang onto his neck and down his back. The boy locked his ankles around Rafe's waist. The boy's weight barely registering, Rafe relocked the door once they were in the hall. Who knew if Demarais made a habit of checking on him? Time was an important commodity.

Rafe moved like a whisper down the stairs and out the garden door. On the street, he trotted with the boy still on his back. His horse waited at a nearby inn, and if the hostler thought it odd a half-starved boy clung to him like a barnacle, he made no mention of it.

After mounting, he settled the boy across his lap, wishing he had a cloak for them both. It had started to mist, the heavy air portending a deluge. Rafe adjusted the collar of his jacket to shield the boy as best he could. It would be a miserable ride.

He left Chevret at a fast clip, the muscles along his shoulders relaxing with every mile. He should feel satisfaction at a job completed, but worries remained. Demarais had left himself wide-open and unprotected. A cruel man, yes, but not a stupid one.

Dawn streaked the sky on the approach to their rendezvous. The abandoned farm lay in a valley not yet touched by the sun's unfurling tendrils. The dark clouds fled to the west, promising a beautiful spring day. Rafe rode the perimeter, birds and squirrels chattering and on the move. There was no trampled undergrowth from clumsy boots. Nothing appeared disturbed. He broke from the trees toward the dilapidated barn, which sat behind an equally rundown farmhouse.

The field, long left fallow, burst with blooming flowers. It was easy to believe in peace in a place like this. Easy to convince yourself there was no war and ugliness in the world. But the boy asleep in his arms would forever feel the effects of being a pawn in this terrible game.

Sunlight revealed the extent of the injuries inflicted on his young body. Bruises, some old, some glaringly new, riddled his legs and face. No wonder Demarais couldn't allow the boy out of the house. And for what purpose? The boy knew nothing. It was pure depravity. Rafe's hold tightened, and the boy stirred.

Sitting up, he looked around in wonder, and then cut eyes to Rafe, the question clear.

"She'll be here soon if she isn't waiting for you already." Rafe didn't care if his mother was guilty or innocent. This boy needed her more than England needed to eliminate one more spy.

He dismounted with the boy cradled in his arms and set him carefully on the ground. The boy took a few unsteady steps into the dim interior of the barn. It was empty.

"My friend is bringing her. We'll wait."

The boy sank to a mound of hay, his knees noticeably trembling. Rummaging through his saddlebag, Rafe pulled out bread, cheese and a skein of water. The boy hovered over the food and shoved hunks of bread into his mouth until Rafe stilled him with a pat.

"Slowly, lad, slowly. I know you're fair to starving, but you'll make yourself sick. It's all for you." Giving a quick nod, the boy slowed, but he never took his eyes off the food as if Rafe might steal it back at any moment.

Every minute that passed increased Rafe's anxiety. Hidden in the shadows, he kept his gaze trained on the horizon. Only when he spotted Gray could he relax. The sun was high overhead when two riders appeared, one unmistakably Gray. The small meal had coaxed the boy to sleep. Soon, perhaps, this would seem like a bad dream.

Rafe shook him awake. The two riders approached through the flowered field. The boy slipped his hand into Rafe's, wrapping thin fingers around two of his larger ones.

The woman dismounted, her velvet blue riding habit swirling a cloying perfume over them as greeting. Gray kept his seat, his mount snorting and sidestepping. The woman snatched the boy from Rafe, hugged, and peppered him with kisses. The boy shared her coloring, but his bony body and rags were in sharp contrast to her well-dressed, well-fed roundness. He stood hollowly in her embrace, not returning the hug. The woman let go of the boy with tears in her eyes, but the smile on her lips set the hairs on the back of Rafe's neck up.

Gray left his horse grazing and stepped into the barn, his gaze darting. Rafe had known Gray since birth. Something was amiss.

The woman looked to Gray. "When can we leave this horrid place?"

The boy sidled back to Rafe and pulled at his sleeve. Rafe knelt down, eye to eye with the boy. While Gray offered vague assurances to the woman, the boy spoke for the first time. In English. "That's not my mama. That's my auntie. They look alike."

The woman had not heard her nephew's confession. The mission hadn't felt right from the beginning. One or both of them had been followed. Rafe rose, closed his eyes and breathed great lungfuls of air. A moment of peace before all hell broke loose.

When he opened his eyes, Gray stared at him, and Rafe shook his head.

"A trap?" Gray asked.

"Indubitably." He kicked a rotten stable door open and pulled at hay and canvas, uncovering loaded pistols, knives, sabers and even a quarterstaff. He stuck two pistols in his belt, along with a couple of knives and tossed Gray an assortment of weapons. "At least it won't be a complete surprise, thanks to your nephew, madam."

"What is this? You promised to save us." The hip she thrust out and the hand that smoothed her hair tempered her faked outrage.

They ignored her. "I knew something was amiss, but she looks exactly like Amelia and had all the right answers." Gray shook his head with a grimace.

"I knew too. Getting the boy out was too damn easy." Rafe prowled the perimeter of the barn and examined the trees for any hint of movement.

Gray stalked the woman into a stall door, asking rapid-fire questions she attempted to parry.

"Where is Amelia?" he asked for the third time.

"In hell. Where all French traitors will go. She was weak. He made her weak. Don't worry, you'll be joining her soon enough." She spit at his feet.

The boy's face had blanched. Even his lips were colorless. There was no time for tears and comfort. It was a time for survival. Rafe tossed him in the loft and instructed him to cover himself with hay.

Rafe sensed rather than saw movement at the edge of the forest. "They're here."

Gray tied the woman's hands with a length of rope and shoved her into a stall. Rafe and Gray faced each other. They didn't need words, hugging fiercely and standing back to back.

The onslaught wasn't long in coming. Men poured into both sides of the barn. Rafe immediately discharged both pistols killing two, and Gray did the same. A few soldiers had muskets, but after accidently killing one of their own in the tight space, everyone reached for blades.

Although outnumbered, Gray and Rafe were better trained, stronger, and experienced. After the first few men went down, fear lurked behind the soldiers' eyes and in their tentative attacks. Rafe smiled, wiping another man's blood from his cheek. The tide was turning.

Movement at the ladder drew his eye. The woman had freed herself and was climbing to the loft. A knife glinted, clamped between her teeth.

"Gray, the loft!"

Gray shot a quick look up and cursed. "Go. I can handle...the...rest." He kneed one man in the crotch and elbowed another in the neck before slashing his belly open with a long-bladed knife.

A soldier with matted hair and twisted lips aimed a punch at Rafe's chest. He was no more than ten and eight. Rafe hesitated a moment, the woman was three quarters of the way up the ladder, then he shattered the bony cap of the soldier's knee with his boot heel. Rafe left him to roll in agony. His screams sent a handful of men retreating through the thigh-high flowers.

Rafe jumped three rungs high and grabbed at the woman's ankles, but she scampered over the top. The ladder was old and rotten, and the next rung snapped under his foot. A high-pitched wail cut to his soul.

Rafe cleared the top, embedded splinters shooting pain into his hands. The woman kneeled over the boy, blood painting a horrific tableau over the hay. Rafe's stomach swooped as if he'd fallen backward, but numb fingers held him on the rickety ladder. Blood dripped slowly from the knife in contrast to the blood rushing like a river through his ears, muffling the clashing metal and guttural yells from below.

Murder bloomed in his heart, streaking out to prod his body into motion. He launched himself into the loft, and the woman kicked out to keep him at bay, but she was no match for his size and strength.

He grabbed at her legs and pulled. She scrabbled uselessly at the hay. Inexorably, he dragged her closer to the edge, and she screamed when she hit the ground. Rafe landed like a cat beside her, but she was up in an instant, throwing herself at him with a viciousness he had never encountered in any man. A burning along his cheek obscured his vision. He rubbed at his eye, clearing blood, but it kept flowing. Jesus, he was going die at the hands of an insane Frenchwoman.

His hands found her throat, and with a sense of justice—or maybe vengeance—he squeezed. She dropped the knife and clawed at his hands. The image of the boy's body bleeding out obscured any gentlemanly inclinations. Imminent death reflected in her bulging eyes. All he felt was satisfaction.

A shot rang out and where the woman's face had been was a bloody mass of skin and tissue. He opened his hands, and the woman body crumpled at his feet. He couldn't seem to tear his gaze away from the destruction.

"I have a bullet for you too, Rafe Drummond. You should have killed me when you had the chance. May you rot in hell." Armand Demarais stood with two pistols, one with smoke curling out the end.

Rafe tensed himself for impact, but as Demarais took aim and fired, a knife flew end over end to plant itself in Demarais's upper arm. Excruciating pain tore from Rafe's shoulder to every extremity. Gray finished Demarais off, his death keen an eerie echo of the boy's.

Every inch of Rafe's body burned, and he lacked the ability to shuffle to the nearest pile of hay. His face throbbed with each beat of his heart, and his vision drew in on itself. The barn disappeared. There was only Gray's face, pulled taut in worried lines, red painting the furrows.

Blood loss took its toll. His brain moved like honey on a winter's day, and his tongue thickened in his mouth. Gray poked and prodded his shoulder. Pressure around the wound increased and eased the pain somewhat. Rafe turned his head to see cloth stuffed into his mangled jacket to stem the bleeding.

Gray's face ducked into his line of sight again. "We have to move, Rafe. The bullet went straight through, thankfully, but you need a doctor. Those men will be back with reinforcements."

"The...l-lad. I wasn't...f-fast enough." Rafe pointed, and Gray nodded, his face aged a decade in the last hour.

"You have to ride, brother. Can you make it to old Mary's cottage? We'll be safe there."

Gray looked desperately worried, which in turn worried Rafe. "D-do I look that bad? I'll make it."

It was a damn miracle he made it to Mary's. Chills racked his body even with the warm sun. He almost passed out half a dozen times and ended up draped over his horse's neck, blood soaking the mane. Once at Mary's cottage, he let himself slip into oblivion.

It was better that way. There was no doctor, so Gray arduously cleaned and stitched Rafe's wounds. Fever set in a day later, and Rafe roved in and out of consciousness.

Gray bribed a smuggler captain to get them back to England and left him in the care of a doctor in Dover. Lily rushed to claim him and take him home to Wintermarsh. Rafe didn't remember much from that time. The fever took another month to run its course, but he was strong and his body healed.

Night after night, he tried to beat the woman up that ladder. Night after night, he woke, out of breath and sweating, never saving the boy.

CHAPTER TWENTY

After Rafe fell silent, Minerva was surprised to find herself on a horse in England. She felt like she'd been by his side in France. If they weren't mounted, she might throw herself in his arms, pepper him with kisses, and confess her love. She cleared her throat. "I'm so thankful you didn't die in France."

"Me too," he said gruffly.

"What was the boy's name?"

"Christopher. Not a day goes by that I don't think of him."

"Rafe, the night I woke you from the nightmare…were you dreaming about that woman?"

His leather-clad hands flexed around the reins. "She had you up in that loft, and I couldn't save you. You can't imagine how helpless I felt."

The sun peeked through the grey clouds, revealing twin stone cairns flanking a grassy, unkempt carriage trail. "Here's the start of Wyndam's estate. Race you there?" It was obvious he wanted to leave France behind. Without answering, she dug her heels into Sparrow's side and leapt ahead of him.

"You minx!"

She leaned over and pushed her mount harder, taking full advantage of her head start. With the stables in sight, she slowed to a walk. He pulled up beside her, their horses chuffing and lathered. She tried to smile at him. He'd trusted her with something precious—his memories. The last thing he wanted was her pity, yet she was having a difficult time keeping from blurting out her love.

"I won," she said in a singsong voice that cracked just a little.

"You're a cheater and lucky Aries was otherwise occupied." The twitching corners of his mouth and the twinkle in his eyes seemed genuine. She shook off her melancholy and smiled tremulously back.

After dismounting, they handed their mounts off to a young groom. New wood abutted greying planks, giving the stables the air of a patchwork quilt. The main house was similar in size to Wintermarsh but centuries older. The remnants of a moat circled the castle-like manor, and a small wooden bridge spanned the empty trough to the front door. Four turrets sat on each corner with narrow window slits. The structure was a mixture of grey and brown stone—rough, jagged enormous blocks. Although charming, it shared a sense of dilapidation with the stables.

"It's like stepping back in time." She walked close enough to brush the back of his hand with a finger.

Out of the door emerged a tall man with sandy blond hair and a lean whipcord body in accord with the wolfhound trotting by his side. A pair of worn, faded buckskins encased his long legs and a patched brown jacket topped a plain white shirt. If he hadn't looked vaguely familiar, she might have mistaken him for a groom.

"Drummond. Splendid timing. I was headed to the paddock. Aries is quite the stallion." The man's Irish brogue identified him as lord of the manor.

"Marcus Ashemore, Lord Wyndam, may I present Lady Minerva." Rafe gestured toward Minerva.

"It's my pleasure to welcome you to our humble, crumbling abode. I'm not sure I had the honor of being introduced in London. You were always surrounded by a multitude of admirers.

No one lesser than an earl could get through the throng." Lord Wyndam bussed the back of her hand.

She demurred with a laugh. "I'm sure that's not true, but it's certainly a pleasure to meet you now."

"I saw gentlemen standing three deep trying to get their names on your card." Lord Wyndam still held her hand.

Rafe took Wyndam's wrist between his thumb and forefinger and shook her hand free. "We get the picture, Wyndam. The horses?"

Lord Wyndam didn't seem the least bothered by Rafe's brusque manner. Ignoring Rafe, he said, "Do you know my wife, Delilah, Lady Minerva?"

"I didn't have the pleasure of making her acquaintance either."

"Yes, all those gentlemen kept you busy, I'm sure. The endless waltzes, the strolls through gardens, the carriage rides." Wyndam cut his gaze to Rafe, lips twitching. "Perhaps you'd like to take tea with my wife while I take Drummond down to the paddock? I'm sure we would bore you. Let yourself in. We're shockingly informal, and our butler is rather hard of hearing."

"Sounds lovely," she said.

She shuffled toward the door. How in the world was she to explain her months at Wintermarsh? Was Lady Wyndam a gossip? There was only one thing she could do…lie her drawers off.

Minerva knocked on the rough wooden door, but as Wyndam predicted, no one answered. She pushed the door open and stepped directly into a large common area. It was unoccupied.

"Hello?" Her soft call echoed off the stone.

Faded tapestries decorated the walls, and two suits of armor flanked the huge fireplace at the far end of the room. Swords, lances and axes hung all over the wall on either side of the armor. The weapons glinted in the slivers of sunlight from the narrow windows. She imagined a medieval knight grabbing a sword straight off the wall to go fend off his enemy.

"Quite the arsenal, isn't it?"

A gasping scream snaked out of Minerva's tight throat as she spun. Her would-be attacker was a woman with thick, straight chestnut hair pulled into a messy chignon and an open, honest face with a dash of freckles across her nose. She was short and slight. Perhaps not beautiful in the classical sense, she was winsome with an indefinable charm.

"Quite impressive," Minerva managed between deep breaths.

"I'm terribly sorry. Did I startle you? I saw Marcus and Lord Drummond head to the stables. Lord Drummond said he might bring you with him when he was here last."

"Did he now?" Minerva cocked her head.

"I'm so happy to meet you finally. I'm Delilah Ashemore." Lady Wyndam bobbed an unnecessary curtsy and stuck a hand out. A vigorous shaking commenced. Minerva tried but failed to stop a smile. Lady Wyndam let go and ran her hand down her skirt, a barely contained nervous energy ready to burst from her tapping toes.

Minerva walked farther into the room. "What a lovely tapestry."

Lady Wyndam outpaced Minerva and ran her fingers along the frayed edge. Her voice bounced with exuberance. "Wyndam's uncle says it's from the fifteenth century. Can you imagine? The first time Marcus brought me here, I thought I was in a fairytale. The rat I saw running across my bed sheets changed my opinions rather hastily."

"Oh my," Minerva whispered.

Lady Wyndam cut her laugh off and took a deep, sighing breath. "Perhaps you'd like to repair to our drawing room and take a cup of tea?"

"That sounds lovely."

One step into the drawing room, and Minerva stopped short. Greek, Roman, Egyptian and Chinese antiquities warred with each other for space. Every nook and cranny was crammed.

"What a charming room," Minerva said rather in awe.

"Charming? That's your polite way of saying odd, isn't it? I rather hate it myself. I was going to move most of it above stairs, but Marcus says given time I'll eventually break it all anyway. Unfortunately, it's all plaster and imitations as far as we've been able to determine." Lady Wyndam wound her way around a huge bust of Caesar sporting a straw bonnet and gestured to a settee patterned in violent red poppies.

Minerva lowered herself, feeling a bit like the poppies might eat her alive. Lady Wyndam plopped across from her in an ancient green velvet armchair. Dust motes poofed up, and Lady Wyndam waved her hand in front of her face, rolling her eyes.

"Good grief. This room is in a terrible state. If I'm being perfectly honest, the entire estate is in terrible shape. Wyndam inherited it a few months ago, you see, and we don't have two farthings to rub together." Lady Wyndam shrugged, slouched back in the chair, and grinned.

Minerva blinked a few times before returning Lady Wyndam's grin. "I'm sorry you're in financial straits."

Lady Wyndam dismissed her with a wave of a hand. "Not to worry. Wyndam grew up in Ireland on a horse farm, and we're breeding horses to sell. We're ever so grateful Lord Drummond is letting us stud Aries. He's a magnificent horse. Wyndam thinks the progeny from Aries and our little mare Starlight will go for top dollar, and then we can update a bit. Although, honestly, I could live in a hovel with Wyndam and be perfectly content."

"That's a beautiful sentiment, Lady Wyndam."

"It's closer to reality than you know. You haven't seen the upstairs." Laughing, she pointed to the flaking plaster of the ceiling. "Please call me Delilah. I'm not particularly fond of it. I mean,

Delilah was a harlot, was she not? But I can't get used to being called Lady anything."

Minerva laughed. Goodness, she liked Delilah Ashemore. Very much. "And you must call me Minerva."

"Let me ring for some tea. You must be parched after your ride." Delilah weaved back to the door and rang the bell pull. After several tries with no answer, she popped her head out the door. "O'Connell, O'Connell."

A creaky Irish brogue sounded on the other side of the door. "Eh? Tea? Well, o'course I heard the bell, ain't deaf, am I? Eh? I'll bring a cuppa, all you had to do was ask, lassie. What? Two cups? And some biscuits? I'll see what that old bat in the kitchen can scrounge up. Back in a jiff."

Delilah backed in to the room, shaking her head. Her heel caught on the worn, faded Abussan rug, and she bumped a pedestal holding a replica of the sphinx. The sphinx tottered and slipped through Delilah's fingers to break into pieces on the floor.

"Blast it! There goes another one. Wyndam's right. I might have this place cleared out by Christmastime." She kicked at the pieces with her slippers, her shoulders slumping.

Minerva knelt down and fit together two large shards. "Perhaps we could fix it."

"Not worth the trouble. We must seem like terribly bad ton to someone like you. I'll never be comfortable entertaining highborn ladies. Marcus says he doesn't care, but I feel like I've let him down." Delilah's sadness enveloped the room like a black cloud.

Minerva patted her hand. "Most of Society isn't worth the trouble, if you want my opinion. Anyway, Lord Drummond thinks highly of you and your husband."

Delilah raised both brows. "I'm not sure if you've noticed, but Lord Drummond isn't exactly Society's ideal of a proper gentleman."

"Yes, I've noticed," Minerva said with humor-laced sarcasm.

Delilah's laughter sent the bleak moment scurrying away.

An older man with dark red hair kicked the drawing room door open with a mud-caked boot and shuffled forward with a rattling tea tray. Large fuzzy red caterpillars shadowed the man's eyes. On closer inspection, Minerva determined they were, in actuality, eyebrows. Similar red hair wisped from out of the man's ears. Delilah transferred the man's burden to a table.

Instead of leaving the room, the man came closer and examined Minerva. "Eh? So I saw Drummond down in the paddock. Is this his woman then?" He thumbed toward Minerva.

Torn between embarrassment and laughter, she covered her mouth.

Delilah took the man's arm and led him to the door. "O'Connell. Really. If you want to be the butler, you must learn some decorum."

"Decorating? What has window coverings to do with anything?"

She pushed the man out and closed the doors, blowing a tendril of hair out of her eyes with a puff of air. "Terribly sorry about that. Wyndam grew up with O'Connell. He's getting rather old to work in the stables, but he can't sit idle and we hoped…well, we'll work him in somewhere, I'm sure."

"It's kind of you to take him in. Lord Drummond seems very fond of his servants as well."

Regaining their seats, Delilah poured and glanced up through her lashes. "Speaking of…Wyndam and I have been ever so curious, what *is* going on between you and Lord Drummond?"

A sip of tea lodged in her throat, and she coughed. Used to the sly machinations of ton gossips, Delilah Ashemore's direct question took her aback. However, far from being offended, she appreciated the woman's frankness.

"I'm not exactly sure. We used to detest each other. But lately, I've found that I rather admire him and," she dropped her voice to a whisper, "he's very handsome, don't you think?"

Delilah clapped her hands. "How exciting. I'm not supposed to notice other men, being a married woman and all, but if I *did* happen to notice another man, I would agree. He's had a rough time of it lately, but he was downright happy when he left Aries yesterday and quite insistent he make it home before nightfall."

"Was he?" The hope imbued in the two words was telling.

"Most definitely. Have you discussed marriage? I'll admit, selfishly, I would love to have you as a neighbor."

Minerva slumped back and plucked at a raveling red poppy. "No. We haven't discussed anything of permanence."

"He holds strong feelings for you. I can tell." Delilah winked and would have said more, but the sound of clattering boots and rumbling laughter came from the entry.

The drawing room doors swung open. With Delilah's encouraging words in her head, Minerva studied Rafe. His lips curled up, crinkling his eyes into a genuine smile. He did look happy. Her cheeks hurt from the force of the smile she sent him.

"Well, m'dear, looks like another horrid knickknack has been executed." Wyndam kicked the broken sphinx under a chair.

Delilah rose and wrapped her hands around her husband's arm. "I'm working on clearing out the room, love. You gentlemen look rather ridiculous in here. Why don't we move to the dining room? Cook should have finished laying out our luncheon. We dine simply here, I hope that's acceptable."

"Simple suits me quite well," Minerva said, never taking her eyes off Rafe.

Rafe offered his arm with a small bow. She lay her hand on his forearm, acutely aware of his heat and hardness. The Wyndams led them down a narrow corridor off the common room. A cold repast was laid out on the buffet in a small morning room. Lord Wyndam popped the cork off a bottle of champagne and poured everyone a glass.

"A toast to Lord Drummond for generously giving our little venture a start," Lord Wyndam said.

"Here, here!" Delilah held her glass high, sloshing the drink over the side.

"Aries did all the work, Wyndam, and you know I don't mind in the least. I wish you all the luck." Rafe dipped his head and took a small sip.

The food was delicious, and the company entertaining. Lord Wyndam's dry humor complemented Delilah's exuberant cheerfulness to perfection. Minerva found herself sharing personal details about her childhood and ruefully confessed the problems she'd faced with Simon and his resulting turnaround over the autumn.

Rafe didn't contribute a great deal. He chuckled when appropriate and interjected a few times, but otherwise his face stayed strangely blank. Even when Minerva coaxed a smile, it wasn't genuine. A hollow pit yawned in her stomach, and she pushed her plate away, her appetite gone.

By late afternoon, only a few remaining grey clouds marred the blue skies. The groom held their horses, and Aries was saddled for the return trip to Wintermarsh. They stood at the edge of the old drawbridge, and Delilah looked first at her and then at Rafe. "Should we expect an announcement to be forthcoming?"

Rafe and Minerva stammered on top of each other.

"Well, I'm not sure—"

"We really haven't—"

"It's not as though—"

Casting an exasperated look at his wife, Wyndam saved more excuses. "It's none of our business, love, and anyway, they're welcome here apart or together. Perhaps we could meet up for a spot of shooting, Drummond?"

Rafe's reply didn't register through the pounding of her heart. Delilah shrugged her shoulders and mouthed, 'I'm sorry.'

The first miles back to Wintermarsh passed in an uncomfortable silence. Not able to stand it, she peppered him with questions about the land and the cottages they passed on their way home. The idle talk reduced the unexplainable tension between them but didn't eliminate it. By the time they left the horses with Tom, she worried what the night had in store.

CHAPTER TWENTY-ONE

Rafe reclined in his huge armchair before a small fire. He clutched his brandy glass so tightly he wondered it didn't shatter. The scratch of a quill broke the silence. Minerva was at his desk writing to Drake.

She had been magnificent today. Charming, lively, warm. She had missed socializing, she'd as much as admitted it on the way home. She missed London and the parties. She missed the art galleries and the museums. Life at Wintermarsh must seem mundane and boring to a woman like her. London would be miserable for him. He hated the parties, hated the perpetual soot and filth, hated the stares on the streets and in the clubs.

For both their sakes, he should end their liaison now. But he wasn't strong enough. She was a tonic as addictive as alcohol. The sharing of his past had somehow lightened the burden that seemed to press him down day in and day out. It made him want to lay himself bare to her, but that path would only lead to more heartache.

As soon as their bargain was over, Minerva would want her old life back. She would leave him more broken than he already was. He could force her away though. He could be the heartless bastard she'd accused him of being months ago.

"What a lovely day. I liked the Wyndams very much. Would

you like me to read to you for a change? Perhaps more from *The Tempest*?" Minerva laid a hand on his shoulder, her sweet smile eviscerating him.

Hating himself, he pressed forward with his plan. The remaining brandy burned a path down his throat, and he set the empty glass aside. "No books. I require physical satisfaction. Are you willing?"

Her hand fluttered off his shoulder to the neck of her gown. She held his gaze, searching. "Perhaps. What did you have in mind?"

"I want you on your knees and between my legs. Take my...cock out and suck it." The vulgar words burned as he made his own hell.

He turned his face away even as his eyes refused to leave her face. He needed to see the disgust and hatred. A barrage of emotions battled on her face. Finally though, she approached. He turned farther away from her. Her face reflected something even more terrifying than hate.

* * * * *

A dark pit had swallowed Rafe while she had been composing a letter to Drake. No, it had been growing all afternoon. But she was beginning to understand him. Fear shone from his stormy eyes, not pleasure in her humiliation. No, he aimed to push her away. He expected her to be angry and outraged, or perhaps, he expected her to cry and run away. In reality, what she felt was arousal and power.

She'd wondered about the act for some time. How could she not, when what he'd done to her had been so delightful? Now she had the opportunity to seize control, and truth be known, she relished it.

She stepped between his parted knees. Every muscle in his body seemed poised for flight. His head was turned to the side as if she'd already slapped him for his impertinence. She leaned over and placed a hand on each of his forearms. His fingers were curled over the arms of the chair, making indents into the supple leather. Slowly, he turned to face her. So much pain reflected in the lines etching his mouth and his eyes. Her heart hollowed, and she wanted to cuddle in his lap to kiss it away.

She steeled herself. The man needed to understand she wouldn't be scared away. Leaning down, she whispered in his ear, "Should I unfasten your breeches?"

His ragged breath skimmed warmly over her cheek. She traced the outer rim of his ear with her tongue and then did the same down the length of his scar into his beard. She pulled his bottom lip between her teeth and sucked. The muscles under her hands rippled. He remained silent.

She dropped to her knees as he had commanded, bracketed by his legs. Their gazes tangled. Like a trapped, confused animal, he looked panicked, not sure where to run. Would he stop her? Starting at his hips, she stroked down the outside of his thighs to his knees. Walking her fingers up the inside of his thighs, she grazed over his erection. His hips jumped.

So far, she had maintained the façade of a controlled, dispassionate seductress. Now, her trembling fingers betrayed her. She fumbled with the discs, silently cursing her clumsiness. He made no move to either stop or help her. One by one, the discs slid free, exposing his heavy, extremely aroused member.

"Are all men this well-proportioned, Rafe? I don't have any basis of comparison, but you seem uncommonly large."

He grunted.

She wet her lips. He had told her to suck his cock. The entire length? She didn't think that would be possible, but she'd try. She tentatively licked the tip, never taking her eyes off his face. His lids fluttered down, and his head rolled back on the chair. She opened her mouth and took him inside.

A groan tore from the depths of his chest, and he curled a

hand around the back of her neck. One of her hands wrapped him tightly at the base, as he had taught her in the cabin, and she danced her tongue over the tip. She sucked him deep and hummed, lost in the sensation and taste of him.

He hooked his hands under her arms, hauled her to her feet and tugged her into his arms. The sudden rise left her lightheaded and swaying. She licked over her swollen lips. "Did I do it wrong?"

"I'm so bloody sorry. I know I keep having to apologize for my actions, my words, but—"

"I know. I understand." She laced their fingers.

"Will you come upstairs with me? Let me make amends?"

At her single nod, he grabbed his breeches up and led her to his room. The snick of the lock reverberated in her ears. The huge bed, with its yawning red curtains, beckoned. But not yet. The residual pleasure of power still thrummed.

He encircled her upper arms with his hands, his intent clear. She stopped him with a soft hand on his chest. Certainly, he could overpower her and take control, but he wouldn't. She was learning. His face wary, he stilled, waiting. She wanted to punish him for having no faith in her. What would torment him the most?

"Go sit on the bed." She nudged him away with her fingertips. He was an immovable object.

"Why?"

"Because I told you to. I'll walk out that door, Rafe Drummond. You'll learn to trust in me, or I'll pack my trunk."

His hands fell to his side, still curled as if they held her. He backed away and perched on the edge of the mattress, looking ready to tackle her if she followed through on her empty threat to leave. She couldn't leave him, didn't want to. Ever.

She paced in front of him, and he tracked her every movement with his intent gaze. "You must learn I'm no weak-kneed, slack-jawed debutante to run for protection every time you lose your grip on sanity. I care for you, you stupid man. Now, it's my turn."

She turned her back on his stare. Was she really doing this? Her heart felt like it might burst into pieces over the rug. She rubbed her hands down the front of her gown, before taking in a huge breath and holding it. She raised her trembling fingers and removed the pins from her hair, dropping them on the rug one by one until the mass cascaded down her back.

* * * * *

Rafe had lost the ability to coherently reason. She cared for him. Why, he couldn't fathom. She should have hit him over the head with something large and pain inducing and stormed out of his life several times over.

Now, she'd upped the stakes and held the trump card. Her hair danced down her back, and the coy glance she sent over her shoulder gave him a clue where this was headed. Torment and pleasure.

She released hook after hook until her dress slumped down her arms, the curve of her spine and shoulders exposed. The gown slipped over her hips to fall to the rug, leaving her in her chemise and stockings. No drawers marred the outline of her buttocks through the thin cloth.

His cock, thwarted in its release, throbbed. As fast as humanly possible, he disrobed and sat back on the edge of the bed, naked and stroking himself. When she turned, her body turned to stone, her mouth parted, her gaze locked on the play of his hands.

"Pray, please continue," he said hoarsely. The outline of her nipples made his mouth water. She hooked her fingers around the straps of her chemise and let them fall down her arms, but caught the material over her breasts.

"You like having me under your thumb, don't you, my lady?" Rafe teasingly repeated the accusation she had hurled at him weeks earlier.

"I'd rather have you over me." Her usual confidence was missing, highlighting her innocence with their sexual banter, but he had a feeling, like with everything else, that she'd be a quick study.

"I very much agree with the sentiment."

"Is this what you want?" She pulled the fabric taut, outlining her already peaked nipples.

"Drop it or I won't be responsible for what happens." He barely recognized his voice.

Presenting him her back once more, she dropped the chemise. It caught at her hips, exposing the barest hint of her buttock crease. She shimmied her hips, and the cloth floated to her ankles. Spinning, she stood with her arms at her sides. Her nearly nude body glowed in the candles. His breathing rasped faster as his hand tightened around his cock.

Pink tinted her chest and cheeks, shyness battling an innate sensuality she was only beginning to recognize and tap. Her breathing was affected too. Her lips parted, and her chest rose and fell rapidly. She leaned over and rolled her stockings down. Her breasts swayed as she trailed her fingers over each bare leg.

Her turn was over.

"Come here, Minerva."

She sashayed toward him, under the mistaken impression she was in charge. As soon as she was within reach, he tossed her in the middle of the bed, ignoring her breathless cry. He came over her like a beast. "Is this what you wanted, woman? Me insane with need and over you?"

He shoved her legs apart and swiped a finger between them. Even in his primal state, he didn't want to hurt her, but once assured she was ready, he thrust deep. He didn't make love to her. He fucked her.

Her throaty groans and whispered words of encouragement accompanied his every thrust. She climaxed, biting his shoulder and raking fingernails down his back. The combination of pain and pleasure drove him over the edge, and with one final sharp thrust, he spent inside of her. They panted, recovering from their bout like prizefighters.

"Was I too rough? Did I hurt you?" he whispered.

"I can assure you, my cries were not from pain. I don't know why you insist on treating me with kid gloves. I like when you treat me like a woman and not a lady." She ran her hands over his back, tracing one long scratch.

"Did I hurt you?" Her eyes reflected true worry.

He fell to his side in a fit of laughter, pulling her close and brushing her hair over her shoulder. "Please, woman. You only wish you could."

"No, I don't ever want to hurt you." She cupped his scarred cheek, her thumb coasting over his cheekbone and across the puckered scar.

He bit the inside of his mouth and tasted blood. His fears sat heavily on his chest, making his words emerge sluggishly. "I watched you today with the Wyndams."

"What did you see, pray tell?"

"A lady who is mesmerizing, charming, effervescent. You must miss the whirl of London and all your friends."

"Friends? I thought we'd established the fact that I only have a handful. I'm admired and imitated. Even a bit feared. But liked? No one likes me."

"Why in the world don't they like you?"

"Might I remind you, Lord Drummond, not so many weeks ago you disliked me more than the entire ton put together. The words haughty, conceited bitch come to mind."

He harrumphed, rolling to his back. "That's completely different. I disliked you because...well, I *liked* you."

She huffed a slight laugh. "That was as clear as fog."

"It's neither here nor there. What I'm wondering...what I've been thinking on all evening is whether you'd be happy away from all of that for…long periods of time." The word *forever* had almost slipped out. He stared at the dark red canopy overhead and held his breath. What was she thinking? Would she laugh? Call him an idiot? Was he mad to consider paying his addresses?

Her face slid into view, her hair pooling around his neck in a beautiful cascade. She didn't laugh or call him an idiot. Instead, she brushed her lips over his brow, his scarred cheek and his mouth. "If I had the right sort of company, I'd be more than happy away from London. Forever."

Would she? He studied her, trying to determine if she hid her true feelings. Only a guileless sincerity showed in her serious blue eyes. A banked fire spread through his chest and drove back the shadows in his heart.

* * * * *

She considered her words carefully. One mention of love might send him running in fear. It would take time to tame him. Did they have enough before their brazen bargain was finished? "I've never felt like this."

"Me either." His quiet admission lifted her heart into her throat. "Here now, I've neglected you."

He rolled her onto her stomach and brushed the hair off her back. It was his way of changing the subject, but before she could protest, he skimmed his big, callused hand down her back. Afterwards. They could discuss the future afterwards.

"Your skin is so smooth and white. So soft." The bristly hair of his beard tickled her side, and she wiggled away. His heavy hand on her back held her down while he did it again, this time eliciting a giggle.

The hand wandered over her bottom, kneading and squeezing. She thrust her buttocks up. With each encounter, her shyness diminished. "Please, Rafe, I need you."

He was as gentle now as he had been rough before. He wandered his fingers closer and closer to her wet center, teasing her. Finally, with a sob, she grabbed his wrist and forced him into her heat, twisting her hips. He eased a finger, then two, inside of her and groaned into her neck.

"That's it, my love, use me. Take your pleasure." And she did, writhing and holding his hand clamped between her legs.

Her climax left her exhausted and boneless. He eased her on her side, facing away from him, and lifted her leg, his cock probing for entrance. She arched her back, and he slid inside of her with a hiss. Rocking her from behind, he lay kisses along her neck and shoulders. Very soon, he shuddered and wrapped her in his arms, both of them sated.

CHAPTER TWENTY-TWO

Minerva's eyes opened to her familiar blue canopy. When had he moved her? Had anyone seen them? Considering his training, probably not. He'd even managed to get her chemise back on. She stretched languorously, wondering where he was.

After dressing and on her way to the study, Cuthbertson passed her a note.

Simon and I are seeing to tenant cottage repairs. Until tonight.

The last two words jumped off the paper. A promise. Tonight seemed a lifetime away. She held the note to her chest with a smile.

Jenny traipsed through the entry, tugging on gloves. "Fancy a trip into Lipton?"

Minerva sighed, grateful for the distraction. "That sounds perfect. Let me get my cloak."

Although the skies overhead were bleak, nothing could contain their spirits. Vicar Appleby would read the first banns for Tom and Jenny at Sunday service. Although Minerva didn't speak of her love for Rafe, she couldn't stop the blushes and the grin when Jenny asked about him.

While the burly young son of the mercantile owner loaded the cart, Jenny shooed Minerva into the inn to get warm while she kept her father company in the smithy.

A fire crackled, heating the small common room. A handful of local men talked in low voices around the window. Taking a seat next to the fire, she tucked her feet close until her toes tingled. Utterly content with the moment and her life, she settled into the chair, a smile on her face.

A dirty, booted foot hooked around the chair next to hers. She looked up, thinking Rafe had somehow found her, but her smile froze into a shocked grimace.

Lord Hampton.

His face was gaunt, and grime and wrinkles masked his jacket's quality. His pants and boots were in much the same state. A fetid, stale odor wafted on the stirred air as he sat. Nausea threatened, driven by a combination of his odor and her fear.

Inclining her head, she adopted her icy ton persona like slipping on a familiar dress, but she curled her hands around the seat of her chair, digging her nails into the wooden underside. "Greetings, Lord Hampton. How are you this day?"

"Don't pretend you're the high and mighty Lady Minerva with me, my dear. We both know what's been going on these past weeks." He spoke loudly and with a sneer.

"Hush, please. I would not discuss that here and now."

"Well, my lady, where would you like to discuss it then? For I have a proposition for you. I hear you're amenable to such." His innuendo dripped disrespect.

"I don't think—"

"I do. You will accompany me to the alley where I have a horse waiting. Then you will be silent as we make our way to my charming little abode in the forest."

"Why would I do that?" She looked around the room but didn't recognize any of the men. Most were too old to be of much help anyway. Still, it was broad daylight in the sleepy village, what harm could befall her? Of course, she'd made that mistake once before.

A knife glinted in his hand, and he played with the edge, a smile tugging his lips. "I thought you may take some extra convincing." Grabbing her wrist, he pulled, but she resisted, her muscles rigid and tense.

He was too strong for her to win their tug of war, and her arm ended up over the table. Ripping the sleeve of her gown with the knife's point, he set the edge against the tender skin of her forearm. A thin red line appeared, and stinging pain accompanied the cut. Tiny rivulets of her blood ran to the table. She stared, her head floating somewhere above the horror.

With his hand like a vise on her arm, he hauled her up and pushed her toward the back of the inn, making sure the tip of the blade stayed pressed into her side. The knife cut through her dress and pricked her skin.

"Be careful, my dear. I would hate to accidently gut you."

How was she to walk on legs that wobbled like an old woman's? No one had even noticed the drama going on in their midst. Minerva ducked out the back door. The alley was narrow and smelled of old vegetables but was otherwise clean. Crates and barrels blocked one end while an old nag, as disreputable as Hampton, blocked the other.

The heavy wooden door shut behind them, and she managed to pull away to the opposite wall. "I assume this has something to do with my brother. Tell me what you want."

He paced back and forth, pulling at his lank, greasy hair, the knife clutched in his hand. She followed its progress back and forth.

"What I want is my bloody life back. Look at me." He held his arms out for her inspection.

"You appear to have fallen in some difficult straits, my lord, but I'm hardly to blame for that. Neither is my brother, I might add."

The knife made an arc that had her scrabbling backwards into the bricks. "Bloody Bellingham. I was poised to make a fortune off that numbskull. Until you whisked him away from London. You even had to pull him from our simple game here and almost get me killed." The tip of his knife was a handbreadth from her nose. Her lungs had stilled, but beneath the terror, a black bird of fury beat its wings.

She pressed her shoulders back and lifted her chin. "Almost got *you* killed? You lying coward. If Lord Drummond hadn't found us, we might be lying at the bottom of a river somewhere."

"You simpleton! I'm not talking about those yokels. I've borrowed a mountain of money from some very unsavory men. If I don't come up with the funds to hold them off, I will be killed in a very painful fashion. They've been on my heels for weeks now, and your brother refuses to see me." Lord Hampton resumed pacing, his fear and desperation palpable.

"I'm sorry to hear that. But I'm still not sure I understand what that has to do with me." She shuffled sideways toward the nag, her back scraping on the rough stone. If she could get close enough, she could call for Jenny, or better yet, Black John.

"I need money. And you are going to get me some." His lips curled upward, but not in a smile.

"I sympathize with your plight, but there's nothing I can do."

"My dear Lady Minerva, I know exactly what has been going on at Wintermarsh. I know the details of the bargain that was struck between you and Simon and Lord Drummond. London Society would be very interested indeed to hear about what you were reduced to do at the hands of the wicked Lord Drummond. Cleaning like a common maid and perhaps performing more intimate chores for the lord of the manor?"

Heat raced through her, squelching the stabilizing anger. "No one would believe your word over mine. You're hardly a paragon of Society. I would discredit you. Claim you're seeking money for your debts."

"No, not me perhaps, but my cousin Mrs. Richard Ogle would be more than willing to listen to my tale. And repeat it." Mrs. Ogle was one of the worst gossips of the ton. She had ruined many a young maiden's chance of a good marriage. The more salacious the rumor, the greater her delight in spreading it. He adjusted the frayed cuffs of his greyed linen shirt. "Twenty thousand for my silence."

"Twenty thousand? Even if I paid you the money, there would be nothing to stop you from coming back for more when you get yourself into trouble again. And you will, you know."

"You'll have to trust my word as a gentleman that I won't ask for more."

Minerva barked a laugh as she slid a little closer to freedom. "As if I would trust your word. You may have been born a peer but you are obviously no gentleman. I won't give you any money."

Hampton slapped both hands on the wall, bracketing her, the blade clinking a few inches from her ear. "Think of your brother's future if word makes the rounds that he was force to muck out the stables to pay his debts. The two of you would be cut everywhere. And Drummond would be ruined as well."

"I don't care."

He pressed his body into hers and trailed grimy fingers down her face and throat. Dirt was packed under his broken nails. She pushed at his chest, but he caught her wrists. "You don't care what happens to you? You know, it's been quite some time since I've had a woman, and you're already letting Drummond between your lovely legs."

She turned her face away so he wouldn't see her panic and forced ton-style haughtiness into her voice. "It's been quite some time since you've had a bath too."

"If you do not agree to my bargain, I will take you right here against the wall."

His spittle dotted her cheek, and she wiped her cheek against a shoulder. "I could scream and have half the town down on your head in an instant." She yanked her hands out of his grip. Her flash of relief died under the knife. Still pressed into her body, he stroked the blade against her cheek, freezing her struggles.

"You're correct. Better to take this somewhere a bit more private. You don't seem to find scars repugnant. Perhaps I'll leave you a few to remember me by." He trailed the knife down her face until the point rested under her chin. He screwed the tip into her skin, and blood trickled down her neck.

For the first time, she feared for her life. In France, Rafe had faced this fear day after day with bravery and strength. Minerva could only cower, her throat closed to nothing, her lungs starved for air. Her head swam, and when he forced her to the nag, her body refused to fight.

"Up on the horse, my lady."

She didn't remember how she got onto the saddle, but within a moment, he was behind her, the knife's point pricking her side.

"If you're quiet and cooperate, I'll not harm you, and as soon as that imbecilic brother of yours pays me, I'll let you go. Is that understood?"

She managed a nod. Hampton guided them out of the alley but turned away from the village center. They soon veered off the road and into a copse. The weak sunlight filtering through the braches made it feel more like dusk than the middle of the afternoon.

It wasn't long before she spotted a cabin through the trees. Decrepit, the roof caved in on one side and windowless. It seemed a more appropriate house for squirrels, mice and birds. Hampton's retreat was in such contrast to Rafe's idyllic cabin, it was laughable. Instead, tears welled and crawled down her cheeks.

* * * * *

Jenny peered around the side of the inn and watched Minerva ride off with the strange man on an old, beaten horse. Was he a gentleman friend from London? A finger of unease trailed down her spine. Minerva wouldn't have left her without word. She ran to her papa's shop.

"Papa, please, something's not right. We need to find Lord Drummond or her brother and at least let them know."

"Now, Jenny mine, I know that you think the lady is your friend, but she's quality, and I've seen them do strange things. It's probably one of her London suitors out to take her for a ride. Most likely, she wouldn't want you spreading tales." Her papa patted her arm.

Jenny bit her lip. Was her father right?

"These folks are different than you and me. Taking lovers here and there is nothing to them. Not that I'm saying that's what the lady is doing, but perhaps she's having a secret meeting, eh?"

She shook her head. "No. I have to get back to Wintermarsh." The decision made, urgency lent desperation to her voice. "Papa, I need a horse. I can't wait for the wagon to finish loading. Anyhow, it's too slow. Is there a horse in the stable I can borrow?"

"Jenny Mitchell, you can't even ride."

"Tom's been teaching me. I can ride well enough. This is important. I feel it. Please?" Jenny laid a hand on her papa's arm and pouted. He threw up his hands in surrender, and she almost smiled. She'd always gotten her way with her papa.

He bullied the inn's hostler into saddling a sturdy gelding. Clenching her jaw, she rocked from foot to foot while the men argued over the tightness of the girth straps. Finally, her papa heaved her to the saddle, a long way off the ground. Vertigo swam her head until she got her feet firmly in the stirrups.

"You have to get the horse back tonight according to the lad here."

"I'll send Henry back with the horse and for the wagon," she called over her shoulder, jouncing down the road. While it was true that Tom was teaching her to ride, her lessons had consisted of walking around the paddock on a short Shetland with Tom handling the reins. Luckily, while considerably larger, the gelding was lazy. So lazy, he wanted to plod all the way to Wintermarsh. She managed to force him into a trot by digging her heels into his side.

By the time she reached the turnoff, her teeth had been shaken loose and her legs trembled from her tight clamp. Amazingly, the horse seemed to know which direction to head for oats and a rubdown and broke into a faster trot toward the stables without her having to attempt a change in direction.

Tom ran to grab the bit. "Jenny, love. What the devil is going on?"

She fell into his outstretched arms. Grateful to be on solid ground, she kissed him.

"What's the matter? Is it your father?" Her pressing kisses muffled his words.

"Not Papa, but Lady Minerva. I need to see Lord Drummond or her brother. Something's amiss."

"They got back not a quarter-hour ago. Come with me." Tom tried to pull her along, but her legs refused to cooperate. Tom swung her up into his arms to stalk quickly toward the house.

Jenny studied her betrothed's profile while she caressed his bristled cheek. "I could get used to this, Mr. Donahue."

"Could you now? Perhaps I'll carry you to bed every night then, Miss Mitchell." Tom's eyes filled with the promise of pleasure. Warmth bloomed in her belly despite her worry.

"I wish we didn't have to wait."

Her petulant tone made him laugh. "We've discussed this countless times. You aren't seducing me into your bed before you make an honest man of me."

"But I love you, Tom. I'll still respect you come morning, you know," she said impishly.

"Lass, it'll be all the sweeter from the anticipation. Trust me." At that, he kissed her nose and climbed the steps to the door before setting her down.

"Can you walk now?" At her nod, he opened the door to find Cuthbertson taking a tray of tea and biscuits to the study.

"Is that for Lord Drummond, Bertie?"

"It is indeed, Tom. Is there something wrong in the stables?"

"Not the stables. Jenny needs to talk to Lord Drummond immediately. It's about Lady Minerva."

The butler shooed them into the study. "Master Rafe, Master Simon, Mr. Donahue and Miss Mitchell need to see you for a moment," Bertie announced them and set a tray next to Rafe's armchair.

Tom pulled Jenny to stand in front of the two men. Thankfully, he kept his hands on her shoulders and his warm body behind her. Lord Drummond couldn't help the way he looked, but the man intimidated her boots off. Her voice wavered. "It's Lady Minerva. We took the cart to Lipton together. I sent her into the inn to stay warm while I was visiting papa. Next thing I knew, she was riding away with a strange man."

* * * * *

Rafe's stomach fell to the cellars.

Simon jumped to his feet, ashen faced. "What did the man look like, Jenny? Did you catch a glimpse?"

"They were on the north road but cut into the woods past old Lizzie's cottage. I never saw his face, but he looked rumpled and rode a swaybacked spotted nag. A hundred if it was a day. Something wasn't right, my lords. She would never ride off like that." Jenny wrung her hands and refused to meet his eyes, but she told the truth.

"Thank you, Jenny. Tom, go saddle Aries and a horse for Simon. Be quick," Rafe said curtly. They were still in riding clothes, and Rafe bellowed for Cuthbertson to ready their hats and coats.

"Rafe. It might be Hampton."

Rafe spun and pinned Simon with his eyes. "Why do you suspect him?"

"He's been sending me notes for the past month begging for money. Ever since the debacle in town. In the last one, he threatened to expose our bargain unless I paid him a substantial amount of money. I told him to go to hell, of course. I can weather whatever he metes out."

"What of Minerva? She would be ruined." Rafe cut his gaze away. Who was he to chastise Simon?

"He's an arse but still a gentleman. I didn't think he would stoop to something so vile. What can we do?" Shaken but steadfast, Simon didn't make excuses or hide.

"We get her back and shut the blackguard up. Permanently, if necessary." Rummaging in his desk, he found the knife he'd taken off Hampton in the summer. He slid it into a sheath in his boot and strode to the door. Simon followed in his wake. After swirling his greatcoat around his shoulders, Rafe shoved his hat low over his brow.

"Do you have an idea where he might be holed up?" Simon twirled his hat, crumpling the brim while they waited for Tom.

"There are abandoned cottages in the woods he might be using. Although they're in terrible disrepair."

"His last letter was rather insulting toward Minerva. We need to hurry." Simon looked to his boots.

Rafe clenched his jaw, barely restraining himself from taking off at a run. "He will die a very painful death if he's touched her. Be sure of that."

He met Tom halfway, grabbed Aries's reins, and leapt to the saddle. Aries was in full gallop before Simon had even gained his mount. Rafe pulled up outside of Lipton. A wavering line of trampled grass led into the woods.

"Here." Rafe pointed along the makeshift trail. They dismounted, leaving their horses to pick at the dried grass, and crept through the woods.

"Can't you be a bit quieter?" Rafe bit out.

"Christ, I thought I *was* being quiet," Simon whispered, hunched over on his tiptoes.

Seeing a derelict cottage through the trees, Rafe stood Simon by a tree and gave him the knife. "Stay here and…keep a lookout."

This was the most important rescue operation in his life, and Rafe couldn't afford to have Simon muck it up. He crept up to the cottage. A paralyzing image of Minerva dead and bleeding out froze him to the side of the window, struggling to breathe. Her cutting, imperious voice carried out the window, shooting life back into his body. Whatever else had happened didn't matter—she lived.

* * * * *

Hampton paced while she tugged against the frayed ropes. Somewhere between being dragged into the hovel and tied to the bed, her backbone reconstructed itself. Escape was her goal, but at the very least, she would stay alive. Rafe was coming. She could feel him drawing nearer.

The charming cottage Hampton called home was falling down around their ears. Mold, excrement, and a heady assortment of noxious aromas filled the air. She breathed through her mouth to keep from tossing her accounts all over the bed. No need to add that to the stew.

"The note has been sent, and I expect a reply soon. I'm not sure how long it will take to raise the money, however, so you might be stuck here for a few days." Hampton played with the wickedly sharp knife, cutting her a sly glance. "How will we pass the time? Do you have any ideas, my lady?"

"I suggest you slit your throat. I wouldn't recommend that

you still be breathing when Lord Drummond finds you," she replied in the voice she used to use to browbeat Simon.

"Yes, your lover. I'm truly shocked. If I knew you were so easily seduced, I would have pressed my suit with you in London."

"As if you would have had a chance, Hampton. Lord Drummond is a strong, capable man, while you are a dissolute, stupid boy who has played with the wrong people and gotten in over his head."

"Boy, am I? I'm man enough to plow your cunt, you little bitch!" Hampton stalked to the bed and leaned in with the knife.

She squirmed back into the filthy, greyed pillows. Instead of slicing her face as she feared, he worked the tip of the knife into her dress at the waist, drawing blood. Then he swooped the tip up, cutting her dress and chemise open. He pulled aside the fabric and bared her breasts, licking his lips. He fondled her, and she wrenched at her bonds. Her wrists burned where the rope tore at her skin.

He fumbled with the buttons of his breeches. The fall fell open, and Hampton pulled his small clothes down to expose his erection.

Minerva stared and did the first thing that came to mind.

She laughed.

"*That* is what you're planning on using to prove your manliness? Goodness me. Granted, I don't have much experience, but you're so small. Tiny, in fact. Might I even say miniscule? You see, I'm used to Lord Drummond, who is…well, not to brag, but rather well proportioned. Huge, as a matter of fact. Enormous, even. Compared to you at any rate."

Hampton's erection diminished before her very eyes. Rafe was correct—she *could* shrivel a man's cock with her acidic tongue.

She gestured magnanimously with her bound hands. "Well, go ahead then. Make sure you let me know when you're done, I'm not sure I'll notice."

He bellowed and struck her across the cheek with an open palm. She winced, but a slap was nothing compared to being killed or raped. Hampton jerkily buttoned himself back into his breeches and retreated to the window, casting murderous glances over his shoulder.

An arm shot through the broken panes. Hampton disappeared out the window before Minerva could blink. Rafe, it was Rafe. A howl of rage was followed by a scream of terror and pain. Minerva couldn't stop chanting his name.

* * * * *

The relief of hearing her voice was acute, but when he heard the slap, a red haze of fury descended. A peek over the windowsill revealed Minerva tied to a bed, exposed from the waist up. Hampton's hands would be cut off first, followed by his bollocks, and then his apparently miniscule cock.

He reacted viciously, pulling the smaller man through the window. Jagged glass cut them both. Pain didn't register. Blood lust sang through his veins as he systematically pummeled the man, starting with his face.

Hampton didn't stand a chance. His ineffectual blows glanced off Rafe like pebbles against a boulder. Breathing hard and wiping Hampton's blood off his knuckles and onto his breeches, Rafe dropped the man to the leafy ground. Hampton was conscious and rolled on the ground, moaning. A few well-placed kicks would finish the bastard off.

While Rafe had been beating Hampton, Simon had freed Minerva. She clutched her bodice together. Her face was white under streaks of grime and smeared blood.

"Did he touch you?" His voice was harsh.

Minerva bit her lip. "Yes, but—"

"Goddammit! I'm going to slaughter him." Rafe picked the man up by the back of his jacket and slammed a fist into his belly.

A rib cracked, leaving him grimly satisfied. More, he needed to inflict more pain. He hauled his fist back, but an impediment halted his forward motion. Annoyed, he threw the encumbrance off.

"Stop it. Please, stop. You'll kill him." The anguish in her voice penetrated his murderous daze. She sat on the ground. The bloody contusion on her temple was stark against her pale face. Her dress had parted to expose a line of white skin to her waist.

He had done that. Not Hampton. He had thrown her to the ground. Hit her. The red haze dissipated. The rush of blood in his ears slowed. Pain from cuts shot along his arm and made his hands throb.

The blackness he tamped down on a regular basis had boiled over. She stared at him like he was some unknown monster ascended from hell.

"Don't kill him. Please. He's hurt beyond all decency as it is. Let him go, just…let him go." Her voice held a trace of fear. Was she scared of him now? She scrambled to her feet and reached for him, but he pulled away. Swaying, she appeared on the verge of collapse.

Rafe turned his back on her. "Simon, take her back to Wintermarsh and fetch a doctor."

"I don't need a doctor, I'm fine." She laid a fluttering hand on his shoulder.

He shrugged it off and stepped farther away. "Go. Now."

"I…I'll see you back home, Rafe. Won't I?"

Home. He had wanted it to be her home and had foolishly imagined her there. Pictured a nursery full of tow-headed children. Pictured teaching them to climb the apple trees and swim in the pond. Pictured her in his bed every night. Ashamed and ill, he almost fell to his knees with the grief of a dream lost.

"Get her away from me. Take her, Simon."

Rafe held Hampton erect by his jacket and waited. Leaves and branches rustled their retreat. Once the woods were silent, he shook Hampton until his eyes opened in his lolling head. "Can you hear me, Hampton?"

Lord Hampton grunted and tried to form words with his battered lips. Finally, Rafe made out what he whispered over and over. "Don...kill...me."

"I won't kill you. You have Lady Minerva to thank for that mercy. But let me issue a warning. If I hear one word of scandal attached to her or her brother, I will hunt you down and take immense pleasure in killing you. I will disembowel you and leave you to die a very slow, painful death. Do I make myself clear?" Hampton tried to nod, his head listing. "If I were you, I would leave the country and never come back. Start fresh somewhere else. Yes?"

Again, Hampton attempted a nod. Rafe let him go, and he fell to his knees and then over on his side, one hand holding his face and the other pressed against his ribs. In a show of undeserved charity, Rafe fished out a few sovereigns and tossed them at Hampton's feet.

Rafe walked out of the woods. Simon, with Minerva across his lap, was on the road to Wintermarsh. What evil had he wrought? He whistled for Aries, mounted, and took off at a gallop toward his cabin.

* * * * *

Minerva allowed Simon to guide her to his horse and lift her to its back. Perhaps Rafe needed some time to let go of the fury he had unleashed on Hampton. God, poor Hampton. Even though he deserved a good beating, the man didn't deserve to die.

Her head pounded, and she rubbed at the ache, her fingers coming away trembling and red. "I...I think I hit my head."

"You did," Simon said grimly, speaking for the first time since he'd released her bonds. "How are you feeling?"

Very faint and nauseous, she leaned into her brother. The

motion of the horse wasn't helping matters. "Not at my best, I'll have to admit."

"Once we're back to the house, I'll send for the doctor." Simon kept the horse to a slow walk.

"Where's Rafe? He should have caught us by now."

"He rode off in a different direction. Perhaps he's going to meet us at Wintermarsh." There was doubt in Simon's voice. He was pale, with tight lines around his mouth and worried, sad eyes.

"Simon, are you all right?"

"I'm so sorry. It's all my bloody fault."

"Your only fault was trusting him. He chose his path and made his decisions. I hope Rafe didn't kill him. Poor Rafe."

"He would have if you hadn't stopped him. Remind me never to get on his bad side," Simon said, making a poor attempt at levity.

"He would never hurt you or me."

"Minerva, he threw you off. That's how you hit your head."

"That was an accident. *He* didn't hit me. The tree did."

"That may well be, but when he saw you on the ground, he looked desolate, sick. He's probably feeling guilty as hell right now."

Her brother was probably correct, but there was nothing to be done at the moment. Tomorrow, however, was another story.

CHAPTER TWENTY-THREE

Two days later, Minerva picked over a plate of food in the morning room, her stomach in knots. Rafe still hadn't come home. The doctor had cleaned her head and told her to eat heartily and rest a day or two. She'd had a difficult time on both counts. Sleep had been elusive, bad dreams troubling her both nights.

Simon walked in and the grim set to his mouth twisted her stomach further. "Drummond's in his study, and he's signed my voucher as paid in full. He released us and ordered his carriage to take us back to London in the morning." She received the document like an order of execution.

Three months ago, she would have danced through the village to have this in her hand. She would have thumbed her nose at Rafe Drummond and been happy never to see him again. Now though, her world crumbled at the release. How could she possibly leave him and take up her old life?

Her eyes brimmed with what seemed her constant companion of late. Kneeling beside her, Simon put an arm around her and pressed his handkerchief into her hands. Sobs threatened to break through her tight throat, and she pressed her cheek into his shoulder.

"Do you love him?"

Coherent words not in her grasp, she nodded and clutched at him even harder. Forcing deep breath after deep breath, she reined in her emotions. "What am I to do?"

"Does he know how you feel?"

"Not in so many words. No."

"Tell him or you'll regret it the rest of your days." Simon grabbed her hand. Their blue eyes met, and the years seemed to pass between them in an instant, leaving them on new ground— even ground. "Whatever happens, I'll be here. I promise."

After retrieving the chess set she'd never given him, she found herself staring at the study door, feeling a stranger. She knocked tentatively and pushed the door open. Standing behind his desk, he gathered papers and shoved them into a satchel as if he were packing for a trip.

"Rafe." Her voice broke. Clearing her throat, she tried again. "I appreciate you releasing Simon from his debt, but why are you packing us back to London?"

Rafe spared her a brief glance before returning to his work. "Your brother has more than paid his debt, and our association has run its course. It's time you returned to London so Simon can transition fully into his ducal role." His voice was as expressionless as if he were discussing crop yields.

Minerva clutched the chess set to her chest as if it could keep her on her feet. "I see. Is it that easy for you to send us…send *me* away? Our association meant so little to you?"

"It was all a game for me. How could you think otherwise? Quite the coup to take the ice princess's maidenhead. How jealous all those London dandies would be to know I rode between the legs of the coldest, fiercest woman in the beau monde." He continued to stack papers, not even bothering to witness his words break her heart.

Doubt crept insidiously in the cracks. "Do you hate me so much? Was my ruination your plan from the beginning?" Minerva swayed, her world tipping on its axis, and grabbed the back of the armchair.

"I was in need, and you were convenient. It was certainly no hardship to use your lovely body. That part was unexpectedly delightful, so you can take that knowledge with you." His voice was rough as if he was forcing the words past a stone barricade.

"Are you going to boast of your conquest? Are you set on my humiliation?" Her voice sounded tinny and far away, but somehow she was still on her feet, still in Rafe's study, her heart shattering. "Are you going to tell everyone how wanton I am? How you made me fall in love with you?"

Rafe's head whipped up, and he whispered, "Minerva—"

"Stop. Not another word. No, no…" She shuffled a few steps toward him still clutching the chess set as if it were her anchor. His eyes had gone from frosty to smoldering, and color burnished his cheekbones. His hands fisted in his papers, his knuckles raw and scabbed and a bandage wrapped his forearm.

Their every encounter scrolled through her head and she couldn't—wouldn't—believe it had all been a lie. He'd nearly killed a man to protect and avenge her.

"If this has to do with what happened with Hampton, you know I'm fine. I hit a tree. You didn't hit me. In fact, you saved me."

Rafe gave a mirthless laugh. "I *saved* you. I almost— Go. I want you gone. Find some nice, unassuming gentleman to marry. Stonewell is still available, to my knowledge."

"You can't mean that."

"I do mean it. I don't want you," he bellowed. At the same time his eyes conveyed a contradictory message, *Please don't leave me.* But he stayed mute and shuttled more papers into the satchel.

Anger seeped from the cracks in her heart, and she clutched on to the emotion like a lifeline. Her muscles trembled from the hold she had on the chess set. Rounding the desk, she shoved it hard at his chest, and his hands took it instinctively.

"You are a fool, Rafe Drummond. I hope this keeps you warm at night." Minerva brought her palm around as hard as she could and slapped him across his scarred cheek. He didn't defend himself or retaliate. She stopped at the door, her hand on the jamb, and took one last look at him before slamming the door. He looked like she felt…stricken.

* * * * *

I know where he is." Minerva paced back and forth in her room, a hand massaging her temple. Her head still pounded. From the accident or her situation, she couldn't be sure. Simon leaned against the bedpost. "He has a cabin in the forest where he goes to be alone. Perhaps if I go and talk to him again, he'll see reason."

"I'm not sure that's wise. As you said, he goes there to be alone. He's probably attempting to pickle himself in brandy and, let's assume I know a bit more about the male psyche than you do, my guess is he needs some time away from emotional entanglements to figure things out."

"What are you suggesting?" She whirled to face him.

"I'm suggesting we leave for London. He's a smart man. He'll straighten things out on his own." Simon gave her a bracing hug.

Minerva wasn't so sure. Rafe's words swirled in her head, tormenting her. One minute, she fully believed them, and the next she denied them with every fiber of her soul. She was confused and uncertain and irrational. Simon spoke logically. Perhaps it would be better to retreat with her pride mostly intact and wait.

"Whatever you deem best." She acquiesced like a child, allowing him to take charge for the first time in their lives together. A seismic shift had occurred.

They had both changed over their months at Wintermarsh. Simon had found an ingrained sense of honor buried under years of resentment, and she'd found a heart buried under years of responsibility. How odd the way life could turn on its head in such a short amount of time.

CHAPTER TWENTY-FOUR

Two months later

It was a miserable, frigid day for travel, and Simon pulled the collar of his greatcoat tighter around his neck to stem the tendrils of icy wind making their way inside. His only bit of luck was the unusual lack of snowfall, although by the looks of the steel-grey clouds materializing from the north, his luck was not likely to hold for long.

The inn was a welcome sight, his extremities numb and his belly empty. The common room was full of local men escaping the elements and assuaging winter boredom. He wrapped frozen fingers around a steaming cup of hot coffee and took a small sip. The heat seared him from the inside out. Burning peat and the bitter coffee colored the air pleasantly.

A commotion at the entrance of the inn turned everyone's head, and a pall fell over the crowd. Simon watched from the bar as he sipped. A heavy-set boorish man who led with his belly examined the common room. "Your two finest rooms, sir. If you have any that qualify as such."

Simon couldn't place the man's accent, but he wasn't local. The innkeeper's agitation was obvious in his jerky movements, but he was a soft-spoken man and his words didn't carry like the brash foreigner's. The innkeeper gestured a young man forward to show the family upstairs.

A woman stood with one arm around a young girl hovering somewhere between adolescence and blossoming womanhood. The girl's brown hair hung thick and straight to her shoulders, red strands flashing when it swung. She took everything in with bright, curious eyes. Her features were pleasant and open, dominated by a pair of large dark eyes. The woman's other arm was around a young boy no more than eight or nine. The mother had a cowed look about her, and based on her husband's blustering, Simon could understand why.

"Wait here while I assess the quality. I don't want to sleep with louses," the man said to his wife.

A red flush raced up the innkeeper's neck. The man pounded up the steps, rattling the bucolic watercolors decorating the wall. As soon as the man was out of sight, the daughter shrugged off her mother's arm and crossed her arms over her chest. She whispered something, which caused a grimace to cross the older woman's face, accompanied by a small shake of her head.

The man thumped his way back downstairs. "'Tis decent enough, I suppose. Quit hovering over the boy, Margaret."

The man grabbed the young boy's arm and twisted it. The boy cried out and reached toward his mother. The girl spoke in a low voice to her father, jabbing a finger in the man's face. She pulled her brother out of their father's meaty grasp and pushed him behind her. The father's lip snarled an instant before he smacked the young girl across the cheek. Her head flew to the side. All conversation and movement ceased in the bustling inn.

When she turned back to look at the man, her eyes glittered with tears, but not of pain—of fury. A red handprint bloomed on her cheek. She stared the large man in the eye and took a step forward, her chin set. The foolish girl asked for trouble. Nevertheless, Simon couldn't help but admire her spirit.

The man was many stones heavier, and Simon hated seeing

the strong prey on the weak. He set his coffee cup down and approached the family who seemed as frozen as the rest of the inn's occupants waiting for the next scene to unfold.

"That's no way to treat a young lady." Simon tried to keep his outward aggression at bay. The last thing he needed was to get involved. He had urgent business at Wintermarsh.

"That's a sharp-tongued shrew, sir, and no young lady." The man swiveled his head to Simon but kept his body angled to the girl.

"Shrew or not, in these parts, hitting young women is beyond the pale," Simon said.

The man's calculating gaze coasted over Simon's tailored clothes. An ingratiating smile revealed an enormous amount of large, yellowing teeth. "My name's Edward Goforth, and we're on our way to Lipton seeking the Penhaven estate. Do you know of it?"

"I do. What's your business there, may I ask?"

"Here's the new Lord Penhaven, right here in your midst."

"You?" Simon choked out.

"No, not me, but my son here. Blake Goforth. Lord Penhaven." He gestured to the boy huddled behind the girl and under his mother's arm.

"Blake Tremaine, not Goforth," the girl said in a clear, strong voice. Her accent matched Goforth's but lilted more melodiously.

Mr. Goforth shifted on his feet, hostility once again directed at her. "Well, not officially Goforth, but since I married your mother, I don't see why you shouldn't take my name."

"Because you're not our father." The girl's eyes spoke of hate, and it was disturbing to see in one so young.

"You impertinent little twit." The man raised his hand and stepped into the blow. Her head bobbed backward as if she'd had practice avoiding his hand. Before he could make contact, Simon grabbed the man's wrist and wrenched it to the side.

"I think not, Mr. Goforth."

"And who gives you the authority to stop me, whelp?"

"I'm the Duke of Bellingham, you arse. You can address me as Your Grace or not at all. If you insist on acting the boor, we'll call the local magistrate." Now he was mad, and if a fight was what the bastard wanted, his fists itched to accommodate him. Bracing his legs apart, Simon cracked his knuckles and stretched his neck as he'd seen Rafe do before their sparring sessions.

"I'm terribly sorry, Your Grace. I suppose such things are better handled in private." He turned on his heel and clomped up the stairs. Halfway up, he barked over his shoulder, "Margaret, come. With the children."

Simon clamped his jaw tight. He could do nothing to protect the girl after Goforth dragged her up the stairs. Margaret, her shoulders hunched, pushed a piece of lank hair behind an ear and followed, pulling the boy beside her. She might have been pretty once, but lines of worry marred her face, and unlike her fiery daughter, she had given up the fight long ago. Or perhaps, the fight had been beaten out of her.

The girl didn't follow but stared at Simon as if she wanted to memorize him. He hadn't done much. In fact, he'd likely made things even worse. He brushed a knuckle over her reddened cheek. "I'm sorry he hit you."

"Honestly, I deserved it. I'm awfully impertinent."

"No woman deserves to get hit, miss. Don't ever convince yourself otherwise, please."

The girl's rich brown eyes widened. She nodded, a small smile curling her lips.

He glanced out the frosted window to see snowflakes floating down. "I'm only sorry I can't do more. I hope I didn't make things worse for you later. Unfortunately, I must ride on to attend to some business."

"Don't worry, your duke."

Simon smiled but didn't correct the blunder.

"I'm a survivor. At least that's what my nana used to say. It was good to see someone other than me stand up to the lout. You've given me a bit of hope. Maybe things will be better here."

"What's your name?"

"Jessica Tremaine."

"You're American?" He had finally placed the accent.

"From Pennsylvania."

Simon took her small hand and bussed the back. "Well, Miss Jessica Tremaine from Pennsylvania, I wish you luck and good fortune here in England."

"Thank you. I believe I'll need all the luck I can get." She held her fisted hand against her chest and flew up the stairs, disappearing down the darkened hallway.

With his coffee cooled, he girded himself to face the remainder of his ride. Halfway out the door, he turned around to drop a few coins in the innkeeper's palm. If things got too out of hand with Mr. Goforth, the innkeeper promised to summon the magistrate. With that final bit of help he could provide Miss Jessica Tremaine, Simon galloped away.

He arrived at Wintermarsh after the short winter's daylight had long since faded. The darkness settled heavily, the moon blocked by the clouds spitting out wet snow. The dark house grew his worries.

In the stables, Tom Donahue was busy blanketing the horses. They greeted each other warmly, informally shaking hands. Aries was in his stall, which boded well.

"Is Drummond at home then?" Simon asked.

Tom shook his head, his tongue clicking. "At his cabin."

Simon muttered a few heartfelt curses as he hurried to the house. He pounded on the door and stomped his feet against the cold. Cuthbertson finally cracked the door open and poked his face out.

"Master Simon. I mean, Your Grace. Come in. Come in. Were we expecting you?" Cuthbertson ushered him in and took his coat.

"It doesn't matter what you call me, Bertie. This seems the only place where I'm not fawned over and treated like I'm separate from humanity. I don't suppose you have a fire going anywhere. I can't feel my fingers, my toes, or my arse. The study, perhaps?"

"Master Rafe isn't here." The butler pursed his lips, radiating disapproval.

"So Tom informed me."

"Mrs. Devlin sends a footman with food, books, and brandy out to the cabin every few days." Bertie led him into the study and had a fire crackling in no time. Simon lit several tapers from the flames. A jumble of papers piled over Rafe's desk.

"Dammit. I was afraid of this. No wonder he didn't answer my letters. He'll continue to wallow indefinitely unless something is done. I'll sort this mess out tomorrow and then go talk some sense into the wounded miscreant."

Cuthbertson heaved a sigh. "That would be much appreciated, Master Simon. I'll have Mrs. Devlin open up your old room, shall I?"

"Thank you, Bertie." Simon stared into the flames. The pile of papers on the desk worried him less than what he'd find in the cabin on the morrow.

* * * * *

Up at dawn, Simon waded through the missives, responding or filing if needed. He checked the ledgers. It would take several more days to get things back to a semblance of normal. Luckily, tenant needs were low in winter or the estate would be in even worse shape. He should take Rafe by the ear and force him to clean up the mess himself. How quickly their positions had shifted. He chuckled darkly.

He would have worked through luncheon if Mrs. Devlin hadn't come bustling into the study laden with all of Mrs. Potts specialties. He dug in with gusto clearing the tray in record time before returning his attention to clearing the desk.

Finally, at dinnertime, Mrs. Devlin reappeared with a hamper. "Good luck, sir. You know the way?"

"I can manage. You don't think he'll run me through, do you?" Simon joked.

"I can't say. Would you like me to find you a saber?" Her serious tone and expression jolted him.

"Let's hope that isn't necessary." His enormous tea was suddenly not sitting well.

Simon found the cabin easily enough. He lifted up the heavy knocker and released it with a bang that echoed through the leafless trees.

"Leave the hamper outside." Rafe's voice was gravelly, as if he hadn't spoken in a long while.

"Afraid that's not possible, Drummond. You've a visitor, but I'm fresh out of calling cards to leave your butler." Simon hoped his weak attempt at levity would get some acknowledgment.

Rafe yanked the door open and examined Simon a moment before he turned around, leaving the door open. Simon gingerly took a step inside the small cabin, which was really one large room. One large room covered with an assortment of items from clothing strewn about to brandy bottles, some empty but most full, lining one wall. Books were everywhere, including stacked on the floor.

"Charming, Drummond. I love what you've done with the place," Simon intoned.

"You're welcome to leave. I certainly didn't invite you." He plopped back into a large armchair. A chess set was open on a side table, and Rafe ran his fingers over each piece. He picked up the white queen and rubbed his thumb over and over its length in a motion that seemed habitual.

As an offer to sit didn't seem to be forthcoming, Simon plucked a pair of breeches, a shirt, and several books off one of the kitchen chairs. Debating what to do with the mess, he shrugged and dumped it all on the floor. Rafe didn't complain, in fact, he didn't spare Simon a glance, his attention fixed on the queen. Simon pulled the chair closer and sat down.

"I thought I'd find you foxed."

"I dried myself out a few of weeks ago. The liquor didn't seem to help."

Simon pretended to pick a piece of lint off his jacket but studied Rafe from the veil of his lashes. "I didn't think anyone could look more miserable than Minerva, but I'd say you've got her soundly beat. She's at least trying."

Rafe's head shot up. "Is she unwell? Tell me." A modicum of emotion made its way into his voice, which cracked with worry.

"With the same illness afflicting you, I dare say." Their gazes clashed.

Rafe couldn't hold his stare and looked back down. "Did she send you?"

"Of course not. She would flay me if she knew I was here. Pride is the only thing sustaining her," Simon said with honesty.

Rafe's jaw clenched. "Then…she's not with child?"

Simon's eyes flared and his jaw went slack. Covering his mouth, he hoped Rafe hadn't noticed his shock. It wasn't outrage but opportunity that made his mind race. "So you ruined her. I could call you out for it."

"You should, I'm a bastard."

"Perhaps this explains her imminent acceptance of Lord Stonewell's offer. Perhaps she's increasing and needs a father for her babe."

"She would dare pass my child as another man's?" He'd

gained Rafe's full attention, and the anger was real. Anger was a good start.

Simon stroked his jaw, treading carefully with his words. "Why do you care? You haven't come for her or fought for her. You've sent no word whatsoever."

"Why the devil would she want me? So I can kill another man for her? So I can completely lose myself in rage and hurt her again?"

Simon rolled his eyes. "If I had your skills, I would have ripped Hampton's arms off and shoved them down his throat. I wouldn't have given him another chance. Knocking her down was an accident. One she readily forgave you for by the way. She blamed the tree more than you. Lord knows, the woman has a sharp tongue that can drive a man to his breaking point. To my knowledge, you've never laid an angry hand on her."

Rafe's jaw worked back and forth, and he clutched the chess queen so tightly Simon wouldn't be surprised if it turned to dust. The silence stretched.

Simon looped back to answer Rafe's first question. "I assume she wants you because she's madly in love with you."

"How could she love me? The things I've done and seen." Rafe sounded pained.

"Have you considered she loves you because of the things you've been through and not in spite of them? You're complicated. Well, so is she."

"I'm damaged."

"Aren't we all in our own ways? Minerva didn't seem to think you were beyond redemption." Simon sighed. "She didn't want to leave, you know. She wanted to march out here and talk sense into you. Perhaps I should have let her. I expected you to sulk a few days and then come and get her. For God's sake, I've never seen her as happy as she was this fall. The way she looked at you...it was downright uncomfortable for a brother."

Rafe grunted.

"And the looks you sent her would set the bloody place on fire. I had certainly entertained hopes." Simon waved his hands around.

"She's too good for me." Rafe sank farther down into his chair.

"Probably." Simon leaned forward, trying to gain Rafe's focus again. "Does Stonewell deserve her as a wife then? In his bed? Bearing his children?"

Rafe sprang forward in the chair, causing Simon to rock back in his. "He doesn't deserve to hold her hand. He's like the rest of them and will never be faithful. Moreover, he's quite possibly the most boring man alive. He'll expect her to become some model of lady-like pursuits. It would crush her spirit. Is that what she wants, dammit?"

Simon shook his head. "Drummond, you've been like a brother to me. I can never express the gratitude I feel for the good sense and honor you forced onto me." He paused to let the compliment sink in. "But, and I say this with the utmost respect, you are a total and complete idiot. And a coward to boot. Even I recognize women like her are rare. She chose you. *You* are what she wants, you bloody fool."

Rafe harrumphed, but his fist had opened, and he stared at the chess piece lying in his palm.

Simon could see him weakening and pressed forward. "You say you don't deserve her, but what I see is a man with faults, true, but a man of honor and strength. Someone I only aspire to be. If you don't go to London now, you'll lose her forever and spend the rest of your lonely, miserable life regretting it."

Rafe closed his eyes, an internal battle raging in the silence. Simon let it. When Rafe opened them, he was intent. "I said terrible hurtful things to her. What can I do to win her back? Will you advise me?"

The hum of relief in his head made him dizzy. "I would be more than happy to help. I already have a plan—a grand gesture. However, I'd suggest the first order of business is…a bath. Drummond, you stink."

* * * * *

Rafe spent his last night at the cabin cleaning up his mess while rolling Simon's plan around his head. He had a week until Viscount Marchant's ball. Simon would ensure Minerva attended. The cream of the ton wasn't yet in London, which meant less stares for Rafe to bear. His stomach fluttered with both nerves and excitement. No matter what happened, he would at least see her one more time.

The next morning, he strode through Wintermarsh's front door, his boots clacking on the marble. Bertie and Mrs. Devlin came running from different directions.

"A bath, Mrs. Devlin. Immediately." For once, his two outspoken servants had nothing to say, their expressions of disbelief nearly identical.

While he waited for the bath, Rafe composed a carefully worded letter to Lily. A twinge of doubt wormed its way in, but Simon was entirely correct—if he didn't try to win Minerva's hand, he would be worthless the rest of his days.

Two footmen brought up a tub, followed by several maids bearing pitchers of steaming water. Once he was alone, he sank down as far as possible into the water and scrubbed the past weeks of grime off his body. After dressing in clean breeches, he stuck his head out the door. "Mrs. Devlin, I require your services!"

She came up the stairs with her usual energy. "Master Rafe. Bellowing in the house. Indecently clad. You've been in your own company for far too long." Although she twitched her skirts in supposed annoyance, her lips curled in a smile.

"Right you are. I apologize most heartily for everything I've put you through over the past weeks, but I must beg a favor. I need my hair trimmed. Could you oblige me?" Rafe handed her a comb and scissors.

"I suppose. I used to cut Mr. Devlin's hair. How would you like it?"

"I don't care. Something pleasing to a woman, I suppose."

"Any particular woman, might I ask?"

Rafe sat and looked at her over his shoulder. "Do you need to ask?"

Mrs. Devlin wore a cat-that-caught-the-mouse smile. "No, I don't believe I do." The pile of hair on the floor grew as she worked. "There, now. You look quite dashing, if I say so myself. What next?"

Rafe ran a hand through his hair, the strands skimming through his fingers. "Next, a shave, but I prefer to do that myself. Thank you, Mrs. Devlin. Could you have Tom ready Aries? I'm leaving for London as soon as I'm finished here."

"Certainly." Mrs. Devlin backed out of the room and closed the door.

He had spent months avoiding his reflection. He grew a beard partly because he couldn't bear to shave himself every morning. But his scar didn't bother Minerva, so why should it bother him? Studying his reflection, he could see past the scar to the man he once was and the man he was now.

After hacking at his whiskers with the scissors, he sharpened the blade of his razor, softened the remaining hair with warm water, and applied the lather. Then, he systematically removed the mask he had grown over the past year.

Rubbing a hand along his smooth jaw, he looked almost unrecognizable. The planes of his face were clearly defined, the cleft in his chin visible once again. He tentatively tried a smile and hoped Minerva would still find him attractive. God, Simon was right. He was a fool.

He packed a few items and left the room with a final glance to his bed. He trotted down the stairs, ignoring the servants who stopped their work to stare. Only Minerva's opinion mattered. Simon leaned in the study door, looking him up and down.

"Grand gesture, indeed. Minerva isn't going to know what hit her. You're looking quite handsome." Holding up both hands, palms out, he added, "I mean that as a manly sort of compliment, of course. Don't get any ideas." Simon winked, a boyish half-grin on his face.

"I'll see you at the ball, won't I?" Rafe cursed the nerves roiling his stomach.

"Wouldn't miss it for the world," Simon said, still grinning like a monkey. "I'll finish up here and be back in London in plenty of time."

"Thank you, Bellingham—" Rafe tried to continue, but only gestured vaguely, "—for everything."

"Of course, Drummond. I hope to call you brother soon enough." Simon held his hand out for a shake, but Rafe pulled him in for a hug and slapped him on the back.

"Aries is ready," Bertie intoned solemnly, but a smile crinkled the corners of his eyes. He handed Rafe his hat and greatcoat. "We all wish you the very best luck, my lord."

Without another word, Rafe galloped for London.

CHAPTER TWENTY-FIVE

I've already accepted for us both." Simon pushed into her room and stared her down with an imitation of her own cutting look. It didn't take.

"Then you can tell them I'm not feeling well." Minerva kept her voice falsely sweet.

He turned cajoling. "Minerva, I would appreciate your attendance by my side. For political reasons. I need the support of my own family on the cusp of something so momentous."

"The cusp of what? What are you prattling on about?" All she wanted was to curl up with a good book and a dinner tray. She didn't want to put on a brave face and make inane small talk at Marchant's ball with people she cared nothing about.

"Lord Wellsey is considering me for a committee assignment in Parliament the next term. It would be quite a coup, being so young and all." Simon picked at a string hanging from his waistcoat.

She gasped. "That's wonderful."

He pulled her wardrobe door open and riffled, pulling out a dress of blue shot with silver adornments. Undoubtedly beautiful, the dress had been stuffed to the back of her wardrobe, the colors a painful reminder of Rafe's eyes.

"Not that one." She took the garment out of his hands and tried to tuck it away, but he wouldn't allow it.

"Yes, this one. You'll look magnificent." He put both hands on her shoulders and looked her straight in the eyes. "Trust me, please. I need you looking your best tonight."

Several hours later, she sat at the Marchant ball in her resplendent finery, bored to tears. Simon hobnobbed across the room, and she listened with half an ear to Miss Cecilia Randolph blather on. "I would faint dead away if Lord Drummond approached me for a dance. You spent the fall at his country house, didn't you? Was he an ogre?"

Her heart constricted every time someone said his name. "Not an ogre, no. Why in the world would he approach you? He hardly ever leaves the country, and when he is in London, he doesn't venture out to socialize with the beau monde."

"Well—" Miss Randolph leaned in conspiratorially, "— confidentially speaking, of course, my papa heard from Viscount Marchant that Lord Drummond requested an invitation for tonight. He may be seeking a wife, but who would want to live in the country all year and have to face him across the breakfast table. Although, he stands to inherit an earldom and is quite rich. Perhaps I'll consider him after all." She tapped her fan on her lips, mulling the idea.

Minerva's eyes narrowed on Miss Cecilia Randolph. Rafe would eat her alive, and if he didn't, Minerva would rip every hair out of the girl's head one at a time. Her heart raced with the possibility, however remote, that Rafe might actually make an appearance. She popped out of the chair, her restless legs demanding movement.

"Here comes Lord Stonewell, Lady Minerva." Miss Randolph sighed. "You're so lucky."

Stonewell did indeed approach with a smile on his face. Minerva pasted on a smile of welcome in return. His warm eyes made her uncomfortable. They wanted things she wasn't sure she could ever give again.

"Lady Minerva, I believe it's my dance."

"I believe you are correct, Lord Stonewell."

Stonewell bowed over her hand and led her to the middle of the floor. He really was a nice man and had been a true friend. Given the slightest encouragement, he would offer marriage.

There were certainly worse choices. True, their conversations were uninspiring, and she wasn't remotely attracted to him. When she had mentioned her interest in financial matters, Stonewell had chuckled, obviously humoring her wild notions. Could she bring herself to share his bed? Perhaps she could tolerate him long enough to bear him an heir. Then she could encourage him to take a mistress.

No doubt, he would make her give up her little project. She'd decided to devote herself to help women find financial freedom. Many war widows possessed a small inheritance and no wish to re-marry. She had formed a small group of like-minded widows. Now she only needed a trustworthy man to help handle the actual investments for them.

She could strangle Drake for hieing off to the wilds of Scotland—in the middle of winter no less. Even if he didn't want to stay and work with Simon, he could have helped her in this new capacity.

Depressed to see her man of affairs—but more importantly her friend—leave, she'd nevertheless wished him luck with entreaties to write if he needed anything at all. She'd even given him a long, tight hug on their front stoop and shed a few tears. Handling her with his typical Scot stoicism, he'd patted her on the shoulder, looking slightly green, and murmured a litany of there, theres.

Positioning herself for the quadrille with Stonewell, she looked to Simon. Had he heard the rumors about Rafe? In discussion with a middle-aged man with white whiskers, he glanced toward the entryway.

Halfway through the dance, a wave of silence crashed over the room, stopping dancers mid-step. Whispers swirled in the aftermath like a swarm of bees. Like everyone else, Minerva craned her neck, seeking the cause.

Standing at the top of a handful of steps was the most devastatingly handsome man she had ever laid eyes on. Dressed in black evening clothes, he scanned the room, his gaze bouncing everywhere until it caught and held her immobile in its intensity. Not that she would have been able to flee on her suddenly leaden feet. Lord Stonewell, sensing her distress, offered her an arm, which she grabbed.

"Lord Rafael Drummond," intoned the butler.

By this time, the musicians had sensed something momentous occurring and stopped playing, a witness to the drama. Rafe walked toward her, his steps unnaturally loud in the silence. The crowd parted like the red sea. Her greedy gaze raked him from head to foot. His hair was short and his beard shorn. He was beautiful.

He stopped directly in front of her, his gaze just as covetous. Then, he lifted her limp, gloved hand to press a lingering kiss on the back. Her other hand was still on Lord Stonewell's sleeve, and the man cleared his throat.

"Stonewell," Rafe said with flinty eyes.

"Drummond. I'm surprised to see you here." Lord Stonewell's eyes had narrowed and he'd assumed a protective stance.

The musicians, suddenly remembering what they were being paid to do, struck up a waltz. Minerva glanced over to see Simon glaring at Rafe and mouthing *dance*. And perhaps the word *idiot*, but surely she was mistaken.

Rafe cleared his throat. "Lady Minerva, may I have the honor?"

Minerva, mesmerized by his turbulent blue-gray eyes,

hesitated and stumbled over her words, "Uh…oh my, dance? I…of course, Rafe, I mean, Lord Drummond."

Stonewell looked back and forth at the two of them and handed her off reluctantly. The dance floor was deserted, waiting in anticipation much like the crowd of on-lookers. With a deep breath, Rafe whirled her onto the floor.

"It's been too long since I waltzed," he said quietly, breaking their uncomfortable silence.

"You haven't lost the skill, but I already knew you to be an excellent dancer." She kept her focus somewhere in the vicinity of his shoulder. If she looked directly at his face, she wouldn't be able to stop her hands from exploring his smooth jaw and silky hair.

"You've lost weight, sweetheart," he whispered.

She darted her gaze to his. A wealth of tenderness and regret shined from him.

"You're still the most beautiful woman I have ever seen. If I didn't think you'd have my hide, I'd throw you over my shoulder and haul you home."

Home. His words chipped at her core of pain, but he wasn't to be forgiven so easily. "You broke my heart, you arse." Tears stung, but she managed to keep them from spilling over. A handful of other couples joined them on the floor, one being Simon, who was trying not to stare at them but failing miserably.

"I know. I broke my own heart. If I could take back everything I said to you that day, I would. I was afraid I would hurt you even worse if you stayed. I was a fool and, as your brother correctly pointed out, an idiot and a coward to boot." His voice was low and gravelly with emotion.

"So Simon is behind your sudden appearance? That's why he was so insistent I attend tonight." Pride stiffened her back.

"Your brother came and talked some sense to me. I spent the first month after you left drunk at the cabin. Even after I dried myself out, grief dogged me. I had no desire to see to the estate or to see anyone, for that matter. I'd guess you coped a sight better than I did." Pulling her closer, he rested his smooth jaw alongside her temple.

She pushed him back. Her defenses were crumbling too readily. "You look different."

"Now that you see the entirety of it, does it disgust you?" He ducked his head as if trying to hide his scar in his shoulder.

"Rafe, no, of course it doesn't." Her hand caught his cheek, and she titled his face back to her. "I meant, you look beautiful."

Beats of music passed before he rumbled, "That's my line."

Now that she'd started, she couldn't stop herself from touching him. "You have a dimple in your chin." She slid a satin-covered finger down his jaw line to the crease. "I never knew."

"I think there might be a spot on my inner thigh you've never seen either…would you like to familiarize yourself with that later?" he asked wickedly but with a hint of desperation.

"Will there be a later? How many times have you pushed me away?"

"God, woman, I would get down on my knees right here in this ballroom if you would consent to be my wife. And if you say no, don't think I'll crawl away in defeat. I'll court and woo you until you surrender."

"Is it to be a battle then, Rafe Drummond?"

"A war if necessary. I'll never allow Stonewell or another of his ilk to have you. You're too good for me, but you're much too good for them. I'll love you and honor you the rest of my days. I'll forever be faithful to you. I can't promise I'll never be an arse. I still have demons. You understand them better than anyone. But for the first time, I feel like they won't pull me down. I haven't had a drop of liquor in a month, and I don't even miss it. We can even live in London, if you desire."

"That's very—"

"Let me finish, before I lose my nerve. You can pursue any unladylike endeavor you desire...financial, charity, even acting a maid at Wintermarsh. Whatever makes you happy. I'll never expect you to embroider or watercolor. I love you, woman. With everything I am and everything I aspire to be." Rafe came to a stop in the middle of the floor and took both her hands in his, holding them against his heart.

"Oh, Rafe." This time a tear managed to escape even as her lips curled into a smile. "Of course, I'll be your wife. I love you so much, you silly man." She threw her arms around his neck and he, most improperly and quite thoroughly, kissed her. Minerva couldn't be sure whether it was the sudden rush of her blood or a simultaneous gasp from the ballroom filling her ears.

"I love you too. Will you forgive me for acting an ungentlemanly brute?" he asked once their lips parted.

Breathless and blissful, she would forgive him anything. "For kissing me? I kissed you right back."

"No, for this." Rafe picked her up, cradled her in his arms, and strode out of the ballroom, the crowd parting for him once again. She couldn't summon any remorse for their scandalous behavior. London could go to hell. They'd be back at Wintermarsh soon enough.

Over Rafe's shoulder, Stonewell stood with his shoulders slumped and his face downcast, the picture of the vanquished. She caught sight of Simon. He waggled his fingers at her in farewell, a self-satisfied smirk on his face.

Rafe climbed into the waiting carriage after her and pulled her onto his lap, forcing her to straddle him. Capturing her face in his hands, he studied her in the dim light. "You're sure you want me? The things I've done...experienced...I'm no saint."

She covered his hands with hers and weaved their fingers. "Has it occurred to you that your past, as difficult and bleak as it was, shaped the man you are now? A strong man who can protect me, who won't control me, who understands me. A man I love." She brushed her lips across his and then skimmed them across his smooth cheek to lay a kiss on his scar.

Sitting up straight on his lap, she tugged her gloves off one by one and tossed them aside. He dropped his hands to her stocking-clad calves as she plunged one hand into his hair and explored his smooth jaw line with the other.

Would she ever get enough of his skin against hers? Leaning forward, she rubbed her cheek against his like a cat. His laughter vibrated his chest against her. "Rafe Drummond, you were handsome before, but now you're downright stunning."

"I'm glad you think so. I've discovered yours is the only opinion that matters."

He slid his hands to her buttocks and pressed her close as their lips met. This time, passion ruled, and soon they were reacquainting themselves with each other's bodies.

The carriage rolled to a halt, jerking them out of their frenzy. "Let's continue this somewhere a bit more comfortable, shall we?"

She managed a hum of agreement through kiss-swollen lips.

She followed him up the steps to the imposing, black door. Was it only months ago she'd left feeling she'd made a bargain with the devil? He pushed the door open and turned to her with a smile full of love. Her heart galloped away. The devil hadn't had a hand in this. A more celestial being had brought them together. And she would thank them the rest of her days for forcing that outrageous bargain.

She walked into his arms for another kiss. Her cloak fell to the floor, as did his greatcoat. She turned her head to the side, and he applied himself to kissing down her neck. "Rafe...Rafe, the servants?"

"Told them to bugger off for the night." He slid the sleeve of her gown to the very edge of her shoulder and down, laying kisses along its retreat.

She took his face in her hands and forced him to meet her gaze. "I'll not forgive you if Mrs. Devlin catches us in flagrante delicto."

His lips twitched. "Your brother offered to put them up for the evening. We are entirely alone."

"Still, should we make our way to your bedroom? I'm not sure finding our clothes strewn about the entry hall in the morning is a proper introduction."

"Perhaps, but I've entertained many a fantasy about taking you against a door. Ever since we were so rudely interrupted by my sister."

She shivered. "You have a door in your suite...and a bed."

"By God, I do." He grabbed her hand and pulled her up the stairs. Laughing and breathless, she ran to keep up.

He wrestled her gown off, destroying a few hooks in his haste. Light stays thrust her breasts up. As promised, he pushed her against the door with his pelvis, kicking her beautiful, mistreated gown out of the way. Plucking her breasts from her stays, he cupped them and ran his thumbs across the nipples simultaneously. She squirmed as liquid heat coated her.

She pushed his jacket off and applied herself to the buttons of his waistcoat. There were too many clothes between them. With his waistcoat gone, she tore at his shirt. He yanked it over his head, fabric rending.

He rid her of her stays, pulled her chemise down to her waist, and rubbed his hair-covered chest against hers. The sweet friction against her nipples shot to her core, the rhythmic throbbing intensifying between her legs.

It had been too long. An eternity. She plucked at the discs on his breeches ineffectually, and Rafe pushed her hands aside to complete the task. His erection sprang forth, and he pulled her chemise up to her waist.

"I'm sorry, sweetheart. I need inside of you desperately." He sounded like a wild creature. "I'll make it up to you later, I promise."

"What do I do?" Her voice carried the same primal ferocity.

"Wrap your leg around me, I'll lift you up." She slid her leg up his thigh, and he grazed his hand up her sensitized skin until he cupped her buttock. He slipped a finger through her wet folds and groaned.

With both hands cupping her buttocks, he lifted her effortlessly, his strength driving her desire higher. Her legs rested on his hips, and he lowered her onto his cock. The exquisite feeling of being filled by him felt like a claiming. A promise.

"I love you." The words came on a gasp of air.

"I love you too." His words wavered with the same intensity of emotion battering her.

Holding her stationary, he took short, stabbing thrusts as if he were loath to leave her in any way. A fine sweat broke on his back and brow. He lowered his mouth to hers, his tongue playing in the same rhythm as his cock.

Tingling shot from where they were joined to her fingers and toes and everywhere in between. Her climax twisted through her body, and she was only vaguely aware when he joined her. He slid them to the floor to lie side by side, her body a mass of trembling muscles.

On his elbow beside her, he brushed her hair away from her face. Her hand was too weak, and her body too sated for even that. Rafe went to work removing her chemise and stockings. Once she was fully naked, Rafe raked his gaze up and down her body and, even with all that had passed between them, a blush spread.

Her fair skin betrayed her, and Rafe laughed. "I love that you can blush with me, sweetheart, even after you played the wanton not five minutes ago."

"Am I really wanton?"

"Yes, and I love it. It might take years before we get through playing out all my fantasies." Rafe kissed her nipple and ran his tongue over it like a big jungle cat.

Tension coiled in the wings, awaiting its cue. "What about my fantasies? When will it be my turn?" Was she bold enough to take his hand and put it between her legs?

Rafe's head popped up, his eyes hooded. "You have fantasies about me? I'm intrigued. Perhaps it's your turn now. What do you want me to do?"

"I want you to stop talking." She forced his mouth back to her breasts and guided his hand between her legs. He huffed a laugh, but she didn't care. Slick with her own arousal and his seed, he toyed with her. Her hips thrust, wanting more of everything.

"Why in such a hurry, love?"

"It's been so long, and I've missed you so." Notes of urgency, longing, and distress colored her words.

His teasing amusement was gone, his voice full of torment. "I dreamed of you every night in despair I would never touch you like this again." He thrust a finger inside her while his thumb rubbed her bud, giving her what she needed. She keened her climax.

When the storm had passed, Rafe picked her up and laid her on the bed, face down with her legs dangling over the side. She was too satisfied to question her position. His erection prodded her buttocks. He ran his hands over her back and entered her agonizingly slowly. Up on her toes, she wiggled back against him.

He curled over her, his hot breath in her ear matching his words. Erotic promises propelled her forward. His thrusts were measured. Held down in a position of submission, she couldn't even touch him, and she gloried in his domination. He snaked a hand under her, his finger brushing her apex. Her sudden climax took them both by surprise, and he spiraled over the same dizzy edge.

Pushing her onto the bed, he covered them with a sheet. She entwined her limbs with his like a vine seeking purchase and fell into a dreamless sleep.

* * * * *

A hand stroking along his jaw and through his hair woke him. Minerva was propped on her elbow studying him, her expression serious. Dawn's light was suffusing the room.

"Do you approve of what you see?" His underlying uncertainty was poorly hidden behind his teasing words.

Her smile banished the darkness like the sun at its zenith. "I've always approved of what I saw. Even when I thought I hated you, you were my ideal of the perfect man. It made everything so confusing."

Clearing his throat, he ran strands of her hair through his fingers. "Do you know what I have in my jacket?"

"A red squirrel?"

Rafe chuckled and shook his head.

"Some of Mrs. Pott's tarts? That would be delightful. I'm finding my appetite much improved."

"You are making no effort at seriousness. A special marriage license."

Minerva looked truly stunned. "For us?"

"No, for the two red squirrels I have ferreted away in my jacket. Of course for us, woman."

"When?"

"Tomorrow. No, actually, today." Rafe laughed but then his smile dropped. "If you want. If you'd rather wait, we can wait as long as you wish. I thought perhaps sooner rather than later would be wise considering…" Rafe waved a hand to the door, pointed at the floor, and patted the bed. "Love, I have to ask, because Simon somewhat insinuated, but looking at you, I don't see…"

She looked bemused by his stuttering and tilted her head.

"Are you increasing?" Rafe blurted out.

"Am I? Oh, my. You mean carrying your child?" Now, it was Minerva's turn to stutter. "Well, no... I mean, after I left, I...I knew it was possible, but then, my courses came...and so I wasn't." She shrugged, her eyes glistening.

"Sweetheart, did you want my child?" His heart was near to bursting, and he gathered her close. "I'll admit when Simon indicated you might be with child, I felt some primal sense of gratification. But when he told me you were going to accept Lord Stonewell's proposal even though you carried my child, I was ready to rip Stonewell limb from limb."

"Rafe, that's so sweet," she said in a tear-blurred voice.

The incongruency made him belly laugh, which in turn dried her tears.

"I did want your child, but I would never have married Stonewell. If I had found myself increasing, I would have retreated to Northumberland to have the babe and raise him or her there, away from the gossips. I wanted any part of you to keep. Why in the world did Simon make you think that I would have passed your child as another man's?"

Rafe reviewed their conversation and rolled his eyes. "Your brother is going to make a brilliant politician. He allowed me to blunder down the wrong path knowing it would spur me into action."

Her brow furrowed, she pushed away from him and pulled the sheet over her breasts. "You only came because you thought I carried your child?"

"No. I came because, although no man deserves you, not even me, I wasn't going to allow some clodpoll like Stonewell share your bed and give you children. If I didn't fight for you, I would regret it all my days. I've lived with enough regrets. I want you. I love you."

"I love you too." They kissed, and he tried to roll her onto her back. He'd woken with a raging erection.

She slapped his shoulder and bolted upright. "You said we

were to be married today. Today. As in, a few hours. I can't, it's too soon. I'd like to have Lily here. And Jenny. And what about your father? And a dress. Rafe, I must have a dress." She ticked off items on her fingers heedless of her nakedness.

He stared at her swaying breasts, the nipples pert and begging for his mouth. Perhaps, he could drag her downstairs in a night rail, make it legal, and drag her back to bed. It sounded a fine plan to him, but Minerva would most likely want something a tad more traditional.

"Now, I hope you don't think I was presumptuous, but why don't you check the wardrobe." He lay back on the pillows and laced his hands behind his head.

Her brows drawing together, she scrambled out of bed and peeked inside the wardrobe as if she expected a red squirrel to come bolting out. She gasped and threw it fully open to reveal his surprise—an ice-blue dress with an exquisitely beaded bodice. The small crystals caught the faint dawn light and reflected it back tenfold. Pleased with himself, he laughed at her hanging mouth.

"How…where…who…"

"Let's see, your usual modiste made it. She directed me to your typical style, and I chose the color. I paid her an obscene amount of money to get it done in a week and keep her mouth shut about it. Do you like it?" He hoped her amazement doubled as approval.

She carefully hung the dress over the door and then bounced back on the bed, peppering kisses over his chest. "I don't like it…I love it. That's the most romantic thing anyone's ever done for me."

Her hot mouth obliterated his good intentions.

It was a good hour later before they emerged from the bedroom. "The servants should be back by now if you'd like to bathe. Jenny, Tom, Mrs. Devlin, and Bertie are here. Father and Lionel and Aunt Edie are still in Scotland, and I don't want to wait. I sent a letter, but I know they'll understand."

The two of them entered the morning room hand in hand. Lily flew over to give both of them hugs, tearing up as she patted his cheek. "If you'd asked me six months ago, I would have bet money the two of you hated each other. I'm so happy, Rafe. I honestly never thought you'd find a woman to put up with your sorry ar—"

"Lily, don't frighten Lady Minerva away. Nothing is official yet." Gray was sprawled on the settee, laughing.

"I'm the lucky one." Minerva looked up at him with undisguised adoration.

"Gawd, you really are in love with the lout. In truth, you know I could never ask for a better brother, and the fact he's marrying my best friend is even better. We'll truly be sisters now." Lily squeezed his hand and extricated Minerva, dragging her down the hall to the drawing room, where the small ceremony would take place.

Her muffled exclamation made him smile. He'd paid a bloody fortune and bought every hothouse flower in London for her.

Gray clapped him on the back. "Well, done. I'm proud of you."

"For what?"

"For reaching for happiness. It takes a different sort of courage to open yourself to someone else. It's downright terrifying to give someone power over you and realize the power you wield over them in return."

"Yes. But it's worth it, isn't it, Gray?" Rafe looked to his best friend.

"Most definitely," Gray replied with a grin.

EPILOGUE

Sitting in his huge armchair in the study, Rafe was ostensibly reading, but in reality, he glanced up every few seconds to watch his wife working at the desk. They had discussed turning the morning room into a second study for her, but he'd balked. He enjoyed sharing this part of his life with her. Not all husbands were as fortunate.

He had girded himself to spend the season in London, so she wouldn't miss the round of social balls and entertainments. However, three days after their wedding, she'd demanded to come home. To Wintermarsh. Rafe had been easily convinced. He'd sent ahead instructions to move another wardrobe into his bedroom, not giving her the option of settling into the adjoining chamber. She hadn't protested in the least.

The month since their union had been the happiest, most fulfilling time in his life. The joy of having her in his bed and waking up with her every morning had exceeded his expectations. Cool and collected while dealing with ledgers and her widows' investments, she was a playful firebrand in bed, as much the aggressor as he was.

But it was during the aftermath of their love making, holding her close, breathing her in and baring his soul that had banished the darkness lurking inside of him. The fitful nights both of them had suffered from were now restful and spent tangled together.

He noticed her re-reading a letter a second time with a wrinkled brow of worry. "You look disturbed, love. What's the matter?"

"It's a letter from Drake. He's met with some trouble in Scotland. I'm not sure how to help him though."

Rafe laid his book face down on his belly and stretched his long legs out, giving her his full attention. "A woman is usually involved when trouble comes to call." He needled her, biting back a smile.

She shot him an irked look. "There does seem to be a young lady involved, but he's not very forthcoming on the nature of their relationship. I hope the chit isn't taking advantage of poor Drake."

Rafe laughed. "*Poor* Drake? He's a grown man and a very self-assured, competent one at that. I'm sure he can manage one woman. What's his trouble then?"

"It involves a possible inheritance. Which is interesting because, although he never really talked about it, I got the impression he had no family. I didn't realize he might have some connections to Scot gentry." Minerva worried a nail.

"The earl and Lionel are traipsing around up there. Sounds like he could use a solicitor and, even in Scotland, I'd say the earl can open some doors for your Mr. Drake."

"That's a fine idea, Rafe." She sounded thoroughly surprised.

"It happens occasionally," he replied dryly.

"I'd say more than occasionally. That was a fine idea you had last night as well, by the by." Her seductive look seared him even from across the room

"Yes, that was one of my more naughty fantasies, I must say." Clouds gathered in the distance promising an afternoon downpour. "It looks like rain," he said conversationally.

Minerva looked behind her at the gathering storm. "So it

does."

"I'm having another fine idea." He stood and held out his hand.

* * * * *

Minerva walked toward him, swaying her hips and pulling the pins out of her hair along the way. The thrumming anticipation that always lingered beneath the surface hurtled to an outright primal need for his touch.

She loved this man. Loved his strength and sensitivity. Loved that he shared every part of his life with her. Most men would abhor sharing a desk with their wife, but he claimed he loved to see her at work here. She had no doubt that he meant it based on the number of times he'd taken advantage of her on top of it.

She took his hand and whispered, "It's my turn, you know."

His eyes were hazy with desire, but he understood her meaning well enough. "Luckily, I know you have fine ideas too, wife."

She drifted her hand to the very obvious display of his affection at the front of his breeches. "I do, I really do. I hope you don't mind if we wrinkle some of your cravats this afternoon."

His eyes widened in a mixture of surprise and excitement. "Not a bit. Let's go." He pulled her out of the study at a run, both of them laughing all the way up the stairs.

.

Ready for more?
A Reckless Redemption...

On the eve of her wedding to man she detests, Brynmore McCann plots to escape the match by ruining herself, but the local lads leave her wholly uninspired. Nearly giving up her plan, she spots Maxwell Drake home after nearly a decade. Although he'd been in love with her sister, Bryn had always considered him *hers*. She can't think of anyone she'd rather have bed her for the first time. But, she never intends for him to discover her identity.

Upon coming home, Maxwell, the unacknowledged by-blow of a local nobleman, discovers his father may have left him an inheritance, and the fairy-lass he spent an incredibly satisfying night with was not the village whore, but the high-born sister of his first love. Wrestling with resentment over her deception, he insists Brynmore travel with him to Edinburgh until they know if she is with child— and if she is, she'll marry him whether she wants to or not.

Complicating matters is the man (or men) out to kill them. As the list of suspects grows longer and his worry deepens, Maxwell falls further and further under Brynmore's gentle spell even though removing the armor from his heart terrifies him more than the peril that threatens them from every angle.

Warning: Contains a broody Scotsman with a tin heart, a fiery-haired lass who knows what she wants, and a night of passion neither can forget...

About the Author

I hope you enjoyed A Brazen Bargain! Although, many readers know me from my Southern-set contemporary romances, the first books I wrote were the Spies and Lovers series! I grew up reading the historical "bodice rippers" of the late eighties and early nineties along with wonderful gothic romances. Now that I have the opportunity to publish all of the Spies and Lovers series, I'm so excited! There will be (at least) four full length books, but I have ideas for more…

Although, I've always read, I never thought seriously about writing until my kids were both in school and I knew I didn't want to go back to work as a chemical engineer. So without telling anyone (even my husband), I sat down one morning after I dropped the kids at school and started *An Indecent Invitation*.

Printed in Great Britain
by Amazon

35941091R00192